AN AMATEUR WITCH'S GUIDE TO MURDER

AN AMATEUR WITCH'S GUIDE TO MURDER

A Novel

K. VALENTIN

alcove
press

Books should be disposed of and recycled according to local requirements. All paper materials used are FSC compliant.

This is a work of fiction. All of the names, characters, organizations, places, and events portrayed in this novel are either products of the author's imagination or are used fictitiously. Any resemblance to real or actual events, locales, or persons, living or dead, is entirely coincidental.

Copyright © 2025 by K. Valentin

All rights reserved.

Published in the United States by Alcove Press, an imprint of The Quick Brown Fox & Company LLC.

Alcove Press and its logo are trademarks of The Quick Brown Fox & Company LLC.

Library of Congress Catalog-in-Publication data available upon request.

ISBN (hardcover): 979-8-89242-342-7
ISBN (paperback): 979-8-89242-343-4
ISBN (ebook): 979-8-89242-344-1

Cover design by Ana Hard

Printed in the United States.

www.alcovepress.com

Alcove Press
34 West 27th St., 10th Floor
New York, NY 10001

First Edition: October 2025

The authorized representative in the EU for product safety and compliance is eucomply OÜPärnu mnt 139b-14, 11317 Tallinn, Estonia, hello@eucompliancepartner.com, +33757690241

10 9 8 7 6 5 4 3 2 1

Para mi abuelita, sé que estarás leyendo por encima de mi hombro.

CHAPTER ONE

"You a witch?"

Mateo Borrero pulls an earbud out, muting the furious screeching and synth blasting his ears to see who's leveled this super creative insult at him. He's greeted by the least surprising answer: a douche-bro hanging out of a truck, halted at a red light. The guy comes in a matching set, another at the wheel, craning around his friend to help jeer. The truck is big, and the douches are bigger. A guy in all-black and eyeliner is a threat to their dicks in some ill-defined way.

Because it's a bad idea to humor assholes looking to start something, Mateo pretends he doesn't see them, even though he unmistakably turned and stared. This flies for all of six seconds.

"Hey, witch bitch!" the guy yells even louder, getting innovative with rhyming now. A real poet screaming from his car. "You deaf, too?"

This is prime *words will never hurt you* territory. They'll get bored if he doesn't react. But his mouth and temper operate at a different speed than his brain. "I heard you, I've just got zero interest in getting blown by a guy in a polo, so I'm pretending I didn't."

There's a beat of silence as the pair try to navigate the meaning of this witty retort, and then a Slurpee cup explodes inches from Mateo's boots. The truck peels off, the poet hanging out the window cackling.

The crosswalk pings, but Mateo stands motionless, searching desperately for calm—three breaths, staring after the truck as it disappears around a corner. He tries not to envision **how nice it would be to drag the poet out the truck window, grate his laughing face off on the asphalt, slit him from belly to neck, reach inside, and squeeze a handful of viscera until it pops.**

The crosswalk light goes through another cycle before he can run his tongue over his teeth and confirm they've returned to their usual human bluntness so he can continue on to work.

He steps through the Slurpee. Cherry. Like a snowman died in traffic.

* * *

The print shop opens and closes late on Wednesdays for reasons no one remembers—and therefore never explained to him—so the front is locked when Mateo walks up at ten till noon. Pizza Lady next door waves as he struggles with the steel grate that separates him from his low-paying-but-needed job. Not for the first time, he longs for a spell that might fuse it locked forever—and give him a million dollars—but the mechanism slides open like it always does.

Wednesdays are the best days of his week, excluding paydays. All of the joy of a cool room that smells like paper with none of the misery of getting up at 6 AM. Stylish sweater stowed and hideous uniform polo applied to body, Mateo surveys the orders from last night. It's clear Angelica was on shift because everything's done and the handwriting is serial killer neat.

He pours a coffee from the shitty pod machine in the back—which is a sin in Seattle, but he doesn't have twenty bucks to waste at an artisanal café—brings out the cash drawer, and uses a boot to ferry the brown rubber doorstop into place between door and frame. The front door sticks, so it's easier to leave it ajar, even if it means flies come in as the days get disgustingly warm.

As a proper, self-respecting goth, he hates the approaching summer. He'll go to his grave in long sleeves and black skinny jeans with too many zippers. It's a stereotypical look for a novice witch—the douche-bros were correct, but he still hates them. When he started practicing brujería, he considered changing his style, but he looks good in black.

Flicking the switch by the door, *Turbo Print and Ship* blazes to life against the front window in neon blue. Glancing at the schedule, he's surprised to see a new name. Doris could have told him. This is probably revenge for caving to his oft-repeated request for staff.

This new guy's late, though. He should have shown up ten minutes ago. Bodes horribly.

Officially open, Mateo retreats to his post behind the counter, sips his bitter coffee, and tries to improve his mood via force of will. In flows a ceaseless mix of office workers who've waited until the last second to print their proposals, college students with homework assignments who just realized their ancient instructors expect a physical copy, and people who haven't used a computer since 1982 but have the sudden and inexplicable need to fax something.

Plastic customer service smile slips into place over black-painted lips. It's his only defense against the masses. As hands do the automatic motions of drudgery, his mind wanders, counting up the extra hours worked this week and calculating the paycheck.

Things are tight again. Always. Mateo's perma-roommate, best friend, and non-blood-related family, Ophelia—who only sometimes exists in this plane of reality—can't even afford her share of utilities, let alone rent. Another roommate would help, but it's tricky to screen for sincerely-okay-with-goth-shit, not just on a superficial level. Though, rent isn't at the top of his list of problems. What he really needs is enough cash to handle his *affliction*.

But every time he gets a little ahead, Ophelia's car dies, something critical breaks in the house, or a collection agency comes knocking about his deadbeat mother's debts.

He has to ring up the next two customers with a close-lipped smile for fear his teeth have gone pointy again. His mother, who conveniently went missing five years ago—happy eighteenth birthday to Mateo—left him a crumbling house with a lien on it, a box of vintage Mister Donut cups, and her demon.

He needs to up his side hustle, but his skill set isn't easily advertised, and he's vowed never to use WorkList again. In retrospect, putting *let's make magic together* on the internet was an obvious mistake that would result in needing to change his phone number.

A customer surrounded by printers asks if the print shop prints things, and Mateo takes three more measured breaths like his mother taught him—ironic—presses the bad feelings down, and relinquishes himself to the flow of stupid, letting it gently wash over him.

At two, the door bangs open, letting in a wash of pizza smell from next door and a scrawny, pale twenty-something with white-blond hair. He looks like he drove with his head out a window, hair messy in a way that can't be fashion. He makes wide eye contact with Mateo that swiftly shifts into surprised confusion. People don't expect goths at retail establishments.

"You're Christopher Nystrom?" Mateo hazards, the level of alarmed disarray pouring off the guy appropriate for someone an hour fifty-five minutes late for their first day.

Messy Hair Guy freezes in the doorway like those videos of deer finding themselves unexpectedly in convenience stores, and it's unclear if he's going to answer or start flailing his stick legs wildly as he tries to flee. "Yeah. No. I mean, yeah, but Topher. My dad was Christopher. *Is* Christopher. He's not dead or anything. Which is . . . I mean . . . that's a weird thing to say. I realize. The dead thing. Not my name," Topher-not-Christopher says, confidence and volume evaporating from his words until he's whispering by the end.

It's *a lot* for a first impression. Mateo considers how to play this because it feels like the wrong word will obliterate Topher. "I'm the manager, and I super don't care that you're late. Stuff happens." This isn't true, but if he doesn't train Topher, he'll never get a lunch break.

"You're Mateo?" Topher makes it sound like an off-brand cereal. *Matt-ee-oh.*

Mateo enunciates it correctly, and sounds only a little derisive.

"Sorry. Sorry about that. And about this. Being late," Topher says, taking one step and then two, finally entering enough for the door to bang back into place against the doorstop. "The bus I was on was supposed to be the express, but it wasn't, and then I was scared to get off, like I wouldn't find the right one. But then it stalled, and we had to get out and get on a different bus, but that was still the wrong bus, and then it got sideswiped in the tunnel, and it was a whole thing, so then I just sort of . . ." He trails off, having run out of air within his slender frame.

"That's some crazy bad luck," Mateo says, his precisely penciled-in eyebrows high.

Topher sucks in a hard breath and holds it, large eyes increasing.

Okay. So. Step one to ever getting a lunch break: Calm this guy down. "Really, it's fine," Mateo soothes, waving a hand at the hip-high door that leads behind the counter. "Come on back. Put your bag in the cubby-thing there." He indicates the cube storage on the far side of the cutting table that was once white and is now various upsetting shades of brown.

Topher's gaze snags on Mateo's matte-black stiletto nails, then hair, then face, and finally lingers on Mateo's shirt. His soft mouth parts as if there's a question he can't figure out how to ask. Probably about the unreality of the combination that is Mateo in black-lipped makeup and a jaunty yellow polo. Mateo gives him a moment to solidify this discordance into a query, but when Topher fails to move or speak, he taps the little door loudly with a polished claw.

Like a small woodland creature, Topher startles into motion and does as told.

Progress. Topher can, if pressed, follow basic instructions.

"I'm afraid you'll have to join me in this high-fashion hell," Mateo says, rooting beneath the register. "The owner requires we wear the shirts." He hefts out a box marked *Employee* in fat sharpie and thuds it onto the counter, gesturing for Topher to come closer.

Topher shifts exactly one inch.

So much for progress. He can't tell if this is high-frequency anxiety or if Topher's one of those guys who freaks at other guys in eyeliner. Whichever it is, it's annoying.

Once Topher reemerges from the back, the bright yellow shirt untucked over his pale gray jeans and his hair slightly tamed, Mateo launches into training mode. "Okay, so, work history. Ever use a register before?"

Topher's head shakes.

"What about customer service? Helping people on the floor?"

Another head shake, his gray eyes getting wider.

"Receiving?"

Topher's eyes go wider still, and he mouths the word *no*.

What the actual hell? Doris wouldn't hire someone with zero experience, right? Except, she would because she's cheap. Probably paying him below minimum wage. He doesn't want to ask but needs to understand how bad the day ahead will be. "Have you ever had a job before?"

Now those gray eyes are saucers, near-perfect circles of alarm, like he's the shocked one.

Fucking. Hell.

"Okay. Okay. Oh. Kay." Maybe he has other skills. Quick learner. Innate ability to color-match that will prove invaluable. "Everyone starts somewhere," Mateo says, impressed that he sounds amiable and not like he wants to walk into traffic. "Let's talk through some stuff."

* * *

It takes one hour for Mateo to confirm that Topher is functionally useless.

Register? Frantic button mashing locks the machine up three times while the slightly inconvenienced customers become hostile. Taking orders? Fails to write down obviously critical information on the easy-to-understand form. Six. Times. Not even a name on the last one. Making copies? Machine spits out solid black pages and makes the place stink like burnt hair.

That last one's not actually Topher's fault, but by this point, Mateo's prepared to blame him for homelessness and corporate tax loopholes.

"How about you straighten up front?" Mateo says in the inflectionless tones of the forsaken, crouching in front of the copier. "Just make things look pretty. If anyone comes in and looks confused, ask if you can help and bring them over to me."

Topher bobbles his empty head in agreement, looking as if he's just survived a war zone when it's Mateo surviving active crimes against humanity. Mateo does a lot of pulling out and sticking back in of parts. Thumb to the *print* button, the machine whirs to life.

He keeps an eye on Topher haunting the front as he prints orders. Topher's doing a lot of picking up and putting back down in the same spot. Like he has no idea how to straighten up.

Holy shit.

Topher has no idea how to straighten up. It's not even a convincing fake of it.

Screaming won't fix this, so Mateo crams the bad feelings into a tight little ball so as to more easily ignore them and finishes orders.

As he powers on the large-format printer, his attention snags on Topher stumbling to put distance between himself and a homemade-cookies-looking elderly woman. It's as far from asking if she needs help as possible. Anti-help.

He can think of precisely one reason Doris would hire this guy, and it's obvious now. Topher's the kid of someone she knows. Another *Shitty Brian*. And like Shitty Brian, this guy's going to be not just useless but extra work.

Mateo waves the old lady over and helps her before returning to orders. He needs their soothing, robotic simplicity. Printing, cutting, and laminating is the only therapy he can afford, but he can't shake Topher's nervous energy. It isn't until the old lady exits, door slamming against the stopper, that he realizes the jittery sensation has morphed into an actual headache.

Pulse picking up, he automatically runs his tongue over his teeth to check for sharpness, which he finds, but he's not angry, so it explains nothing. What the hell is happening? He puts both hands on his forehead, like he expects to find a gaping wound to explain the strange ache. Not just strange. Unprecedented. In his twenty-three years of life, he's never once had a headache.

One of the benefits to Mateo's *affliction* is that he's incredibly resilient. His body can't hold on to discomfort or injury. Never had a cold. Doesn't worry about flu season. Even a broken bone will mend in about an hour.

This has nothing to do with his novice magic and everything to do with the fact that his mother turned him into the clandestine vessel for an ancient evil. And no, he doesn't know why. She never wanted to talk about it, and she isn't the kind of person who you ask things twice. His infant body must have been the only human-shaped receptacle on hand. Not that he's got a whole complex about it or anything.

Which means this sudden headache is amazingly alarming. It's gotta be a magic attack. Probably. Like, ninety percent sure. It'd be weird if he started getting normal-people headaches out of the blue, wouldn't it? Unless the headache is a new symptom of his degrading human body losing out against the thing inside of him—like the dreams, the fugue states, and the shadows in mirrors and at the corners of his vision.

This thought's too real, so he focuses on the magic-attack angle again. Maybe someone's found him. Maybe he's been sloppy in his warding and someone picked up his demonic scent. But the shop's empty except for Topher, who's staring dimly into the bin of poster tubes like he can't work out their function.

Topher.

Mateo's mom used to tell him there were demon hunters out there—to get him to do the dishes. Maybe Topher's a demon-hating wizard and this is *his* magic headache attack.

But why the hell would a demon hunter get a job here?

Not that Mateo can talk.

The headache is very real, though. Something is happening, and the backs of his eyes are throbbing in a way he's never experienced. If this is somehow Topher causing it, then he's way worse than Shitty Brian.

CHAPTER TWO

An hour of careful, side-eyed observation and Mateo's bored again.

It's not that he wants a demon hunter fight. Zero idea what that would even be, especially when they're both of the *never thrown a punch in their lives* physique. But he'd welcome it over the newly discovered joy of performing his job with a raging migraine.

He tells Topher to take a lunch, and all Topher does is speed walk up the street like an uptight, suburban housewife—all jarring, high-stress motions. No threat there, just ridiculous looking. The tension in Mateo's skull slacks with every power-walked step between them. As far as evidence of aggression goes, it feels circumstantial.

Pulling out a granola bar—hemp, sunflower, and pumpkin seed because Ophelia does the grocery shopping, and she's disgusting—he leans on the counter and tries to reason out the unreasonable as a lone customer circles the bubble mailers.

If it's an attack, it's a weak one. Only mildly inconvenient and defeated by clocking out and going home. Could it be that Topher's so annoyingly useless that he's forced a normal human headache through a demonically altered body? Plausible but not likely.

It really probably is his human body dying around him.

Demon, sprite, faerie, god. They're all technically the same thing: an entity from another plane of reality. The ones dubbed *demon* are just the ones most incompatible with human life.

Mateo's housing one of those.

A typical demon possession has some notable hallmarks: All-black eyes, bone-breaking contortions, vomiting demon gunk, and speaking in tongues. Real *The Exorcist* stuff. The human body can't handle containing any of these creatures. It starts to break down pretty rapidly—props to his sucky mom on mitigating that. He's lived for over two decades since she locked something inside of him. Which has to be the worst world record to hold.

But whatever she did is failing. *Missing time, seeing things, invasive and violent thoughts, loss of control of his own body* kind of failing.

And using magic makes it worse.

Which begs the question: why would he want to do magic on the side if doing magic makes it worse?

Funnily enough, time makes it worse too. He can either wait to be overtaken by the thing inside him or scrape together enough money with the only questionable skill he has and hire someone to get it out. And the people who might be familiar with his specific problem—and not immediately kill him for it—are expensive and far away.

A real damned-if-you-do, damned-if-you-don't scenario, but the literal kind because no signs point to good stuff happening to his soul once he fully loses control of himself.

A soft buzz, and he scoops up his phone from the counter, knowing it's Ophelia texting because he doesn't communicate with anyone else. It's a picture of what must be their last DRIVE! Energy drink, held upside down and empty over the sink. Mateo fishes out his wallet, counts six dollars, does a little rent-dinner-paycheck-timing math, and then texts her back a sticker of a cartoon skeleton tenderly holding a bright pink heart.

Hemp seeds and sixteen fluid ounces of cranberry chemical is Ophelia. He wouldn't tolerate such a hypocritical combination from anyone else.

Thumb hovers over the keyboard as he considers asking for help. They're codependent but in a cute, probably psychologically healthy way, and he feels better when she's involved. But what would he even ask? Hey, could you flip through one of those books in terrible old Spanish that we're both bad at reading because our parents never taught us Spanish and check the index for *demon vessel gets a headache from a potential demon hunter with no life skills?*

That isn't what he'd ask, of course. He'd ask her to swing by. One look and she'd know if Topher was of the spell-wielding variety. Ophelia possesses both horrible taste in drinks and the Sight with a capital *S*. But he can't risk it. Not when he doesn't know if Topher's a threat.

Bubble Mailer Guy stuck his hand inside every mailer, found them wanting, and left, so Mateo searches online for anything about his now-faded-probably-dying-but-maybe-magic-attack headache.

Halfway through an article on negative energies, someone whispers. "What's that?"

Topher's directly in front of the counter.

Mateo full-body jolts in an obviously startled way that Topher doesn't react to. Which is cool and super normal of Topher. Not that Mateo's a master of his surroundings, but the only noise in the shop is the smooth jazz his mind filters out due to years of inhumane exposure to the same six songs. He hadn't heard the bang of the front door hitting the doorstop.

"Article on dark energies, according to some guy named *GoodVibesOnlyPaul*," Mateo answers truthfully, learning that his reaction to being startled is disconcerting honesty.

Topher's bug-eyes get buggier, and he starts a full chihuahua, trembling all over. It's the worst response—until those pale lips, barely a different color from his anemic skin, part. He's going to say something. A spell. A threat. Random weirdness. Doesn't matter. Mateo takes an unconscious step back, certain something he doesn't want is about to happen.

The shop door bangs open, and a rumpled CEO or poor college student—no visual difference in downtown Seattle—stands there with a phone pressed to his ear. "You sell paper?"

CEO, then. And it's the most beautifully brainless question Mateo's ever heard. He vaults over the hip-high divider to get around the counter and away from Topher, ecstatic to show a person with literal stacks of paper on every side of them where the paper is.

* * *

Paper Dumbass signals the start of the after-work rush. The flow of customers is constant, and it's five after seven before the *cha-ching* of the final customer brings with it the suffocating weight of aloneness with Topher.

Mateo walks to the front, flips the lights off, and pulls the security gate down and locks it.

"I just have to do the drawer stuff," Mateo says, voice startling himself because it's booming in the heavy silence. "Can you watch the front?" This isn't a thing. Both the gate and the door are locked, but Topher bobbles yes, and Mateo flees into the back with the cash drawer.

By the time he zips up the day's earnings into a black deposit bag and inserts it into the safe, he starts feeling ridiculous for getting worked up. The headache went away. Anything could have caused it, including something internal. There's a demon in him, for fuck's sake, and he's blaming that dipshit. The only proof is coincidental timing and that Topher's awkward, weird about guys in makeup, and never learned a single life skill that could help in a work environment.

More than that is the fact that Topher just worked an entire five-and-a-half-hour shift without a single murder attempt. Unless he's a long-game demon hunter serial killer, odds are he's just a nepotism-hire weirdo.

Nightly deposit done, Mateo steps out of the backroom just as Topher's quiet voice says, "—going home. The car seemed familiar. It might be from my neighborhood."

Easing through the door, Mateo doesn't let it slam shut. He tries not to think too deeply about his automatic spy-mode response.

Topher is in the dark, facing the front window, bathed in the blue wash of light from the glass. A phone is pressed to an ear, his posture rigid and motionless as he listens to the other side of the call. Seeing Topher still when he's been mild-panic-frenetic all day is unsettling.

"No. I didn't see her face before it was . . ." A pause. "Off her face," is what Mateo is positive Topher says next. Which is absolutely the fucking worst. Like that, Mateo's certain Topher's a demon hunter serial killer again, nonchalantly discussing his latest kill with a friend demon hunter. Or maybe the gravity in his voice means he's reporting to his demon hunter boss. Maybe he's in a demon hunter union. At least he sounds somber about un-facing a lady, like maybe if he kills Mateo, he'll be a little sad about it.

Topher's free hand balls into a fist at his side, and Mateo tenses. The silence extends a moment more before Topher says, "No. I won't. This conversation was a courtesy and now it's over. I think you should talk to my lawyer from now on." It's textbook *murderer deferring to lawyer* application of the phrase, tone firm and quiet.

Topher lowers the phone and stares out the window.

Being the vessel for an ancient evil sounds impressive until you consider that Mateo's mother forbade him from learning magic. Since her abrupt departure, he's self-taught what anyone could if they'd spent years spying on their scary witch mom and unearthed the real spells in the glut of bullshit how-to witchcraft books on Amazon. He's three-quarters through a practical guide on crystals he'd been feeling pretty good about until now. It hadn't covered anything about keeping his face on his face.

With all the care he can muster, Mateo opens the door just an inch and then pushes it closed loudly as if he's just walked in. "All done. I just gotta get the trash."

Topher turns, blinks as if just waking up, and nods.

They spend the next few minutes wordlessly rustling around in the darkness, getting original outfits back on and bags collected while Mateo fervently hopes Topher won't speak. But the silence is unnerving too. It's pregnant with a nameless dread, like Topher's head might tip back and a demon tongue will come lolling out.

He's not sure how Topher went from demon hunter to demon—no, it was definitely the *face off* stuff. Topher doesn't have any of the signs of being possessed, but strong demons are meant to be able to hide it for a while.

Is a demon possession better or worse than a demon hunter? A demon might be cool with Mateo—birds of a feather. Or might totally hate him. His body's trapping one. That's probably a real dick move in demon circles. Though, this might have nothing to do with magic. Topher might just be a good old-fashioned serial killer. No reason to discount a classic.

His brain is spiraling as he shoves his polo into one of the cubbies. Almost out of there. Just gotta walk out the back. Then it's someone else's problem. Like Doris, who he has to convince to fire this guy without explaining the real reason why. Maybe he can do a *him or me* threat. Except he can't. Too big of a chance Doris would fire Mateo. He's paid under the table on account of not having a soc, ID, or taxable proof of legal existence and she likes to remind him she's doing him a solid paying him anything at all. She's fun like that.

Grabbing up the day's trash, he motions for Topher to give him a minute. The back door is a heavy steel thing that takes all of Mateo's body weight to shove open. Gross back-alley night air washes over him and feels fantastic. Like escape is imminent.

The only sounds as he disposes of his armloads in the appropriate bin are his boots squelching in alley-yuck and his heart thudding an experimental riff in his chest. He doesn't want to go back inside—considers what would happen if he cut through the alley and went straight home—but that feels like Topher would still be there in the morning, waiting with his serial killer eyes and a bunch of people's faces.

Irresolute on his escape plan, he slams and locks the bin.

"If you make a single sound," a woman says, her voice impatient and very close as a knife suddenly enters his peripheral vision, angled at Mateo's throat, "I'll kill you."

CHAPTER THREE

Mateo turns with cartoon slowness. The most displeased office lady Mateo's ever seen stands disconcertingly close. Her black hair is slicked back so severely that it resembles paint applied directly to her scalp. She's in an impeccably white pencil skirt, with a high-necked white blazer on top. Her dark red lipstick is perfect, eyebrows razor sharp, and her eyeliner could kill a man. She's kind of amazing, but it's hard to appreciate because of the knife in her hand.

No. Not knife. Dagger.

Fancy handle with intricate patterning. She's holding it like one might if they were about to stake a vampire. Is *this* a demon hunter?

"Wallet," she demands, enunciating her point by taking an aggressive and frankly unwarranted step toward Mateo.

Okay. Not a demon hunter. Unless they multitask and mug demons first.

At six foot three, Mateo towers over her, but it doesn't matter. She's doing a back-alley mugging in all-white with a dagger and it's real unstable behavior he can't match the energy of. So, it's with the utmost care that Mateo reaches around to his back pocket and slips his wallet out. He's doing exactly what he's been asked to do, but the mugger takes another step and presses the tip of the blade to the skin of his throat.

"Slow," she demands flatly, leaning in close enough for Mateo to feel the word.

The worst he's tested his healing against is a fractured ulna when he fell off the roof as a kid. Having his throat slit feels like a whole other level he's not mentally prepared to explore tonight, so he doesn't take another breath until his wallet is snatched from his fingers.

The mugger steps back and flips it open, blade kept level at Mateo. She's way too calm, and an irrational desire for a frantic mugging rises like acid in Mateo's throat. The sober professionalism feels fatal. A red-polished thumb riffles, looking for choice credit cards or an ID to identity theft, neither of which Mateo possesses. There're some sandwich point cards. Clairvoyance isn't a power Mateo has, but he's certain that when she sees only six crumpled dollars tucked in the flap, he's getting stabbed.

Ignoring the money, she eyes the point card for way too long, then turns her dark gaze on him. "Where's Ignacia Luisa Reyes Borrero?"

"What?" Mateo asks way too forcefully while under knife-threat. But now he's taking her in with proper context. The outfit, the manner, and the magic-ass-looking dagger make a specific sense. She's a witch. It's been a while since anyone magically inclined cropped up looking for his mother. Never so aggressively, though. Nothing about her expression says she wants to repeat herself as he puzzles over this, so he adds, "I have no idea where she is. She's been MIA for almost five years."

Mathematically lipsticked lips thin in displeasure. "Who are you?"

Unexpected follow-up in this very on-purpose situation. Why does she know to ask him about Ignacia, but doesn't know Ignacia's his mom? He opens his mouth to lie—doesn't feel like he should tell a woman trying to knife him about his complicated familial relationships—but four things happen in rapid succession:

A deafening crash way too close. The witch lashes out. The knife stabs into the arm that he jerks up in defense. And someone grabs Mateo's other arm and pulls.

He stumbles a few steps and realizes it's Topher that has him, frigid fingers dragging him away from the woman and down the alley. A wild look back and she's braced against the wall. A giant terracotta pot lies shattered at her feet, dirt and plant matter scattered about. She's staring after them in what he can only imagine is fury but it's too dark to see.

They explode onto the Belltown evening streets where traffic and prying eyes live. They run a block before they both start to flag. They get one more before the wordless agreement of two people who don't workout passes between them. Mateo keeps looking back but doesn't spot a stiletto-wearing pursuer. Rounding one last corner, they collapse against the side of a coffee shop.

Five minutes of gulping air as people walk by pointedly ignoring them, and nothing codifies in Mateo's brain. He has no clue what just happened, and the meat of his bicep is throbbing. A buzzing tingle sits beneath the heat, like rubbing Icy Hot into a first-degree burn.

Topher is squatting beside him and having a rougher time of their extremely pathetic marathon—which causes a brief, petty, and utterly undeserved feeling of triumph in Mateo. He is better at running than someone who is also bad at running.

Focus up. Black blood is dripping down his arm. His sweater sleeve, conveniently also black, is soggy with it. As discreetly as he can manage, Mateo starts wiping his hand on his also-black pants. Hopefully, the combination of goth and dark street means Topher didn't realize he was slashed in the chaos. If he doesn't draw attention to it, his new plan of walking briskly away from Topher forever might still fly.

"Did you see . . . what the fuck?" Mateo manages eloquently around his wheezing.

Blond head tips back, pale cheeks flushed with horrible physical exertion. "The . . . roof . . . a pot," Topher says with effort, pausing to pull in loud breaths. "Fell. Scared her."

Thank fuck for bad landlords who allow dangerous rooftop gardens. The timing of that was insane, though. And if it had hit anyone, they'd be super dead.

"Who mugs retail workers? Notoriously-flush-with-cash retail workers." Mateo sounds affronted, glancing at his hand. It's not perfectly clean, but it can pass as dirty now.

"You were cut," Topher says.

Mateo's gaze snaps back to Topher, huddled on the ground but staring up at him with his worst expression yet. At no point has Topher looked anything but on the verge of an existential anxiety crisis, but now his unnerving gaze is steady, saucer eyes featuring a new, glossy edge.

Fuck. Fuck, fuck, fuck.

"No," Mateo says too loudly. "She missed." He offers a relieved smile. It occurs to him three seconds too late that his teeth get sharp when he heals.

Gaze still steady, Topher whispers, "I came here to find you. I think you can help me."

CHAPTER FOUR

In the dimly lit bathroom of the Downtown Expresso, Mateo's arm is raw and angry but nowhere near as bad as it was. Only a long divot sits where the blade sunk in, and a deep heat in the meat of the muscle. A freak-out needs to happen about someone showing up at his job to violently shake him down about his mom, but he can't deal with that yet. So he wrings the blood out of his sleeve as best he can with a dozen gauzy paper towels and then shoves them to the bottom of the trash.

Favoring his injured arm, he pushes out of the bathroom. Topher is vibrating at a table in the back of the café, a to-go cup in each hand. Mateo gives the café a quick look for Dagger Lady, then drops into the seat across from Topher, trying to play it like this isn't terrifying.

Topher presses both cups across the table at him. "I didn't know what you like. I got a triple tall cappuccino and a caffe generra with whip. I can get something else, though. Anything else. Many elses. Or food. Croissant. There was a donut. It looked old."

One of the drinks sounds like sugar, so Mateo takes it, watching Topher wrap both hands around the cappuccino.

Someone should slap it away from him. The last thing this guy needs is caffeine. But the same can be said for Mateo, heart still jackrabbiting in his chest. Whatever Topher wants, he's seen Mateo's secret. This is now as close to discovery as he's ever been. It requires no great imagination to get to experiments-medical-types-might-like-to-run-on-him.

Not that Topher said anything about selling him for parts to the highest bidder. He'd distinctly said he wanted help. With no idea what to say, Mateo waits for Topher to explain anything.

Topher drinks his coffee like a mouse with a prized morsel of food, both hands lifting it and a lot of small, rapid sips. "There was a WorkList ad."

"I pulled that." There's no world where this is a confused, sexual proposition situation, but Mateo's mouth moves on defensive autopilot.

"I know," Topher says, squeezing the paper cup hard enough that the lid pops up on one side. "I just . . . I need help. A lot of the other magic people ads were really long and had all of these weird credentials and certificates I've never heard of, and I couldn't look most of them up, and the ones I could were made on really bad free websites that didn't even use basic website templates, so they were really ugly. Like with gifs. And your ad sounded . . . normal. Like, not made up or conceited. And you didn't have any social media or a site or whatever. And the last line of the ad made me laugh."

Mateo makes a low sound of emotional distress in the back of his throat. How can he be embarrassed, freaked out, and annoyed all at the same time? He sips his coffee while trying to pick a lane. "I didn't list my place of employment in the ad." Annoyed won.

Topher's skin, which had faded back to the alabaster pallor of an anemic ghost, flushes so entirely it's like his hue setting got slid all the way to magenta. "I know. I'm sorry. I screen-grabbed the post before you took it down. When I tried to call, the number was disconnected, so I hired someone to look up who the number belonged to. A professional someone I mean. That sounds bad. I mean, it was bad, probably. I'm sorry. I just . . . I really need help, and I don't know who else to go to."

Most of the components of that sentence are alarming, but there was a bright shining nugget in there: Hired.

As in: With money.

New eyes consider Topher as Mateo takes another sip of his sickly-sweet drink. Topher is brandless and styleless, but maybe that's money. There are different kinds: Gucci/Hermes/Louis Vuitton rich—which is easy to spot—versus *so rich your clothes look like whatever the hell*. Those kinds of rich people are so rich that a plain gray t-shirt could cost thousands of dollars.

Mateo licks his lips, trying to rejigger the situation in his head, wanting it to make sense. "But why did you get a job at the print shop?"

Topher's gaze averts so fully that he actually whips his whole head to the left. "I . . . I came in a week ago to talk to you but . . . um. I mean, I saw you and . . . I mean, there's nothing wrong with, um . . ." He starts and stops, looking like he wants to flee the table.

Mateo relaxes a little bit. "Right. Goth posting about magic. Looks fake."

Topher's head bobbles in agreement, his relief at being understood palpable.

"So, you saw my ad." Embarrassing. "Tried to contact me, couldn't, hired someone to track me down." Scary, but meant money. "Popped in to talk to me but got nervous from my cool style." Understandable given the context. "Decided the easiest thing to do was get hired and feel me out." Insane. "Worked a shift." It was hard not to say *badly*. It was hard to say *worked*. "And now we're here?"

Topher bobbles.

"*Here*, meaning you want to hire me?" Mateo asks slowly.

Another bobble and Topher deflates, shoulders slumping and eyes lowering to his cup as he starts spinning it between restless hands.

Mateo gives him the moment he obviously needs. Because . . . money.

When Topher's pale eyes find Mateo's again, they're wet. "That lady mugging you was my fault. Bad things happen around me. I've gotten five people killed in the past few months. Eight others really hurt."

Mateo's never seen someone's eyes get so wet without tears falling. Must be the sheer surface volume available to the liquid. Some of that is bullshit, though, since Dagger Lady definitely had nothing to do with Topher.

Reading his expression, Topher's voice gets quieter. The dam holding back the volume of water in his eye gives out, and tears slide free. It's a silent crying that doesn't involve the rest of Topher's face, just twin rivulets streaming. "I know how this sounds. I tried to get the police to arrest me, then I realized there'd be people trapped in a cell with me. But something's really wrong. It's definitely me causing these horrible things, but no one believes me."

This guy might be deranged. But if Topher's story's true, it sounds like a curse. Doesn't take a magical genius to figure that out—which is great because that's not what Mateo is. And it wouldn't take a magical genius to uncurse him, either. Meaning Mateo can theoretically handle it. He can theoretically handle anything if the price is right.

"Nothing's guaranteed. I do a consultation first. Five hundred for this talk, and we'll figure out pricing from there," Mateo says, tone matter-of-fact, like he does this all the time and isn't reaching wildly for numbers.

As soon as it's out of his mouth, he's positive the ask is too high, but Topher nods tightly.

It would be inappropriate to cheer, what with all the death and crying, so Mateo focuses on the still-throbbing knife wound to remain sober. Money is good, but curses are a big deal. They can kill and maim. Doom bloodlines. Not that Mateo's bloodline isn't already absolutely fucked. Healing from a slashing seems really cool until you realize that's magic. And that flare of magic will cost him.

Every time he uses magic, the world's shittiest prize wheel spins. He could win: More blackouts—no clue what he does during them. More anger—going to become a real problem soon. That horrid dream—please no.

But no one else is offering him a bunch of money, so whatever danger this curse represents, he's game to deal with it. "Elaborate on how people are getting *hurt*." Mateo says.

"All sorts of ways," Topher says, trying to make the world's smallest, waxiest napkin do anything about his tears. "An air conditioner . . . horrible. Tree branch . . . speared. A *For Lease* sign got caught by the wind. It was arrow-shaped. A wiggly inflatable arm car dealership thing."

Holy actual shit. Mateo desperately wants to ask about the wiggly arm guy, but Topher's not done, and it feels kind of insensitive, maybe.

There's lots of car crashes: the bus thing that very morning, multiple intersections, at a drive-thru, and even in front of Topher's house days ago. Topher hesitates on that last one, fingers drifting up to his damp cheek as he whispers. "That woman died. Very badly."

The face off!

Okay. Wow. If any of it's real, that's a lot.

However much he can get out of this guy isn't worth dying for. Unless it's, like, really a lot of money.

The lack of reaction to the consultation fee is a bright blaring siren call in Mateo's mind, drowning out the fact that he was just knifed. If he's doing this, he needs to get paid even if he can't figure out what's happening or fix it.

First, show that he's compassionate. "That sounds difficult." Second, say some shit to sound smart about it. "If it's a curse, and I'm assuming it is right now, it has some interesting characteristics. Abnormal, even." Solid.

And it's only sort of bullshit. He didn't put the ad on WorkList with nothing to offer. Being raised by a powerful bruja who was also a shit mother meant that he'd heard and seen a lot of things he was forbidden from seeing and hearing. He'd picked up some stuff.

Topher's eyes become watery balloons again.

Hope. And a willingness to pay for said hope.

He's on the line. Mateo just has to not reel too fast or jerk the line or however the hell fishing works.

"If it's a curse," Mateo says, taking the last sip of his coffee to work out something cool to say, "That means someone cursed you." Fucking obviously. "Got any enemies? Make anyone mad? Classmate? Or a coworker at whatever your real job is? Anyone hate you?"

Like a wet dog left alone in the rain, Topher's head dips. "No. I mean, not that I can think of. I finished school two years ago, and this stuff only started about three months ago. I don't have a job. I mean, I did today. But normally, I don't. I don't talk to a lot of people. But. I mean . . . I'm also not very good with people sometimes. Most times. All times. So. Maybe? But not that I remember it being bad enough for all this. The, uh, killing."

Useless. Okay. Other routes. "What about your parents? Do they have any enemies?"

"My dad works on Wall Street."

They share a beat of silence.

"Right. So, dad pissing someone off is an angle," Mateo says. "What about mom?"

Topher bodily curls around the cup, intensifying the sad dog look into ASPCA-commercial levels. This dog has never known love. Dramatic music's already blaring from the overhead speaker. "Probably nothing to do with her. She left a little before Easter. Left my dad, I mean. I mean, she left the house, so . . . she left me too, I guess. Technically. But, I mean . . . it's him she was leaving. Not me. We haven't really talked since. But she's busy. She has a busy job."

Jesus. This guy is a bunch of yikes topics. Also, he'd just basically said his mom did it. Curse stuff starts happening right around the time she bounces? Not answering calls? Sounds sus as hell. He can't say that, though, or he won't be able to run up the bill. Except now he has no idea how to respond because that was a slightly too intimate information dump he'd absolutely asked for.

"Okay. This gives me a place to start." Nailing it. "I'll need you to email me some basic info. Your parents' full names, any close family or friends, and any of your father's business partners or associates' names." Wall Street guys had partners and associates, he was pretty sure.

Topher bobbles his head.

"And just to be perfectly clear," Mateo says, needing to stress this disclaimer so hard. "I don't know if I can help you."

Topher bobbles again, the song overhead crescendoing.

Channeling every crime procedural Ophelia's made him sit through while painting his nails, Mateo says, "Put me on retainer for a week. The rate is—" A pricing structure for magical research based on knowing the guy's dad works on Wall Street forms. "Two grand. Half now, half at the end of the week."

It's too much. It's deranged. Mateo braces for Topher's shock and then outrage.

"I don't think I have that much on me right now," Topher says, like there was a possibility he could have that much on him right now. Phone is in hand without a thought, tapping away. "The banks are closed . . . you probably don't take card. I have PayNow?" Topher's suddenly striking, engaging, beautiful, and not-too-big eyes look at Mateo questioningly.

"PayNow works," Mateo manages as Topher hands over his phone so Mateo can type in his username with hands that want to tremble. He hits enter, and the cell in his pocket chirps. As he fishes it out, he has to use every ounce of self-control to keep his customer service smile in place and not just, like, cackle. A one. A five. A pair of zeros. Four-dollar twenty-cent service fee subtracted. It's the most beautiful email he's ever received.

This is a plane ticket to Puerto Rico amount. Extended stay in a bad hotel amount. Track down someone who might understand what his mother did and not automatically try to kill him for being an abomination amount.

"Cool. Very cool," he says, which isn't the pro response he'd hoped for but at least he hadn't screamed it in primal joy.

Once outside, coffee cups tossed and a multitude of possibilities suddenly attainable, Mateo offers a goodbye handshake. A thing he's never done in his life, but it feels like something a professional should do. "Give me a few days, and I'll be in touch."

Topher power walks out of sight, and the café front becomes uncomfortably devoid of life. Mateo checks up and down the street for Dagger Lady, wishing he'd borrowed Ophelia's car. Long-term-fix might be brewing with this cursed rich guy, but that doesn't do anything about his mom's enemies showing up in the dark.

Keeping his head on a swivel, he hurries home.

CHAPTER FIVE

"Phee!" Mateo shouts, tossing his ruined sweater onto the ancient moss-green couch that's always existed in the living room. It's pitch black in the house, so he flips switches as he goes down the narrow hall toward Ophelia's bedroom. He's halted by the sound of running water as he passes the bathroom. No crack of light visible under the door. Shit.

They've lived in close quarters for half of their lives, his tween years made up of sleepovers in each other's beds. When his mom bounced, and Ophelia's family died, it just made sense that she'd move in. No discussion. They'd packed her up the night of the funerals.

Which is why he shoves the door open without warning. "Ophelia? Are you—shit, you're not here." Metaphysically speaking, at least.

Her body is right there, standing motionless in the shower, face tipped up toward the water. No reaction from his intrusion, even when he shoves the pebbled plastic curtain aside and reaches in to turn the frigid spray off. The water heater went to shit a few months ago, so he's not sure if the thing's acting up again or if she's been gone long enough for the hot water to run out.

This would be real horror movie vibes, as she's unresponsive, dead-eyed, staring up at nothing, but he knows exactly what this is.

Accidental astral projection again. Traveling.

He spends the next few minutes maneuvering her slippery body out of the tub when he isn't strong enough to lift her. It isn't pretty. They end up in a pile on the bathroom floor, Mateo's pants soaked as he pats her cold cheek a few times, repeating the chant they agreed upon: "Ophelia De La Garza, come back to me, or I'll throw away your disgusting chips."

The third pat makes her close her milky-whited-over eyes. The fourth pat gets those same eyes twitching beneath lids. "Don't you dare," she mumbles through barely functioning lips. Eyes, now unreasonably pale blue, slide open. Dark lashes flutter as she blinks a few times, the transition back to her body always groggy and difficult.

He has a million things to tell her, but all he can do is cradle her, trying to rub warmth into freezing skin, as if that'll melt the brick of ice that forms in his chest whenever he finds her like this.

"Feels like I shouldn't have to point out that leaving your body while standing in a running shower feels like a super bad idea, bu-u-u-t." Defaulting to disapproving is the only way he knows how to deal with this as he reaches for her towel hanging from a hook beside the shower.

Ophelia only has two kinds of smiles. The nice one comes out for puppies and a variety of snacks with the word *flax* on the package. The shitty one has too many teeth and zero mirth and can wilt a man from thirty yards. She graces him with the shittiest one yet. "I don't come into your shower and tell you how to be a functioning member of society."

Mateo's chest thaws a little, pressing dark lips to her forehead briefly. One of her frozen hands finds his arm. Squeezes. It's all either of them will allow after one of these incidents.

The topic of Ophelia's condition, much like Mateo's, is rife with uncertainty. What they do know is that Ophelia and her whole family were astral projecting—common enough for a family of Travelers. They'd been exploring a plane Ophelia had never visited before, led there by her older sister, Juliet. And something found them.

Most witches have to use tokens to communicate with the powerful things that live in other planes of reality. Something imbued with intention and crafted specifically for that entity. Using a token is a lot like talking to someone with bad cell reception. But Travelers can send their spirits to those other planes. It gives them direct contact with these extradimensional beings; which means it also gives them direct contact to very real danger.

The details of what had happened are unclear, lost to the trauma of being trapped out of her body for an extended period of time. But they'd all died. Juliet. Their parents. Ophelia.

Three days later, Ophelia woke up.

The rest did not.

And ever since, Ophelia sometimes floats away, like a critical part connecting spirit and body was severed. Each time Mateo finds her empty body, he manages to coax her back. So far. But he's terrified that it's like the shitty water heater. It'll work until it doesn't.

There's no point in talking about it. They don't know how to fix it. One of the totally emotionally healthy reasons they're such good friends is because they're both so undeniably fucked that it feels right that they go down together.

She extracts herself from his arms, stepping gingerly around his legs, and starts to towel off. She fully doesn't get out of his way, drying herself nearly on top of him, so he has to crawl on hands and knees out of the bathroom to avoid having her butt in his face.

"Did you get my drink?" she asks, wringing out her hip-length, bad-bleach-job hair into the sink—not an insult. She loves her dark roots showing.

"No, I didn't go to the store, but shut up," Mateo says, getting to his feet. He's sopping wet, so he starts undressing in the hall. "I got knifed and made fifteen hundred tonight."

"At work? Are we criminals now?" she asks, stepping out of the bathroom towel-less with her hair in a vast, messy bun. She won't express concern or excitement until she understands, so he follows, stripping off his soggy pants and tossing them at their tasteful hallway floor hamper.

"This new guy showed up at work—" he starts and has to wait for her to finish making the universally recognized *bow-chika-wow-wow* insinuating sex as she disappears into her room. It doesn't even make sense, but he tells her to shut up again and then shouts everything through the paper-thin wall between their rooms as they get dressed. No detail is spared. Topher's startled-bird-like weirdness, the headache, how shit Topher was at working, the well-dressed Dagger Lady looking for his mom, the knifing, and Topher's stalkery tracking Mateo down.

They end up at the kitchen table, Ophelia pressing cold fingers to the pink line that's the only thing left of the knifing.

She releases his arm, considering him. "Add me as a consultant. Get double the pay."

"Ophelia De La Garza," Mateo says slowly, scandalized. "You're a fucking genius."

"Don't I know it." She takes the seat in front of him. In their boxy kitchen, she always looks unreal. Five foot nothing, skin the tone of wet sand, and eyes the exact shade of the sky over the ocean at sunrise. The point where the orange ends, but there's a washed-out blue before the real color of the sky begins. They used to be brown. Another facet they don't understand.

Getting a few grand could change things.

They're both in a bad way. The very real possibility of her drifting out of her body and being unable to find her way back again is a fear so many magnitudes larger than his fear of what's happening to him. But his demon problem puts a target on both of them because nobody likes demons. If he's found out by the wrong people, they're both in danger. Also, it stops him from being able to freely use magic. If Topher's money can buy him an exorcism, he can become a proper brujo and maybe learn the kinds of things that could help her.

For a second, they're hopeful.

But then Ophelia asks, "What about Dagger Lady?"

Mateo grimaces, the pain in his arm gone but that problem persists. "Yeah, I dunno. She found me at work, which maybe means she knows where this house is and followed me." It's not like she pulled up employment records.

Ophelia sucks her teeth for a moment, squinting. "Yeah, probably that. I might have seen her. Couple of days ago. Some pant-suited lady was on the lawn when I came home."

Mateo gapes at her. "Why is this the first time you're mentioning her?"

"Oh right, because a random lady on the lawn for, like, two minutes, is an extremely notable occurrence in this house of magic and demons," she says sardonically. Which, fair. "She didn't try to stab *me*. She just stared when I pulled in, then walked off."

"She can't get in, so at least there's that," he says, extremely hating that this crazy lady had been so close to Ophelia. Moving houses so his mom's criminal associates can't find him would be ideal, but the house is warded all to hell, keeping him safe from wider demon-hating-people detection.

Not that he can hide away inside forever, either. He has to go to work. And if Ophelia leaves the house, she'd also be in danger, since Dagger Lady proved tonight that anyone Ignacia-adjacent will do for knife-based interrogation.

"Wild coincidence that a rich weirdo and Dagger Lady both found you at work today," Ophelia points out, and they stare at each other.

It *is* a wild coincidence. Considering how earnest and upset Topher had seemed—and how bad he was at working—Mateo can't imagine he was putting on an act. Or fathom a reason for one. Dagger Lady didn't need help. She was doing a fine job of scaring the shit out of him.

"I think that's what the curse does," he says, leaning back in his chair. "Makes unlikely, shitty situations happen to people around him."

The first edge of concern enters her voice as she asks, "You had protection wards on?"

"Yeah. She didn't know what I was," he says. You'd probably bring more than a fancy dagger to a demon fight. "Just thought I knew where Ignacia was."

He doesn't want to get distracted from the possibility of a real payday by his mom's residual bullshit, but he also can't pretend he wasn't knifed. Especially when it could happen to Ophelia. "Okay. As my newly appointed assistant—"

"Additional consultant. Sexist," she interrupts with her shitty smile. They both let the appropriate level of seriousness slip away from the conversation.

"As my newly appointed unpaid intern," he returns with his own shitty smile, "You have to help me brainstorm how the hell to uncurse this poor, wretched, extremely wealthy soul."

"I'll have a look at him, I assume."

There goes the faint sheen of levity. "No. No way. Even if it mighta been my mom's shit, I got stabbed being around Topher. And the headache? What the hell even was that?"

"Has the curse ever caused a medical emergency?" she says with raised eyebrows.

Genius. Maybe Topher's curse was trying to give Mateo, like, an aneurysm or stroke or other bad brain thing, but his demonic healing wouldn't let it. "You're getting a promotion," he says, pulling out his phone, opening his notes app, and typing out the medical question for Topher. There could be additional casualties Topher wasn't attributing to his curse—which is grim. "But that super makes me not want him near you even more."

"What's he gonna do? Kill me again?"

Mateo makes a pained sound deep in his throat. She won't talk about it, but she'll make horrible jokes all the goddamned time. "Now you're fired."

She leans back in her chair, the metal base like a pair of C's connected at the top and bottom. They'd found a set of them on a corner about a month ago and dragged them home. They smelt unrelentingly of hairspray. "This is forty-five hundred. We can put protection wards straight up your ass if that'll help. I have to look at him. Dagger Lady, too, if she shows up again."

Another groan, but he starts a list on his phone. It feels professional to have a list, and they're professionals now. "Fine. Protection wards up *your* ass. What else?"

They end up on the living room floor atop a forest green area rug Ophelia thrifted to stop them from tripping on the half-missing floorboard between the couch and the coffee table that has its own gravitational pull. The carpet is the nicest thing in the whole house.

Ophelia decides she's their tech support because all the books are horrible to read unless you love dry academia in a language you're not especially well versed in. A thing he doesn't love either, but she called *not it* first.

Both hunching, Ophelia over her old laptop—from a deluded summer of their fifteenth year when either of them thought college was a possibility—and him over a wide array of books he can only sort of read, they brainstorm and research.

The Topher list ends up looking pretty good: search the Nystrom family online to see what dirt can be had; an exhaustive list of which protection wards to put on them; which cleanses, scrubs, and smudges they could try on Topher; have Ophelia look at Topher; and a tarot reading never hurts.

Easy and reasonably crafted to string Topher along effectively. While helping him. They're not monsters.

Except on a technical level—where he's got a demon in him and she's an undead spirit walker or something.

CHAPTER SIX

He's always impressed with how much blood the meat suits hold. Like they're under high pressure, barely contained, everything waiting to flow out at the smallest of punctures. Which he gleefully does, licking the ensuing warmth that dribbles down his arm. He even laps at the wood floor, relishing every sweet copper drop, grit, and the exquisite tang of fear that seasoned the blood before spilling out. There's no shame in this act, only joy.

And hunger.

And a confusing sense that he doesn't want to mess up his clothes.

Reaching deeply into the meat, he pulls, delighting in the tension, the give, the eventual slow tearing as a kidney comes free. A half-remembered biology lesson flits through his mind, dragging him out of the simple pleasure of eating. He doesn't stop, though, pressing organ to lips and biting. Juice and pleasure fill his mouth with a groan, and something shifts, no longer savoring but devouring, ravenous as he takes one bite and then another. Both hands reach in, needing the next morsel waiting and ready so there's no moment without this taste on his tongue. Care evaporates as questing claws meet resistance, solid masses of muscle and bone he has no patience for. He tears, breaks, wrenches, separates joints, and cracks bone, forcing everything down his throat.

He doesn't slow until the body's a deboned fish, only major junctions, spine, and the flayed skin he has less of an interest in—though he'll eat that too. As he sits back, snapping a rib and shattering it between teeth, a nagging thought urges him to look up.

To look at the face.

To understand who he's eating.

As if that matters.

But a tension starts in his stomach, threatening to make the meal come back up.

He looks.

The space above the hollowed-out chest confuses him, pleasure and horror warring as he presses a blood-covered palm against the cooling cheek, manipulates the slack expression into a self-pleased smirk. Then, an approximation of a cackle. He can't make either as dickish as the real ones.

None of these thoughts make sense to him, and frustration swells.

Concentrating, he catches just beyond the front teeth with two claws, pressing against a cooled tongue before slowly pulling down. The cheeks stretch, then tear, and he doesn't stop until the jaw cracks and pulls free.

CHAPTER SEVEN

Mateo leans over the toilet and retches salty black demon-goo into the bowl, amazingly glad that he just cleaned the bathroom. It takes ten minutes for the gag reflex to subside, the feel of hot meat sliding down his throat vivid under the harsh yellow light of his tiny bathroom.

He searches the black film on the surface of the water for flesh or bone that isn't his.

The dreams aren't new. They started as grotesque flashes of feasting at the edges of his sleep, a hazy memory of salty richness on his tongue. Disturbing but easily dismissed.

By the time he was a teen, the dream found him every few weeks. Never the entire eating, but some section of the act.

And the need.

The details change—and by *details*, he means the victims. He stays the same. His hunger. The pleasure. The thrill of every bite.

Lately, he's had the dream every night. It encompasses the entire meal and persists in high-definition detail when awake.

The sound of the jaw cracking fills his brain, starts the back of his throat salivating again, and his stomach tries to empty itself of something that isn't there.

Or, at least, something he really hopes isn't there.

Flushing, he gets unsteadily to his feet but catches his pale, blurry expression in the mirror. Eyes wide, skin sheened in sweat, hair pressed flat on one side and sticking up on the other. *Hot*, he thinks of Ophelia saying and has to fight the urge to go to her bed, curl up behind her, press his face to the back of her neck and hold on to her until he feels like himself again.

It's a dangerous thought, teeth sharp in his mouth.

He stares too long, and the shadows come. Tendrils of pure black, seeping from his eyes and mouth, out of his hair, and off of his skin. If he asks anyone but Ophelia, they don't see them. But they're getting worse. Everything is getting worse.

And just like Ophelia won't talk about that night, he won't tell her it's escalating.

That if he stares too long in the mirror, he can't see himself.

That the dreams come every time he sleeps.

That he's calling them *dreams*, but he's pretty sure they're real.

That he's going to spend the next hour on the internet searching for the douchey guys from the truck the other day—an impossible search, too soon, not enough details, and there wouldn't be a body to report anyway.

CHAPTER EIGHT

Mateo drags himself out of bed extra early the next morning for Topher's appointment, which is heinous because he'd slept poorly and it's his only day off that week.

Throwing open all of the windows and doors as the sun only barely lights the sky, he sprinkles rue and salt over every inch of the floor.

If curse-boy is coming over, he has to re-up the wards on the house. They were composed by his mother to let the demonic energy that is Mateo in and out. Vampire-style, no one can enter without permission. A permission that can be revoked, at which point the person is violently expelled through the nearest exit, even if that's a second story window. Ask him how he knows.

It's kept his mom's associates out, including Dagger Lady, whose bright white power suit he hasn't caught even a suggestion of since the back-alley stabbing. She could be anywhere or given up entirely and he has no way of knowing.

Broom and vacuum follow, moving from the front to the back door. Smoke next, white copal resin, and then a bundle of herbs—white sage and lavender with a bit of rosemary shoved in for good measure. Nothing wow about any of that, standard witch stuff found in a million blogs with titles like *Positive Energy, Positive Mind.*

It's the blood stuff that pushes everything into the dark arts territory.

Pocket-knife in hand, he drags the blade across the pads of his fingers and presses a black smear to the small symbol carved above each door and window, systematically moving from room to room. His mother used to do it with an extremely magical looking dagger. Handle pointing up, she'd have him wrap a fist around the blade, held a small white plate with a golden edge beneath to catch the blood, and then she'd yank the blade up through his grasping fingers.

It had sucked every single time.

On his first go of it by himself, he'd been scared the dagger was a critical element. Torn the house apart looking for it—except in her office where he absolutely wouldn't search.

Turned out the wards didn't care how they got the blood, so long as they got it. Lucky him.

The visible symbols are just the point of connection for the ritual. The meat of the protections are painted against the bones of the house and plastered over. He can't get to most of them without ripping into drywall, except the ones in the roof crawl space. He's spent a lot of time, flashlight in one hand, phone in the other, studying them. It's exactly like staring at quantum physics when you only got through multiplication in your self-taught homeschool.

The last set of wards go on Ophelia and himself.

Ophelia sleeps like the dead, which is both normal—she's always been like that—and unnerving. She's just as capable of slipping out of her body and getting lost in another plane of reality in slumber as she is wide awake, but a dread born of vivid memory seizes him whenever he has to wake her, terrified she'll be cold to the touch.

Assuring himself of the steady rise and fall of her chest first, he drags her legs out from under the comforter and traces symbols onto the soles of her feet with cascarilla chalk. Minimal kicking for his efforts. With much more difficulty he does this to her wrists, arms snaking out to drag him into bed with her. By the time he gets to her chest where the last ward goes, she's fully awake but refusing to rouse because she knows there's work to do—she's on the payroll via a carefully crafted text explaining her skills and fortuitous availability.

He leaves her there faking sleep because warding himself is a whole thing.

Cascarilla is used to protect against things like being possessed by demons, but he's already possessed. Unfortunate. Still needs the wards, though, so he has to prepare them special.

On him, the purpose is less about protection and more about hiding him from anyone who might sense the demon. It can't be stressed enough how much other magic people don't like demons. Which you'd think would mean every other magic person in town would be down for helping him get an exorcism, but please refer to the frowned-upon blood magic his mom used.

A few weeks after his mom bounced, and after a particularly scuzzy-looking ex-client came knocking, Ophelia had decided they should follow the client and see what they could learn. Ophelia had just figured out a new form of projection—her family was still alive and training her at the time—and had wanted to try it out. All she needed was a good look at their aura and a personal item of some importance and she'd be able to track them. She'd forced this plan by having already stolen the wallet of the scuzzy guy.

They'd ended up in front of a nightclub with opaque windows, a large, solid, high-gloss black door, and a sign that read CARD. A quick phone search described the club as having mediocre drinks and sticky floors. The odds were high they'd get turned away, since they weren't old enough, but the guy at the front had simply said, "Show me," and fanned out a strangely miniature deck of cards face down, with a humorless stare.

Ophelia plucked out a card with a sun on the face. Whatever *sun* meant was good. This had been clear because it was directly contrasted by the grim reaction the bouncer had when Mateo pulled a blank card. They were let in with a lot of side-eyes thrown Mateo's way.

Inside had been a club with mediocre drinks, sticky floors, and magic practitioners tucked into every booth and table lining the walls. No one had been dancing despite the blaring techno and the straight-up laser light show projecting onto the lacquered dance floor.

Sitting at the bar with rum and cokes, Ophelia and Mateo had become the center of attention.

It was the blank card.

It meant he was hiding his magic, and everyone wanted to know why.

Having a maliciously secretive mother meant he was savvy enough not to let anything about his situation slip, but as the people around him chatted and prodded, the absolutely wrong answer to what kind of magic he used became alarmingly clear: anything having to do with demons.

Associating with demons was considered vile. Even blood magic was pushing it, since blood magic was often tied to demon powers.

Which was super unfair because the difference between something dubbed a *demon* or dubbed a *god* is pure human-biased semantics. Higher magic requires siphoning from something else, and borrowing power doesn't come for free. So, when the cost is mild, like devotion or homage, everyone's like: Great. Love it. This one's totally a good one.

And when the cost is something high, like blood and death, everyone's like: Oh no. Don't like that. Obviously, it's evil.

And yes, he calls the thing inside of him *evil* all the time, but he's allowed to over-reduce and generalize because one day it's going to kill him. It's actually really annoying when everyone else ascribes morality to things that don't think in corporal or even mortal terms. *Evil* isn't the same thing as *bad for a living, breathing human*. It's whatever the human does to get the power, or with the power, that's capable of good or evil. His mom, for example, isn't evil because she does blood magic. She's evil because she's a gigantic asshole.

Finding out the local magic scene thinks you're an evil abomination and ought to be dead is a real bummer, though, so he'd never gone back.

But he thinks about the combination of disgust and fear on the faces at that club every time he readies the cascarilla. His mother's preparation was really dramatic. Magic-ass dagger, candles, smoldering herb blend, and the slow mixing of blood and cascarilla with mortar and pestle.

He'd improved the process by buying a spritz bottle and filling it with water and his blood once a week. He needs to apply the wards every time he leaves the house or he risks detection, and who has time for blood rituals first thing in the morning?

Last night, during his curse research, he'd compiled a list of protection spells and cleanses for Topher's situation, so he gets to brewing those. It takes four knocks for him to realize the sound he's hearing is a person at the door and not a kitten softly batting a stuffed toy into another stuffed toy.

Mateo finds Topher standing outside the front door. His hair is once again in the disarray of a violent tumble out a highrise, hand raised to attempt another ridiculous feather-soft kiss of knuckles.

At the sight of Mateo, Topher withdraws his fist toward his chest and then opens it into a weak wave, like he's not sure what to do with his limbs now that there's someone there to see that he possesses them. "I'm early. Too early. Sorry. Is this too early? I can go away. And come back. More at the time. The right time, I mean. The time we agreed upon. Which isn't now."

Ophelia, miraculously roused and somewhere in the living room, lets out a mean laugh that Topher absolutely hears. This very rich guy they're trying not to offend's see-through complexion is suddenly bright pink.

Mateo pretends that hadn't happened. "Now's fine. Come on in."

Like at the print shop, Topher takes one step in but goes no further, gaze skittering around the room, glancing off of every candle and crystal Mateo had artfully sprinkled around. The room is full Halloween, all of Mateo's mother's performance pieces dragged out from the front closet. Eventually, Topher's attention snags on the mantle.

The out-of-commission fireplace is the single most cursed looking thing in anyone's house anywhere.

A simple framed picture of a shriveled-orange of an old woman with a stony-eyed stare sits at the center. She's Mateo's grandmother or great-grandmother—he never met anyone in his family and his mother wasn't chatty. But she called this old lady abuelita with a pronunciation that included a silent *shitty* at the start. Two additional and exponentially worse frames flank the surly old woman. The things inside of them are posed like a portrait from the shoulders up of something seated, but the shadowy forms are difficult to look at, the eye naturally sliding away.

Abuelita is surrounded by candles, incense, trinkets, figures, and a shallow bowl of water. All of which he upkeeps once a week, exactly as his mother had. He doesn't know this old lady, but he likes to think that she's just as disappointed with her lineage as he is.

"Come on," Mateo says when it's clear Topher's stuck, coaxing him like he has a piece of cheese and Topher's a little skittish dog he wants to urge close enough to pet.

It's at this point that Topher sees Ophelia but also realizes he has shoes on. This short-circuits his brain. It's a whole thing. Another wave of apologies spews out of him as he backs up into the door, frantic to remove his shoes.

Ophelia watches with dangerous amusement. She's probably Looking at Topher, with a capital L, but her expression makes him think she's coming up with a sick burn.

In an effort to hinder that, Mateo hustles Topher into the living room to sink onto the couch, taking the low stool on the other side of the coffee table for himself. "Okay. So, we texted a bit about our progress. Research, mostly." They'd looked into the accidents Topher had described. But then learned Topher's dad's house was legit a mansion and spent a lot of time on an old Fillow listing admiring the pool. "Every culture has curses. Meaning there's a wealth of information out there, which is fantastic, but it also means we've gotta sift through that information in order to pinpoint the exact flavor of what's happening to you so that we can figure out how to deal with it. We can narrow it down in some obvious ways, though. What's afflicting you seems to be bad luck, but bad luck curses don't usually cause bad luck to people around the hexed."

Topher nods, eyes googly and huge again, but Mateo doesn't think it's because of what he's saying. Ophelia is standing just inside the room, leaning against the wall closest to their bedrooms. Topher's gaze keeps flicking to her in abject terror. It could be a curse thing, afraid he's going to hurt her. It could be a Topher thing, other people too much for this flimsy, washed-out rich boy to deal with. But he suspects it's just Ophelia.

Objectively speaking, she's terrifying, even if she barely comes up to his chin. Armored in little airy maxi dresses and flip-flops, she makes men and women alike cower. Ophelia is cute in the same way a small, pink pocketknife is. Her mass of hair is a cloud of soft browns and blondes in direct contrast to the coldness in her eyes and the hostility of her smile.

Since dying, her mystique has only gotten worse.

"This is Ophelia, the colleague I mentioned," Mateo says a little louder, gesturing at her.

"Yo," Ophelia says without moving, and Mateo realizes that he should have had a customer service conversation with her. She's never held a job in her whole goddamned life, and she's basically a nightmare gremlin given cute human girl form.

"Hello," Topher whispers, and he's doing that trembling thing again. Is this excitement? Fear? Deep desire? Difficult to decipher what a bug-eyed trust fund guy might be into. Whatever. Not his concern. Time to focus on the money in his digital pocket.

"First thing we're going to do," Mateo says, drawing Topher's attention back to him. "Is a cleansing ritual. There's a lot of different cleansing methods, but I want to start with something a little higher up the scale, since what's happening to you is pretty hardcore."

Ophelia, transformed into a rarely seen level of helpfulness by the concept of money, puts the gallon pitcher Mateo had brewed earlier on the center of the table, and Mateo places a white candle between the pitcher and Topher. He lights the candle with a cheap blue mini torch, and they're ready to go.

People want magic to be glitzy rituals, chanting, and lights flickering. With higher magic, those things can happen, but it either means you've done something super wrong and you're about to die, or you're tapping into something from another plane of reality.

The basics aren't flashy.

They're smoke, breath, and intention. A hand to chest or temple and the silence of trying to understand and communicate with things unseen. Simple candles, common herbs, and light. But people don't pay for what feels like you walked into a Bed, Bath, and Beyond, grabbed a hundred-dollar candle, and then did Lamaze breathing with them. The performance is critical.

"This is a brew made from espanta muerto," Mateo says, exaggerating the flavor of the words. "The ghost chaser plant. It's a bitter herb that's good at breaking curses."

Topher's hands slowly reach toward the pitcher and Mateo realizes he thinks he's meant to drink a gallon of brown liquid. "No, it's for a bath."

Topher's hand freezes an inch from the pitcher, eyes becoming glassy orbs. "I have to take a bath?" He looks around the living room like he expects a tub to be there.

Mateo tries to remember how his mother swung this sort of thing. Ignacia Luisa Reyes Borrero was a lot of things. Extremely powerful witch. Subpar mother. Con artist. Cheat. Thief. Murderer. Middling cook. Okay with a house plant. Terrible singing voice. By twelve, Mateo had seen her stab a man in the face, rip a spirit from a little girl's body with her bare hands, and lie to every single person she'd ever met like it came easier than breathing.

While her nighttime business had been of the deals-with-dark-creatures sort, she paid the bills—when she felt like it—the same way any witch for hire does.

Husband cheating on you? She could hex him. Or her. Or other him. Client's choice, as his mother was without opinion on any and all morality issues. Been cursed? Not a problem. She could cleanse it, offer a variety of protection spells you definitely needed to see her every two weeks to re-up.

Absolutely worst role model possible, except perfect for this, which is making him feel all sorts of ways he refuses to feel. "It's like in movies when the sports guy wins the big game and someone pours Gatorade all over him for some god-awful reason. Not a bath-bath. We'll do it in the bathroom tub and you'll get privacy and a towel. We have to do this first, though." He indicates the candle. "Look at this flame for ten seconds. Great. Now close your eyes and keep picturing that flame; try to empty your mind of everything else, and think about asking for aid in purifying this pitcher of water."

Topher had closed his eyes, but they open, brow furrowed. "Ask you?"

"Not me," Mateo says. "Are you religious?" Topher's head shakes a no. "That's okay. Anyone who pretends to know exactly what they believe is lying." Mateo startles himself by saying something his mother loved to say verbatim. That fount of bad feelings wells up again, but he shoves it away and searches for his own thoughts. As someone with a demon inside of him, his relationship with the concept of a higher being is a little weird. "Whatever actually powers life, sentience, souls, be it magic or a fluke of science, there's an energy there. In you and me and everything that lives or dies. You're reaching out to that energy. You're asking the things that create, to help. Think about it like that."

Topher vibrates a moment more but then murmurs *okay* and closes his eyes, lashes long and startlingly stark in their paleness.

"Intentions are important here," Mateo continues in a soft tone, gaze shifting to Topher's pale lips as they move in silent beseeching. "Seek help. Humbly. Earnestly." Sprinkling more cascarilla into the liquid, he lets Topher beseech for a moment more and then drops him off in the bathroom.

Ophelia, a vulture perched on the arm of the couch who's been watching something slow-moving and desperate, doesn't wait for Mateo to ask what she thinks. "He's magnificent. I thought he was going to hurl when you got all smooth-talking new age at him. He fully stopped breathing for that."

"Gawd, you have no idea," Mateo delights, crossing to her so they can talk mad shit in whispered tones. "Legit, I think he's never seen a computer or talked to a person before. Everything I asked him to do was followed by—" He indicates his own face, trying to make his eyes wide. "I can't even do it. My eyelids lack the power. Like a pug. I was afraid his eyes were going to pop out. I mean, some of it was trying to avoid killing people probably, which—okay, very nice of him. But also, I wish I'd filmed him trying to use the register. Watching that was the most painful thing I've ever experienced and I'm weighing it against the stabbing and that time I fell off the roof."

He expects her to laugh and add on, but she's looking at him, brow furrowed and shitty smile tilting the edges of her lips.

"What?" he asks defensively.

"Nothing," she says like it's absolutely something, teeth flashing in one of her more ambiguous, yet still shitty, smiles and he's not clear on the meaning.

Oh. Maybe she'd really thought Topher was magnificent. Mateo had yet to ever guess her tastes correctly, but maybe something in Topher's chihuahua mystique had piqued her interest.

Before he can decide what to do with this startling revelation—and make fun of her for it—she tilts her chin toward the hallway. "He's taking a while."

Outside the bathroom door, Mateo strains to hear the splashing of water he expects at this point in a cleansing. Can't even hear the rustling of fabric which might make sense if Topher's going slowly because he's trying not to touch anything he doesn't have to. It's probably the worst room Topher's ever graced with his million-dollar presence. There was only so much Mateo could do to make a bathroom older than the incorporation of Seattle look nice. Broken tiles, a missing cold dial on the sink—maybe he could have replaced that—and a window that's been painted over since before he was born. It has a very *Motel 6 putting on a brave face* spirit from all the little towels he'd rolled up and placed on the counter.

Not wanting to rush the guy, Mateo starts scrolling on his phone, skimming tarot articles for choice verbiage. But Topher keeps not emerging and it's been silent in there for at least ten minutes. It doesn't take that long to strip, hose down in the tub, dump the cleanse on yourself, dry off, and pull your clothes back on—the baby-simple instructions he'd given Topher.

Maybe the shock of poverty gave Topher a heart attack.

Except, maybe something really did happen in there. There *is* a possible curse. What if it finally finished him off? That would be such ass.

An Amateur Witch's Guide to Murder

Mateo has no idea how to get rid of a body, and it'll look so suspicious if he reports it. The house is full *hello Satan* right now and Topher looks like he shouldn't have even entered the zip code. Also, there's the matter of Mateo not existing, legally speaking. Weirdly, his mom hadn't registered her demon-spawn child, so he doesn't even have a birth certificate to prove citizenship.

Pressing his ear to the door, Mateo listens with breath held. Nothing. No signs of life at all. It would be exactly his luck that the rich guy who'd promised a payday dies in his fucking bathroom.

The combination of dread and certainty reaches critical mass, and he knocks.

And gets silence in return.

CHAPTER NINE

Thirty never-ending seconds pass before the door cracks open and one of Topher's bug-eyes fills the space. They stare at each other, Mateo waiting for Topher to say anything.

"I think I did it wrong," Topher whispers.

"Huh?" Mateo articulates, unable to fathom how he could pour liquid on himself wrong.

The google-eye quakes. "I forgot . . . I forgot to, um. When I did the pitcher . . . I was thinking. I mean, I wasn't thinking. I should have thought. But didn't. So. Um. I forgot to, um . . . I still had on. I mean, I didn't take off . . . my, um . . ." Topher's cheek is blotchy neon, and it takes three times before Mateo catches the soft word he keeps ending the ramble with.

Underwear.

Topher got into the tub and undressed but left his underwear on because of course this barely held together bundle of gawky twigs and scared-rabbit reflexes in the guise of a real boy could no sooner strip stark naked in a stranger's bathroom than in front of a crowded theater.

"Why didn't you just throw them in the trash and put your pants back on?" Mateo has to ask, dismayed at this level of unnecessary honesty.

The strip of Topher-face he can see retreats from the crack. Probably to die. Eventually, a small voice says: "The trash can isn't very big. And I thought, *what if he looks in and sees it there?* Not that you look in the trash. But it's a small can. That would be . . ." A heavy moment loaded with whatever the hell Topher thinks might happen if someone saw his underwear in a trash can passes. "I mean, it's a weird thing to do. Leave wet underwear in someone else's house. And what if something else you want me to do needs me to take off my pants? I'd have to explain that I've got no underwear on and they're in the bathroom, wet, in the trash. I just . . ." Mateo thinks Topher's clicked off, but he starts back up, even more quietly. "I mean, I know probably none of that would happen. It wouldn't happen. But maybe."

Plastic smile slips into place and Mateo intones serenely, "It's a mistake anyone could have made." No one. No one else could have done this. But with Ophelia's additional rate it's so much money. Four. Point. Five. Grand. Eight point five grand if he can stretch it into next week.

As if his hand is disconnected from his body, Mateo lifts it, presents it palm up to Topher through the little crack. "Give them to me. I'll toss them in the laundry and give them back later. No problem." And then he waits for a very rich man to place a sodden, wadded-up ball of underwear into his hand because he guesses that's where his life is right now.

Back in the living room, Topher sits on the couch looking exactly like an extremely shy guy who's been forced to openly free ball it in a stranger's house.

Mateo can't let this new awkwardness linger, because Ophelia's a shark and she might come for this man's blood. "You getting anything?" he asks so that she won't say anything else.

"He's weird," she says, and again Mateo wishes he'd had a talk about decorum in front of rich people who they want to make them rich. "There's a . . ." she's looking at Topher in that horrible way of hers, blue jadeite gaze penetrating his body. Topher looks on the verge of dying from the scrutiny. "Presence," she finishes after a lengthy pause.

It's not what Mateo expected. "Possession?"

She shakes her head, but then tilts it, unsure. "No . . . not exactly. But not unsimilar either." A shrug. "Unique. I've never seen anything like him."

Not as helpful as he'd hoped, but also not a huge surprise that she couldn't glance at Topher and solve all their problems. Like Mateo, Ophelia's suffering from *no one taught her the shit it would be really good to know*. Her training terminated with her dead entire family.

"Next up is a tarot card reading," Mateo says, trying to keep things upbeat. "Ophelia's going to watch in case she can glean anything else. And the cards might give me more insight into what exactly is afflicting you. Have you ever gotten a reading before?"

Topher shakes his head, expression apologetic for no reason.

"That's fine. I'll explain as I go," Mateo soothes, picking up his deck, purchased online while at the height of his teen goth phase—a less sophisticated version of the twenty-something goth phase he's currently in. The deck is solid black on one side, while the face of the cards are various stackings of skulls, roses, ravens, and knives. The art's not great, as his tastes were shit as a teen, but it's the kind of thing he only thinks about when they're in his hand and it's too late.

He passes the deck to Topher and talks him through what to do and is relieved when Topher's trembling hands manage decent shuffles without dumping the deck on the floor.

Past, present, future. Self, situation, challenges ahead. A simple three-card read is what Ophelia and he decided on.

Taking the deck back, Mateo draws and places three cards between them.

Three of swords, the devil, and death. None reversed. Objectively speaking, it's a pretty shit pull. Mateo studies the cards a moment, not because he needs to but for suspense.

He indicates the three of swords with a flourish, picking the card up as though reading from it and not memory. "This is the past position. The self up to this moment. Three of swords. You've been lonely. There's been a separation in your life that you've grieved, and these events, the heartbreak and sadness, affect you today."

Topher told Mateo that he has no friends, and his mother is MIA. There should be some skepticism or at least an eyeroll. But, like loads of others who sat on this very couch before, all Topher does is suck in a breath, eyes becoming saucers. The world's easiest mark.

Mateo continues, setting the first card down and showing Topher the middle card. "Present. The situation you find yourself in now. The devil card." He pauses for dramatic effect, and Topher stops breathing until he continues. "There's a negativity in your life, something you're doing, or something you've allowed to be done to you." A pause to squint at Topher, not out of showmanship this time, but because something is wrong in Mateo's vision.

Trying to dismiss the illusion, he looks down but there's a miasma over his hands that's not really there, except in the way that his blood is actually black. This isn't the time for his demon bullshit, so he presses on. "It's harming you." He forces a swallow. "It's . . . not the thing causing the death and destruction." Breathe even. **"An agitation."** Ignore the growing darkness flickering at the edges of everything. **"An aggregation. A culmination of catastrophe soon to be."**

"Teo?" Ophelia says, but her voice is muted, garbled, underwater and very far away.

Mateo wants to ask why she sounds so fragile, but instead sets the second card down and picks up the third. **"Future. A future. A challenge. A change. A chance. A transformation. The death card. Death is the ultimate transformation. Of mind. Of body. Of flesh to something else. It is endings. Because the mortal flesh is only a sweet shell, a house, a cage that chokes and squeezes and rends for something greater than. Something more. Something endless and new that will not rot or fade or . . ."**

A blink, and he's in a different position, staring at the ceiling. He shifts only to realize he's on the living room floor with his head cradled in Ophelia's lap. Topher's to his right, squatting just a foot away with a roll of paper towels held between two hands.

"What?" Mateo muffles because Ophelia's holding a wad of towels to his face.

"Your nose started bleeding and you passed out." She pulls the towels away enough for him to see they're soaked in black. "After you started rambling about the virtues of death."

He sits up with her help, and though it must have only been moments, he has the drag of waking in the middle of a dream on him, thoughts distant and head heavy.

"It started at the end of the second card. Do you remember reading the last card?" Ophelia asks, on her feet but with a hand on his shoulder like she's afraid of breaking contact.

"Yeah, I think so." He's never lost time in front of anyone. "Did I stop midsentence?"

Ophelia's hand squeezes and she hesitates. "No. Not midsentence. You went on for a while, then you stood up and got the three-tone chime off the altar and started playing it. Then you slumped to the side. You were out for a few minutes."

Mateo gapes, staring at the little handheld bar chime set on the table where it hadn't been before. Dread settles over the numbness in his head. The chime is for calling something to him.

"I'm sorry," Topher's quivering voice says, on his feet with paper towels still clutched to his chest, somehow thinking this is his fault. He looks extraordinarily worried—not just in that *how does this affect me* sort of way Mateo expects from a rich guy dealing with the hired help. It doesn't get more run-of-the-mill than a tarot reading so Topher trying to take the blame is ludicrous, strangely sweet, and beside the point.

Client. Money. Get it together. Whatever bullshit that was, it's a Mateo bullshit, not a Topher money bullshit.

Can he still think, talk, and stand? Yes. Back to work.

Mateo offers what he hopes is a normal smile, realizing too late again that his teeth are sharp. Shit. Topher's already seen them. Just go with it. "Nothing to be sorry about. That wasn't your fault. I was tapping into the spirit realm." True, technically. "Possessed." Absolute truth. "And getting higher-level insights." Sure as hell hopes not, but at least it was a good show.

He moves to stand, and Ophelia and Topher both hurry to assist. It's like two children helping a wayward scarecrow.

"Never mind me," Mateo says, looking at Ophelia. "You get anything else?"

Her face flips through a series of complexities, invisible to anyone but someone well versed in all the ways she doesn't show what she's feeling. "His energy settled after the cleanse."

"Settled how?"

"Calmed down. It was swirly. Now it's not."

"What does that mean?" Topher asks, grip tightening on Mateo's arm—which he's totally still holding—staring up at Mateo in the most valid alarm of the morning.

Mateo has no idea what that means, so he smiles again, remembers his teeth, and stops. "That we've made some progress." He says this with a confidence he doesn't feel, off-kilter from his episode, and Topher—staring up at him in saucer-eyed worry, diligently clinging to his arm in support—isn't helping him reestablish his professional cool.

"What the hell . . ." Ophelia says softly, and he turns to her. She's sitting where Topher had been, the tarot deck in her hand. The three cards are still on the table, same pull but facing her like she'd rotated them to look. Her pale eyes lift to him. "I just got the same pull."

"What?" Mateo says, because that's all his brain can manage right now.

"This isn't his spread." She taps each card. "This is mine. Shuffled. Redrawn."

Mateo gently extracts his arm from Topher, squats in front of the table, and takes the deck back from Ophelia, sweeping her pull into it. He shuffles, really good, even scatters them on the table for a moment so things have a better chance of reversing and splits the deck six times before doing his pull.

Three cards laid out in front of him.

No.

The same three cards laid out in front of him.

Three of swords, the devil, and death.

This was supposed to be a fun, curse-breaking money grab, not whatever portentous fate-entwined situation this just became. Mateo casts an uneasy glance at Topher, who doesn't understand enough about what's happening to be as disturbed as Mateo now is. It doesn't get more definitive than three impossibly identical pulls.

Whatever's happening, it's happening to all three of them. Together.

CHAPTER TEN

Mateo gets Topher as far as the doorstep—wanting him out so that Ophelia and he can flip the fuck out about what just happened—but can't work out a good way to hurry him along without sounding as deeply distressed as he is.

"Yeah. So. We're gonna do some more research, and I'll call you as soon as we've got next steps," he tries, head a little swimmy now that he's moving around. Not great, body.

Topher's nodding intently, gaze flicking around Mateo in what Mateo hopes is deep trust in his overpromised abilities. "You don't have to push yourself. I mean, if you need to take some time. I can wait."

Not deep trust, then. How bad does he look? For all Mateo knows, he's crusted in nose blood, bleary-eyed, and wan. Topher's saying to take his time—which is great for billable hours—but showing weakness this early in the curse-breaking-process feels like a mistake.

"Really, I'm okay," Mateo says, leaning on the doorframe in his best approximation of a very okay and casual guy. "Just need to get a little food in me. Maybe a nap. Do some laundry." Shit.

He hadn't meant to joke about the wet underwear waiting for him, heat flaring in Topher's pale cheeks in response. Grimacing, he tries to course correct. "Sorry. Too soon?"

"By a century," Topher replies, surprisingly witty for how shell-shocked he looks.

"I'll never mention them again," Mateo assures him, but then—out of a spontaneous and morbid curiosity—is unable not to add. "Except when I hand them back to you."

Topher's gaze does that jittery thing, then he blinks once, hard. "I'm going to go before I do anything else stupid. Good night." A suffering pause because it's broad daylight, followed by a self-aware nod, choosing to double down instead of correct, and Topher flees.

What a weirdo.

Mateo closes the door, walking wearily back into the living room to meet Ophelia's concerned gaze. There are so many things to deal with suddenly. Never mind the losing time, passing out, demon-speak thing—not that he shouldn't be thinking about that—it's just that he super doesn't want to. But getting the same pull three times is cryptically fated.

All three of them pulling the death card requires some pragmatic troubleshooting. The death card doesn't usually mean *death*. It means *change*. But also, sometimes it *does* mean death. And the demon inside him sure had appreciative opinions about that card in particular.

Which is why a few minutes later Mateo is jogging in place, trying to warm up to his own bad idea.

In front of him is an office door.

Ignacia Luisa Reyes Borrero's office door.

AKA: the office of the world's most powerful dark bruja.

Not that anyone ever said it so plainly. A procession of scary people peppered his childhood, the sort of sordid individuals you cross the street to avoid, even in broad daylight. No one element in common between them, except that force of presence that lets you know without words that you should avoid eye contact.

And every one of them walked into the living room and prostrated themselves to his mother, showing the deference only megalomaniac dictators with penchants for random executions require. Soft-voiced pleas for assistance delivered to the five-foot-one bruja like she might end them for a raised tone. Mateo hadn't been allowed out and hadn't developed a habit of sneaking off until he met Ophelia, so he eavesdropped a lot, and the conclusion was easy to draw.

Everyone was scared of his mom.

"This might not have anything to do with Dagger Lady," Ophelia says, a few steps behind him. There's a subdued quality to her words, a rare moment of raw uncertainty. For all of his suspicions about his mother, Ophelia's actually Seen her magic. She'd tried to explain it once, expression like she'd chewed raw sewage. In the end, she'd shaken her head and said, "It's bad."

"Dagger Lady knows where the house is, tried to stab me, and saw Topher run off with me. Feels like she could three-way murder us all. And Mom had a who's who of clients and associates," he says, stalling. "Dagger Lady might be in that book, and any information about her could be useful. And I haven't seen the address book floating around. It's gotta be in here."

The room's sat untouched since the day his mother walked away. The threat of her coming back and seeing him in her stuff is an effective deterrent, even five years later. The door's not even locked. She wasn't the sort of woman who locked something when a ward that could maim or kill would do instead.

He flashes Ophelia a forced smile before pushing the door open.

The room's been opened a dozen times since his mother stopped coming home, but Mateo's never worked up the nerve to step across the threshold. Which feels both ridiculous and well informed. He isn't allowed inside. She isn't here to stop him. He's worried about it anyway, like she'll walk in just as his sock touches the naked wood floor. Which would be great and awful. She might know what's happening. She probably wouldn't help.

Sweating, Mateo steps in and fumbles on the wall for the light. Pitch shadow flashes into a dim orange glow that barely illuminates the corners. Blackout blinds block the two windows that would otherwise let in the early evening light.

Peering around, it might be an eclectic college professor's office. There's a heavy wooden table in the center that's polished to a liquid gloss, marred on the four corners where the wax of a thousand candles has melted and been scrubbed off. Two squat, blood-red chairs hunch around it. They look comfortable, fat, and well-used, but he doubts anyone's ever felt at ease sitting in one with his mother across from them. The customers she scammed got the living room. The real-deal clients got to come into this room, and they weren't asking if their wives were cheating or if they should start a new Pilates routine.

He doesn't go any further, half expecting her to leap into view like a cheap jump scare. Which isn't a thing she ever did, so he's not sure why the expectation's there. She'd done so much worse. The memories are hazy, and like the dreams of cannibalism, he's never sure if they're real memories or products of his dually inhabited psyche being incapable of dealing with something he hadn't understood.

Wood floor, on his back, and very young. He can never move, and there's a yellowed smoke heavy in the air, making him choke. The pain is a single note piercing the haze of the nauseous paralysis blurring the world as she carves pieces of him away.

In the office, nothing moves except a bead of sweat rolling down his upper lip, and he bats it away.

One step and then two, floor creaking, and he reminds himself she can't hear him. She's not here. Wax and incense, Florida Water, with something beneath that catches in his throat.

Oh. It's blood, he realizes as he takes a third step. She always smelled a little like blood.

The room takes up the entire second floor of the house, and yes that means he's been living in a house where he's not using half of the available space. It functioned as her bedroom too, but he's never seen her sleep and there's no bed. There's no dust on anything, as though even it was afraid to enter her space.

The walls are lined with dark shelves, neatly stuffed with books. Any bit of non-book-covered wall has framed photos, all difficult to look at. A glance at the spines on the shelves proves they don't hold the address book he's after, so he goes for the closet. It's the kind with sliding doors, but the doors have never been attached in his lifetime. Instead, heavy crimson curtains hang in their place. He's seen hints of what's inside, crept up and peered through the open door. She always caught him, head turning, small frown on her always frowning mouth twitching, and the door would slam.

"Careful." Ophelia's voice scares him. She's squatting outside the room, the skirts of her sepia dress pooled around her. They'd agreed she shouldn't go in unless absolutely necessary.

Delicately, he catches the edge of the curtain and slides it over, holding his breath until he has it all the way to one side. Any resemblance to a closet within is gone. The space is filled with shelves of trinkets, pictures, symbols, herbs, bones, veils, boxes, and books.

Every inch of it is warded with tiny symbols. They're even scrawled into the back wall and around the closet frame. All drawn with blood. His blood, he realizes with a start, not thrilled that he can tell this by smell. Even less thrilled when he realizes his teeth are sharp.

This is the real-real shit. The kinds of things he's not supposed to mess with.

Slowly, like the closet might bite him, he slips his phone out of his pocket, turns on the light, and starts examining every row. A brass key has a wide berth, a series of symbols carved into the wood around it. A mortar with some sort of iridescent sand within. A scrying mirror that he's extra careful to avoid looking at. A definitely-not-human skull with horns. A wide black candle that's impossibly burning a soft white flame. Item after item, and he has no idea what any of them are.

A thin, green book catches his attention, not because it looks extra magical, but because it doesn't. It's tucked against one corner of the second to last row. It's exactly what he wants and his heart leaps, except his gaze drags to the bottom row that isn't a row but the underside of the bookcase. It's impossibly dark down there. The light he's shining has no effect even though he's moving it around, trying to catch the space in its beam.

Something is wrong and it's already too late.

This thought forms crystal clear in his brain and is then tossed aside as he reaches a hand into the dark space. It doesn't matter. **He needs what's in there. It's his. It's always been his and she took it from him.**

The tips of his nails meet resistance, but he pushes against it, heart thudding in his throat, applying pressure until the opaque blackness parts and then spills up his hand and starts swallowing his arm. It's freezing, but he only understands this in a distant way because **he needs what's inside of the shadow.** Feeling around, he meets more coldness, piercing needles of ice rushing up to his shoulder. He's on his knees with no memory of getting on the ground, still clawing into the dark space, **knowing it's in there and he has to have it.** The cold is traveling up arm, to neck, down back and chest, and up his face, engulfing him.

Something is happening to his meat, he thinks with no urgency, still pawing around at the extremes of his reach. It's then that his nails catch on to something, and he strains, dislodging it. A primal victory shudders through him as fingers close around something solid.

It's not until he pulls it out, revealing a small black book, that he realizes he's on fire.

CHAPTER ELEVEN

Being on fire is exactly as terrible as it sounds.

Stop, drop, and roll has been ingrained on the psyche of every American kid, so Mateo's disappointed to find that his first instinct upon being engulfed in flames is to thrash around without much rolling. In his defense, this awareness of being on fire is poorly timed. It came at the moment he was most engulfed, but before the fire had burned through enough tissue and nerves for adrenaline and shock to take any edge off.

He is pain. No faculties available to think.

This useless flailing lasts a moment that also might be forever, and then he's being doused in something frigid that's like breathing in hairspray while spraying it directly on an open wound. It sucks but is less bad than the fire, so it's technically an improvement.

He must've blacked out, because he's suddenly staring at the ceiling, Ophelia leaning over him, expression grim. She sees he's awake and pulls in a hard breath. "Teo? You okay?"

"Not even almost," he rasps, voice like he gargled glass.

They get him into a seated position, and he has to double over for a long time, coughing up black—which is normal—and white globs—less normal. Eventually, he realizes he's in the short hallway outside of the office, and he's coughing up fire extinguisher foam.

"What happened?" he wheezes.

Her expression flickers in that way it does only when she's really upset, like she can't keep it neutral despite a lifetime of unshakable success. "You were looking around, got down on hands and knees to dig under the shelf, and stopped answering me. Then you were on fire. But you kept digging like you couldn't tell or didn't care." She swallows and he realizes she's cradling one of her hands in her lap, bright eyes wet but no tears. She doesn't let anyone see her cry.

He reaches for her but it's a terrible idea, every motion stretching tender flesh taught, forcing out a gasp as he crumbles down again. Makes the knife thing earlier feel like a scratch. Panting he manages: "You're hurt?" He has to settle for being still but saying concerned things.

Her throat works for a moment, trying to tamp down whatever emotion is trying to escape, before: "It's fine."

"Let me see," he demands—like that'll help. It doesn't help. She shows him her right hand, palm bright red and shiny. Blisters are already forming, and the surface is swollen and raw. She'd grabbed hold of his burning body and dragged him out. "Phee."

She grimaces, lipstick smeared from heroics he'd missed. "You look way worse."

"You're sweet," he says, closing his eyes, horrified at the way the lids drag against his eyeballs like bonito flakes sticking to a hot pan. "Please go deal with it. Neosporin and gauze. Do we have gauze? Fuck. I have to just sit here. For a while."

She leaves for a time, and he swearingly manages to lie down on the floor. Gradually, the flash-fried fingers of his left hand—a perfect replica of a cursed monkey's paw—straighten, blackened skin unwithering. It's grotesque but entrancing. And it really fucking hurts, nerves screaming back to life as warped skin and bone slowly slide and pop back into proper pliability.

As far as he can tell from the minimal movement he's willing to try, that hand got the worst of it. He suspects his face is overdone too by the way his cheek sticks to the floor when he shifts but he'd rather not confirm that one, and he's trying not to think about his hair.

His gaze travels beyond his soon-to-be-jointed fingers and focuses on the pool of white and char in the center of the office. Like a drunk memory, the feeling of something beneath his fingers urges him upright, gasping loudly as things pull and crack and ooze anew. Crying doesn't come easily to him either, but getting onto hands and knees and then crawling into the office forces a few tears to join the mess of his face, burning on their journey down his cheeks.

In the center of the liquefying fire extinguisher spray is a black book. Not black in the traditional sense of the word, like his clothes, hair, or lipstick. Black like the stuff he spits up and bleeds, devoid of dimension, like he's staring at a lightless, square-shaped hole in the ground. But he knows it has form. The tips of his utterly ruined stiletto nails scraped it, dragged it out.

It's his mother's spell book.

His tongue runs over dry lips, a cracked layer of skin sliding free, and he spits it onto the floor. The black spell book is roughly the size of his open hand—**would fit so nicely there**—which is how he knows it's magic compelling him. If not for how much being on fire hurt, he'd have his fingers on it again already.

A bandaged hand descends in front of his face, and he snaps out of a daze he hadn't realized he was in. Ophelia is squatting beside him, and he's surprised to find they do have gauze. A competent wrap encircles her palm, and she's removed her lipstick entirely.

"What the hell?" she asks correctly.

"No, I know," Mateo says, having a hard time keeping his gaze focused on her. "Do you wanna touch it?"

She lifts an eyebrow critically but looks at the spell book. "No. You do?"

"So much," he says, licking his lips again, relieved the skin stays in place. "It's her spell book. I can't believe it's here."

Leaning over the foam, she peers at it. "It kinda looks like you. Magically speaking."

His gaze skitters to the fire extinguisher. "Is that thing empty?"

"I didn't use the whole thing, but I don't know how much is left. But also. Don't."

"I know." The point of coming in here wasn't to kill himself with his mom's evil-ass spell book—though, it's disconcerting to realize it's been in the house the whole time. And difficult to think around. **All he wants to do is press his hands to the cover, look through the pages, hold it close.**

Death card.

Focus.

Shaking himself, he says, "Before I burst into flames, I saw the address book on the top shelf." He squints at the now normally-shadowed underside of the shelves. "I think the fire was a ward on that bottom area, not the whole thing. To keep anyone from getting the spell book out of there." **To keep *him* from getting the spell book out of there.** There's a certainty in that thought that makes his head swim, gaze losing focus.

Except, this certainty makes zero sense. She wouldn't have wanted anyone to find her spell book, not just him.

Giving the shelf a wary once-over, Ophelia gets the fire extinguisher in her good hand and braces it between bare calves so she can trigger and aim one-handed. "Try not to run around if you catch fire again. Also, I hate this."

"Not loving it either," he says, crawling around the foam and sitting in front of the closet shelves. The little green book is unassuming, which hopefully means no fire. "Count of three."

"One—" she says, and he reaches for it.

Gets it.

Has it.

Neither of them moves, eyes wide and alert on each other. No fire. No nothing.

"Thank fuck," he says, sitting back on his ass and examining the blank cover. The whole thing is less than a quarter of an inch thick. "Reading anything off it?"

"Nothing," Ophelia says, not releasing her grip on the extinguisher.

"Count of three," she says.

"One." He opens the book to the middle.

And sees a name, *Sven LaRue*, a phone number, address, email, and the word *inútil. Useless.* His mother's favorite word. He flips through a few more pages. "This is it."

Ophelia holds out her hand for it and he passes it over. She's abandoned the fire extinguisher to balance the book on her lap and flip through it. "Now what?"

"Check addresses. See who's local. Maybe someone's listed as *Dagger Lady* and it'll be easy," he says, shifting closer so he can see despite his burnt misery. Her hands are more functional, so she gets to turn the pages.

Six are local. He doesn't recognize any names except Braulio Blanco, who is distinctly not a lady but a smarmy con-man who had a falling out with his mom years ago. Not that he expects to recognize the name of the lady who tried to stab him, as he'd never seen her before.

After a difficult balancing and agility exercise of button mashing with barely functioning fingers, they translate all of the locals' notes. None scream *will knife you in a back alley*. As far as they can tell, they're clients, middling witches his mom wasn't impressed with, and one has a Metsy shop that sells incense. All have photos readily available on the internet. None of them have the rage-precise eyebrows of Dagger Lady.

Total dead end. And all he got for it was both of them burnt all to fuck.

He closes the book and holds it in his lap, then catches sight of his hand. Mostly whole, though covered in shedding, burnt-up skin. His nails are totally trashed, now shriveled bits of plastic he starts ripping off even though it hurts.

"Fuck," he says quietly. And then again, much louder. Teeth press unevenly against each other, sharp and useless as his blood buzzes in his veins. Fixing him. Feeling hotter than usual. Like maybe getting knifed then getting badly burned tallied up two points against him in his unknowable scoreboard of demon possession.

What good is a book filled with magic people when they're probably all assholes like every other magic person he's ever met? It's not like he can call each of them and ask if they attacked him. And now Ophelia's hurt. That's completely his fault. The opposite of what he's trying to do here. Throwing the address book would feel good, but that's one of those things people do in movies that's nonsense in actuality. Throw the book, kick the desk, knock the probably cursed finger bone off the shelf for a moment of impotent power.

Looking to the wall of books, he wonders if there's something helpful there. And how many times he'll set himself on fire trying to check.

Finally, he turns to the spell book on the ground like it ever left his awareness. It's a second heartbeat, cocooning around his own and buzzing with his blood. He tries to feel past the thrall. His mom hadn't taken it with her. Had hidden it. Warded it. From him. But how did she know the book would call to him? He'd only ever seen flashes of the spell book. She'd kept it close, kept it closed, tucked it away if she saw him nearby.

She'd so clearly never wanted him to have it.

So, it seems extremely bad that it's here while she's missing. Like it means her missing wasn't on purpose. Which is a slew of complicated feelings he doesn't want to deal with.

His thumb finds the steady pulse beneath his jaw. It should be galloping because his teeth are sharp. There's an asymmetry to his thoughts and his body's reaction, a cold and distant terror at what it would cost him if he tried to use that spell book, being smothered by the sureness that **he should**. That **he's supposed to**. He tries to examine the thought, but it's like the murderous ones that rattle though his brain. Slippery. Impossible to grasp onto and examine. Some part of him, or the thing in him, really thinks he should use his mother's scary-ass magic book.

"Your aura's freaking out," Ophelia says softly, and Mateo rips his eyes from the spell book. Her complexion is waxy, like she's not slept or eaten, and the image of her corpse flashes in his mind. Like it was yesterday. Like it could be today.

He can't use that book. If the demon wants him to, it's bad. And if he lets himself get taken over, he can't save Ophelia.

Getting to his feet isn't easy but he still offers her a hand and hoists her up as his re-forming nerves scream. "Let's keep brainstorming the Dagger-Lady–tarot-pull problem. I don't work till tomorrow night, so we've got time."

Time is the one thing he doesn't have—none of them do with the ill-omened death card in the air—but she doesn't point that out. As they settle in the living room for a night of research, he pretends the spell book, still on the floor of his mother's office, isn't pulsing gently at the edges of his awareness, keeping time with the beat of his heart.

CHAPTER TWELVE

Mateo is low-key freaking out as he takes his spacious window seat and buckles in, watching the stream of boarding passengers. Seems like too many people, but no one else looks concerned. He starts counting them but has no idea what a reasonable number is, so he stops.

It's 5 AM, which should be illegal. Especially because Ophelia and he had been too restless from yesterday's misadventures to focus on research. Persisting just long enough for Mateo to not look like he'd made out with a campfire, they'd gone bar hopping until last call and haven't slept yet. While walking home from the bar, they'd had a brilliant idea.

They should talk to Topher's dad.

Just, like, interview him. See what's up.

Because they'd both been drunk, they'd texted this idea directly to Topher and even though it was 2 AM, he'd agreed. With the obscene powers of a huge bank account and the info from Mateo's fake ID—Topher hadn't commented when he'd listed his name as Matthew E. Borrero—Topher got them a flight. Sobriety had come to Mateo an hour later—another demon-vessel perk. Ophelia has only really come back to the world of reaping what you sow in the past thirty minutes. She sits across the aisle, the seat beside her empty, huge sunglasses hiding bloodshot eyes as she checks every compartment around her for free things.

"We switched seats," Topher whispers beside Mateo, failing at buckling in an impressive number of times before getting it. "I was going to have an empty seat beside me. Because people too close might be bad with my thing. But I thought maybe she'd like to sleep. Not that she can't sleep next to you. I mean, not to imply that you guys are okay sleeping next to each other. Or not okay sleeping next to each other. On a plane. Only talking about planes. Where you sleep other times is—" Topher has the sense to cut himself off, eyes wide and desperate.

Jesus, this guy. "It's okay, I get what you mean. We were up late researching." Which bars had better tapas. If Topher wants to keep up this awkward chat for the whole flight—curse, demon, and death card be damned—Mateo's not going to survive.

Speaking of not surviving, there *is* the matter of Topher's curse, and how utterly brain-dead it is to get into a plane with him after the tarot pull yesterday. But he can't explain to Topher that they'd drunk-texted him, so here they are. In an attempt to mitigate this bad idea, Mateo hyper-warded Ophelia and himself and, upon pickup, made Topher get out of his ride so he could aggressively rub a damp and perfumed egg all over him in a last-ditch effort to remove more bad energies.

He needs to distract himself but there's nothing here but Topher and a small pinprick hole in the window he now can't stop staring at. Isn't that how the Alien got killed once? Sucked out of a hole? Is that a space thing or an air thing?

"Sorry it's so early." Topher's quiet voice blessedly draws his attention from what is probably a perfectly normal hole in a window that's going to be in the sky, apology all over his face. "You texted and I bought the next available flight without thinking. Set the pick-up and drop-off. Reserved a hotel. I almost booked dinner at three different places because I don't know what you like to eat. What either of you like to eat, I mean," he continues, gaze intent but curling a paper menu up into a thin tube between restless fingers.

Now Mateo feels a little bad he'd been getting wasted while this guy stressed. As someone who'd just recently lit himself on fire while looking for an address book that was only ever going to be so helpful in the first place, he perfectly understands the desire to *do*. "I get it. Sometimes it's nice to do anything that feels a little bit like progress."

The wideness of Topher's eyes diminishes as he nods.

Mateo's pretty sure that means some concerns have been soothed. So, in general solidarity with Ophelia on free food matters, he adds: "For the record, neither of us are picky eaters." The overhead announcement muffles that they're waiting for a maintenance approval—which is deeply distressing to Mateo. Not wanting to give power to the cool phobia he didn't know he had because he's never been on a plane before, he keeps talking, "How'd things go once you left my place?"

Topher's face does something it's obviously never done before. It's like in Bambi when baby-Bambi tries to stand and then walk, but it's happening with Topher's mouth in the form of a smile trying to figure out how to exist. "Nothing bad. I got back to the hotel without any accidents. I even ate in the hotel restaurant for dinner, and nobody choked." Cool to clock another thing he should be wary of.

Shit! Had they solved the curse? Disappointment wars with being a decent human being while this sad guy offers the world his very first smile over not getting people murdered. But even if the curse has been removed, they still don't know who cast it, so there's still a job here. Remind him. "That's great. We can set you up with a local place that has all the cleanse ingredients. That's important while we don't know who's responsible."

Topher bobbles, his newborn smile solidifying. "Okay. Yeah. Okay."

Smiling-Topher might be more alarming than looking-freaked-out-Topher. Mateo doesn't know what to do with the raw positivity being directed up at him. Stringing Topher along aside, if that cleanse really did do the trick, he's a little pleased with himself. Not to be petty, but somewhere his mom is hating this for him, so he smiles too.

And Topher smiles even more.

Too much.

It gets weird fast, and now Mateo's playing smile-chicken.

Luckily, a dead-eyed flight attendant moving through the motions of buckling, oxygen masking, and inflating a dirty yellow vest interrupts them. It's rote warnings, repeated since time immemorial, but it feels like it's a little hard to breathe in there. Do they limit air in cabins? Is that a plane thing? It's okay. He's fine. Because it would be amazingly unprofessional to freak out on a plane next to your client who you asked to fly you to San Fran—one of three offices the dad could have been at. Thank fuck he wasn't a five-hour flight away in New York.

Ophelia catches the flight attendants' attention as soon as he's done with his spiel. "I'm going to sleep but I want any and all food and drinks. Just make a pile. Beer." Message delivered, she slumps in her seat, and the plane starts moving.

Mateo enacts a The Thinker pose, pretending he's not in a tube about to rocket into the sky. Everyone says you're more likely to crash in a car than a plane. Except cars can't fall out of the fucking sky, and most people don't have a death-causing-curse guy strapped in beside them.

"You can hold my hand if that'll help. I mean, because sometimes that helps. It might help. When I was little, that helped," Topher offers, those wide eyes trained on him in concern.

Mateo wants to say that's not necessary, but then loud hell noises start up and the plane lurches forward, gaining horrible speed. It's not a decision so much as a necessity, and Mateo two-hands Topher's arm like he's been tasked with keeping the limb in place or dying. They ascend for approximately ten years before stomach-lurching sensations finally level off.

"Sorry," Mateo says in a strangled voice, prying his fingers off of Topher. He glances to Ophelia and for once thanks the whole goddamned universe that she's got her legs bent over the seat beside her, head lolling against the window, dead to the world.

"It's okay," Topher whispers.

It's not lost on Mateo that Topher's just said the thing he keeps saying to Topher. And that's twice now—first time was the Dagger Lady situation—this wraith of a guy has been more together than Mateo in a stressful situation. It feels out of character, but Topher did seek him out and fly to another state to hire him, which kind of makes him an industrious man of action, as insane as those descriptors are when he's looking at Topher's cat-that's-seen-a-cucumber gaze. And it's really emphasizing what a shit job Mateo's doing maintaining his just-fabricated professional persona.

But at some point, the plane needs to land and there's a cursed guy beside him, so Mateo might as well make it thrice. "I'm absolutely gonna need to do that again on the way down."

CHAPTER THIRTEEN

Having never been further than Mount Rainier National Park, a two-hour drive from his house—forty-five minutes if Ophelia's driving—Mateo squints in acute goth pain as glittery water and too blue sky make themselves known outside their arrival gate. Ophelia's gigantic shades have transformed from hangover-obscuring to correct for the environment.

They follow Topher, who power walks them to the pickup area in front of a line of identical black cars. His head bobs around on his skinny neck with purpose until a tall, well-built man in a suit steps out of the wall of vehicles. He introduces himself as Quincy. Amazing lashes and a startlingly dulcet speaking voice. His suit is department store off-the-rack but tailored. The kind guys own only on the off-chance they'll get invited to a wedding. Nice but not *nice*.

Quincy collects Topher's expensive-definitely-leather backpack, holds out a hand for Mateo and Ophelia's very-not-expensive-definitely-vinyl backpacks, and then herds them into a big, organized-crime vibes SUV. Doesn't miss a beat when Ophelia holds out a hand like an old-timey starlet wanting assistance and doesn't react to her gremlin-crawl into the backmost seat.

"We meeting your dad now?" Ophelia asks as Mateo and Topher settle into the seat in front of her, which is super regrettable. Mateo had been hoping not to sit next to Topher, not sure what to do with himself after the cumulative twenty minutes of handholding. Not that there was even a reason to be weird about it. Just two business professionals holding hands while one desperately prays to any gods of aviation he can think of. Standard guy stuff.

Topher's not making it weird. He's fighting his seat belt.

"My dad said he'd be available sometime between one and five." Topher's putting all his concentration into seat belt buckling because he's said something insane.

"That's a four-hour window, hours from now," Ophelia is incapable of not pointing out.

"Yes. Well. Yes. But he's busy. I mean, he's always busy," Topher flusters. "But he said he'd meet. And I said it was important. Really important. So. So he'll probably talk to you. I mean, if he's not too busy. But he'll really try to, I think."

Maybe the dad doesn't believe the curse stuff, but the idea of this frantic baby ostrich of a guy goggling in distress at a parent and getting a four-hour window is pretty shit. Two data points on dad: Wall Street and this. Huge asshole energy. "We'll make it work," Mateo soothes.

Quincy pulls smoothly into the line of cars leaving the airport, and Mateo relaxes a little. The cleanse is keeping things in check, and asking a few questions can't be that difficult. Looking around Topher's house for clues also feels like an obvious thing to do. Bonus, there's no chance any of them will get stabbed here, since Dagger Lady's a state away.

And sure, his mom's spell book is in his carry-on bag where he'd stashed it last second, but it's not as irresponsible as it sounds. He's not going to use it. It's just not smart to leave it exposed in an unattended house. Everyone's safer if it's with him.

* * *

"Can you get jetlag from a two-hour flight?" Ophelia asks as they ride the elevator to the lobby.

"They call that a hangover," Mateo says, double checking that his tie is straight.

They'd hit the magic shop for basic supplies and then their structurally questionable hotel, ninety-nine percent glass folded in a high-gloss accordion shape in an earthquake-prone state. It hadn't collapsed on them as they stole a nap in one of the beds of the four-whole-ass-bedrooms suite Topher inexplicably got for just the two of them. Nap was followed by reapplying protection wards and figuring out how best to look professional but not boring.

All of Mateo's nice-enough-to-wear-in-a-Wall-Street-setting stuff is second-hand designer, purchased with great persistence of spirit on an auction site for a fraction of their actual price. Black Alexander McQueen on the legs, black Fendi button-up, and a black Philipp Plein tie—which sounds like a lot of black because it is. Ophelia only owns gauzy ankle-length dresses that hit the perfect balance of boho whimsical respectability, so she didn't need to do anything special. Also, she's cute, so can roll into most places in a paper sack with live birds in her hair, dropping f-bombs, and it's fine.

Questions currently thought up to ask the dad? Zero. But at least they look good.

Topher, already waiting in the lobby, raises a hand as they approach. He's changed since that morning, the generic tee, jeans, and sneakers traded for a dropped sleeve V-neck sweater, chinos, and wingtip boots, all in gray. It's surprisingly stylish and transforms him into the posh rich guy he actually is. Even the afternoon sun shining through the lobby is interpreting this as a higher form of Topher, casting angelic rays only on him, his near-white hair glowing.

The illusion lasts all of twenty seconds.

Once they're close enough, Topher speaks in an earnest theater whisper with eyes wide and vibrating at Mateo. "You look great." Realizing he's delivered the comment with way too much intensity, Topher starts to malfunction. "You both do, I mean. Look great. Not that you looked bad before. You didn't look bad before now, you looked good then too, but differently good, and now you look like a different, not better but definitely different kind of good, and, I mean—"

"Looking spiffy yourself," Mateo somehow says to stop this torrent despite never having used the word *spiffy* in his life. Eager to end whatever either of them is doing here, Mateo puts a hand on Topher's back and herds him out the exit. "Consensus is we all look amazing so let's go."

He's surprised to see Quincy behind the wheel when they crawl into their ride. Maybe you rent the expensive rideshare drivers by the day? Doesn't matter. He's gotta think about what to ask a rich old guy about his son being cursed. Family history? Has he pissed anyone off lately? Except Mateo's dragged from his concentration by Topher's buzzing beside him.

He's doing that thing where you grasp one hand with the other again and again, like a cartoon worried person or an arthritis flare. Anxious about his dad is Mateo's guess. Relatable. Mateo always hated talking to his own mom. Only did it when absolutely necessary.

As if that was his dictate and not hers.

Plane-compassion debt still past due, he wracks his brain for something distracting, wishing Ophelia hadn't again stolen the backmost seat, because she's better at small talk. Or, not actually better, but not him, so *that's* better.

He decides he can ask about Topher's shoes, which he's pretty sure are obscure designer and expensive, but Quincy speaks in an unhurried deadpan. "Hold on."

They all look forward and see a semitruck skidding across every lane of the five-lane freeway, an impassable truck-death-wall hurtling toward them.

CHAPTER FOURTEEN

This vision of metal death is snatched away as they're thrown hard to the left.

The car three-sixties across two lanes of heavy traffic.

The shout Mateo tries is cut short by the seat belt pulling taut.

They spin at high velocity for an eternity before jolting to a stop on the shoulder. The world darkens. A split second of panic that Mateo's having another episode, but it's the semi's shadow as it skids by close enough to roll down the window and touch. Then they're in the harsh California sun again. The world still spinning, Mateo whips his head around to follow the wall of jackknifed semi. It continues down the freeway in a scream of metal against asphalt. A few cars make it around the truck like they did, but none so flawlessly.

One makes it under. Which isn't a good way to go.

The back of his throat gets sour with fear, but he turns to make sure Ophelia's still whole and buckled in. She is, but she's not looking toward the squealing and crunching. Her eyes are on Topher, who's curled into a ball beside Mateo like he expects every impact to be theirs.

"Hey," she says softly, inscrutable gaze on Topher. "I don't think we got the curse."

* * *

The concept of sticking around to talk to the police is floated by Topher alone, and the three nos—thanks, Quincy—have it.

Which is why they're parked at Nystrom Sr.'s office with a despondent Topher unwilling to get out of the car, legs drawn up and forehead against knees. Can't blame the guy. The curse is still in play, and it just sent a handful of people to critical care and the morgue. Mateo's doing an amazing job envisioning piles of money so he won't think about how many people just died or how close the crash was to Ophelia's fragile human body. He wants to re-up her wards, maybe have a fight about how she shouldn't be here, but has to deal with this first.

"Heeey. That was . . . a lot." Mateo starts. Topher's upset about hurting the people around him, so Mateo can't feed him the platitudes that come naturally. Instead he says, "This isn't your fault. Whatever's causing this, it's not you. It's something happening to you. The best way to keep everyone safe is to figure out who's cursed you and stop them."

"What if nothing can stop them?" Topher says, and if Mateo wasn't so close, he would have missed the miserable muffle.

How do you make a sad, soft boy happy?

He has no idea.

Practicality then.

Topher, jelly-limbed and without any sense of rigor, allows Mateo to peel one of his arms away and excavate the side of his face. "That's not how this stuff works. There's a reason for what's happening. If we can find the reason, we can fix it." Probably.

Topher's eyes squeeze shut. Mateo's afraid he'll need a round two of this not very good pep talk, but then Topher unfurls, lowers his legs, and gives Mateo another of his very intense looks. This close, the light gray of Topher's eyes is more pronounced, no hint of blue or green, pupils wide and dark like he's on something. Probably near-death fear. But when Topher speaks, his voice is unexpectedly calm and resolute. "Sorry. You're right. I've been upset and not doing anything for months. That doesn't help."

"That's the spirit," Mateo says and pats Topher's knee like Topher's his new stepson he's just been introduced to on the day he lost the big game. At around the third pat, he realizes Quincy is staring at him in the rearview mirror. Right. The driver can totally hear the words about curses. Not wanting to deal with whatever judgment might be there, Mateo relegates the paid-driver's bulk to his peripheral vision. Whatever. It's not like he'll ever see this guy after today.

They pile out of the car.

Ophelia, in a rare moment of delicate compassion, puts her hands on Topher's cheeks like someone might do before a kiss and commands: "Three deep breaths. In for five seconds. Out for five seconds. Starting now."

Topher, startled into compliance, does exactly what she says, silently goggling with arms limp at his sides and eyes perfect circles. That neon flush heats Topher's cheeks again, and why not? Ophelia's terrifying, but she's also cute, and obviously into this guy who's obviously into her, which is, like, great. Probably a conflict of interest or whatever—professionally speaking—but otherwise fantastic for everyone.

It's this moment Mateo realizes his tongue's been absently worrying over the tips of sharp teeth. From the near car crash, he guesses, and doesn't think about the time delay there.

"It's just a conversation. You can do this," Ophelia concludes.

"Right," Topher whispers readily, and Ophelia releases him. It must be hell to blush that easily and visibly, and Mateo feels a twinge of something that must be sympathy. Loving Ophelia is like loving a rocket ship. One day it's going to shoot into space while shedding noncritical parts that will then hurtle back toward the planet, burn up on reentry, but sometimes take out a cow.

"I'm not sure how long I'll be," Topher says, and it takes Mateo a confused moment to realize he's talking to Quincy. It's the first words Topher's directly spoken to the man.

"That's fine," Quincy says, offering Topher a tissue and then running his paid-driver hands through Topher's chaotic mess of hair, forcing some order into it. "I've got a book."

Topher, unreactive to the extremely personal hair thing that has scandalized Mateo, nods and they start toward the towering office. But Mateo's distracted, fully staring at Quincy now, watching the man get back into the SUV.

It's only then that it occurs to him that Quincy isn't some random day driver. "Topher, do you, like, *know* know the driver?"

"Oh, yeah. Yes. Quincy's worked for me for a few years," Topher says distractedly, leading them through a heavy door and into a lobby that looks like a Roman statue threw up all over it. Every inch is gray-swirled marble except for the inches that hold a line of security guys.

The rigid postures and serious business vibes bring his attention distressingly back to the fact that he still hasn't thought of a single thing to ask Topher's dad.

CHAPTER FIFTEEN

The inner lobby of Christopher Nystrom's office is worse than the downstairs lobby. Worse here, meaning expensive and like a place Mateo should be shot for occupying.

The walls are covered in ugly abstract art that either took someone ten minutes or ten years to make. A literal golden door bars them from accessing the office beyond. The far side of the room houses a plastic-lipped receptionist baked into the wall in a to-go-style window. His orange-tan face gives Mateo a head-to-toe look, purses his lips to say something passive aggressive—for sure—but then catches sight of Topher. That smile stretches back into place. Despite Topher's tumbled bedhead and mouse-on-uppers energy, he's got some inherent money-scent this man is sensitive to, and they proceed to have a polite conversation.

"Conference room three," Plastic-Lips Man says before a soft chime sounds. Inexplicable. Until the golden doors start to swing open.

They've been deemed worthy.

Behind the door is aggressively boring. Rows of cubicles form an endless grid. The edges of the room are lined with glass-enclosed offices with wall-to-ceiling windows letting in the too-bright day. Everything's transparent. You couldn't scratch your nose without it being visible from seventeen different seats. Absolute hell. It's the first time in his life Mateo's grateful for the dark, burnt-hair-smelling back room at work.

Conference room three sits tucked in a far corner—or as tucked as you can be with an unimpeded view of the world around you. A massive table takes up most of it and reflects the sun painfully. Mateo walks to the window, taking in the insane view. There's water all around Seattle, but this is sparkly California water.

"There's drinks and food and stuff," Topher says, flitting about the room, trying to get an angle all around the office, presumably to spot his father.

"Where?" Ophelia asks because she can always be counted on when free is involved.

Topher seems to have forgotten that he spoke, pressed to a glass corner on tiptoes with his head on swivel. "Where?" he repeats, diverting his attention back to them in confusion.

"Where's the drinks and food and stuff?" Ophelia drops into the seat at the head of the table, because of course she would.

"Oh, sorry. Sorry." Topher throws one more forsaken look toward the glass wall before focusing. "I'll go get . . . or I'll find someone . . . or . . ." He's locked in an infinite loop of existential indecision, seesawing between the door and the lone phone at the center of the table.

A towering man in a relentlessly navy but well-tailored suit stomps up to the conference door. He's in his fifties or sixties and composed of a series of tightly stacked cubes. Square head, broad chest, graying hair in a nothing style that is also a square. No particular point of interest to call out, so he probably loves

Ralph Lauren's fall catalog. In size alone, it's hard to conceive of his relation to Topher.

Something on Mateo's face alerts Topher, and his loop is broken as he turns and wilts.

The guy—Christopher Nystrom Sr., for sure—points at Topher and then hooks a thumb to the left. He doesn't perceive Mateo or Ophelia, only gives Topher the constipated expression of someone who's been waiting hours even though they're early for his four-hour window.

Topher whirls back to them, hands held up . . . as if either of them has made a move to follow and he needs to stop them. "I'll be right back. I didn't get to explain anything. Or, I mean, I didn't want to on the phone. And I probably need to explain some things. I mean, I don't think he'll be very receptive if he doesn't know what's going on."

"It's okay," Mateo soothes, and Topher flits out of the room, carefully closing the door behind him so it doesn't so much as click. The dad is already gone. He hadn't waited for Topher's brief words to them, so Topher has to hurry after him. During Topher's pitiful work shift, Mateo had thought the power walking was a weird Topher quirk. Now he thinks it has to do with keeping up with his jerk dad.

"He's a peach," Ophelia says.

"Seems really supportive too." Mateo takes a seat, running his tongue along his sharp teeth. Demon doesn't like the asshole dad much either. "Did you see what happened in the car?"

"The weird swirl of stuff on Topher exploded out right before the truck fishtailed," Ophelia says, her gaze still following Topher. "Then it slowly came back."

They'd been pretty sure about the curse, but now they're for-sure-for-sure that it's real.

"Get anything off the dad?"

"Not him specifically." Ophelia rummages in her purse, extracting a cherry lip balm and applying it over red-painted lips before continuing. "There's a lot of weird energy around here. I'm not sure if he's the one practicing or it's just someone else in this office. Or multiple people. There's too much energy for no magic to be happening, but not enough to pin it on one person. Witches usually look like witches. Unless they know how to hide it." She gestures at Mateo, presently sporting the very ward she's talking about to mask his demon stank.

"Oh shit. Someone's been doing magic but also trying to clean it up," Mateo whispers, examining the cubicles outside the conference room. No one's paying them any attention. Why would they? If the curser were the too-pink guy in the ill-fitting DKNY button-up in the closest cubicle, he'd have no reason to think the pair of random people left to rot in a glass box were out to get him.

A knock on the glass directs their attention to the door. It's neither of the Nystroms. It's a jacquard Alexander McQueen suit. Black on black, so the iconic logo pattern is subtle and only visible when it catches the light. Matching jacket and pants Mateo would murder a bus full of children going to a *Sad Kids Who've Never Known Joy* charity party to wear. Beneath is a crisp white button-up. A double monk strap pair of Jimmy Choo's with a rounded toe finish the look.

Flawless.

There's also a guy in all that, but the wearer is an afterthought. Mateo's never experienced someone so well dressed. Well dressed and bald. But in a stylish way. Like it's a choice and not an outcome of genetics. Maybe both. He's working it either way. He's also staring at Mateo, waggling his fingers in greeting, and opening the door. "Hey. Sorry to interrupt. Are you guys waiting on someone?"

"Your outfit is amazing," Mateo says because it has to be said. He can't think past it.

Well-dressed man smiles sharp lips, wielding a cupid's bow that could cut metal. It's a good smile. Like he understands the soul-deep sincerity in Mateo's words. He's gotta be early twenties too. All these wealthy guys his age should be pissing Mateo off, but this one gets a pass because he's now the best human being Mateo's ever seen.

"We're waiting for Mr. Nystrom," Ophelia says because she's not being seduced by an outfit.

The guy's artfully plucked eyebrow lifts. "Really?"

"We don't seem the type?" Mateo says and is rewarded by that smile again and the guy stepping in, offering his hand. Which Mateo stands and shakes. "Mateo Borrero."

"Ethan Robillard. New clients?"

"Mr. Nystrom Jr. is *our* client," Ophelia says, surveying Ethan before introducing herself. It's a surprising level of interest. Nothing about Ethan lines up with the scattershot diagram of her tastes that Mateo's worked out over the years. She tends to like cutesy across all spectrums. Unless she's seeing something in his aura—the thought he should have jumped to first.

"I've heard tales of drinks, food, and *stuff*," she says, still angling for free things. Or a non-Nystrom-guided look around because she's a genius.

Ethan seems amused. "We do indeed have drinks, food, and stuff. You've got time for a tour?" He asks Ophelia but then looks at Mateo.

"You tell us." Mateo tilts his chin in the direction the Nystroms went. "Nystrom Sr. and Jr. went to chat. That an all-day affair?"

Ethan looks at his watch, one of those bulky things that represent the last stage of *rich* for any man, when they've run out of things they actually want to buy but recognize that the archaic devices hold power over *olds*. "Ten minutes until Nystrom the Senior's in a meeting I'm also in."

"How long will you be trapped in that?" Mateo asks.

"Scheduled for four hours," Ethan answers readily. "Traps me till the end of the day."

They're being blown off by Topher's dad. He never had a window to talk to them.

"We'd love a quick look around," Mateo says.

* * *

With only ten minutes to spare, Ethan provides a very economical tour. The fancy-money-people office features a nap room, a chill room, and a room where one whole wall is expensive bottles of booze—where Ophelia wants to linger so Mateo gives her a *we're working* look and she concedes.

On the main office drag, their tour guide indicates the boring old guys who can't talk about anything but stock portfolios, the boring old guys who can't talk about anything but tax write-offs, and a corner that holds a trio of younger guys who can't talk about anything but sports ball of various forms. A whole floor full of people Mateo would rather fling himself into traffic than talk to, so it's a real shock that Ethan seems so completely self-aware and funny about it.

They end up in a large kitchen-slash-cafeteria, a catered lunch still steaming in metal bins. Ophelia helps herself, a woman with no working definition of shame; she has two plates, and they both know that neither is for Mateo.

"What do you do here, other than give opinionated tours as a ruse to guide forsaken people to the free food?" Mateo asks, picking up a paper plate but not doing anything with it.

Ethan, hands in the pockets of his nice pants, looks both completely at ease and totally out of place in the harsh Walmart Superstore lighting of the space. He smiles and throws the question back at him. "For my excellent tour, you should go first."

A reasonable cover doesn't come to him but in Ophelia's shows the investigators always just say who they are, and the bad guy gets jumpy. If Ethan's suddenly nervous, he's the bad guy. Easy.

Except Mateo's never verbalized this thing before. It's not embarrassment so much as an acute awareness that he's about to learn if he hates this man. Mysticism is a polarizing topic. People believe or they don't, and both sides can be really annoying about it. "Occult specialist," he says, bracing with his customer service smile in place.

An eyebrow lifts, a half-smile forms, and Ethan waits for the punchline. When it doesn't come, he finally says, "For real?"

"For really real," Ophelia says dully from somewhere behind Mateo.

Ethan still looks like he's waiting for Mateo to yell *psych*, but he's not being a dick about it. Yet. "Unexpected. Like . . . what does that mean? Haunted dolls?"

Mateo lets out a laugh. "Why haunted dolls?"

"I don't know. I saw *Annabelle* last week. It was all I could think of," Ethan defends. No grand villain revelation on his face before he indicates himself. "Now this is going to sound boring. Financial advisor." He elaborates when Mateo's expression mists over. "I say a bunch of numbers at people until they relent and let me put their money into the stocks I want to. There's a bunch of research involved, analyzing risk versus benefit, and math. But it's sexier if you imagine Wall Street, and me yelling 'buy, buy, buy' and 'sell, sell, sell.'"

"Isn't Wall Street in New York?"

"You're getting hung up on the details," Ethan says, gesturing to the nearest cubicle, where someone in a boring suit is staring dull-eyed at a screen. "Don't picture that. Picture the buying and selling. Add me holding a fistful of money and shaking it in the air as I trade."

He should be asking Ethan what he knows about Christopher Nystrom, or other work-related questions, but it's few and far between that he has an enjoyable conversation with someone other than Ophelia. "Are we talking ones or twenties?"

Ethan leans close, smirking as he whispers. "Let's say hundreds."

"Your meeting," Ophelia says, standing by the end of the buffet now with three small biodegradable plates neatly stacked and balanced in one hand.

Ethan leans away and checks the time. "My meeting," he agrees. "I've gotta run." He does that slick business-guy thing where he gets a business card out of his inside jacket pocket with a flourish. It's nearly a magic trick. Mateo's aware that the outfit is making the wearer's actions acceptable to his mind, but knowing doesn't change the effect. Ethan offers the card to him, but then pulls it back a bit when Mateo reaches for it. "You available tonight?"

"Why? Do you have a haunted doll?" It's a joke . . . but also not. Is this what networking is? If this guy's intrigued by the idea of *occult specialist*, Mateo should humor him. With that impeccable suit, his paycheck has to be ten times what Mateo's making.

"I could probably find one," Ethan answers easily.

"We have to check with our client," Ophelia—again from somewhere behind him. Mateo turns to look at her, startled by how generally helpful she's been. She has a piece of cake in her hand, so at least there's some sort of balance.

"Let me know," Ethan says with another smile, letting him take the card before leaving.

A hurried feeding later, and Mateo leads the way down the hellishly glass-lined hall back to conference room three. The stench of something brined and rotting assaults him and his steps slow. "What the hell?" He manages not to gag only because his teeth are suddenly sharp and he's afraid they'll be visible if he yaks. There's only gray-carpeted floor and little metal trashcans all around. Nothing to explain the stench. And no one else is reacting.

"You can see the ward?" Ophelia asks, and Mateo whips around to look at her. Her expression is slack, pale eyes focused on something beyond him. The conference room.

"I don't see anything. You can't smell that?" he asks, turning again to the conference room and approaching. The space beyond is visible. And empty.

"I don't smell anything." She moves to step around him, but he blocks her.

Carefully, like slowness can offset unknown magics, he opens the door. "Where?"

Ophelia slips in after him, tilting her head, gaze unfocused on the table. "Under it."

Mateo squats, and there's nary a festering bowl of blue cheese in sight, but that's what it smells like. This close, there's another smell beneath it. Sweet like candy but also a little savory.

His eyes land on a smudge up where the leg meets the underside of the tabletop. It's dark and still wet against the stainless-steel legs.

Not candy.

Blood.

It's on the other table leg across from him, and without looking he knows it's on all four. Completing a circle. It wasn't there earlier. No smell and Ophelia would have mentioned seeing a blood magic ward. They hadn't been out of the room for more than fifteen minutes. Which means someone had been watching. Waiting for them to leave.

"Blood magic," Mateo says quietly, and doesn't need to look at Ophelia to know she's frowning.

It's not that totally innocuous blood magic spells don't exist, it's that he doesn't know any and can't think of a positive reason you'd paint one onto the bottom of a table the moment someone left the room. Whatever the ward's meant to do, it's probably not friendly.

Also, blood magic is a weird pairing for someone working in finance. There's loads of magics out there that focus on spells for wealth and success. Gentler, more precise magics, asking specific entities for assistance with specific goals.

But blood magic isn't a scalpel, it's a sledgehammer. You don't use it to enhance your odds of getting a promotion. You use it to maim the competition.

And, most troubling of all, nothing about Topher's curse implies it was cast with blood magic . . . until this moment.

Mateo stands, turning toward the offices beyond. A sea of heads tipped down, staring at monitors. No one's paying attention to them, even though someone definitely ran in and did this.

Somewhere close by, waiting and watching, is a blood magic witch.

CHAPTER SIXTEEN

Before they can decide what to do about the unknown yet ominous magic blood circle, Topher's pasty form appears in the doorway. "I have some bad news, dad wants to resche—" he starts but Mateo has a hand on Topher's back, herding him out of the conference room and down the hall double time, Ophelia in their wake.

Topher, incapable of stopping anyone from doing anything, allows this, not managing a question until they're in the elevator and heading down. "Did something happen?"

"Saw the writing on the wall," Mateo says, hitting the button for the lobby with too much force. He's sharp-toothed and mighty keen to get Ophelia and Topher out of here. It's not that he wants to keep Topher in the dark so much as ominously and futilely telling him, "There's defo a scary witch running around your dad's office, and we have no idea who it is, but they just tried something" doesn't feel super helpful at this juncture.

Leaving very quickly feels more prudent.

"I'm sorry," Topher says in distress, letting Mateo continue to usher him around, out the elevator, through the lobby, and into the too bright day. "He's just . . . he's having a hard time with things since mom left. But he said he'd come home after work and talk."

Wants it in the private space of his home. Almost like he doesn't want to talk to two magical specialists about curses while at work.

Which, honestly, could be a perfectly reasonable stance if you don't believe in magic and think your son brought two con artists to your place of business.

But also, it looks sus as hell and someone is definitely doing magic in that office.

"It wasn't a total loss. We got free food," Mateo assures him as they pile into the waiting car, giving Topher another awkward knee pat once they're seated. The wide-eyed look shifts from apologetic to normal-near-panic, which must be better. "We wanted to check out your house anyway."

Mateo uses the ride to puzzle over how and why someone went for them in the scant few minutes they'd left the conference room. Coincidence feels unlikely, but anything but a coincidence also makes no sense because no one knew they were coming. Was the target Topher? He might have been on his dad's calendar.

This thought keeps his teeth distressingly sharp the whole traffic-laden trip across town.

Eventually, Quincy parks in a cobbled driveway split down the middle by a fountain filled with naked lady statues endlessly pouring water from vases.

It's Topher's dad's mansion. Ophelia's out of the car first, taking pictures.

Topher's fuchsia again, looking like he wants to pull Ophelia away but wouldn't dare touch her. "Sorry about the, uh . . ." He can't bring himself to say "naked ladies" so trails off, then powers ahead. "They came with the house. Mom hates them. Dad . . . he likes them, so . . ." Topher's taking psychic damage standing near the statues, so he hurries to the front door, punching in a code on a keypad to let them in.

Mateo's still trying to think through this blood magic complication, but there's an honest to God foyer on the other side of the door. Marble floors, gaudy frames featuring more unclothed women doing manual labor, and no obvious use for the large space. Until Topher opens an unseeable closet to one side of the door and indicates they should de-shoe.

Ophelia has on those girl shoes that are made of half an inch of fabric and wishes so she kicks them off into the closet like an animal, then walks ahead into the house.

"Holy shit," Ophelia's mild voice calls as he follows Topher into the living room.

More pale marble and questionable art abounds. Cutouts in the walls hold things like a single sterile white apple. An L-shaped couch sits in the center of a slate-gray rug, and neither looks like something a human ass is meant to interact with. A low coffee table made of glass threatens in front of an open fireplace that runs the length of one wall.

It's the most actively hostile room Mateo's ever been in. A nightmare of a deathtrap, every surface high-gloss or sharp, and they're standing in it with a cursed guy.

But that's not what Ophelia was reacting to.

She stands in front of a wall-to-ceiling window and stares into the yard, where a pool dazzles in the dying San Francisco light. "I'm going to investigate the backyard," she says to no one because she doesn't wait for a response before wandering deeper into the house.

Topher takes a step as if to follow, but Mateo catches his shoulder. "She's fine on her own. Looking for auras and trace magics." Ninety percent chance she goes directly into the pool without doing anything else. "When I got background information from you, you said you didn't really know any of your dad's associates, right?" A bobble of agreement. "Have you ever interacted with any of them, though? Not best friend stuff. A handshake. Quick conversation. That kinda thing?" A curse could be cast in a million different ways.

"I only really talk to the receptionist," Topher says, still looking worriedly after Ophelia. "But just to ask where my father is. And only a few times. I don't go to his offices often."

"Any of your dad's suited peers been around the house?" he tries. Considering the MIA mom and that Topher's the one cursed, one of Christopher's rivals might be trying to hurt the man. Get him off his game for business reasons Mateo can't guess at because he doesn't know how finance jobs work.

Topher nods. "Some. I don't really, um, I mean, dad has an office here, but I'm usually in my room." Right. The naked-lady house with the least human-friendly living room known to man didn't imply a close family dynamic.

"Show me around," Mateo says, steering Topher deeper into the house. "Since someone cursed you, there might be signs of it in the house. Maybe even a focus to amplify the effect."

"Oh. Yeah. Yes. The . . . uh, whole house, or?" The panic of a layperson asked to disarm a bomb overtakes Topher. "I mean, the whole house is fine. It's just, there's a lot of rooms. We don't use most of them. They're guest rooms. Except we never have guests. And there's a lot of bathrooms. Fifteen. More bathrooms than rooms. Do you want to see the bathrooms?"

A sheen of sweat sits on Topher's brow, and Mateo's realizing that without direction, a faucet spins wide open and Topher spews uncertainty. "Let's start with your room, then check out your dad's office."

It gets Topher moving, and Mateo follows through two more living rooms, a can-sit-the-last-supper-twice-over-sized dining room, and a massive and functionless area before the stairs. Topher provides stilted narration as they walk, also unclear about the function of most of the rooms.

Hand on knob, Topher goes to lead him into his bedroom, but then stops so abruptly that Mateo bodily bowls into him and has to catch himself on both Topher and the doorframe.

"Sorry. Sorry," Topher says, arms spread wide, also braced against the doorframe. "I didn't, um . . . I mean, I left in kind of a hurry. I don't know if, I mean, it's probably fine, but . . ."

Mateo backs up a few steps, hands raised in surrender. "You can make sure your room isn't a mess. I'll hang out right here."

Hunted mongoose eyes vibrate in desperate gratitude, and then Topher slips into the room, pulling the door shut soundlessly like he stood there with both hands on it and eased it closed with breath held. A real loathing starts in Mateo's gut about a dad he only saw for twenty seconds, and he has to yoga breathe his teeth back into bluntness. They're getting sharp at everything today. Which isn't great. In the past few days, he's done a lot of minor magic—and a lot of healing. He'd napped at the hotel, and it had been dreamless, but he's dreading tonight.

Topher opens the door, and it's clear that rich people are exhibitionists, another curtainless floor-to-ceiling glass wall that overlooks the backyard. All the furniture's matching matte gray, the bed huge and neatly made and stacked high with nonfunctional pillows. This whole house is an impersonal yet expensive hotel. There's almost nothing that could be out of place so Mateo can't imagine what Topher cleaned up. The only signs of life are a neat stack of math books on the dresser beside a framed photo of Topher, his dad, and what must be his mom.

Walking to the frame, Mateo picks it up. Mom's gotta be Mateo's height or taller, towering over her tiny son and normal-dude-height husband. Long, colorless hair flows down to her butt. She's like if a high-fashion model got upscaled—meaning she's not just large but a little weird looking. Thin mouth, small nose, high cheekbones, and a narrow chin. The air of a startled bird with the same large, watery eyes as her son. He doesn't need to ask, but he does to be conversational. "This your mom?"

Topher nods, back pressed to the window, giving Mateo as much space as possible.

Setting the frame down, Mateo squints around the room. "I'm going to rummage around. Is that okay? The focus I mentioned could be anywhere."

Topher hesitates, eyes darting around like he's trying to remember where he's stashed every sordid secret. He eventually nods, and Mateo begins his riffling, desperately hoping he doesn't run into anything weird. There's something wildly unpleasant about shoving your hands in someone's underwear drawer while they mutely watch you, so Mateo gropes for conversation. "You really haven't talked to your mom in three months? Since the curse started?"

Another pause. "I know we talked right before she left. Maybe once right after. I didn't realize what was going on with me right away. Things steadily got worse and worse as more accidents happened, but she was having a hard time too. I didn't want to make her worry."

The timing of Topher's mom going MIA had made her seem sus. Not that moms can't just split—insert self-deprecating joke here—but the unpleasant dad and the blood magic is causing another theory to form. Like maybe the mom isn't alive anymore. "Were you and your mom close before your parents split?"

A soft hum of thought from behind him. "I think so? She's nice, and smart, and funny. By the time I finished school, she seemed way busier than before, so we didn't get to hang out as much. I think it's that thing, you know, when the kid goes to school, so the parent gets to work."

Mateo, having never gone to school or had a pleasant mother, did not know, but nods. "What's she do?" He moves to the closet, pausing to gape at the massive size. A bed could fit inside. It's so tidy, too. Everything hung up is shades of gray, and all of the hangers are identical.

He realizes Topher hasn't answered yet and leans back out. The sun is starting to set behind his pale form, making him difficult to look at, but he's fiddling with his hands again. "I don't know," Topher eventually says. "I . . . I think it's something like what dad does. Something with money. That's probably weird that I don't know, isn't it?"

The last thing this guy needs is for the single positive interpersonal relationship in his life to be criticized. So, Mateo shrugs. "I don't really know what my mom does, so I can't judge anyone." This is starting to bum them both out, though, so he steers toward something soothing. "Maybe she just didn't think of mentioning it since she started while you were busy. By the time you were done with school, it was old news to her." He's pretty sure that's how people work.

Another little hum. A thing he's realizing that Topher does when he doesn't know how to reply. Mateo, having done his best, leaves Topher to his sad and starts groping around in the corners of the closet. He's immediately distracted by the clothes. The button-ups and tees are brandless expensiveness, soft fabrics, and the suits off to one side look custom. A closet full of perfectly tailored or handmade things is such an insane power move.

"Can I ask a question?"

Mateo drops a sleeve like he was caught trying to steal it and not just checking out the stitching. That anxious face peers into the closet, waiting until Mateo gives permission.

"How come you were okay after getting cut?" Topher's warbly voice asks. "And you had teeth. Different teeth. Pointy teeth. Twice. When we ran and during my tarot thing. And your blood was black. Is that a . . . a spell or?"

These are completely reasonable questions Topher should have asked days ago. That doesn't mean Mateo wants to answer them.

"Yeah, a spell," Mateo says, skirting around Topher, wanting out of the closet and away from him. This is a professional situation terminating in a few weeks. Can't have Topher out there knowing things about him. He's obviously got no one to tell—except his jacked personal driver—but still. "Really high-level protection spell. It's on Ophelia too. That's why we're not stressed being around you." It's more like a conflation and simplification of information. There *are* protection spells in place.

"Oh that's—I'm so glad to hear that." Mateo only feels a little bad that Topher looks genuinely relieved, eyes tracking Mateo out of the closet and to the bed but staying rooted in the closet doorway. "It would be horrible if something happened to you while you were helping me. I mean, or ever. Ever would be bad too. But it would be my fault if it happened from this. And

I'd feel bad. I mean, I'd feel bad if something happened to you even if it wasn't my fault."

"Thanks," Mateo says loudly to halt the flow. How can someone be so rich, so bad at talking, so sad, and so relentlessly nice? Wanting a distraction from a level of human decency he can't match, he starts delicately lifting the comforter of the carefully made bed like that could be hiding anything and tries again. Something easy. Safe. Simple. "You like math?"

"Math?" Topher repeats in confusion.

Baffled right back at him, Mateo gestures at the stack of textbooks.

"Oh. Yes. I mean, I do, but those aren't math books," Topher says, wandering to the stack to pick one up and show Mateo the front. It reads: *Structures, Algorithms, and Systems.*

Squinting, Mateo drops the comforter. Aren't algorithms math? Oh no. He's suddenly the stupidest person in this room and can't ask what the title means because Topher's looking at him pleasantly like he's supposed to know. And he's paid Mateo a lot of money. Based on context clues of the bad CG graphics sci-fi-ish cover he says, "So, like, computer things?"

Topher nods and Mateo wishes he could high-five himself. "I double majored in computer science and business," Topher explains, setting the book back down and flipping the cover open idly. "I really liked the computer science classes. Business was because of my dad. Those classes were boring but it's good to have a solid business foundation."

"I do hear that," Mateo says because it feels like he should agree. But a distant alarm is sounding in his skull—a dim realization as he watches this very rich and well-dressed guy leaf through textbooks fondly. Computer science and business are smart things. Despite his inability to function in the ecology of a print shop, Topher might be smart. If he starts trying to talk about either of those things he majored in, it's going to quickly become clear that Mateo's only barely rocking a GED certificate. Okay. Easy. Just keep the conversation on Topher. "Where did you go to school?"

Gaze darting up from the book, Topher hesitates before saying, "Massachusetts Institute of Technology."

"Oh?" Mateo says, baffled as to what Topher's expression means. Maybe it's a bad school? Kinda sounds like a trade school so maybe that's embarrassing for rich people. Not wanting him to feel bad about a thing Mateo absolutely doesn't care about, he adds, "I got really nervous you were going to say Harvard."

That insubstantial smile flickers over Topher's lips as he says, "It's a pretty good school for computer stuff."

Okay. He's gonna call that a successful human interaction. Having no cool information about Massachusetts, computers, or business to carry this conversation further and unable to pretend looking at the top of the bed is still happening, he squats and goes elbow deep under the mattress to root around.

Fingers brush against something. There's an uneasy moment where he's positive it's going to be a sex toy he'll have to diplomatically hurl across the room, but what he has in hand is a little figure of a woman. It's definitely magic-adjacent because he doubts Topher keeps cryptic figures under his mattress for fun, but before he can ask, a navy-clad figure fills the doorway.

"Why the hell is there a girl in my pool?" Christopher Nystrom Sr. asks. The large man doesn't wait for an answer, turns and stomps away, expecting Topher to follow—which Topher does, an apologetic look thrown to Mateo before he's jogging after his father's back.

Mateo stands but doesn't follow. Not because he's unconcerned with this guy's hostile attitude toward his own kid, but because he's extremely concerned—a sharp-toothed, swimming head, heat in his stomach, and a mass of something thick and virulent seeping into his quickening heart kind of concerned.

Claws could so easily sink into the father's body, root around, seek out the most delicious parts—the consistency of firm, hot Jell-O. It would be so easy to separate organ from the rest of the meat, and the squelch of insides ripping would be intoxicating. Liver or spleen first, pressed to lips for a relishing moment before teeth shred with ease. Pleasure would fill his mouth, the blood a delicious condiment. Au jus. A candied taste to accent the snap of flesh, the heady, salty richness of a meat so recently pulsing with life.

Bracing against the doorway, he sways.

A blink and he's in the living room, Ophelia's hands on his chest, like she's stopping him from going forward. Her washed-out robin's egg eyes are wide and directed up at him. She's in a swimsuit, which meant she'd come with it under her dress. **She's sublime and undimmable, even after death.** This thought feels alien in his head, not because it's untrue but because he doesn't typically think in such dramatic terms. The world blurs briefly, and he finally thinks to look beyond her, to understand what's happening loudly a few feet away.

"Please, just talk to them. I know you don't believe me, but things are really bad. And they're helping. Please," Topher begs, using his flimsy body to block the way to the foyer.

Christopher Nystrom Sr. looks like if a slightly doughy linebacker ate another one. Muscle under a thin layer of dude who works in an office. He's unmoved by his son's desperation. "I don't know what lies these swindlers have fed you." His face is pink with anger as he turns to direct his hostility at Mateo. "But I'm not biting. Get out of my house before I make you."

They need to leave. Mateo's heartbeat is an assault on his rib cage, and the edges of his vision are dimming. He's transfixed by the thin layer of skin holding in all that meat. **So easy to puncture along the gut and let everything spill onto the floor. Hot juice and organs. He could reach in, pluck free, sink teeth into, and then he wouldn't have to hear the meat's voice anymore.**

Warm hands cup Mateo's cheeks, drawing his attention down to Ophelia's sedative gaze. Steadying him. He forces himself to focus on her perfect halo of wet curls from the pool, even as his mind stutters with reconceptualizing the rest of the scene.

Not meat. A man.

The agitation in the room is teetering in his skull. Christopher is staring at him, daring Mateo to say something so he can kick his ass. But the dream that may or may not be a memory of his hands buried in guts comes unbidden and he starts salivating.

An ache works its way to his awareness, the little lady figure in his hand gripped hard enough to hurt. Forcing fingers open, he stares at it, Ophelia's attention on it too.

"What?" she asks softly.

A maddening thought occurs to Mateo. The little lady figure is familiar, even though he has no idea who it is, and something about this familiarity means Christopher is lying. He needs to leave this room now, but they need to ask something. "The mom?" he whispers to Ophelia. She's the biggest unknown. The central mystery. The thing that seems so unresolved here.

Ophelia turns to Christopher and says loudly.

"Where's your wife?"

They all see it.

Christopher Nystrom Sr. has the same highly reactive complexion as his son. The pallor shifts, skin that was furious red, blanches.

For one solitary moment, he looks guilty as all hell.

Then it flips back to anger. He puts a hand on Topher's shoulder and bodily moves him out of the way. "Out. Now."

CHAPTER SEVENTEEN

Whatever vibes they bring with them as they get into the SUV, Quincy gleans enough to pull out and head toward their hotel without direction.

"When's the last time you heard from her?" Ophelia asks Topher gently.

"Maybe two—two and a half—months ago," Topher says, a hollow quality to the assertion because he's not sure. "With all the stuff happening, we weren't talking much."

"Why don't you try her again?" Ophelia coaxes; followed by the muffled sound of a call ringing and ringing before cutting off without even a *leave a message*. Mateo, eyes closed and still trying to get a hold of himself while slumped in the furthest back seat, counts twelve attempts.

"She's probably busy," Topher says softly from the middle row.

"Probably," Ophelia returns, and they all listen to him dial again.

Mateo wants to say something soothing. Anything to offset the reality that anger issues plus what sounded like an impending divorce divided by a mom going MIA usually equals a husband killing his wife.

But he has to leave it to Ophelia.

The carnivorous thoughts have stopped which is great, but a salivatory bitterness coats his tongue, and he's afraid he's going to vomit. That's two moments of lost time in as many days. When he'd blacked out during the tarot reading, he'd at least been using magic, so it made some sort of sense, but this time he hadn't been doing anything.

Except watching Christopher be an absolute dick to Topher.

Something about seeing that guy be so dismissive about the literal death and mayhem following Topher around had really pissed off whatever's inside Mateo. The demon's extreme investment in Topher's familial drama and well-being wasn't on his bingo card for the week. It'd be embarrassing if it wasn't so homicide-adjacent.

Jamming palms against his eyes, he can feel a breathless sort of volatility just below the surface, and he spends the ride trying to yoga breathe the demon away.

By the time they pull up to their hotel, Mateo's pretty sure he's not going to hurl.

They cluster outside the car, not quite ready to part ways. The situation is not only unfinished but also unstarted, because none of them want to put words to the unmistakable guilt that shuddered across Christopher Nystrom's face.

Quincy waits a few respectable steps away, like sound doesn't travel an arm's length.

The evening air is amazing on Mateo's heated skin, and he briefly fantasizes about sitting somewhere alone to get his blood settled. There's a twitchiness, like he's had too much caffeine.

"I thought, I mean, I hoped," Topher tries haltingly, wrapping arms tightly around his middle. "Just a few questions. When it's so important. He knows all about the accidents. I don't know why he can't see what's happening. I really thought if we were all just there, and we asked, he'd talk. And I know mom's a sensitive issue but . . . but that was weird, wasn't it? The way he . . . I mean he looked like . . ." He doesn't want to say it.

"Yes," Ophelia says softly.

It isn't the answer Topher wants, and he doesn't know what to do with it, staring unblinking at the side of the car. A missing mom must suck so much worse when she loved you.

Mateo looks to Ophelia, and his eyes tell her everything he doesn't want to say: *Yes, something almost happened there but I'm okay.* And underneath that is a *holy shit* at the father's reaction. There's also a question between them, and it's scrawny, quivering a few inches away, and actually paid for the way too big suite they're staying in. An incline of his head and a lift of her chin. They're agreed.

Even though all he wants is to lock himself in his room and have a little freak-out, Mateo turns to Topher. "Maybe you should stay with us tonight. We have some findings to discuss."

* * *

Sitting on the arm of the hotel living room couch, Mateo balances a plate of pizza he doesn't want on his knee and tries to work out the most professional way to start a conversation about Topher's probably dead mom.

Quincy is still with them because Topher invited him along. Meaning the driver might be the closest thing Topher has to a friend, which is both sad and going to get weird when they start talking about blood magic. But it's Topher's dollar.

Ophelia, beside Quincy at the low coffee table, uses the moment Topher dips into the bathroom to explain the dad's reaction in the mansion. Now everyone is up to date, uncomfortable, and unenthusiastically eating pizza.

Turning to Topher, Mateo watches him try to maneuver the world's dullest plastic knife through a tomato-smeared slice on a flimsy paper plate that's resting on his pale-gray-panted lap. It quickly becomes too stressful and forces Mateo to broach the terrible topic at hand.

"So," he begins, making Topher start, knife slipping and nearly sliding sauce onto his pale gray shirt. Mateo stifles a scream for the shirt and Topher gets it under control. "We should probably try to find your mom. Like. In a hurry."

Topher abandons his slice on the low table in front of him before turning his round eyes on Mateo in miserable question.

"In case she's more receptive to questions than your dad," Mateo adds quickly, evading the probably-dead-elephant-in-the-room, afraid those enormous eyes are going to overflow again.

"And to make sure she's alive," Ophelia says around a bite of a toppings-less slice, the cheese and sauce discarded into a disgusting pile on her plate.

Mateo gives her a *holy shit* look, which she fully sees but ignores.

"I don't know your dad, mom, you, your life, or your personal chauffeur that stunt driver-ed us out of harm's way a few hours ago," she says, still chewing. "But I know guilt and lies, and your dad's full of shit. And there was magic all over your house."

"What?" Mateo, Topher, and Quincy all say.

"There's protection spells on that whole place," She abandons her crust on the table between them. "Weird ones. Like . . . nonstandard. Daddy Dearest came home before I could really study them, but even if I'd kept looking, I'm not sure I'd get anything more than that. Custom but nothing like your mom's." The last part is said to Mateo.

Which probably means they aren't super evil. But it's also the most buck-wild thing Ophelia could say. A warded house that didn't reject Mateo shouldn't be a thing. *Don't let demons in* is a pretty standard thing practitioners want. Could imply the wards are shit, but that's not what Ophelia said.

Focusing on Topher, who's blanched so completely that the blue of his blood is visible through his skin, Mateo says, "Has your curse ever popped off at home?"

Topher starts. "No. Nothing's ever happened there."

"Okay. So. Maybe the wards are keeping you safe at home," Mateo muses, looking back to Ophelia. "Do the wards feel like the same magic as the office?"

"*Totally* different," Ophelia says with feeling. Meaning the wards on the house aren't blood magic.

"There was magic at the office?" Topher whispers in dismay.

Mateo digs around in his pocket and unearths the little lady figure he'd found under Topher's mattress. Balanced on his palm, she's barely an inch tall.

"That's magic as all hell," Ophelia says.

"It was under Topher's mattress."

"Is it the focus? For the curse?" Topher leans in close to examine the cute, simplified features. She's little more than the suggestion of a woman with long, straight hair.

Ophelia takes it carefully between fingers, looking between it and Topher for a bit. "It's the same energy as the wards on the house. And similar, but not the same, as what's coming off of Topher, but . . ." Her eyes drift partially closed, the out-of-place blue of her irises fading. Dread ices Mateo's veins as he readies himself to jump forward and catch her if she slips away.

A tense moment and she blinks slowly. "It's—" She draws in a breath, frowning minutely. "It is a focus, but not for a curse. There's nothing negative about it." Her hand unconsciously comes up to rub an eye, like she can scrub away whatever she's seeing.

Taking the figure back, Mateo says, "It's a focus for a god then."

"God?" Topher parrots in alarm.

"Lowercase g." Mateo runs a thumb over the smooth face of the little wooden woman. "These are usually on altars. The idea of higher magic is: Light the right candles, incense, perfume—whatever that entity likes; recite the right words, which can be a spell, intention, dance, song, or power word; and then you can briefly connect to one of these entities. It's for channeling powers or communication. This is a specific entity, but I don't know who."

A lot of blinking as Topher tries to absorb this. "But why was it under my bed?"

Mateo shares a look with Ophelia, both hoping the other's figured it out, but no dice. "I would guess it's trying to protect you too. If it matches the magic of the wards on the house it might be an amplifier for those. But then, what the hell is going on with this curse? Why would someone go through all the trouble of cursing Topher but then protect the real estate?"

"I have no idea, but I think we're dealing with multiple casters," Ophelia says.

"One protecting and one cursing?" Mateo asks.

"That's not the distinction," Ophelia says, ticking them off on her hand. "Protection wards on the house, lady figure, and Topher's curse look similar. They're all the same kind of magic. I don't know what the blood ward at the office was going to do, but the curse on Topher looks completely different than it—not the same type, skill level, or intensity of intention. At least two different magics at play means at least two casters."

"How is that possible?" Mateo starts to pace the length of the living room. "Do multiple people have vendettas against Christopher? Is that what this is? No. That doesn't explain his guilty-as-all-fuck reaction back there. Now I'm not sure if the blood ward at the office has anything to do with Topher at all. But then, it has to. It can't have been cast because *we* walked in the door. We're total strangers to all this and warded up the ass. No one would have a reason to target us."

"One or both of his parents has to be a witch," Ophelia says.

They all look at Topher but he shakes his head mutely.

Reaching for the figure, Ophelia says, "Let's just ask whoever this is what's going on."

Mateo closes his fingers over it with a sharp, "No. Not you." There's no world where he lets her get into contact with some unknown, possibly hostile thing. It's not just demons capable of possession, and Ophelia's hold on her body is tenuous, at best. "I can try to contact it."

"No, you can't," she counters because he obviously shouldn't be using magic willy-nilly after the tarot thing and the near-freak-out in Christopher's house. "I'd be better with it."

"You don't know that," he snaps.

Now they're staring at each other, an old argument about who should risk themselves to fix their situation sucking the air out of the room. They shouldn't have this conversation in front of Topher and Quincy, their instability would be laid too bare, but neither of them can deny that there's something they could each try. It's extraordinarily dangerous to summon unfamiliar spirits—especially when one of them has a hard time staying in her body and the other has a hard time staying entirely human. Inviting an unknown into that is asking for trouble.

"We can try to find the mom first," Mateo says. It's a Hail Mary play. The mom's probably dead. But if she's not, she could know something.

Ophelia smiles without humor because Mateo's the auto-winner of this argument, the little figure held tight in his hand and he's not giving it over.

Looking to Quincy, Mateo says, "Beyond Topher calling, texting, and emailing, anyone have any ideas how to find her?" He's hoping—because of the Tokyo-drifting—that Quincy knows a secret way.

But it's Topher who speaks. "I could check her emails, see if she's met with other people, and see if she's been using her credit cards," he offers almost too quietly to hear, cheeks scarlet.

"What? How?" All Mateo can think is that Topher and his mother have joint accounts, like tweens too young to have their own account sometimes do.

Worrying hands together, Topher says, "I can hack her accounts."

Topher could have said "I'm actually my own missing mother" and it would have been less unexpected. The space between thought and speech is nonexistent in Mateo right now, so the room gets his real-time realization. "You didn't hire someone to track me down. You tracked me down. With hacking. You hacked me?"

Topher, eyes glued to the largest window in the room, looks like he's considering going for it to free himself from this confession.

"Cool," Ophelia says.

"I'm sorry," Topher says desperately to the window because he can't bring himself to look at Mateo. "I didn't know how else to figure out if you were legitimate. You don't have social media so I looked at your emails but you don't really email anyone so I started looking at your purchase history and that was pretty encouraging but then I realized you don't have a real birth certificate, ID, or medical records, and that's weird but I don't know your citizenship status and I thought if you did know magic that maybe you wouldn't have those things anyway, like maybe you don't adhere to the laws of man so then I thought—"

At this point in the never-ending run-on sentence Quincy puts a hand on Topher's arm, startling him into silence.

Holy shit. This mouse boy could see his internet searches. What about texts? He has no idea how hacking works, but Ophelia and he text 24/7. The thought of someone reading those is mortifying. Also, this guy knowing about his lack of ID stuff is pretty concerning, but mostly it's the texts. Shit. They send pictures sometimes too.

"Focus," Ophelia says, but something in his face shows the psychic damage he just took, and she assumes the lead. "Topher, hack your mom. See if you can contact her or find someone else who knows how to or that she's talked to lately. Any locations where she might be. Where she works. Lives. Last place she did anything. Teo, set up a date with that guy."

"What guy?"

"Back pocket."

Mateo pulls the card out of his back pocket. Ethan of the great suit. "Why?"

"He's our inside man. Ask about Christopher. Ask about anything weird at work. Ask if he's seen a wizard and can give a description. Use your wiles."

"Wiles?" Topher repeats with the same dismay Mateo feels.

CHAPTER EIGHTEEN

Dive bars are Mateo's thing. Chock-full of rowdy people he can talk to once and never again. Too loud to hold a proper conversation, but he can briefly feel like he's part of the human race without actually making any meaningful connections. All while getting plastered. Wonderful. Highly recommend. Great at it, even.

Flirting at a dive bar? Not a fan.

Flirting at a fancy bar playing soft elevator music with too many lights? Mateo's nightmare—the nonliteral kind.

It's a thing he has zero interest in, though Ophelia swears he's good at it. But he's not flirting. It's just the customer-service-honed affability he wields like a weapon when it can extort a free drink or an extra plate of fries. The second he's aware it's eliciting sexual attraction, he'd rather test out his healing ability against oncoming traffic.

Which is why it's so unfortunate that he's at the fancy hotel bar. There are totally open tables he could sit at, but Ophelia was adamant that he should let Ethan coax him to a table. He's two drinks in and trying not to chug the last gulp of his rum and coke before Ethan shows up. Also trying not to think about what Topher hacked, that he's suddenly involved in a murder mystery, that he keeps having demon episodes, that someone tried to blood magic him today, and that somewhere there's still a dagger-wielding witch waiting to be dealt with.

Ophelia sits on the other side of a window, poolside, sharing a table with a twitchy Topher who was adamant he keep watch with her. She was fine with it because it meant he'd cover her bar tab. Topher's got his laptop from Quincy's car and is staring at it.

Quincy—not obligated to stay for what didn't involve driving—went home for the night.

Ophelia makes eye contact and sips the bright blue daiquiri in front of her. Another sits in front of Topher but he's ignoring it in favor of his computer, fingers clacking away at the keys.

Maybe a third drink wouldn't hurt. As if hearing his desperation, Ethan's impeccably dressed form pushes through the door. Mateo mourns the loss of his previous outfit, but only for as long as it takes him to realize Ethan's now wearing Les Hommes—bomber jacket, graphic tee, unnecessary zippers all over the pants, and boots. Everything black. It's difficult to stay on his stool, wanting to meet him halfway and run his hands over the pattern of metal studs all over the bomber. Mateo only gets truly excited about stylish clothes—and money. Ethan happens to represent both, and it's alluring. Mateo definitely wants in his pants, just not the way that usually means.

"Hey," Ethan says, looking Mateo up and down—okay, it's definitely, definitely flirting—before eying his one empty and one near-empty drink. "I didn't take that long."

Mateo checks his phone. "Twenty-seven minutes. You're lucky I'm still upright."

"I dunno about that," Ethan says, smile sharpening.

Mateo finishes off his second drink so he doesn't have to formulate a reply to that really good but unmistakably sexual setup he'd accidentally provided.

"Let's grab a table," Ethan says, then knocks on the bar top, slick as shit, and catches the bartender's attention. "Another of what he's having." He scans the bottles neatly lined up behind the bartender. "The Gordon & MacPhail for me. Neat." Ethan doesn't wait for the bartender's agreement, just turns and heads to the closest open spot.

Is this annoying or charming? Mateo can't focus correctly beyond the Prada boots. He doesn't even care about Prada, but they're chunky-soled with a pouch above the ankle and he's trying to gauge Ethan's shoe size. Shit. Now he's too aware that he's being seduced by clothing and he's not sure what to do. Go with it for authenticity in exploitation-flirting, he guesses.

"If that was a really impressive whiskey you ordered, it's totally lost on me," Mateo admits as he slips into a velvet half-circle chair around the high gloss table Ethan moved to.

Ethan smiles. "It is a really impressive whiskey." There are three seats to choose from but Ethan takes the one next to rather than across from Mateo. They're both tall and the table isn't meant to hold more than a couple drinks and a bowl of expensive artisanal pistachios, so their legs are crowding the space beneath and are right up against one another's. Which is probably flirty too. "It's one of those bottles old guys buy to impress a table of other old guys."

Mateo makes a *tsking* sound. "See. Your first mistake. I'm only a little old. I could see if that guy wants to come over?" He gestures with his chin at a booth across the room where an ancient man talks too loudly to a woman who looks to be smiling indulgently.

"Give me a few minutes to work up the nerve," Ethan says as a waiter drops off their drinks. Ethan pushes the whiskey across the table at Mateo with a lifted brow. "Try it."

Mateo wants to chug his rum and coke but the rules of polite society dictate he mustn't, so he'll gladly taste the expensive stuff. "What's each sip run? $5?"

"Might even be $10."

Mateo sips then pulls a face as a cloying yet smoky taste burns his throat.

"What the hell was that?" Ethan asks, mock-offended as he takes the glass back.

"Tastes like every whiskey I've ever had." Mateo lifts his own glass slightly. "I'll stick with my low-to-mid-shelf rum and coke."

Ethan pretends to look around for the waiter. "Just going to call the waiter back so I can send a bottle to that old guy and be properly appreciated."

"If you wanna impress me, let me try on your jacket." The sincerest thing Mateo's said all week. He's pretty sure it would fit.

Ethan stops pretending to look for the waiter and focuses on him again. "Maybe in the morning." He's just tease-flirting and Mateo knows it, but his face must have done something because Ethan leans back slightly. "Too far?"

Shit. Mateo sips his drink. "It's fine." He knew he'd be bad at this and he's being bad at this. "How was work?" The urge to slam his head into the table is strong.

Ethan leans back all the way and allows the blatant redirect. "I actually got out of my meeting early. Christopher was even more worked up than usual. Made me wonder if it had anything to do with my new favorite occult specialist."

That's interesting and conveniently the point of why he's here. "What's he usually like around the office?"

Ethan seems to consider as he takes a sip of his whiskey, but then he sets it down, folds his hands in his lap, and levels a more pointed look at Mateo. "I'll answer that, but then you have to answer one from me."

Ophelia's faith in his wiles has been poorly placed. Ethan clocked this for what it is. A ruse to gain information. He doesn't seem annoyed, though. "Okay," Mateo says dubiously.

"Christopher Nystrom's an asshole who baselessly thinks he's the smartest person in every room he enters because he's made a few good investments. If he had a heart attack and died, I'd have a little party in my office. With balloons and everything." Ethan says it without heat, but Mateo believes him. It's the bone-deep hatred only people forced to work alongside assholes can manifest. Rage and exhaustion all mixed up. Also, he's met Christopher.

Ethan leans close again. "Now tell me, what's baby Nystrom hired you for that you're so interested in daddy?"

It's a completely fair question but he needs to reestablish some sort of confidence level here because this guy is seriously shrewd and Mateo's like a dipshit lamb trying to seduce a wolf—and the wolf keeps clocking all his bullshit. "Doctor-patient confidentiality," he tries.

Ethan leans toward him, smile flickering. "Play fair."

Mateo struggles for the least informative thing he can say. "Trying to pinpoint the cause of some bad energy. Christopher seems like a bad dude." This close he can smell the whiskey on Ethan's breath. It's not unpleasant. Also not helping. "Ever met Mrs. Nystrom?"

"She's, like, an eleven and he's a six, tops," Ethan says, picking up his whiskey again. "I don't get it. Money, I guess. She doesn't come around a lot. Haven't seen her in a while.

He definitely cheats on her. Pretty sure he hits her. Baby Nystrom's basically a poster child for abusive parents. A stray "boo" might kill him. Christopher seems like that kind of asshole. Controlling, overbearing, bad temper. Flies off about any and everything."

It's the kind of salacious office detail he's after, and a completely fair deduction of Topher's disposition and the likely cause of it, but Mateo doesn't want it to be true, and hearing it adds the weight of reality. And to the idea that this curse is the dad's fault—if not his actual doing. The thought of that jackass hitting Topher makes that earlier fury threaten to seep into his brain again. He shakes some ice into his mouth, crunching to force focus around his newly bleeding-heart demon.

Ethan's watching Mateo over the glass. It's an interrogating look, not terribly different from Ophelia's. He's going to ask something Mateo would rather not answer. "Can you do magic?"

Mateo forces his plastic smile. "Everyone can do magic. It's a natural energy in everything."

"Bullshit answer," Ethan rightfully says, then leans even closer so he can whisper again. It's completely unnecessary. The background tunes are soft, ignorable Muzak, but his voice has a different quality when he speaks quietly. And he knows it, because he knows exactly how slick he is. "I think you're trying to pump me for information but aren't quite mercenary enough to invite me to your bed to get it. Which is too bad, because that would be effective. We can work with this, though, but you're going to have to give me more than you're trying to."

Shit again. He'd flown too close to the sun and burst into flames—neck and ears hot from that too-frank assessment. The best solution would be to thank Ethan for the drink and retreat. He's probably gotten all the office gossip he's going to.

Confirmation the dad is a piece of trash and the likely source of the curse in some manner isn't nothing.

But Mateo hesitates.

It's pointless to want to leave things pleasant between them. Mateo's going back to Seattle soon. Even if he likes talking to Ethan, there is a fucking demon inside of him that's probably going to burst out and kill him sometime soon, he's having weird episodes where he's saying and thinking crazy things, and he dreams about eating people. He's not exactly a catch.

Mateo glances toward Ophelia even though he can't see her from this angle. "Okay. Fair. Yes. I can do magic. And no, not right now. It takes preparation and ingredients that look an awful lot like cocaine, so I couldn't bring them on the plane."

"You're not local?" Ethan asks, surprise registering for the first time since his mention that he was an occult specialist. Maybe disappointment too. It's a charming reaction.

"Flew in for the dad-chat. Not sure when I'm going back. Soon."

Ethan tips the rest of his whiskey into his mouth and sets the glass on the table. "You should call me again before you leave. And show me your magic."

"That sounds like a line."

"It is."

They stare at one another, smiles threatening. Before Mateo can think of a zingy parting line so he can flee, a series of shrill screams sound from the pool area and he's on his feet.

The only thought in Mateo's brain as he crosses the bar and slams the door open hard enough to crack something in the flimsy hinge, is that Ophelia's out there.

She's inexplicably crawling out of the pool, still in the orange gauzy maxi dress she'd pulled on for her and Topher's drink. It and her hair are plastered to her as she stands and tries to wrangle her mane out of her face.

Other things are happening, but Mateo can't recognize them until he confirms there's nothing wrong with her other than the clear topography of her chest being flashed to the world through wet fabric. Without his suit jacket, he starts untucking his shirt as he crosses to her so she can cover up. Ethan presses ahead, pulling off his bomber and putting it over her shoulders.

She accepts the jacket without thanks and grabs the front of Mateo's shirt. "I just pulled him out," she says, holding to him tightly to make sure he understands she's fine. Just wet.

Mateo lets out a shaky breath and forces his eyes from her. Topher's kneeling behind her, over a man who's wet and lying on his back. Watery Pepto-Bismol blood is seeping all around the man's head, fanning out across the tile. Half a dozen hotel guests gawk from tables and chairs. There's no world where Ophelia screams. One of them was likely the screamer.

She'd dragged a bleeding guy out of the pool?

"Hit his head and fell in," Ophelia says, teeth chattering, the evening air only a little chill but it's probably the adrenaline.

Topher has his ear to the prone man's mouth. Unsatisfied with what he hears, he positions his hands on the man's chest and begins an impressively professional looking bunch of chest compressions. Mateo looks around frantically for hotel staff. For the price of the rooms, every waiter should have a gold-plated medical degree. A blazered woman followed by two hotel security guards finally comes barreling through the same door Mateo did.

Topher's hauled up by a guard and pressed into Mateo—as gently as possible because even in an emergency this hotel knows you shouldn't push rich people. Mateo takes hold of Topher's shoulders and bodily backs up with him. Blazer Woman is trying CPR now.

It doesn't matter, though. She gets the same response Topher did, meaning nothing.

Another death.

That's at least seven. Topher's vibrating under his fingers. Probably feels like he killed that guy even though all he'd done was sit by the pool with Ophelia.

Wide eyes turn up to Mateo, wet, but not crying. There's not even desperation there anymore, just the unfocused blankness of someone who's just found out they're terminal. Mateo knows exactly what this is. He's seen it in Ophelia and himself.

He's just witnessed Topher lose hope.

Ophelia squeegees water off her face with a hand and leans on tiptoes to speak close to Mateo's ear. "Topher found a lead on his mom."

It's probably bad that the client did the detective-ing here, but it doesn't matter anymore. He keeps trying to use money to obscure the danger here, but this is bad. It's a lot of bodies. Now there's blood magic and some dickhead abusive dad murderer. And he remembers the tarot. How they all pulled the death card. Death doesn't necessarily mean death, but sometimes it does.

Why isn't he thinking about that more when Ophelia's right here, so easily killed?

Fuck figuring this out. They need to leave.

CHAPTER NINETEEN

It's not eating someone that unsettles Mateo's sleep as he tosses in the luxe hotel bed. It's the memory of the cold dead weight of Ophelia's corpse.

At that point, his mother had been missing for nearly seven months. Collection agencies were sniffing around and her acquaintances in the dark arts had been steadily popping up looking for her. Mateo had been trying to deal with the possibility that his mother wasn't coming back while skating by on odd jobs, trying to find someone willing to employ a poorly homeschooled eighteen-year-old without a GED and no references or work experience.

Ophelia had lived next door since they were little. It was completely normal for him to let himself into her house, which he'd done that day with a mind to complain to her about getting the stink-eye from some guy who worked at the kitchen store in the mall. Like you needed a master's degree to sell yuppies overpriced chicken motifs.

He hadn't noticed her parents' bodies in the living room. Hadn't noticed Juliet's either, walking past her room with no interest.

Ophelia was into grunge at the time, so she'd had on a fleece plaid button-up, crop tank top, and cutoff shorts, hair its natural dark brown, one knee-high sock with a red stripe, the other with two black ones. Her nails were a chipped gray paint that matched his because she'd done both of their nails a few nights before.

Before they'd met, she'd lived in an astral projecting, third-eye, hippy-dippy commune—a legit cult. Something had happened and her parents had fled the Oregonian forest for the outskirts of Seattle with their two kids. To his neighborhood.

Ophelia's room was dark, her body on the bed. She practiced Traveling all the time. He'd meant to lie down next to her, wait for her to come back into her body like he'd done dozens of times before.

But lights on, it was clear she'd been dead for hours.

The smell made him gag before his brain fully registered how purple and plastic her skin looked, like someone had pulled it too tight and painted her the wrong color. It wasn't his first time seeing death, but it hits differently when you love that person more than you love anyone who's ever existed.

He stood in her doorway, just staring at what could have been peaceful slumber if not for the blatantness of her death. He'd been pretending his mother leaving was fine, pretending he wasn't terrified of what his life would be, of what would happen to him, of what he might do to other people—do to Ophelia, specifically. So much worry that he might do something to her.

There were a million lies he could tell himself to distract from the unknowable dread of his future because Ophelia was right there with her shitty smile and her bad hair, making him live in the world, if only with her.

He only wanted to be in it with her. If she wasn't there, there was no point to it.

Lights switched off again, he'd crawled into the bed beside her.

Sometimes he dreams about those three days, every detail as apocalyptic as it had been at the time. Holding her first stiff and then limp body, how heavy she felt, how excruciatingly light, the coldness of her death-blanched skin, the reek of days-old excrement and urine, like cabbage and peeled eggs, as he drifted between sleep and awake and hoped the awake would just stop.

She'd eventually—inexplicably—woken up, but he'll never rid himself of those wretched seventy-two hours.

Which is why he sits wide awake on the hotel balcony with no hope for sleep, wishing he smoked so he'd have something to do while goth-ing about in the middle of the night with fangs in his mouth. Not like he can get lung cancer—he assumes. He should take up smoking. He's going to take up smoking. Except cigarettes cost a lot.

What he really needs is something to silence his thoughts. Ophelia hadn't even been in danger at the pool, except by her proximity to Topher. She's a good swimmer, and the scream hadn't sounded like her at all, but just the weight of the conceptual harm to her is making him really aware of every breath he pulls in and he can't get his teeth to unsharpen.

There's not even room to worry about the last interaction with Ethan, how he's not even sure he said bye, just ushered Ophelia and Topher away from the cooling corpse. If they don't learn something actionable at the mom's house—Topher found the address before the pool debacle—he's going to call it. Say sorry to Topher, walk out on the other half of the money. Fuck the tarot reading. He doesn't have to play along with the conceit that they're in this together. That requires a healthy respect for fate, and fate's been especially shitty to him.

Ophelia will be pissed. Say he's being dense, which he is. And he's not loving the idea of leaving Topher in whatever this fucked-up situation is—those sad tarsier eyes are going to haunt him forever.

In answer to this internal resolve, he catches motion. The balcony is enclosed but runs the length of the suite, which means the other suites along this side have balconies too. Frosted glass separates them. It's in this frosted glass he sees the reflection from inside—of Ophelia. Exiting Topher's room.

As if sensing him—she probably can—she makes her way out to the balcony. There are two padded seats, but he moves over and she sits down, half on his lap, and he puts his arms around her. She's in a sleeping gown like the main character of a seventies horror flick, and her skin is warm from a shower. When he puts his face in her hair and closes his eyes, he can smell lavender from the hotel's shampoo.

"You're freaking out," she says.

He wants to deny it but there's no point. "You're seducing Topher," he counters.

She cranes her neck to look at him with a critical expression that could strip the outer shell off a bowling ball.

He flashes teeth to hide the wince. He'd been joking but also maybe not. She's not denying it, which has the added effect of making him double down. "I thought we were playing *state obvious things*."

"You're a riot," she says, but settles her cheek against his shoulder again and he relaxes. "I was checking on him. He's pretty freaked about his dad and the pool thing."

Oh, right. Checking on him was a viable option he hadn't considered in the slightest. Also a disconcertingly compassionate option for Ophelia, which makes him feel like a double asshole about it.

They don't say anything else about Mateo's alone-on-a-balcony freak-out. They don't have to. She's made herself clear in the way she obviously actually gives a damn about Topher, a previous-to-this-moment conceptual impossibility.

She won't be dipping. And Mateo can't go without her. There's no world where he convinces her to do anything she doesn't want to, though he considers it for as long as one full minute. Her proximity to death is a sour taste at the back of his throat, but he doesn't verbalize it. Because that won't matter to her. She's in this. They're in this.

Her even breathing and warm body curled against him eventually smooths his teeth. Like a hibernating racoon, she can sleep through a car alarm going off, so he slips out from under her unnoticed. Sleep isn't going to reclaim him—especially now that he's thinking about Topher's conceptual freak-out she'd mentioned. The truck accident and the drowning means at least two bodies added to the tally, plus the guilty dad thing. It's probably professionally courteous to check on him. Or at least try.

The knock Mateo does is reminiscent of Topher's, barely audible in the stillness of the suite. He kind of hopes Topher's already asleep and won't hear it.

But the door cracks open, and then swings wide, Topher in a puffy white bathrobe with the hotels golden initials embroidered on the right chest area in a script so fancy it's illegible. His hair's damp but still somehow defying gravity, skin pink from a hot shower he must have just left. The same lavender from Ophelia's hair is all over him.

Mateo had been trying to rile Ophelia, but suddenly he's concerned she really was in here seducing Topher.

Which . . . she can do.

What does he care? He doesn't care. At all. She can sleep with whoever she wants, and Topher can sleep with whoever he wants. They can sleep with each other and that's fine. Great, even. For reasons he can't think of right now.

This last thought jostles any innocuous well-wishes out of his brain, and what comes out is a stilted, "How's it going?"

Topher's pale lips purse slightly in what can only be confusion. Instead of slowly closing the door in his face, the other manages a much more normal: "Okay. I mean, kind of. Except the not sleeping part. You?"

"Right. Same." Zero follow-ups enter Mateo's brain so they're just staring at each other.

"You can come in if you want," Topher says, stepping back and keeping the door wide.

Mateo's so grateful for a next action that he enters before realizing this is going to prolong the interaction. Too late, the door closes and Topher's slipping around him, moving to the minibar, opening the small fridge, and picking up one of the bottles to look at the label.

"You can't!" Mateo says in automatic alarm, hand reaching as if to stop Topher even though he's already done the damage. Topher stares at him with his round eyes, so Mateo has to add: "It auto charges if you take anything out of there."

They both realize the absurdity of this concern being directed at Topher—a guy so rich that the concept of *minibar extra fees* has never entered his realm of consideration.

"Right, sorry, that obviously isn't a worry—" Mateo starts.

"Oh, sorry, yeah, no, it's okay, I mean—" Topher also starts.

And now they're both deeply embarrassed in a way that doesn't entirely make sense, and apologizing over one another.

Topher cuts them off by pressing the small bottle into Mateo's hand, a premixed old fashioned. "I just thought maybe we could have a drink?"

"I would love to have alcohol right now," Mateo says with too much feeling, taking the bottle and retreating across the room with it. Desperate for something to do with his body, he takes one of the low oval chairs by the window.

Topher takes another bottle from the fridge and wanders closer, looking out the window.

Neither of them says anything for a few sips before Topher breaks the silence. "Sorry about today. This probably isn't what you thought you were signing on for."

Despite the exchange of ten incoherent apologies a moment ago, this one flips the irritated switch in Mateo's brain. "Nothing that happened today was your fault. Not a moment of it. You're cursed. And your dad's an asshole. And whoever's doing this is the one who needs to apologize and then sit on a steel spike and spin while I kick them repeatedly in the dick."

Topher goggles at him a moment, and then that baby deer smile flickers and an exhale that sounds suspiciously like a laugh happens. "Descriptive."

"Ophelia could have done better. She's the queen of blue humor," Mateo says. If this thing is happening between Topher and her, he might as well act like a proper wingman.

"You've been pretty funny so far," Topher says politely.

Blessedly, it gives Mateo an avenue of conversation. Flashing his teeth, he says, "I think you're confusing humor with the affected self-defense mechanisms of the average underpaid retail worker. Perhaps undetectable at your yearly income rate."

It came out harsher than he'd meant it, but Topher doesn't look offended as he replies. "What's the threshold, do you think? Under 80k?"

Surprised and a little delighted that Topher's willing to joke, Mateo smirks and leans forward. "Wow. 80k? Can't even guess a low salary. I thought you were good at math. You saw what Doris was offering hourly."

Topher grimaces, obviously doing that math. "Oh no. Right. Okay. Much lower. Got it." He takes a sip of his drink, humming a little into it and stepping closer, looking seriously contemplative. "So how does it work? Do you think if I divest enough, at some point, I'll just become funny?"

"Like a survival instinct?"

Topher nods.

"Absolutely," Mateo relaxes a little, liking this stupid hypothetical and that Topher's playing along so thoroughly. "Though, that's only one of many retail worker self-defense types."

Maybe getting a little booze into Topher helps him relax. Instead of stuttering and goggling, he rises to the challenge. "What's another type?"

"You know when you go to the grocery store or the drugstore or whatever?" Mateo pauses and squints at Topher, unable to imagine him shopping. "Wait. Do you actually get your own prescriptions and stuff? Do you grocery shop?"

Smiling around a sip, Topher nods.

"Okay, so you know how that conversation's always excruciatingly chipper? Like the cashier's stoked about everything you're buying, and the holidays, and the weather?"

"That's a type?"

Mateo nods emphatically. "That conversation's painful, right? Like all you wanna do is stop having it, pay as fast as you can, and leave? It's the most powerful type."

Another startled little laugh escapes Topher. "I don't want that one. I'd be too good at it." He makes his eyes really wide—like *really*—smiling too hard, borderline manic. When he speaks, his tone's a little higher pitched and breathless. "Oh wow. We had this? Wow. I've never tried this one. Is this new? I've tried all the brands. That green one, that one's the best. I can't believe they made a new one. Oh, I'm so excited. I'm going to get one at lunch. Where did you see this? Aisle five? Wow."

"Oh my god," Mateo says, not expecting an impersonation, let alone one so horrifically believable. "I have shivers. You *are* too good at that. I'd take my own life right there at the counter. That had to be based on a real checkout. What were you buying?"

"A canned coffee," Topher says, dropping the insane eyes but the smile lingers as he takes a step closer and sets his drink on the desk beside Mateo.

"Classic," Mateo says, while realizing there's a lot of visible thigh when Topher moves. A quick scan of the room, and he spots Topher's clothing neatly folded and stacked on the bed. Because Topher hadn't packed anything from home, he'd come with them change-of-clothes-less, and he'd just gotten out of a shower.

Meaning Topher doesn't have anything on under that robe.

He turns back to Topher, only to find him closer still, right in front of him, the height of the seat Mateo's in making him below Topher's eye-level for the first time. Topher's just standing there, smiling, looking down at him, ass naked under that robe.

It's a wild thought to have right before Topher leans down and presses lips to his.

If asked before this moment how Topher might kiss, Mateo would have said: *a bird peck*. Or: *a total miss*. Possibly: *no kiss at all and Topher would combust at the thought*. He'd have also said: *Topher initiating said hypothetical kiss was impossible. A thing of fiction. Ridiculous*. And, lastly, he'd have said: *Why the hell are you asking me? I've got nothing to do with it.*

But the warm press of lips is happening to him, unhurried and disconcertingly self-confident, with a hint of something spiced from his cocktail. When Topher finally leans back from the kiss, Mateo's not sure if his mouth had done anything during it—not sure what it's doing now either. His brain is the sound of a train braking, the scream of five thousand feet of metal against metal, taking an eternity to shed the inertia to come to a full stop.

Topher's still just, like, right there, staring at Mateo, except Mateo's not great at this sort of thing—*thing* being feelings, affections, or physical anything. He avoids these things when at all possible, and he's got no idea how he walked right into this.

It's so quiet he can hear outer space.

Someone should say something.

Probably him. The kiss was Topher saying something.

No response is forthcoming. The train is still going top speed. It's blown through the brakes. It's out of control. It's going to derail. "What's happening?" is what Mateo lands on, which is the actual fucking worst. At least his tone is confusion and not bone-deep hysteria.

"You're so funny. And nice. And hot," Topher says softly, undeterred by Mateo's notably bad reactions to everything happening. "So, I kissed you."

Hearing Topher say the thing he'd just done makes Mateo's chest, neck, and ears heat like a simultaneous and instantaneous sunburn. The calm execution and response from Topher is making it worse, knocking Mateo wholly off balance when he was struggling here to begin with.

"Ophelia?" is what Mateo asks next, looking toward the closed door like he can see her from here. He's not even forming a proper question, trying to communicate through desperation his conceptual confusion because Topher obviously likes Ophelia.

"She's really cool," Topher says, the usual quiver slipping into his words as he adds. "But I think you're really amazing." This important message conveyed; Topher backs up a step.

It's the ideal moment for Mateo to say something. Anything. Maybe even have a thought. Except his train has finally ground to a full stop, and it's a total loss. No one has survived. He can't think of what to say or do here.

Eyes slowly widening, something in Mateo's frozen-rabbit manner registers to Topher. "Were you not . . . ? Is this not . . . ?" Topher starts and stops, unable to land on what exactly he wants to ask there, the situation getting so much worse as Mateo's stunned demeanor combines with Topher's frantic realization that only one of them was prepared for that. He backs up another couple steps, hands raised in surrender, eyes their widest yet. "I'm so sorry! I thought—I misread—because it's so late! I wasn't trying to—"

They're both going to die here if Mateo doesn't get out of this room. "It's okay!" he says in a tone he hopes sounds *okay*, moving swiftly toward the door with a hand up in a dorky wave goodbye for some reason. "Good talk. Good drink. Good—" What in the actual fuck was he about to say there? "—night," he finishes, stepping out and solidly closing the door behind him.

The only noise in the suite is the soft whir of traffic filtering in from the cracked open balcony, Ophelia's hair visible through the glass. Mateo stands there, back to Topher's door and gaze traveling to Ophelia again and again as though her passed out form can help.

A booty call. Topher thought that was a booty call—because it's, like, 2 AM. Meaning Topher thought Mateo was of the booty-call variety. Also meaning Topher himself is of the booty-call variety. And by the transitive properties of all that, it means Topher is down for a booty-call from Mateo. Does anyone even say *booty-call* anymore? That is the least important detail but is easier to think about, so he lets that stress him out too.

Wait. Ophelia's visit was only twenty minutes ago. Had they had the same confusion, or was it somehow only Mateo giving down-to-fornicate energy?

What in the actual hell is today?

He puts a finger to his lips, mimicking the pressure of Topher's lips and then flushes again because it's a weird thing to do.

Okay. So. He'd misread that. Like, a lot.

Which is . . . something.

Something he's not going to deal with right now because it doesn't change anything. Not really. Maybe. Probably. Ophelia doesn't want to leave. And Topher—despite whatever the fuck just happened there—still needs help. If they're in this, he'll be in it all the way.

Even if it means accelerating his own condition.

Starting toward the balcony, he has every intention of curling back up with Ophelia to wait for the sun, but jolts to a stop as he reaches for the handle. Turning slowly toward his room, the soft pull of his mom's spell book tucked in his bag startles something hungry in his blood.

And then he's in his room, cross-legged on the bed, no memory of walking across the suite or closing and locking his door.

The spell book is comfortably open in his lap, to a page filled with his mother's small, neat script. With dry-mouthed alarm, his eyes slide over the words, trying to make sense of them. He can only read every third or fourth word, his spoken Spanish shit but his reading is even worse.

But eventually he understands.

It's a summoning spell.

So very carefully he closes the spell book, puts it back in his bag, and stuffs it into the closet safe.

CHAPTER TWENTY

Sitting over a room service breakfast he agreed to out of a lack of willingness to temper Ophelia in any way, Mateo stares at a satellite view of Topher's mom's house, projecting the air of a professional who's definitely not going to be weird about their misunderstanding last night. He'd had a lot of hours to—not *think about it*, that implies he's *thought about it*—but to conclude that pretending it hadn't happened is the only solution. Which is easy. They have a clear job to do today. No time for deep psychological overanalysis of anything.

It's still early, but the additional hour or so to mentally acclimate that Mateo was hoping for is shattered when Topher steps out of his room. He's in his outfit from the day before, mussy-headed, barefoot, and startled to see them at the six-chair dining area of this insane hotel room.

Topher's eyes round. "Good morning," he says, simultaneously looking cheerful and grimacing, the little smile on his lips in physical pain.

Ophelia, who's scooping a wretched seed and porridge goop into her mouth with the sluggishness of someone sleepwalking but really dedicated to getting every free meal, grunts in greeting. Which means Mateo's the one who has to act like a normal functioning person here.

"Morning," he says back, again doing a stupid little wave, which is his thing now, he guesses.

"I just have to . . ." Topher says mysteriously, edging toward the suite door but unwilling to take his eyes off of Mateo. He reaches with one hand behind him, catches the door handle, and opens it. For a split second Mateo thinks he's going to run away, but on the other side of the door, waiting patiently, is Quincy. At this point, Topher's forced to turn away.

A whispered exchange between the two and then Quincy hands a bag over and comes in, eying their breakfasts and finding the QR code for the menu.

Yes. Amazing maneuver, Topher. Now they can't possibly bring up last night.

Topher disappears into his room, and Quincy joins them at the table with a quiet hello that's reciprocated through dull nods.

Relieved he's managed to avoid any sort of interpersonal conversation, Mateo returns his attention to his phone, on which he's uselessly looking at a roof, like that's helping anything. He pans around the streets just for thoroughness and is about to attempt to eat some of his scrambled eggs when his phone vibrates with a text.

It's from Topher, and reads: *Could you come talk to me in my room?*

Mateo's not done reading it before a second pops up: *You absolutely don't have to.*

And a third: *If you don't feel comfortable that's totally alright.*

Closing his eyes briefly, Mateo wishes for a strength of character and spirit he doesn't have and wordlessly leaves the table.

Ophelia doesn't move, but he's pretty sure he can feel Quincy's eyes on him as he walks across the suite. He doesn't bother knocking. If this has to happen, he's going to brute-force his way through it as fast as possible.

Topher's sitting at the desk, phone still in hand, and startles to his feet at Mateo's sudden arrival. He's changed clothing—what Quincy was probably here for—and is now wearing a pair of extra-wrinkled skinny jeans, cuffed at the bottom, and a longline t-shirt with a curved hem and raw seams. It's all grays again, with an excellent fit. Mateo appreciates his aesthetic loyalty, wants to say as much, but that's not what he's here for.

Holding both hands up, palms toward Topher to stop him, Mateo tries to make this painless. "Look, this isn't necessary. It was late. Everyone was tired. We'd had a day. Accidents happen. We'd been drinking." There. Every excuse possible. Easy and done.

He expects Topher to do a google-eyed nod and free them both, but Topher frowns, gripping his phone to his stomach. "That was really inappropriate of me. I think you're cool, and I just . . ." A pause, looking fantastically grim. Mateo almost cuts him off, the level of suffering on Topher's face too much for what was just a deeply embarrassing mistake. But Topher presses on. "I jumped to something insane because . . . I don't know." A mirthless little smile slides over his lips. "Wishful thinking, I guess. But there's no excuse. I put you in a weird spot where I owe you money for things and you might not feel like you can tell me to back off. I want to make it clear that I won't do anything like that ever again." Topher fiddles with his phone a minute, then turns it around to display a confirmation email to Mateo. In case Mateo doubts his sincerity, he guesses. "I've already booked my own suite, so I'll get out of your hair today.

Or, if you'd prefer, I can pay you the amount we agreed upon right now and call this done."

It's the most words he's heard Topher speak in succession without backpedaling or corrections, and it's disconcertingly earnest, and very concerned about Mateo's feelings in a way no one but Ophelia has ever been. It's not just nice. It's an out.

All of the money and none of the risk.

He'd been a foot out the door just last night. Could probably get Ophelia to accept it if Topher were *telling* them to go. No reason in the world not to take it.

Except it leaves Topher to figure this out alone.

"For the record, it didn't occur to me for even a second that you might pressure me, and that's not because I lack imagination," Mateo says, neck heating at even alluding to *the event*. "Also, for that same record, it's not *insane*. You're a nice, smart guy with a pretty choice wardrobe. I'm not, like, offended or anything. I'm just not very—" *Human* is probably the best way to end that sentence, but he can't say that. "It's fine. Really. You don't have to get out of here. We're cool. It's cool. I'm cool and you're cool."

Finally bobbling his head in a nod, the unhappy downturn of Topher's mouth smooths away. "Okay. Okay. Great."

"Also, you did buy me dinner, so," Mateo for some reason jokes, even though he'd totally managed to smooth this over already.

Topher's eyes go briefly very wide, and Mateo's horrified he'll have to frantically explain that he makes stupid jokes as social lubricant. That he's not really implying Topher felt like he owed him something for paying. But then a smile flickers across Topher's lips. "Actually, I bought you breakfast too," he says, skirting around Mateo to leave the room but calling back, "Which we should probably go eat."

Every time Topher jokes back, Mateo's wholly unprepared for it, but seeing that smile loosens the pressure he hadn't realized was building in his chest. It takes him a moment to recognize the pressure as heat; the heat as how his body feels when he's getting angry in a demon-esque way.

Except he's not angry.

Tongue to teeth, he confirms they're sharp.

Had staring at Topher's doe-eyed contrition made the demon mad? A really concerning reaction, demon. What is that supposed to mean? Does the demon hate apologies? Does it just hate seeing Topher upset?

Or maybe it hates idiots who turn down free money.

Unclear how he's feeling about that exchange, Mateo follows Topher to eat his cold eggs.

CHAPTER TWENTY-ONE

Ophelia clocks it as soon as they exit the car. Mateo catches the coppery sweet and decaying yogurt sour smell within a few feet of Linnéa Nystrom's beautiful row home. It's just like at Christopher's office. Four dark smears along the doorframe, crusted into brown from age.

There's a blood ward on Topher's mom's front door.

"Same magic as at the office," Ophelia says, all three of them keeping a few steps away from it in the sheltered porch. Quincy's waiting in the car two blocks away but Topher's vibrating beside them, gaze locked on one of the blood smears on the frame. Mateo hadn't wanted Topher there, but it's his mother and he's worried. Couldn't be dissuaded—even though the most likely discovery within is her body.

"Can you tell if it's, like, offensive?" Mateo asks, scouring the frame with his eyes, trying to understand the symbols. Anything to give him a clue what it does.

"I don't think it is," Ophelia says slowly, that subdued quality to her voice that means she's not entirely with them. "The one in the office would have done something. This one's . . . passive. Not very much intention to it."

Mateo doesn't know any passive blood magic spells. Anything he'd ever seen his mom do was of the maim variety. The wards on his own house were technically passive, but they were non-blood spells altered with blood to be more murder-y.

Meaning, there's only one way to find out.

He slaps his palm flat on the door.

"It reacted," Ophelia hisses, and Mateo braces, expecting flames or knives or something.

But nothing happens.

Glaring, Ophelia says, "We don't know what that did."

"Then we better be fast." He says it like he'd been confident.

Pushing him aside, she crouches in front of the door while he stands extremely conspicuously between the covered porch where she's forcing the lock and the rest of the world.

"Got it," Ophelia says, rising from her crouch and backing up.

Mateo moves in front of the door and pushes it open. Nothing happens, so he steps in.

It shouldn't be surprising that Linnéa's rich too, but the different flavor to her fortune is striking. Christopher's home was the flavor of wealthy that was purchased full price and put on show so everyone understands how many more digits exist in his bank account than yours.

Linnéa Nystrom's wealth feels cozy. The row house had to run multiple millions, but it's not the biggest on the street. The foyer has a warm pale wood and floral motif. There's a simple coatrack, hung with a lady's long wool coat and scarf. A pair of off-season boots are pressed to one side. It smells like flowers and fresh-cut grass, and as he listens in the foyer for sounds within, he tries to work out what could be making that pleasant scent.

When he doesn't drop dead, Ophelia and Topher slip in behind him.

They give Topher a moment to stare around, but the sudden watery look in his eyes makes it clear the townhouse feels momish to him. They've got the right place.

Mateo cranes around the stairs to look beyond. A few doors, one must be the garage, and a room lined with floor-to-ceiling bookshelves. He takes the lead.

No body on the floor of the garage, no pentagram painted on a wall in blood, no sacrifice in the middle of the library. There's a candle that smells like fresh grass, so there's one mystery solved. None of the stink of the blood magic on the door is inside. It's a perfectly normal home.

A silent yet heated conversation later and Mateo is still leading the way even though Ophelia in her tiny paper-thin girl shoes would be quieter on the creaky stairs. Extremely recently they've been made aware that getting knifed and burned isn't a game ender for him, so he gets to win every *who should lead* fight.

Topher takes up the tail.

Keeping to the wall edge of the stairs, Mateo steps as slowly as he can in his chunky boots. Every third step produces a soft creak followed by them pausing to listen. Nothing stirs each time, so they continue up.

The second floor has a kitchen and dining space. It's been redone, but not into minimalistic modern hell. Might even be the original cabinets. *Shabby-chic.* Rich people's poor people play. Not a lot of places to hide here. Mateo checks the fridge because he's seen enough horror movies to have the passing thought that sometimes the body's in there.

Thank fuck it's not.

One more floor. Up they go.

A new smell reaches him just before the top, and this time he knows what the unfettered sweetness means.

The third floor is airy and bright, a large window letting in the midday sun. It also highlights the stark rust streak of dried blood on the eggshell couch, splashed across two cushions and onto the white area rug beneath.

CHAPTER TWENTY-TWO

"Shit," Ophelia whispers from behind. Her hand finds the back of Mateo's arm, holds on at the elbow as she peers around him.

As much as he'd been convinced that something had happened to Linnéa Nystrom, the blood still startles him. He's seen a good amount of death in his twenty-three years, and he doesn't even know if the owner of the blood is dead, but his pulse quickens at the thought of the likely outcome.

Ophelia and Topher are behind him, so he shifts his stance so neither can get past on the stairs.

Break into the blood-magicked house—this really was his worst idea yet. Topher's seconds away from seeing blood that must be his mother's. Seconds away from losing the little bit of family he has who actually cares about him.

Mateo turns to Ophelia and whispers urgently. "Both of you go back to the car. Please. I'll check up here, and then we'll figure out what to do."

Displeasure surges behind cerulean eyes, red lips in a tight line. "No."

"What's happening?" Topher whispers.

Ophelia turns and catches Topher's shoulders. "There's blood."

Topher goes very still, blinks hard twice, and then finds Mateo's eyes. "I want to see."

The irrational desire to protect Topher takes hold, but if her body's somewhere in here, it's not like he can hide it from Topher for long.

They all step into the living room and approach the blood-splattered sofa. Up close, it's grim. Blood's like that. A russet splatter, worse than if it was bright red because that means it's been sitting there a while. Whatever caused it has fully happened.

Ophelia stays beside Topher, his hand held in hers while Mateo regards the splatter from a few different angles like he can CSI it. He ends up squatting in front of the main streak. It's not *someone bled out here* amounts, but it's also not *minor accident* quantity. Looks like a cup at least. A splatter of something that gushed.

His fingers get less than a millimeter away before he realizes what he's doing and yanks them back.

Why was he trying to touch it?

But he knows why.

He wanted to taste it. Still wants to taste it, mouth salivating.

His thoughts are two frames of a movie overlaid but slightly out of sync, a double image that's difficult to look directly at. The urge to lean forward and press his tongue to the taupe cushion is debilitating. It's at once an obvious, natural reaction to the situation and an incomprehensible ripple of bone-deep revulsion as he forces himself to stand.

This is not the time for this bullshit. He can't be sick in a murder scene, and Topher's right there. Mateo forces his attention away from the blood. Anything but the blood.

It's a comfortable living room otherwise. There's even a fleece blanket folded poorly on the small coffee table with a book, pages-down, on top of it. Like someone got up while reading and never returned. Romance something. Smoldering guy all up on a pale lady with pointy ears who is also smoldering. It's unsettling learning that Topher's mother likes romantic fantasy—not because there's anything wrong with that, but because her husband didn't strike him as a romantic—and also, she's probably dead.

They need to get out of this house, but they haven't found a body yet. To his left, there's a closed door, to his right there's a short hall with another closed door. Moving to the door in the room, he braces for the violent stink of death and turns the knob. That fresh grass smell greets him, a large candle on a raw-edge wood shelf above the toilet. A bathroom. Tasteful marble and simple tile. No blood. No purpled and bloated form curled up in the clawfoot tub.

He pulls the door closed then realizes he shouldn't be touching anything here. For a heart-pounding moment, he uses his sleeve to wipe the handle, and then makes a stern mental note to do the same at the front door.

One room left. Topher's still just standing there, eyes on the blood. Mateo catches Ophelia's eyes, moves his chin toward the hall with the last door, and she nods. Sleeve over fingers, he goes to the door and turns the knob, squinting but not actually closing his eyes because what would be the point of this if he doesn't look?

Main bedroom. The grass scent is mixed with an artificial floral smell, like a bottle of perfume was regularly used in here. Queen-sized bed, neatly made with a floral quilt on top. It's what he imagines moms' rooms look like when they don't dabble in the dark arts. Pastels, neutrals, and a jewelry stand with dainty necklaces—not a one made of bone.

No body.

Thank fuck, but also oh no. Where the hell is Linnéa Nystrom, and why is there blood in her living room?

He spends a few nervous minutes gently ransacking the place. The closest he gets to a secret is when he realizes his hands are in an undies drawer and closes his eyes in an attempt at respect. Mattress gets a thorough check but there's no little lady figure.

Straightening up, he has nothing to show for his efforts. It's a normal bedroom. No obvious signs of magic, white, black, or otherwise, and Ophelia hasn't said anything, so no non-obvious signs either. Topher's mom's secret home is neat and cute and makes him think she's a lovely woman who he hopes isn't dead.

Pulling the door shut behind him, Mateo hurries back to the others. The sun is harsh on Topher's still bowed head, making his near-white hair glow. He's still in front of the couch, eyes on the blood stain. He hadn't moved at all. Ophelia's out of sight, but the bathroom light beyond Topher is on, door open. Probably looking for clues or checking out the medicine cabinet.

This idle thought—and an eagerness to tell Topher he didn't find a body—is blown out of Mateo's brain as the last step from hall into living room brings someone else into view.

Standing a few feet behind Topher, in the center of the living room, is a whole other person.

"What?" is all Mateo can think to say.

Topher, head snapping up, focuses wide eyes on Mateo. But when Mateo's obviously looking behind him, he whirls to stare at the stranger.

Ophelia, wad of toilet paper in hand, steps out of the bathroom then. Whatever she was doing with the toilet paper is forgotten. Now they're all staring at this person.

They're in head-to-toe black, dressed like if Demobaza and a Jedi had a goth dystopian love child, with a shroud pulled tightly over the face and a hood pulled low over that. It's not the sort of outfit you wear about town unless you're on your way to the anonymous techno goth end-of-days wizard club that probably exists in San Francisco. They are bewildering in this sunny living room.

"Blood magic," Ophelia says softly. Followed by, "The ward was a signal."

Mateo's attention sharpens, as do his teeth. He shouldn't have needed Ophelia to say it. The candied scent of blood floats in the air. Much more than the little splatter can account for. This is the blood magic practitioner who warded the door. Maybe the table at Christopher's office, too. They'd done something to Topher's mom and then set a ward to let them know if someone showed up.

An accusation curves Mateo's lips, but before he can get it out, a creak from the stairs draws everyone's attention.

She's in all-white again, though it's a different outfit—a long-sleeved top and perfectly pressed wide-leg trousers that look tailored to her aggressively discerning form. The back-alley Dagger Lady from Seattle who tried to shake Mateo down about his mother stands inexplicably at the top of the stairs. No dagger in hand but everything about her demeanor conveys displeasure.

And just like that, this charmingly airy living room murder scene is crammed full of people who shouldn't be there. Everyone stands in a baffled T-formation, Dagger Lady, the blood magic wizard, and Topher making up the stem with Ophelia and Mateo flanking Topher like whatever the top of the T is called.

"What!" Mateo repeats way louder.

"The other magic," Ophelia says, less softly.

"That's the lady who stabbed me," Mateo says.

"*Accidentally* stabbed you," the lady who stabbed him says like that's better.

"What is happening!" Mateo says louder still.

"I was following you," Dagger Lady—who is not presently holding a dagger but is still Dagger Lady in his brain—says. "And then saw the most suspicious thing ever." She indicates the evil wizard. "So, I came in."

"You fucking followed me from Seattle?" Mateo is shouting now.

It almost drowns out Topher's soft, "But who's this?"

This—the evil wizard—turns back to Topher.

There's a beat where no one does anything but look at each other. Dagger Lady at Mateo, Mateo at Dagger Lady. Evil Wizard at Topher, Topher at Evil Wizard. Ophelia at Mateo and Mateo at Ophelia, and then both of them at Evil Wizard and then Topher.

Then the Evil Wizard lifts a black-gloved hand in the direction of Topher like they want Topher to stop where he is.

The same part of Mateo's brain useful for avoiding bar fights and maneuvering around customers' shit moods realizes something's about to happen. It's not a rational thought based in anything concrete, but it comes with a wash of rage, teeth sharpening further in his mouth. Whatever this Evil Wizard fuck's about to do, it's directed at Topher and **that's an outrage.**

Mateo surges toward Topher and shoves him sideways, at Ophelia. Topher yelps, Ophelia swears, and both are propelled through the still open bathroom door.

With Mateo now standing where Topher had been, something hits him.

It's exactly like what slamming into a wall at freeway speeds would feel like, a solid force knocking air out of lungs and his footing out from under him. The bloodied couch is right beside Mateo. What was once a secure and sturdy obstacle between himself and a large window overlooking the backyard, becomes a comical tabletop situation. His body slams into it somewhere around the knees and sends him tumbling over it and face first into the window.

And then rapidly face first through the window.

And then rapidly face first into the charmingly concrete paver backyard three floors below.

CHAPTER TWENTY-THREE

When Mateo's eyes open next, he's pretty sure his head's trying to twist off his neck. Eyes haven't even focused before he's leaning over and vomiting. It's horrible for all the usual reasons vomiting is horrible, but it's doubly bad because something is really wrong on the way up. He's half choking, drowning on the black bile trying to evacuate his body because it's hitting a structural complication.

After retching for a while, an awareness of fingers in his hair seeps in. Someone trying to keep it out of the way. An arm around his shoulders as well, stopping him from rolling down into the vomit on what he belatedly realizes is the floor of a car. Quincy's car.

At some point he's coaxed back, head on a lap that he assumes is Ophelia's until quivering gray eyes appear above him. "We're almost there," Topher whispers.

"Phee?" Mateo chokes through a blood-coated mouth, thick with mounting alarm, not sure why it isn't her.

"I'm right here. Don't worry," she says quickly, and he turns toward her and it's a mistake. The scream only cuts off because breathing is so difficult, and he nearly slips back under before his vision un-narrows enough to see her in the passenger's seat beside Quincy. More than the terror of the poor state of his body is seeing her expression. Pinched brow, grim line of lips, and the lipstick's smeared down the right side of her mouth. It's not easy to disturb Ophelia's expression but it's a chaos of naked emotion right now.

"You fell out the third-floor window," she says, and for a beat it makes no sense. Until it does. Magic people suddenly in the room. Evil Wizard tried to attack Topher.

Mateo tries to sit up, an automatic response to the remembered fear, but his body has other ideas, and the reality of his condition exerts itself. When he was nine, a shrieking coyote woke him in the night. Probably hit by a car and left to die. He'd been neither bold enough to ask his mom or rebellious enough to sneak out to find it, so he'd lain awake for hours listening to it scream. The sound he makes as he crumbles back onto Topher's lap is a lot like that.

When he can pull in a breath again, he uses it to helpfully declare, "Oh, fuck."

"I'm sorry," Topher says softly, so blanched he's blue.

He's fussing at something on Mateo, and it takes his screaming brain a while to realize Topher's positioning Mateo's extremely broken arms in a less terrible way. He's too afraid to tilt his head to see it better, but from this angle, it's like a sleeve filled with loose sticks. Why can't he feel what Topher's doing? It seems like he should understand without visual confirmation, but there's a sickening numbness rolling through his body, blanking out large spots even as every nerve fights to let him know how bad it's feeling.

"No hospital," Mateo says to Topher's face, the thought occurring to him like a gunshot, piercing through all the other concerns.

"I know. Just lie there. We're getting you somewhere safe so you can rest," Ophelia's disembodied voice soothes.

"Are you sure we can't call someone, at least?" Topher asks urgently.

"I'm sure." Ophelia's voice is hard. "No one can know. He can't go to a hospital. And if you try to take him to one, I'll crash this goddamned car and drag him away myself."

A beat of silence, the threat barely making sense as she's not driving, but Ophelia is Ophelia, so it's also amazingly credible.

"I don't like this." Quincy. For the first time his mellow tones are stressed. Makes sense. Someone's dying in his back seat.

It's meant to be a glib thought, but is it? Is this dying?

This seeps into his brain, and like a switch he shuts off again.

This state is only a momentary reprieve from existing because he jolts awake what feels like seconds later, half out of the car. Quincy's got him under the armpits and Topher's on his knees in the car, trying to help slide Mateo's body out. It's the new worst thing he's ever experienced, topping falling out a window onto his face.

Trying to assist is out of the question so he just focuses on gasping instead of screaming—it's not clear if he manages.

He cuts out halfway up a dark flight of stairs, and then he's on a couch, staring at a lightly textured ceiling with no concept of time or place. The numbness is gone, which is heartening and awful. He can feel his body so he's positive it's all there. But he can feel his body so he's positive it's all there in a bad way.

And there's heat, familiar flames licking through his blood, engulfing his neck, down his back, and up his right side.

A quiet yet fervent conversation is happening somewhere to his right.

"—seems difficult for you both," Quincy's voice says, followed by the unmistakable accent of ice clinking against glass. The man's regained his calm, but there's an edge to his words, like the customer service neutrality is being ultra tested and only barely hanging on. "But I'd like a more thorough explanation about the part where he fell out a very high window and broke his neck but is rapidly getting better on my couch. And about the blood."

"It's magic," Topher says in the purest tone, like that explains it all.

But the silence that follows means it's not what Quincy was hoping for.

"It *is* magic," Ophelia says, and more ice clinks. Drinking. Everyone's drinking, which seems fair. "His mom's an extremely powerful witch. She did something to him. A ritual. And since then, he heals." Every word of that is true, if lacking fundamental details.

"That's insane." Quincy says the words calmly but with feeling—and that feeling is the hysteria of stepping outside to enjoy the stars and having to deal with an alien invasion.

"We didn't know how powerful it was. He's never been hurt so badly before. But he doesn't know what his mom did. And she's been missing for five years, so he also can't ask her." The sound of glass against hard surface with urgency. "This is a secret. Whatever she did, bad people will want it, and he doesn't have a way to give it to them."

"We'll keep your secret," Topher answers readily.

Quincy, less immediately but eventually says, "I thought you were con artists."

"Yeah, no. Magic's real and it's kind of shit," Ophelia says evenly.

It seems like they've reached a—not consensus, but Quincy can't freak out when no one else is. Ophelia made Mateo's situation sound adequately sympathetic and that he's lying in ruin on the couch helps. So, Mateo—still too scared to move in any way—asks the room. "What happened to the Dagger Lady and the Evil Wizard?"

A rustle of her skirts and Ophelia's leaning over him. "After you fell, the wizard tried to shove past the Dagger Lady, but she *did* something." She emphasizes *did*, meaning magic. "It flared around her and the wizard, and then the wizard ate shit down the stairs. Then ran. Dagger Lady chased after. We ran to the backyard to help you, and by the time Quincy got the car in the driveway, there was no sign of either of them."

Most mystifying series of events ever laid out for him.

"So," Mateo starts slowly, swallowing a few times to get his voice going. "The Dagger Lady who showed up in Seattle cursed Topher, but also put a protection ward on his dad's house so curse-things won't happen there, left a little lady figure under his bed—maybe to extra protect him—and has been stalking me. Or Topher. Or both of us."

"If she's involved with Topher's situation, why was she looking for your mom? Why did she follow you? What do you and your mom have to do with anything here?" Ophelia asks.

It's a great and pertinent question. "Blood magic," Mateo says. "Blood magic is the only common element. My mom uses blood magic. I use blood magic. Whatever the hell is happening around Topher has at least this one asshole using blood magic. An asshole I am officially dubbing *Evil Wizard*, by the way."

"I don't understand how any of this works," Quincy pipes in, out of line of sight and Mateo's not going to move his head.

"But blood magic sounds bad. Could this lady in white—" Topher's voice softly corrects to *Dagger Lady*. The pause before Quincy continues is so tired. "Could this *Dagger Lady* be going after people using blood magic? Like, a magical vigilante?"

"Yes," Ophelia says, and the certainty in her voice sends confused alarm through Mateo's exhausted body. He tries to sit up, but her hand is flat on his chest, keeping him down as she speaks to Quincy. "Blood magic isn't automatically bad, but a lot of magic people think it is because it puts the user in contact with demons. Until pretty recently, the most powerful practitioner out there was a blood magic witch, so no one could really say shit about it. Just by being terrifying, she kept things in check. But she's missing. It's causing a lot of problems. And a lot of new assholes popping up, thinking it's a free-for-all to do whatever they want. Dagger Lady *could* be a vigilante. Someone taking things into her own hands because of the influx of blood magic users."

She looks down at Mateo finally, and there's no apology on her face.

Learning that his terrible mom's presence had kept the peace sits weird in a chest already hollowed out by her inattention and cruelty. When could Ophelia have even found out about this magic stalemate situation? But the answer's obvious. Any time. He works and she doesn't. And once upon a time they'd found a club full of magic people and Mateo had been too scared of discovery to go back. She wasn't scared of anything.

Everyone does the obvious math of what Ophelia's not saying. Topher breaks it, voice warbling, "Is the missing super powerful blood magic witch Mateo's mom?"

Blue eyes stay directed down at Mateo, so he answers. "Yeah."

Her expression softens when he doesn't freak out, the fingers on his chest no longer splayed to keep him still but simply holding him. "The Evil Wizard has to have something to do with Christopher, because of the blood magic in his office," she says, giving him something else to focus on. "And the Evil Wizard has to have something to do with Linnéa, because of the blood magic on her door."

"Dagger Lady could have made the same realization, that the Evil Wizard has to be connected to the Nystroms," Mateo says, eager to think about anything but his own life. "She could have put the curse on Topher to flush the Evil Wizard out. And she warded the house because she wanted to spare Topher killing his housekeeper or gardener or whatever."

Mateo tries to remember the build of the Evil Wizard, beyond his own shock. The outfit had been layered, loose, and billowing. Probably a guy. Could be a large woman. They'd had some height. "I don't have the imagination required to put him in a store buying that outfit, but could the Evil Wizard be Christopher?"

The only thing for sure is that the Evil Wizard isn't Ignacia Luisa Reyes Borrero. She's just over five-foot and did magic and grocery shopping in crop tanks and linen pants.

"Maybe," Topher surprises them all by saying quietly.

"But Christopher was with Topher while we were getting a tour from Ethan," Ophelia reminds the room. "Christopher couldn't have put the wards in his office."

Another thought occurs to Mateo. It doesn't really make sense but also almost does. "The Evil Wizard was tall, could get into Christopher's office, and did magic on Linnéa's house, where we found blood but no body. Is it possible the Evil Wizard *is* Linnéa?"

The silence following his question is Topher trying to grapple with the possibility that the person who just tried to murder him was not only a parent, but the one he'd thought loved him.

Dead or trying to kill him. Both are shit options.

"No," Topher says quietly, and then with more certainty. "No. She wouldn't hurt me. Something's happened to her. I think . . . I think it's time I go to the police."

CHAPTER TWENTY-FOUR

The next few hours are spent floating in and out of consciousness, his body desperate to sleep off breaking his neck. One of the times he drifts closer to awake, whispered, heated words fill his awareness.

Naturally, he doesn't give any indication he's listening.

"This is stupid," Ophelia says vehemently, and Mateo inwardly flinches for whoever she's talking to.

"Maybe," Topher's surprisingly not-on-the-verge-of-crying voice responds. "But it's *my* stupid to deal with."

"If that wizard comes back, you won't be able to stop them. He survived that fall. You won't," Ophelia says evenly.

A long silence in which Mateo imagines Topher disintegrating under Ophelia's blistering scrutiny, but when Topher speaks, he's quiet and firm. "That's exactly why you need to leave. I'm not going to let him get hurt again. Not either of you. I'm going to file a missing person report in the morning. I already got you tickets. A car's coming to take you to the airport tomorrow afternoon. I'll keep you in the loop, but I don't want to worry about something happening to you while I'm trying to find my mom."

Mateo braces for some sort of Ophelia-based verbal execution. Not that the ask is unreasonable, but Ophelia's not the sort of person you say no to—ever, but most especially not once she's decided on something. Never mind that getting the police involved isn't great for a lot of reasons. Most obviously that the police can't do anything about evil wizards throwing people out windows with magic.

"Please get him away from here," Topher adds into the ensuing silence.

It's a sniper shot sort of plea. Possibly the only thing Topher could say that Ophelia can't counter. It's not shocking that Topher realized he could use them against each other in that way, but it is shocking that he'd actually do it.

Also, Mateo's starting to feel sort of bad that he's eavesdropping on this. He considers protesting, backing up Ophelia so Topher doesn't try to handle this extremely unhandle-able situation alone, but Topher's concern can be flipped. The Evil Wizard could just as easily have shoved Ophelia out that window. Mateo doesn't want her anywhere near this, and there's no world where she leaves without him.

"Fine," Ophelia says, the word more forceful than it needs to be. That's the end of that conversation—also the end of anyone else saying anything. The apartment grows quiet, and Mateo dozes again.

It's nearly two in the morning when he chances movement. First an arm, a leg, and eventually a head turn. Everything is stiff, like what he imagines doing a five-hour CrossFit class featuring a lot of jarring, neck-based movements would make him feel like. It's wretched, but nothing like the pain of a few hours ago.

Sitting up leaves him panting and shaking, but he manages, and takes in Quincy's living room. Large flatscreen. Faux fireplace. Respectable bookshelf that's half Xbox games. Ophelia's asleep on a recliner to his left, curled up tight in a blanket, like a caterpillar that gave up halfway through its transformation. The long fabric of her dress escapes the confines of the blue fleece and spills onto the floor like unused wings.

Beyond the living room is a kitchen . . . and also Topher staring.

He'd seemingly gone still when Mateo had started to move around—why Mateo hadn't spotted him—but he continues to be still even after Mateo looks right at him.

"Bathroom?" Mateo asks in a whisper even though Ophelia can sleep through a shout. Topher points to a dark hall off the room, so Mateo gets to his feet, teetering slightly, his right leg protesting bending. When he looks up again, the hall is lit and Topher's standing to one side of the opening, awash with sunny bathroom light. Mateo hobbles past, avoiding eye contact because Topher's looking at him with a new intensity. Fear or more anxiety would make sense, but if anything, Topher seems calmer than ever before, an expectant gopher out of its little hole.

There's no room in Mateo for whatever this is, so instead of thanking him for turning on the light, he wordlessly shuffles into the bathroom and locks the door after him.

It's not like he thinks Topher will come in, but some alone time would be great.

Until he sees himself in the mirror.

Holy shit.

If he ever wants to up his goth game, the way to do it is to fall out a window. What's normally sun-starved light brown skin is ashen with sickly purple undertones in the harsh light, like he stopped breathing an hour ago and hasn't worked up the will to give it a try again. His lipstick is mostly off—Ophelia must have cleaned him up some—and his naked lips are bloodless. A bruised and weary darkness sits deep enough around his eyes to suggest empty sockets. Puts his normal eyeshadow to shame. A dark welling of black blood sits on the inside edge of his right eye. Strong strung-out Jack Skellington vibes, especially because the black Dolce & Gabbana dress shirt he'd been wearing is scuffed and tattered from the fall and his subsequent dragging.

Tearing his gaze away, he peels off his ruined shirt, fingers finding the back of his neck, sides, and front, carefully touching the tender but unbroken skin. It's especially bad down the right side, along the arm he'd seen in loose pieces, and the front of his neck. Bruised all to hell, but whole. The blood dried hours ago and crusted into various places, mostly his hair and below the neckline of the shirt. There's a dried clump on his forehead, probably where he hit the pavers.

The trembling starts without warning, and he has to grip the sink, and then sit on the edge of the tub so his legs don't go out from under him.

It's a bizarre sensation, freaking out while refusing to admit you're freaking out.

He's okay.

He almost died but he's okay.

But then why is he crying?

And why can't he stop thinking about the impact, convinced he heard his own skull crack on stone, or the fleeting consciousness, choking, the way swallowing had felt like forcing glass through a twisted and bent straw, how his mouth still tastes of blood and his nose still smells of copper and he will never get the formless sensation of his arm minced and twisted up out of his brain?

It's not like the movies where there's this amazing healing factor that makes the hero able to fight anything no matter the damage. He'd been absolutely fucked up and then very slowly unfucked—still slowly unfucking—and it's the worst miracle in the world that he'll never be able to complain about to anyone because at least he didn't die. Except he doesn't know what he's doing to his body. Or soul. It's not good, for sure. He's known from go that every bit of magic he uses is a risk, adding to an unknowable bucket of bad that could overflow at any moment. And he has no idea what happens when the bucket fills. There's no way to know how much of himself he's just lost.

So, he cries quietly in the bathroom, turning on the faucet to obscure the second wave of ragged breathing when he realizes that his teeth are sharp again. It's not like he's looking for a deep sense of belonging to all mankind, but this classifies him as inhuman. He is twenty-three, and it's ridiculous to cry about this very-not-new situation, but he still does it for a while.

Once he's cried himself out, he takes a shower.

Just as he starts to pull his battered clothes back on, the world's softest knock sounds on the door. Topher. He doesn't want to talk, but the part before he broke his neck was Topher seeing a room splattered with his mom's blood, so Mateo cracks the door.

"Quincy found you stuff to sleep in," Topher whispers, pressing fabric at him.

"Thanks." Mateo takes the sweatpants, closes the door, and drags them on with the measured motions of the very old. Quincy's close to his height but with more girth—also known as muscle—so they're big but fit well enough with the drawstring.

Another glance in the mirror, but he can only assume he looks better after washing up because his reflection has a swath of darkness where his face should be. Just the shadow silhouette. Luckily, he's well beyond his emotional limit so he can't get upset again and instead wanders back to the living room.

"I made tea. I mean, I made enough for two. Like, in two cups. I mean, I made two cups of tea, and if you want one, you can have one. But if you don't, I can just put it in the sink. Or drink two. It's just tea. I mean it's Quincy's tea so I don't want to waste it, so I'll probably drink it, but I can drink two teas," Topher rapid-fires from the kitchen, caught in a quantum state of picking up and putting down the mugs to accommodate whatever Mateo decides. This guy's mom is probably dead—or maybe wants to kill him—and he's fretting over tea.

"I'll take a tea," Mateo says just to free him, joining Topher in the kitchen.

Topher presses the mug to him. Chamomile. Too hot to drink, but they're both standing there staring at each other, so they both try to take a tongue-melting sip because burning your mouth is better than this awkward silence.

"Can't sleep?" Mateo tries, because he's bad at small talk not about a purchase or getting something free, but it feels like he should say something to Topher after the day they've had.

Topher shakes his head, tries to sip his tea again, but it's still too hot, and he puts it down. "We were taking shifts," he says, but has to expand when Mateo stares at him blankly. "For when you woke up. Ophelia went first, then Quincy."

Oh. That was . . . something. *Nice* is probably the word he wants. But instead of letting it form fully, he becomes aware of how weak his legs feel. "I gotta sit."

He means it as an invitation to join him, but suddenly Topher's at his side, taking his mug with one hand and elbow with the other, helping him hobble to the couch. Topher retreats briefly to get his own tea, but then surprises Mateo by sitting right next to him.

"I got you tickets back to Seattle for tomorrow evening," Topher says, slowly spinning his too hot mug between his hands.

"Thanks," Mateo says automatically, pretending he didn't already know. The idea of leaving makes it feel like he's talking to a soon-to-be-dead guy. The demon reacts in a distressingly subdued way by making Mateo feel like a cowardly shithead about it.

Think of something encouraging. Even a hollow assurance will work. All Mateo's done is take thousands from Topher and is about to leave him with a murdered or murderous loved one to deal with alone. The tea is finally cool enough to sip, so Mateo uses it to search for nice-person words.

"Do you think *your* mom's dead?" Topher asks, and it blasts away any feeble platitudes forming in Mateo's brain. Topher realizes how it sounds and gives Mateo an even more startled look than Mateo's giving him. They're not a pair of deer in headlights. They're both the headlights. "I'm sorry. I didn't mean—I was just thinking, because they're both missing, and there was blood, so I was thinking. Not that you were ever thinking. I mean, about yours. Not that you have a reason to think that yours—"

He keeps going and Mateo can only stare. Topher is trying to have a scared-about-my-possibly-dead-mom conversation and he's fantastically bad at it and so concerned he's going to upset Mateo that he can't get a coherent sentence out. There's no need for the alarm, though. Mateo's an empty husk of exhausted existential dread. Which is why it's so impressive when Topher peters out and Mateo excavates what he hopes is a smile and says, "Have you seen your mom in a dream since she went missing?"

"A dream?" Topher repeats, some of the tension releasing from his panic-face. "No."

"So, this isn't a promise or anything, but there's this belief. When a loved one dies, they come to you in a dream. It might take a few months for their spirit to gather enough energy for the manifestation, but once they have it, they let the people they love, who love them, see them dressed in white in a dream. It's to let their loved ones know that they're at peace."

The softest gasp from Topher, like he'd desperately wanted a salve for his mom's terminal situation but hadn't expected Mateo to have one.

And now Mateo's profoundly uncomfortable, not sure why he said it. False hope is so much heavier than no hope at all. It's a kind of weight that increases exponentially the longer you hold it, and at some point, you have to put it down or be crushed.

He wants to retract it, to remind Topher that the likely outcome of seeing blood in a house where, moments later, an attempted murderer showed up, is probably death. That an abusive dad and a missing mom almost always means a murder. But Topher asks, "Did you ever dream about your mother?"

"No." It sounds like a positive so that baby deer smile creeps onto Topher's lips in response and Mateo can't say that he only dreams about eating people and Ophelia dying. Never anything else. Also, Mateo's not sure he counts as a loved one to Ignacia.

Topher, urged on by this misunderstanding, goes back for more curiosities. "The, um, spell? That lets you heal? Did your mother do it before she left? So you'd be safe?"

Perfectly logical conclusion to make if you'd never met her.

His face must have done something because Topher flinches back. "Sorry. Sorry. We don't have to talk about it."

"It's fine," Mateo says for reasons beyond him. He'd rather go out a window again than talk about this, but the alternative is lying down on this couch with nothing but his own terrible brain to keep him company. Hell, maybe someone else's family drama will distract Topher from his own. That's almost like being nice and supportive. "Ophelia said my mom is a crazy powerful blood witch, right?"

Topher bobbles.

"She isn't just powerful. She's the scary person other scary people are scared of. When I was a kid, like, my whole childhood, I was convinced that if I said one wrong word, she'd kill me. Not an exaggeration. I'm talking ritual murder."

"But . . ." Topher says, shifting closer, searching Mateo's face. "It's healing, isn't it? So, she must have wanted you safe?"

Despite having a crappy dad and the questionable nature of his missing mom, Topher's struggling with the idea that a mother could be terrible. To be fair, shoving a demon in your kid is a whole other level that Topher probably lacks the imagination for, even after a day like today.

This is a bad topic. Just blow him off and go to bed. A million excuses flip through his brain. Hell, even agreement is fine. It doesn't matter what Topher knows. It doesn't matter if he lies to him. He's lied to him a dozen times already. Say he must be right, say moms are complicated, and say good night. He'll probably never see Topher again after tomorrow, a thought that sits sourly in the back of his throat.

"It's not a protection. She didn't do it to keep me safe. This kind of magic has a cost, and she's not here to pay it. I am," Mateo says instead of a lie, unable to even be shocked at himself because he's too tired to be anything but honest.

Topher pulls in a loud breath, eyes doing that jittery thing they do when someone's thinking. He even puts a cold hand on Mateo's, probably trying to come up with a soothing line to follow that ill-advised truth-adjacent yet still vague comment. Good luck with that, Topher.

"You saved my life today," he says with an unexpected firmness, leaning closer so they're making a lot of direct eye contract.

For a fraught few seconds, Mateo thinks Topher's going to kiss him again—and Mateo doesn't lean back, doesn't shout, doesn't hold up a hand to block the other. He only stares between Topher's pale lips and gray eyes.

But then Topher continues talking, tone earnest, squeezing his hand. "Whatever the cost is you'll have to pay for doing that, I'll pay it with you, if I can. I promise." At this point, Topher seems to realize he's made a bold declaration about things he doesn't know jack shit about, while being really touchy. His cheeks go scarlet, and he releases Mateo's hand. "Sorry. I just mean, I want to help."

Instead of thanking him and sharing a moment of honest human connection, Mateo says, "Wow. He really thinks he can buy his way through everything." He's truly horrified at his own pathological need to avoid all sincerity.

Topher cracks a smile, releasing his hand and standing. "My platinum card has no limit. I usually can." This important reiteration of how unexpectedly Topher's always-down-to-clown delivered, Topher snatches the mugs from the table and whisks them away to the sink. He doesn't look at Mateo as he rinses them or as he loads them into the dishwasher. He does look at Mateo just before leaving the room. A second of full and horrible eye contact and that weak smile, and then he's gone.

The silence that follows is filled with more fraughtness as Mateo diligently doesn't analyze whether he's disappointed or relieved that nothing happened there.

At least he's no longer thinking about the nearly dying thing, when the hell Dagger Lady or Evil Wizard will pop out again, or the Schrodinger's missing mom who's either murdered or attempted murderer.

Now he's thinking about how alone and defenseless Topher's about to be.

CHAPTER TWENTY-FIVE

The next morning, Topher delivers a flimsy yet plausible story to his lawyer as he perches on a bar stool in Quincy's kitchen, not eating a plate of eggs they've each got in front of them. The warbling quality of Topher's voice and his overwrought yet deeply repressed disposition sells it. It helps that the core elements are true. Not that Mateo's overanalyzing every single thing Topher's doing today.

They keep it simple: Missing mom, blood in house, and Topher's overwhelming ignorance. Mateo and Ophelia are entirely omitted.

Call done; they head back to their hotel so Topher can gather up his things from his sleepover and Mateo and Ophelia can wait around for their flight that evening.

In his room, Mateo drags on his last outfit, a bone-deep weariness weighing his motions and lingering whiplash down his neck and spine. He's whole, functional, and on the road to normal by the time he brushes out his hair and puts some lipstick on.

No one's talking, except the bare minimum for logistics, so when Mateo goes to the living room, he nearly backs out again because Topher's the only one there. He's seated on the edge of the couch, bouncing a leg, and fiddling with his phone.

Having come to no emotional consensus about the events of the past few days, Mateo's been dealing with it by avoiding all eye contact with Topher. That wasn't flirting last night. That was heartfelt emotions—the worst kind—and requires introspection he's extremely bad at even when there's not a near-death experience and a magical murder mystery in the mix.

That habit of Topher's to not fully enter a room is rubbing off on him as he oscillates between living room and bedroom. But it would be wildly too dick not to say anything at all. Question mark of emotions aside, he's taken a lot of money from this very nice guy who's just trying not to hurt the people around him.

"All packed?" Mateo asks even though he's pretty sure Topher only needed his laptop.

Topher's head pops up, eyes large and steady and unnervingly on him as he nods.

Mateo should have backed out of the room. Or done what he hadn't managed last night. Be sympathetic. Show some level of basic human consideration to another human going through a difficult time. "Are you sure I shouldn't come with you? For, like, emotional support?"

It's the least sincere offer he's ever made in his life, and he's flabbergasted that it came out of his mouth. He's not stepping into a police station unless someone's got a gun to his head. The sentiment is true, at least, that he wishes he had some way to help, but he's going for the window if Topher says he'd like him to come along.

That little smile flutters and Mateo nearly takes another step back. "I'll be fine," Topher says in his rarely experienced level tone.

It occurs to Mateo only then that Topher likes a plan, even if it's a bad one. He's a million times more chill when there's steps to carry out. It's a useless realization because it doesn't help him come up with a next thing to say. This conversation is still happening and now it's his turn to speak, and they sure are staring at each other a lot.

"Cool," Mateo goes with, and inside his head he's screaming for Ophelia. What the hell is she even doing, and where is Quincy? Why did everyone leave? Can he leave?

Topher's phone *bings*, thank fuck, and frees Mateo.

"Oh, that's him. My lawyer, I mean," Topher says, pocketing his phone. "I should go. I'm going to go. He's gonna meet me there. Quincy wanted to do one last drive."

Quincy and Ophelia finally come into the room, as if everyone was giving him time to self-inflict maximum damage. There's a moment where Topher stands, and Mateo should step forward and offer an arm pat or *something*. Would it be weird to hug him? He's never hugged anyone other than Ophelia. Topher cradled his bleeding body in his lap, and they've held hands.

It wouldn't be weird.

Would it?

Wouldn't it?

Doesn't matter. He waits a beat too long and Ophelia wraps her arms around Topher from behind. "Be careful," she says, on tiptoes to kiss his cheek. "And text after it's done. We'll text when we're home." It's a lot of civil and even helpful words from Ophelia, and it startles Mateo.

Topher turns around, not pulling out of Ophelia's arms, and gives her a proper hug. This also startles Mateo, something close to jealousy but without the barbs rising in his chest. Like he wishes he'd taken that initiative, managed the same comfortable interaction, but is simultaneously relieved that someone else did. But also shocked the someone is Ophelia. And shocked again at the easy reciprocation.

As he's being fivefold startled, Topher leaves, and Quincy gives a nod, then follows.

Alone at last with Ophelia, Mateo collapses onto the couch, head tipped back and arms wide across the back. Ophelia tucks in beside him and neither of them say anything for a long while, dozing right there in their fancy hotel room.

It's a little after noon when he rouses, blinking slowly in the too bright room. "Are we bad at this?" he asks softly, so if she's sleeping, she can keep sleeping.

"We're amazing at this." Ophelia answers immediately, wide awake and shifting against his side so he looks down and she's looking up at him. "We found out his mom is missing, found the scene of the crime, found a bunch of suspects, found weird magic shit all over, and flushed out two bad guys. That was in a day and a half. We should both get a promotion."

Mateo makes a dying sound in the back of his throat. "I wanted to solve a fun death-causing curse, not get lost in a . . . brokerage firm conspiracy missing mom murder spree . . . or whatever the fuck." He jams the palms of his hands against his eyes. "I don't like leaving this so unfinished."

Ophelia reaches up and brushes fingers against his cheek. "How you feeling?"

Mateo presses his face into her fingers. "Still tired. Neck's a little shitty, but it was worse before the nap."

She stares at him a moment with her pale eyes. "That was scary."

It's a lot that she'd admit it—earth-shatteringly devastating, actually. Not to be dramatic. He wraps his arms around her, speaking into her still chlorine-smelling hair. "I'm sorry." Even though it wasn't his fault. In Quincy's car, she'd looked back at his shattered body with such naked fear, a state so unnatural to Ophelia that it was obscene. **For that glassy-eyed terror, lipstick smeared just below the quivering line of her hallowed lower lip, someone would be made to suffer.**

The theatrics of the thought strikes him as disorienting, but fundamentally correct, so he ignores that it doesn't feel like it came from him. He's getting used to that.

They don't say anything for a bit, holding tightly to each other. And then, because they both lack the facilities to deal with their complex negative emotions in a healthy manner, she says, muffled against his chest, "What's going on with you and Topher?"

Grimacing on reflex, he admits, "We had an awkward thing the other night when I went to check on him." She'd see through any lie, but he doesn't want to tell her the details when he doesn't really get what's going on with her about Topher.

She dislodges herself enough to check her texts, taps the ringer a few clicks louder, and puts her phone face up on the coffee table. "Be more specific."

Stalling, Mateo also checks his phone. Still nothing from Topher, but he has no idea how long filing a missing person report takes. Eyeballing the pod coffee maker, he gets up to fiddle with it—and flee Ophelia's direct proximity. "The timing was kinda weird," he begins slowly, nervous that he's about to upset her. "It was 2 AM, and I said I couldn't sleep, and he offered me a drink, and . . . and he kissed me."

A sharp laugh and he turns to look at her.

"Right? Isn't that insane?" he says, laughing too. "We were joking about—it's hard to explain—like, it was about retail self-defense mechanisms." He waves the details away, almost throwing the little pod in his hand with the motion. "Nonsense conversation. Whatever. But he was being kind of funny, which, who knew? Not me. I was reeling about that revelation, and he just went for it."

"I bet you were surprised even though he's been tripping over himself about you since second one but you're too stupid to notice," she says with the same pleasure she has in her voice when she orders a beer.

Huh. That holds no resemblance to the reality of the past week. Topher's nervous about everything. How's she ascribing it to him and not the curse, missing mom, or crap dad? But Ophelia is, despite all odds, better at people-ing than him. It's not like he thinks she's wrong, but he doesn't know how to finish that thought without being the one who's actually wrong.

"He's probably just looking for a warm body during these trying times," Mateo defends weakly.

"Yeah, he really strikes me as the hookup type," Ophelia says with a taunting edge.

He tries to imagine a suave Topher, getting ass all around town, but his brain rebels against the concept. Not that Topher hadn't been—in retrospect—kinda slick in the moment. Kinda slick during his apology and the pay-the-price motivational speech too.

But.

She definitely has a thing for Topher. Her tastes have always run cutesy. She'd only become friends with Mateo because they'd met during his pastel phase. And Topher's basically a little plush rabbit. The kind that moves and blinks but the battery's fried, so it just vibrates with its disproportionately too-large plastic eyes. But, like, not in a bad way. Pleasant enough.

He spins all this around in the tumble-dry setting of his brain for a minute as he finally inserts the pod in the coffee maker.

"You like him?" he asks, immediately realizing he doesn't want the answer.

She smiles.

Not the shitty smile. It's the flax smile.

Topher is held in the same esteem as a pack of bland seeds she'd shove a newlywed for. Ask him how he knows. He's so stunned he doesn't put the mug in his hands under the coffee maker spout and has to scramble to get it positioned when coffee starts spitting onto the table.

"Do *you* like him?" She prods from the couch, on her knees now, facing the back of the chair with arms folded along the top edge as she watches him make a mess.

He sops up bean water and frowns, trying to consider Topher in some ill-defined way. It's not as though he dislikes Topher—he loves the parts that have all the money—but now Mateo's thinking about the vagueness in his chest. When he was a kid, he blamed his unclear feelings on the demon. Like it was blunting the world, making other people less interesting than everyone else seemed to find them.

Then he'd met Ophelia.

Their friendship was a slow-motion car accident. The kind where everyone gets a good look at everything, knows exactly who ran what or failed to brake, before two chrome bodies wrap around each other and destroy both vehicles and everything inside.

But positive. Ish.

They were each other's first anything and everything, good and bad. It was like trying to compare the brightness of a flashlight to the sun when the sun had already blinded him.

And then there's whatever the hell's happening lately with the demon. It's reacting to a lot of Topher-adjacent things.

Like right now, he realizes with a start, teeth sharp.

But why? Because he was asked something about Topher? What the fuck, demon? It certainly felt some sort of way about Topher. Positive or protective or something. And if that's happening, how's Mateo supposed to filter through that to figure out how *he* actually feels?

He doesn't answer for so long that Ophelia asks a different question. "What about Ethan?"

"What about Ethan?"

"You forgot about Ethan," she singsongs it, making fun of him. "The man that said right to your whole stupid face that he'd give you information if you slept with him."

He cringes, not sure if his pain is at the forgetting or just that she's saying the sex part with her human mouth, and he hates it. "I forgot about Ethan," he admits. "I was kind of busy falling out a window. Oh shit." He abandons his coffee attempts and goes to his room, grabs something out of the closet, and returns. "I stole his jacket." He presents the studded Les Hommes Ethan had thrown over Ophelia's shoulders after the pool incident. It's still beautiful even if it also smells like chlorine. "I meant to call him or something. Or leave it with Topher."

"Free jacket," Ophelia says, sprawling on the couch now.

"This thing had to be a grand," Mateo says, normally a fan of getting a free, expensive jacket, but Ethan had been nice, if playing at a different league or bracket or whatever sports metaphor makes sense for guys that are casually suave at sleeping around.

Wait. Ethan had been all slick lines, but Topher had kissed him. Isn't that the stronger come on? Why is he less disoriented by Ethan's advances, which were, comparatively, better?

He digs out his phone, not a fan of how much he doesn't know what he feels about anyone except the amazing, studded jacket in his hands and the horrible girl on the couch. None of it matters anyway. He's not looking to date random guys. He'd probably end up eating them. "We've got a few hours still. I'll shoot Ethan a text." Mateo pretends not to check whether Topher messaged again. "And we weren't fired so we should go back to researching."

Ophelia makes a guttural, dying noise but retrieves her laptop.

It takes two hours and a pizza before they're bored out of their minds. Mateo swipes an especially ad-laden site away and checks the time. "It's almost two-thirty. That's too long just to report something, isn't it?" Unless this was Topher's conflict-averse way of firing them.

"I texted half an hour ago," Ophelia says, giving him a meaningful look. Surely, he'd text back the rabid and beautiful lady. "Call him."

"Why me?"

"Because he's so hot for you."

Mateo pulls up the last text from Topher, but his phone starts chirping before he hits Call.

The caller ID reads *Slick as Shit*.

"It's Ethan!" he yells for no reason.

"Speakerphone!" Ophelia yells, also for no reason.

Mateo hits speakerphone and answers. "Hey!" Too loud. Bring it down. "Hi. Hello." It's not that he's excited to talk to Ethan or anything, but this is something happening after hours of nothing happening. It's a coincidence that he's avoiding all eye contact with Ophelia right now.

A pause on the line—probably laughing at him—before Ethan says, "Hey to you. And wow, the nerve. Trying to skip town without showing me your magic tricks *and* stealing my favorite jacket?"

"Dick move, I know." Mateo bodily turns from Ophelia, as if that makes a difference when it's speakerphone. It's awkward to talk with her hearing every flirty thing Ethan says. "My flight's soon, but I think I can leave it at the front desk. In exactly the same condition you last saw it in. Which means it smells like chlorine because I'm scared to try to clean it."

"You're leaving?"

"Yeah. We're close to wrapping things up with Topher," Mateo lies.

Another pause on the call. "You know baby Nystrom's in jail, right?"

Now Mateo meets Ophelia's equally startled eyes. She tosses the wet, cheese-less pizza dough she was about to bite onto the table, wipes her hands on the rug like an animal, and drags her laptop to herself.

"What?" Mateo says, crawling off the couch to peer over Ophelia's shoulder as she starts searching for local news.

"Coverage started a few hours ago. Said he was brought in for questioning and then arrested," Ethan says.

On Ophelia's screen is a closed caption video of a perky Californian with platinum blond hair. Topher's face sits in the upper right corner, like one of those night mode stills of a raccoon in someone's trash. Mateo reads the headline below the picture three times before it registers correctly. *Trust Fund Murderer.*

"Who'd he murder?" Mateo asks slowly, touching Ophelia's screen like that'll help or prove anything. She opens a second video, and a slim guy with too much gel in his hair makes a perfect Hollywood-concerned-face as he says something about the charges.

"His mother," Ethan says as the screen doubles down with a caption: *San Francisco native charged with killing mother.*

CHAPTER TWENTY-SIX

Topher's phone gets through half a ring before a voice picks up. "Mateo?" A guy. Not Topher. Takes Mateo a second to place the voice because he's never heard it through a phone.

"Quincy?"

"Why'd you wait so long to call?" Hella accusatory.

Ophelia's eyes meet Mateo's across the now empty pizza box.

"*He* was supposed to call *me*," Mateo defends. Quincy's tone is understandable but alarming because it's on edge to a degree not present even when dealing with Mateo's broken neck situation. "We saw the news. What the hell is happening?"

What the hell was happening: Quincy had gotten Topher to the station, no problem. Just as he pulled over, preparing to let Topher out, the car was swarmed by police. Like they'd been waiting for him—a black Mercedes-Benz isn't a rarity in the fancy areas of San Francisco, though, so they had to know what Topher looked like. Topher had the presence of mind to chuck his phone at Quincy, and Quincy had the presence of mind to jam it into his jacket pocket covertly. Which made them both geniuses but also marked the end of anything Quincy knew about Topher's arrest directly. He said he was a normal rideshare driver and had been prepared to show the sticker, but they hadn't cared about him, just told him to leave.

After having an existential crisis in his car—Mateo's interpretation, not Quincy's words—Quincy had gone inside and tried to ask if the lawyer, a Mr. Moreau, had shown up. Whoever was working the desk didn't know he was the driver from the earlier thing, thought he was there about an accident, and said Mr. Moreau was probably at Saint Francis. Quincy called the hospital, lied, and eventually got someone to tell him that Mr. Moreau hadn't made it. Meaning Topher's lawyer was in a fatal car accident while he was on the way to meet Topher.

That was over four hours ago.

Quincy, unsure of their flight time, had gone back to his house with Topher's phone, failed at guessing the password enough times to stop trying it in fear he'd brick it, and waited for them to call.

They sit on the open line for a full minute without comment, Ophelia's hands pressed over her mouth and eyes locked on her screen where she'd paused it on Topher's gaunt-faced mugshot. The idea of this pale, scrawny guy getting a mugshot is insane. The thought of him sitting in an actual jail cell is impossible. It's like he's been told that someone shot a goose into space. There's just no reason. Why would you do that to a goose?

A flush heats Mateo's skin, something between outrage and naked fear taking hold. This is so beyond bad. This is their-goose-is-in-outer-space levels bad. "We all know there's no way he killed his mom, right?" He has to ask.

"Absolutely no way," Ophelia says at the same time Quincy says, "None at all."

"Okay. Good." Mateo absently tongues one of the sharp teeth in his mouth, focusing on the constant thrum of his mother's spell book. The pool of endless weariness he's been floating on since breaking his neck dries up as he decides. "I've got a really bad idea."

CHAPTER TWENTY-SEVEN

Things go awesomely for exactly twenty-two minutes.

It's like the spell book wants him to use it, his shit Spanish inexplicably more than enough to flip through well-used pages, dismiss spells that have nothing to do with the situation, and land on the perfect one.

The same summoning spell he'd opened the book to when he'd lost time in the hotel.

But he knows why, now.

The little woman statue he's been carrying around in his pocket goes onto the hotel coffee table as does a careful arrangement of witchcraft goods a dead-eyed delivery person dropped off ten minutes ago. White chime candles, incense, water, a few oils, a bowl, and a mix of herbs. He only runs down to the hotel lobby twice, for a marker and for a knife, but then he's scribbling his intentions onto the candle, carefully forcing blood into wax, onto herb, and between points on the table.

The instructions are easy to follow, his fingers working like a musician's over piano keys, perfectly in time with a song that's been playing in the back of his mind forever. Working with the spell book feels right. Feels natural. Like drawing in a full breath for the first time in his life. None of his previous spell work felt wrong, exactly, but none of it felt this right.

"I'm ready," he says, sitting down cross-legged on the floor in front of the spell book he's carefully placed in the center of the table.

Ophelia's been helping, knows what he's proposing, and has yet to voice the displeasure evident in her every motion, because she knows the simple truth to their lives that he spends a lot of time denying. No one else is going to save them. They have to save themselves. And *themselves* includes Topher right now. Which is why there's no argument or admonishment in her voice, just very reasonable concern. "She hid it for a reason."

"Fuck her reasons," Mateo says softly. "She did this to me and she's not here." He looks at Ophelia.

It's not worry creasing her brow, but the same shifting rage boiling in his blood. She's not mad at him, though. It's their situation. Their lives. How useless and powerless they always are. Which is why she gets to her feet, moves to him, and squats before wrapping her arms around him. "Don't die," she says.

Then she's out the door, down the elevator to the lobby, giving him space enough to not feel like she'll be caught up in whatever happens.

Alone, Mateo turns back to his mother's evil-ass spell book to triple-check his work. It's correct, but the assuredness flutters like the candle he's just lit as he considers the words he has to speak. If he messes this up, he doesn't know what will happen. If he lands it, he's also not sure what will happen. The little lady statue he found beneath Topher's bed is an obvious source of information that they don't have the luxury of ignoring anymore. Whatever this entity is, it has something to do with everything, and Ophelia doesn't think it's bad. If he can do this correctly, he can summon it. Communicate with it.

Unless he's wrong. Unless he's not reading the book correctly. Unless he's amped up on nearly dying and overreacting to Topher maybe being in jail forever, and he's staring at a book he can barely read and making things up.

It's going to cost him. There's no way using a big bad spell from his mom's scary book isn't thee most *using magic* thing he can do. There's been a distance in his head since the fire. A growing haze over himself he's been trying not to think about. There's no way this is going to help that.

Except Topher is in jail. It's a stress fracture in his critical thinking skills, tripping him up. No matter the cost, he has to use magic because it's all he can do to help Topher. This is fact, like that the Earth spins and the sun rises.

Just do it. Now.

Using the knife, he slices into his palm and dribbles more of his black blood onto two of the open flames and the smoldering pile of herbs, reciting the spell in his bad accent.

A blink and the room, the world, around him is gone. Blacked out. Replaced by nothing and the sensation of plummeting. Part of him—**a him he suddenly doesn't understand at all**—is terrified of this velocity, this lack of substance. **A larger part of him thrills at the familiarity and strains against shackles that feel so close to breaking.**

Something is shining in the dark, warm and radiant and **trying to hide from him**. He focuses on this dim speck, the faintest glow within an endless night, and calls to it.

The answer is immediate, the faint glow intensifying, the dark replaced by light that's just as blinding in its completeness.

She's answered the summons. A piece of her is here with him and it burns. She's angry, fury overwhelming the connection, nearly forcing him out of this liminal space. The immense pressure of outrage almost hides the flicker of fear beneath the surface, an anxiety this call has caused her.

It's this fear that undoes him. Reminds him that a part of him is terrified, doesn't know what he's doing, is playing with a dangerous book that isn't his, and now this thing has seen him, and might be able to find him.

In the hotel room, his skin is a poorly sewn together sack, his edges coming unthreaded, unable to hold him in. His eyes are closed, head tipped back, and black ichor forces its way out of every orifice. It dribbles most profusely out of his eyes but even sweats out of his pores.

It all goes wrong like a shot in the heart—a full-body jolt of searing pain at his core.

Except he doesn't die.

The all-encompassing white is replaced by the soft yellow light of the hotel room. The pain quickly fades, but its intensity steals the breath from him, leaves a ghost of heat in his chest. He pitches forward, gasping, still dripping profusely.

Which is how he realizes his mother's spell book that probably held the secrets to everything he needs, is missing.

Gone.

Disappeared from right in front of him on the table.

He sits there, panting from the memory of pain, agog and uncomprehending. No clue how much time passes as he tries to process what just happened or how or where an entire evil book could go. He'd so definitely summoned something, connected with it just long enough to register that it wasn't happy to see him there.

Everything else on the table is scorched all to shit. There's a smoldering pile of ash where the statue was, and he has a sense the thing he'd summoned did that. He'd made her angry—which feels like a bad thing to do to something that felt that powerful—but he'd also made her scared.

More critically, did the book burn too? There's no remnant of the pages, no ash, no paper stink among all the other stinks of charred remains and wood. He can't even be scared that he's absolutely fucked the surface of the expensive hotel table, a problem that would have sent him into hysterics not twenty-four hours ago. Losing the book is the worst thing that could happen.

Except it's not.

Because he sees his hands next. He stares at them, heart kicking a chaotic beat of confused revulsion against a rib cage that feels different.

He gets to his feet and nearly goes right back down. Something is wrong with his legs. "The proportions," he thinks wildly, stumbling into the little writing desk at the edge of the main room, scrambling to get himself to the bathroom, to understand what's happening. He smacks his head solidly against the top of the doorframe, which is amazingly dense in this panicked moment and utterly incomprehensible.

He's a tall guy, but not that tall.

He ducks, gets into the bathroom, but seeing doesn't help. A brief look in the mirror is all he can manage, his normal dizzying reflection pulsing in a new, alarming way, and he can't stand to look at it.

He'd gotten the gist, though.

It's extremely bad.

CHAPTER TWENTY-EIGHT

Ophelia tears the price tag off the largest pair of lobby gift shop sunglasses she could find and hands them to Mateo. Little rhinestones that he'd normally be repulsed by line the edges, but he puts them on without complaint, and she considers him. "You just look famous and bad at hiding it."

Bold-faced lie. She's being positive, which is a sure sign that things are shit. He is to *famous person bad at hiding it* as she is to *sparkling and peppy*.

"Think he'll notice?" Mateo asks weakly and Ophelia cracks her shitty smile. She's trying her best to act like this isn't super bad so he's trying his best to act like he believes her.

Of all the nonsense things he's done in his life, trying a spell from his extremely evil mother's extremely evil spell book that had recently lit him on fire was truly the most top-tier dumbassery. Every waking moment of his life he's been afraid of the thing hiding inside him. Now it's not hiding. He'd coaxed it out. Undeniably a dude with a demon problem—sitting on a couch in a hotel room wearing shades, a medical mask, a beanie, women's wool gloves, and a XXXL hoodie declaring his love for the vibes of San Francisco that Ophelia found up the street.

And he's destroyed the little lady figure, maybe alerting something scary where he is, and lost the spell book.

A knock at the room door and Ophelia bounds over to get it. Another sign he's living his worst life because she's being exceedingly helpful.

Mateo's customer service game is strong, maybe one of the best, but the way Quincy steps in, pauses at the sight of Mateo in a baffling assortment of face- and body-obscuring accessories, nods in greeting, and turns back to Ophelia without a series of frantic questions is a thing of legend. Topher better pay him well.

"Anything new?" Ophelia asks, which is good because Mateo's not quite worked out how to talk well around all the teeth in his mouth.

"No." There's weariness in Quincy's tone. "Christopher isn't answering. Not that I think he'd be helpful. I called the law firm of the dead lawyer and got assurances someone else was sent to represent Topher, but that's all they'd tell me." No one wants to talk to the driver.

Ophelia wanders to the AC controls and blasts them, which Mateo appreciates deeply through his stifling layers and fogging up shades. "Any clue where Nystrom Senior is?" she asks.

"Usually work at this time of day, but his kid is in jail," Quincy says with another glance at Mateo. He so super wants to ask. But again, Quincy's too Customer-Service-powerful, and shifts his gaze back to Ophelia. "I stuck around the jail for a while, but Christopher never showed. Maybe I missed him, but—" He doesn't finish. They all know. Christopher's a dick, so it's highly probable he didn't come to his son's aid.

Ophelia, phone to ear, holds up a hand for quiet. After a moment, in an impressive polite-society voice, she says, "Hello, I'm calling for Mr. Nystrom. This is Cynthia on behalf of McBrian and Associates Law. Mr. McBrian is on the line with an urgent matter." Silence for a few beats and then, "Very good. Thank you." She lowers the phone. "Left forty minutes ago."

"Could be going home. Could be going anywhere," Quincy says, looking despondent. He'd probably hoped their arrival would help, but at the end of the day, they're all the hired help.

Careful to enunciate each word, Mateo asks, "What are you thinking, Phee?"

"That Christopher knows something, and we suddenly have a persuasive way to force it out of him." She looks pointedly at Mateo.

Right. Mateo would absolutely love to scare the shit out of a middle-aged asshole like this. It's a brilliant plan if they can find Christopher—but also, what's Mateo going to do right after that? And right after that? He can't fly like this, which ruins any plan about going to Puerto Rico and scouring the island for brujas who might know what his mother did. If it wasn't so hard to use his phone with claws, he'd be researching container ships. Didn't Dracula travel that way? Isn't it bad that he's narrowed his life choices to the same ones as Dracula?

Beneath the medical mask, his mouth is filling with black goo, the sensation oddly soothing, and he suddenly can't remember why any of that matters, his thoughts drifting out of focus. What's he supposed to be doing? **Figuring out how to find and eat Christopher.**

No. Wait. Shit.

Figuring out how to find and *scare* Christopher.

"Do you think—" he asks, mentally shaking himself and awkwardly digging his phone from his hoodie pocket. His hands have an unnatural length and it's difficult to find purchase on glass with sharp tips covered in cheap glove. "—Christopher would answer someone from work?"

They both turn to regard him, Quincy nearly breaking, eyes flitting between Mateo's hands—which seem wrong—and the mouth he can't see because a mask is hiding it. Blackness is definitely seeping from the edges.

But Ophelia speaks first. "Ethan? That's quite the ask."

"My wiles," Mateo says, as if he possesses any. Especially right now. But they could drive all the way to Christopher's house, bogged down by traffic, and Christopher might not be there. Every minute wasted is another minute the most beat-up-able and super-cursed guy in the world is trapped behind bars with other people.

He fumbles with his phone, trying to get to the call menu. It's not the kind of situation you can text about. Ophelia crosses to him and takes the phone, dials Ethan, puts it on speakerphone, and holds it out for him to talk.

Two rings and a voice says: "You still in town?"

Mateo does a probably horrific wide-mouthed grimace beneath the mask to get the words out clearly. "Yeah. Trying to help." Only sounds a little like he's talking around a hoagie.

"And you're calling me in the middle of that because of the oppressive guilt you feel about stealing my jacket even though your boss is in jail?"

He keeps forgetting Ethan's exactly the kind of guy who'd call him on every bullshit thing he tries. It's gotta be straightforward. "I need a favor."

"He needs a favor," Ethan repeats, but he doesn't sound put out so Mateo presses on.

"A big favor."

"Not really selling it . . . but now I'm curious."

Mateo meets Ophelia's eyes briefly. There's no good way to ask this so he just says it. "I need to talk to Christopher. In person. But he's not answering my calls and he's not at work."

A long pause. "You want me to call a senior broker at the place I work and wheedle out of him his physical location so you can . . . ?"

It's such a reasonable question and he can't possibly answer in a reasonable fashion. So, he doesn't. Ethan hadn't seemed that weirded out about the possibility of magic existing. He hopes that holds true. "Topher hired me because he's cursed; his mom is either dead, missing, or is the evil wizard who just tried to kill me; and Christopher knows way more then he's saying. I wanna strong-arm him into telling me what the hell's happening."

An even longer pause. "I sure do think you're hot, Mr. Occult Specialist, but I'm going to need a little more than these mad ravings and promises of assault to put my job at risk."

It's not like he's suddenly developed a deep bond of trust with Ethan. That takes more than some flirting and a pseudo-date that ended in someone drowning. Hell, he's not sure what that takes. The person going back in time and being Ophelia, probably. But Ethan's been alright so far. Enjoyable, even. Understanding in a weird situation. Against all odds, Mateo kind of likes talking to him. There's a brief reticence at incinerating that tiny kernel of something like friendship, but this is an emergency. They're out of options and have zero leads. Christopher's the only one who might know what's happening, so they need to get to him.

Executive decision, then. It's his horrible secret. Might as well use it to convince a broker that magic's real so he should help them.

Mateo pointedly doesn't look at Ophelia as he asks Ethan, "Can you come to my hotel?"

CHAPTER TWENTY-NINE

"Holy shit," Ethan says, back pressed to the closet, as much distance between himself and Mateo as possible. He would have gone for the door if Quincy wasn't standing in front of it.

Speaking of, Quincy watches the reveal with a widening of eyes and thinning of mouth, but is otherwise unmoved. Consistently solid. Mateo would applaud the man if not for the claws.

He lets Ethan have a good long look—even though the cornered and strangled cat expression on Ethan's face is hurting Mateo's feelings. Like, not really, but also, kind of.

Not that he blames the man.

Pitch-black talons sit at the tips of eerily long fingers, which are themselves a disconcerting hardening of dark flesh without real transition from skin to nail. A matte black that's difficult to look at extends from claws, up arms, and fades into the normal tone of his skin near his shoulders. Oily orbs of shadow replaced his eyes, no whites or brown irises visible, and they're leaking Mateo's black blood. It's running down his face and smeared across his cheekbones from him trying to keep it in check. Dark mist is lazily rolling out of his hair, off his skin, and even coming from his mouth if he leaves it open long enough. Ophelia said it smells like a snowy day, which is the most normal thing about the new look.

The teeth are the worst of it—which is saying something because it's all bad. Rows and rows of razors, his mouth a black-hole nexus of scary the human eye can't stand to look at. Mouth, tongue, and teeth are the eye-averting black stuff, so it's difficult to understand what's happening there. A real *Babadook* situation, but not so sausage-gloved. *Edward-Scissorhands* with less metal and more nightmare-horror-made-flesh-and-teeth.

In short: It's a lot.

"Sorry," Mateo says after a moment, the act of talking making Ethan flinch. "There's not a good way to preface: I look like a demon."

"You could have just said you look like a demon." Ethan draws in a breath and lets it out noisily. Doing a passable imitation of Topher's google-eyes. "*Are* you a demon?"

"That's such a good question I wish I had an answer to," Mateo says, ignoring Ophelia's displeased attention from a side chair. She'd hated this plan, but there hadn't been an alternative, so here they are with a guy he barely knows in hopes of threatening another guy.

"Like . . . you don't remember what happened, or?" Ethan asks.

"More like a magical mishap I don't understand," Mateo tries, knowing these are shit explanations but he'd rather not do a life-story dump right now.

"A . . . spell? Backfired?" Ethan tries to guess.

Ophelia's flat voice says, "Magical show-and-tell has to happen later. Topher's in jail and if we're going to do something about it, we have to do it quick."

Mateo gives Ophelia what would be a pained look on a human face but probably just looks like he's threatening her. They're asking a lot of Ethan, so rushing him isn't going to help. "I can explain some of it later. It's not going to be as informative as anyone would hope. But right now, we need to find Christopher. You've seen Topher. A man like that can't be in jail."

Ethan looks between Ophelia and Mateo, even peers at Quincy like he needs the assurance that at least some of the people in the room are still people. He spends some time nervously wiping his mouth before asking. "How do I know you're not evil?"

Such a fair question. Mateo's full eldritch horror meets *Freddy Krueger* shadow creature . . . and it's only their second bad date. He's not even dressed cool. Ethan's got nothing to hold on to.

"I promise I'm not evil, I just want to help Topher," Mateo pleads while trying not to open his mouth. Nothing undercuts an *I'm not evil* declaration like a mouth full of shark teeth.

Ethan nods once.

Then again.

Slips out his phone and dials.

And really sells it.

A potential client who's loaded. Hush hush on the details—obvious code for super illegal. Feigns a deep desire for Christopher's advice. Promises a cut after ego stroking that borders on flirting, impossible to follow math, and mysterious investment words. *Optimize* is said upward of sixteen times but he'll never know what was optimized. Money, he guesses.

Absolutely debased behavior that neither Ethan nor Christopher seems uncomfortable about. Begs the question: What the hell do brokers even do?

He hadn't thought it would work, because Christopher's son is in jail for murdering his wife, but the scumbag takes the bait with zero emotional distress. A meetup is arranged, client details too salacious for phone conversations to be had in the privacy of Christopher's house.

They have a plan. Good cop/bad cop. A classic. Though Ophelia is going to have to play out of character as good cop.

It's a group effort to get Mateo out of the hotel room. Quincy gets his car, Ophelia takes the lead in case she has to dissuade any interested parties from the elevator door to the curb, and Ethan takes the rear. Which just means he follows briskly while looking completely freaked out.

If anyone notices, they don't have time to react before they're all in the car and racing to Christopher's house. Mateo rides on his back, in the furthest row of seats so Ethan doesn't have to sit beside him. The mask is in place to hide his teeth, but he has to keep wiping at the black shit coming out of his eyes and it's easier to do that without glasses or gloves. Ethan's watching, though he's trying to be discreet about it.

Bet he didn't think the goth he was trying to get into bed was a straight-up horror show.

Oops. One glib thought too far, and Mateo's reeling again. It's not like he super cares what Ethan thinks. Except. Kind of it sucks that he's scared. A correct reaction to this nightmare persona, for sure. And it doesn't matter anyway, because Mateo's here to collect paychecks, not new people to damn alongside him.

The ride is silent except for the low-key tunes coming out of the stereo. Eventually, Quincy pulls over and Mateo sits up, giving his cheeks one last wipe before putting the shades back on.

"You're not actually going to hurt him, right?" Ethan asks. It's nice that Ethan can hate the guy and be concerned about the actions of the demon he's helping into his house.

"No. No. Totally not," Mateo says in what feels like too much defense. The idea of hurting Christopher is very appealing, which is why he's been carefully not thinking about it since the *eat him* slip.

They gauge the range of Christopher's front-door peephole, and then stand off to one side as Ethan approaches the door. The man looks like he's suffering a hernia, uncomfortable, stilted steps toward the door. He tosses Mateo a brief wild-eyed look that makes Mateo feel really bad for getting him tangled in this mess, and then hits the doorbell.

A long wait, Ethan unconsciously backing up one step and then two. When the door swings open, he reaches some limit, turns, and flees.

Which is mad confusing to Christopher, who stares after Ethan, lips parted in question before thinking to step forward, maybe call after his retreating form. But Mateo and Ophelia sidestep in front of him.

Christopher's still in his suit from work, though the tie and jacket are gone. Booze is heavy in the air. Whiskey. Rich guys and their whiskey. His eyes are bloodshot, and if Mateo didn't know he was a dick, he'd think he'd been crying.

Those red eyes widen, the beginning of a fear that's hard for the man to register properly with Mateo's mask, glasses, hat, and gloves obscuring so much. The door starts to slam, some base sense of self-preservation rocketing Christopher's arms into action before his brain sorts anything out. But Mateo steps forward and catches it. It's not strength that makes Christopher jump back. It's an animal part of the brain noticing the very wrong proportions to the thing approaching him.

"We need to talk," Mateo says, taking advantage of Christopher's confusion and shoving the door all the way open. Moment of truth. The house is warded, and he's not sure if he'll be able to enter this time. He'd been distinctly less of a full-ass demon twenty-four hours ago.

He steps across the threshold, breath held.

Nothing happens—except Christopher backs up another step. Whatever parameters the ward is protecting against, Mateo doesn't trigger them. No time for wondering why. He's bad cop.

"You can't," Christopher says like a spoiled child with their golden Hot Wheels truck taken away for the first time ever. It's a statement of general outrage that either has to do with the wards allowing Mateo in or the fact that no one's ever dared do anything other than exactly what he wants.

It's not proper fear, though, and that's what Mateo wants. **Trembling. Begging. The understanding in his hateful face that his bag of blood and bone only has a few breaths left.** With the next step, Mateo reaches up and pulls off the mask and glasses. "I said we need to talk."

The little color in Christopher drains away, reminiscent of his transparent son. The man nearly slips on his ugly polished entryway as he tries to put space between them. Mateo doesn't allow it, matching every backward step easily with his long legs.

Behind him, the door closes and locks, followed by the gentle slaps of Ophelia's girl shoes. "You shouldn't run from him," she says mildly.

"You can't come in here," Christopher declares uselessly.

The calm sitting in Mateo's chest is like one of those fancy melting ball desserts he's seen online that look super impressive until you pour molten chocolate on top, and they reach a moment of total structural failure and violently collapse. He means to say something to defuse his feelings, lob a passive aggressive starter at Christopher about him leaving Topher in jail, but what pours out is vitriol and shadow, in a powdery voice that usually exists only inside his head: **"Christopher Nystrom, why have you forsaken your blood?"**

CHAPTER THIRTY

Christopher's pink mouth opens and closes like a damp-lipped carp dragged to land, trying to reply and flee while too scared to turn away from Mateo. A strangled gasp is all he manages as the back of calves hit the low couch and Christopher sits down hard.

Mateo doesn't stop advancing until their legs are touching, and then he peels his gloves off, revealing claws made for rending flesh from bone. He'd had vague plans to put on a show, act up the demonic appearance, but he needs no pretending. It's taking all of his concentration not to test if his claws slice through meat as easily as they do in his dreams.

"I'd tell him what he wants to know," Ophelia says serenely, staying behind and to one side of Mateo. "He's been in a mood about you leaving Topher in jail all day."

The thought that she's clarifying his absolutely deranged *forsaken blood* word choice flits through his mind, but he can't hold onto it; is confused by it. How else could he have said that? **Christopher is a traitor to his blood, a flesh pest that tried to own something he should not, and he's due suffering for the impertinence.**

"I th-thought he'd b-be s-safer there," Christopher stammers, scooched back as far as the stiff cushion will allow.

But it doesn't matter because Mateo presses closer still, the raw, senseless rage spilling out of his mouth in tendrils of darkness as he whispers against the man's ear. **"Pretense."**

It isn't loud, but Christopher does a full-body flinch, then slurs out a series of frantic words. "It's Linnéa it's Linnéa's fault you need to talk to her I don't know what she did, but this is her fault—it's always her fault!"

"It's her fault for dying?" Ophelia asks in an unimpressed tone.

"She's not dead," Christopher snaps, like he's annoyed at Ophelia's tone and can't remember to be scared because a tiny woman said something he didn't like.

Which Mateo extremely doesn't like.

He has hold of Christopher's face with no memory of reaching for it, the large square chin solidly between too-long fingers, the needle-tips of claws threatening over bloodless lips. **"Speak with reverence, or I will take pieces until you can do nothing but scream."**

"She—she's not actually dead," Christopher mumbles, Mateo's grip too dangerous for him to move his jaw much. "I mean, maybe she is. Maybe by now. I don't know. Someone's trying to—to flush her out." A sheen of sour sweat sits on his brow and his skin trembles like the film on pudding left out. **Easy to puncture, reach in, and scoop out what's inside.**

Ophelia drops onto the couch beside Christopher, her **stunning corpse-eyes** watching Mateo briefly before saying, "Who's *someone*?"

The tremor intensifies, the frantic pulse beneath Mateo's touch ratcheting up. "I don't know," Christopher whimpers. "A few months ago, she started ranting about someone looking for her. Wouldn't say who. Wouldn't tell me anything. Demanded a—" Hesitation. Word correction. "A divorce."

Ophelia leans in, not missing the pause. "What did she actually want?"

The skin under Mateo's fingers is slick, not just with sweat but with the black ichor dripping from his eyes. Christopher's trying not to let it get in his mouth, trying to look at Ophelia but also finding it hard to not look at Mateo—but also unable to keep focused on his nightmare visage. His trembling intensifies, and he asks in a high tone, "You've bound him?"

"Yes," Ophelia says. Lying to shitty men is her specialty, so it costs her nothing to do so now.

But whatever terrible thing *bound* means triggers a bone-deep shudder in Mateo that fragments his thoughts, half hateful at the word and half soaring at Ophelia's thin expression. **He needs only her approval to slit this mealymouthed rodent from belly to throat.**

"C-call him off..." Christopher stammers, the whites of his eyes visible around the entirety of his quivering irises. Something Topher got from him. **That Mateo could take. An easy press, the flesh of an eye begging for rupture.** "And I'll tell you anything you want to know."

"Tell me now," Ophelia says. "Or I'll have him smear you all over the room." Merciless delivery that makes Mateo squeeze tighter, small pearls of blood bead up where claws dig into pink skin, **hoping Christopher won't answer, hoping he'll say something cruel so Mateo can keep squeezing.**

A breathless keen like a whistle with a hand cupped over the end issues from Christopher's mouth before he says, "Linnéa was bound to me. She wanted me to break the contract so she could run."

Another shudder choked with loathing ripples through Mateo as he tries to focus on the words while transfixed by the thin skin of Christopher's throat. **It'd be so easy to find the jugular, wrench it out, stop hearing his wretched voice, and watch all that blood**—the rest of the thought terminates like vertigo mixed with a sledgehammer to the skull. The beads of blood on Christopher's neck and cheeks are streaming, the tips of Mateo's claws buried in flesh.

Christopher's a caught rabbit, eyes wide, unwilling to move even to breathe.

Mateo casts wild eyes to Ophelia. Her larimar gaze holds his for a moment, but they can't both have a psychotic break right now, so she continues in an even tone. "Did you break her contract?"

Words can't happen while Mateo's squeezing. Mateo knows this, but it takes real effort to force his horrible hand to release Christopher's jaw. To take a step back. To let the reality of what he'd been doing—**what he still hopes to do**—register.

An explosive breath escapes Christopher now that he's free, fretfully touching the dozen dribbling punctures on his neck. "I had to. She said she'd ruin me. Kill off my clients, my business partners—everyone I'd ever met—if I didn't release her. Then she was gone."

"Not a very good contract," Ophelia says like she's chastising him.

Christopher looks chagrined as he wipes the blood from his cheek and it comes back black with the stuff Mateo dripped onto him. He frowns and uses his pants to clean his fingers. "It served me fine for twenty-three years. She was happy enough with her son. Whatever mess she's gotten herself into did this. That's on her, not me."

It's difficult not to react to this shitty framing of events, the callous reference making it sound as though Topher's not his own too. *They need this information*, Mateo's repeats silently to himself, folding his arms tightly across his chest like it'll stop them from doing anything else.

The moment of not being actively threatened makes Christopher revert back to thinking anyone needs to deal with him on an even level and he asks, "What is he?" Meaning Mateo, who he's brazenly peering at now—though still can't keep his eyes focused on him.

"You first," Ophelia says, reclining, as if she discusses owning people all the time.

"The old name for her kind is Hamingja," Christopher says, and Mateo's positive he's said it wrong, but hell if he knows the right way. "Luck spirit."

Like walking through one of those automatic doors that blast air to keep bugs out, clarity buffets Mateo. Linnéa's not a rogue blood witch gone bad. She's some sort of supernatural entity. Something that looks human but isn't.

"What about Topher?" Mateo asks, startling Christopher, who seemingly forgot he can talk and had been talking a lot of scary words just a moment ago.

"What?"

"Your son, you stupid donkey's **cock**," Mateo says almost normally, but by the time he gets to *cock* his voice is grainy and soft and utterly not his own. **"He has beseeched you for aid, has pled with you for support. You have dismissed and gaslit, you piece of shit."**

Worst dad of the century has the dignity to look uncomfortable, which feels extra bad because it implies an awareness of how not-an-asshole might act. "What am I supposed to do about it? I told her if she left, something might happen with him. That boy's always been off, but he's never had her powers before. I can't stop it. And it's not going to hurt him anyway. Or me. I did ask about it." In the deep well of that shitty soul, Christopher dredges up a bucket of defensiveness. Like, bare minimum he asked a single question about his son that was mostly about his own safety, so someone give him an award.

"Don't you have anything useful to tell me?" Ophelia asks, sounding bored to tears, and it draws Christopher's attention back. Man reacts well to negging, which is the worst.

"Whoever's after Linnéa is powerful. She's ancient. I've never seen anything threaten her before," Christopher says, sounding both simpering and put out. "And they have connections. We're still married. I haven't been called in to identify the body or anything. Whoever's doing this is trying to flush her out with Christopher Jr." A pause, sensing the rapidly turning mood—not that the mood had ever been anything but turned. "He *is* safer in jail. If she's actually dead, there's nothing to be done about his powers. Better a bunch of criminals in his blast radius than innocent people on the street."

It's okay if people in jail die is certainly a take, but Mateo can't be surprised by anything this guy says anymore. More importantly, so much makes sense now.

Linnéa was under threat and wanted to leave, to protect herself, maybe even to protect Topher. She'd ghosted, tried to hide, or something got to her. Meanwhile, and poorly timed—or because of her departure—Topher's powers start popping off. And Christopher doesn't tell his son anything. He'd left Topher out in the informational cold, so Topher ran to Mateo. And maybe somewhere in their searching, they'd drawn the attention of who was after her—the Evil Wizard.

This clarity is the moldering cherry on top of the trash sundae that is Christopher Nystrom. He could have helped his son in a dozen different ways but chose not to.

It's so easy to stalk forward and catch one of Christopher's hands. To force it into his mouth. To use the incomprehensible dexterity of teeth to shear meat and bone and remove the middle digit. One sweet morsal drops onto his tongue—tongues? The chew is perfect, delicate bones shattering and then down his throat smoothly with a wash of blood turned honeyed syrup to his pallet. Mateo burns to take more, but this meat sack has a task to do first.

He releases Christopher and the man thrashes on the floor, screaming about the missing finger.

Ophelia presses to Mateo's side, and he puts an arm around her waist and his face into her mass of hair. **She'd like him to do more—he can feel the hate of her blood—but she holds her savagery inside better than he ever has, and they wait together for the screaming to turn into desperate whimpers.** A throw pillow stuffed against the missing meat slows the flow, and eventually Christopher looks up at them, wet-eyed and trembling.

Appropriately terrified at last.

"The safest place for Topher is in this house," Mateo says calmly, the whispering tone overlaying the words. **"Bail your son out of jail, or I'll come back for more than just a taste."**

CHAPTER THIRTY-ONE

They're all the way to the marbled foyer when the vertigo makes him stagger. Ophelia, still tucked against him, tightens her grip, gets him to the front door, his back leaned against it.

"Did I just . . . ?" Mateo tries to ask in whispered panic, reaching a hand to his mouth, but recoils at the sharp coldness his horrible hand encountered there.

Ophelia grasps hold of his cheeks, looking up into his terrible face with grim determination. "You did. But it's okay."

He wants revulsion to overtake him, the taste of blood and salty skin still in his mouth. But he can't summon nausea, a cold nothing where there should be a lot of some sort of complex human emotion. The absence leaves him trembling, but not properly freaked out. "I fully said I wasn't going to hurt him," is all he can think to say.

"You improvised. I'll handle it." Ophelia takes his bizarre hand into hers and pulls him with her, out the door, and back to the car where Quincy and Ethan wait.

Expectant eyes turn to them—more on Ophelia than on him because he's still hard to look at.

"We got him to talk." Ophelia recounts what Christopher revealed about Linnéa and Topher. She talks around Mateo eating his goddamned finger, instead saying they had to get a little rough when Christopher wouldn't answer.

Quincy looks strangled about the revelation—finding out his boss is part magical luck spirit was not on his schedule for the day.

"This is probably where I get off the ride," Ethan says uncertainly. It's got nothing to do with him, so it's exceptionally fair that he looks like he desperately wants out of the car.

Mateo gets his little medical mask back on and then struggles with the gloves a moment before getting out of the car with him. They wait quietly as Ethan summons a rideshare, Ophelia and Quincy giving them the pretend privacy offered by being inside a car with open windows.

"Sorry things got . . . weird," Mateo says weakly.

Silence greets his feeble attempt. It's not like Ethan can say, "It's cool, no prob, we should still hang out some time." And it's not like Mateo can say, "Wow, wasn't this crazy, but it's temporary, and my whole deal isn't normally this messed up so we should definitely talk again."

Eventually, a black car rolls slowly toward Christopher's front gate, the driver looking around in that way only rideshare drivers and kidnappers do. Ethan lifts a hand to the rideshare but finally turns fully to Mateo—a thing he'd been avoiding. "But, like, *are* you a demon? Or witch or . . . warlock?" The words are difficult to get out, like he can't believe he's asking it but can't not when Mateo is standing right there looking undeniably evil.

It surprises Mateo because it's not a sprint into anonymity. "It's complicated," he says, which is the worst answer, and he sees Ethen's expression close off. There's no world where he gets into it right now, even though Ethan's owed something like the truth.

Ethan smooths the front of his perfectly smooth button up—Armani, with fussy red piping along all the edges—looks at the car, looks at Mateo, the car, and Mateo. "Maybe once this situation, which I'll deny all involvement in, is wrapped up, we can talk?"

"Perfect. Excellent. A plan." Mateo just barely stops himself from a fourth confirmation, relieved at an olive branch in all this.

A crooked smile flicks across Ethan's lips. "You are the weirdest occult specialist I've ever met." And then he's gone, into a car and out of this magical murder mystery. Which is something Mateo has to deal with so he can't really linger on the sensation Ethan's ambiguous and non-negative departure fills him with.

"I should drive Christopher," Quincy says, he and Ophelia both getting out of the car. "Make sure he actually bails Topher out. Get them back here after."

It's an amazingly above and beyond offer. "You're a solid guy, and I hope Topher's paying you so freaking much an hour, but maybe you should tap out." Mateo holds up his gloved hands as evidence of how out of control the situation is. "Shit is getting weird. And there's at least two magic people running around causing chaos, one that threw me out a window."

A pause, every worry in the entire world cycling through Quincy's stalwart gaze. But then he shakes his head. "Topher's a nice guy. I've been working for him for four years. It's all I can do and the least I can do."

Ophelia adds, "Quincy's kept Topher whole so far." She means the Tokyo-drifting. "And it's not like we can chaperone." Right. A demon shouldn't walk into a police station. Never mind that it's probably a bad idea for him to be in an enclosed space with Christopher right now—also super awkward. And Christopher's as trustworthy as a snake filled with smaller, shittier snakes. Someone should make sure he doesn't skip town.

This plan leaves Mateo and Ophelia carless and inside Christopher's house. Not a dynamic Christopher deeply loves, but he's not in a position to say no. There's a lot of question in Quincy's eyes as he herds Christopher with his haphazardly bandaged hand into his car and away.

Sitting in the living room trying not to drip demon ichor on anything, Mateo and Ophelia regard each other.

"Don't freak out," Ophelia advises, and he gives her a tired smile that she probably can't interpret as such because of his nightmare teeth.

"I'm not. Which is kind of freaking me out," he admits, sitting back on the couch and staring at the ceiling. Three sensations war inside of him: dread, indifference, and more dread at the indifference. And they're all useless. Actionless. Soon, Topher will be safe in this house, but it still means there's an evil wizard somewhere out there who's inexplicably after Linnéa and Topher. Linnéa's still MIA. Possibly dead. And Christopher's confession has nothing to do with Dagger Lady. Is she also after Linnéa? Or is she really after the person after Linnéa? A blood witch hunter. A new thing he has to be wary about that he hadn't known existed yesterday.

"Phee," he says, a wild thought occurring to him. "Do you have the address book?"

Digging in her purse by way of answering, she holds up the thin green book.

"We'd assumed that Dagger Lady was a Seattle-local, but she could be from anywhere. Look for anyone from San Francisco," he says.

With a raised eyebrow, she starts paging through the address book. She gets a little way into the back half and swears. "Linnéa and Christopher Nystrom are in this fucking book," she says hotly, turning it for him to see.

Linnéa Nystrom sits on the left page, a note under her name that says: *Mejorar o disminuir las probabilidades*. Luckily, his mother's handwriting is neat, and the internet exists. He struggles with claws on his phone for a moment before Ophelia takes over.

"It's something like improve or diminish odds. Luck," she says with a grimace.

"Fuck," Mateo says. "Fuck us. We had this the whole time."

Christopher Nystrom sits on the right page. Mateo doesn't have to look anything up to translate the one-word note. *Inútil*. His mother considered the man useless too.

Ophelia flips to the end, but then doubles back to the front, pausing on a page a dozen in and reads aloud: "Ulla Kindell. Mejorar o disminuir las probabilidades."

Same exact note as for Linnéa. "What the hell does that mean?" Mateo says more aggressively than he means, but seriously. "Like, what? A rival?"

"Or relative," Ophelia adds. "Nystrom's Christopher's family name. She's San Francisco local, too."

"Fuck it. Let's call," he says.

Ophelia dials.

Ulla picks up in the middle of the first ring. "Who is this?" The voice is unmistakable. One thousand percent Dagger Lady, and she sounds even less pleased than when she was stabbing him.

Locking eyes with Ophelia, they have a silent back and forth where it's clear neither has an actual approach in mind now that they have her on the line.

Honesty it is.

"I'm the guy you've been stalking and tried to stab in Seattle. That Linnéa Nystrom's son Topher hired to uncurse him. Except Topher's not cursed—I've just learned from his crap-dad. He's magic. And maybe you are too? And he's in jail for his mom's murder, except no one knows if she's actually dead. But he definitely didn't kill her if she is. And someone *is* after her, but that someone isn't me because we both saw who was probably that person push me out a window. Linnéa seems like she was nice, and the Nystroms and you were in my scary witch mother's address book of magic-people contacts so I called you because I can't figure out what the hell you have to do with anything except you have the same magic description as Linnéa."

Silence greets this which is super fair.

"Who's your mother?" Ulla Kindell asks acidly.

Interesting first question, and it's his turn to pause. Shit. He hadn't thought about what it might mean to tell her how they're related. Probably nothing good. But Ulla hasn't hung up, so he goes for it. "Ignacia Luisa Reyes Borrero."

Sharp breath. Not good. Or very good.

"The boy who fell out the window is Ignacia's son," Dagger Lady says slowly, like she's testing out the concept. He'd have preferred *young man* who fell out the window, but that's fine. She's thinking, and thinking might lead to explaining anything. "Topher's . . . like us?"

"I'm pretty sure." Promising. *Us* implies she has a connection to Linnéa. And she's talking about Topher like she knows who he is. "Actually, it might be less good luck and more the bad kind. Since his mom ran off, a lot of people have died in his proximity. Topher didn't know who you were, and I don't wanna get all up in your business, but I need to help him, and I can't help him if I don't know what's happening." Bold statement because he might not be able to help even if he knows exactly what's happening.

The pause is longer this time. Mateo can feel his claws growing, which is a disconcerting reaction to stress. A splatter of the black stuff his eyes are leaking falls on the phone's screen. How is that helpful, body? He's afraid to wipe it away because he might accidentally hang up.

"Where are you?" she asks.

He sits up straighter. "Christopher Nystrom's house."

A soft *huh* that might be consideration or might be confusion and then, "I'll be there in half an hour."

CHAPTER THIRTY-TWO

"The thing about Linnéa," Ulla Kindell says as a hello, pausing to take the longest drag on a cigarette Mateo has ever seen as she stands in the center of Christopher Nystrom's living room. "—is that she's cryptic. Magic eight ball nonsense. Never answers a question outright when she can say something that sounds like she's staring into the river of time, the silly bitch." She makes every consonant sound like a swear.

No clue what the *river of time* is. Doesn't matter.

Ulla doesn't care if they understand. She's come to unload months of Linnéa-related stress directly from her neat, white BMW to this midstream conversation. They'd had a plan—Ophelia fetches her from the front and warns her about Mateo's condition—but Ulla hadn't knocked, had stalked right in, and taken no notice of his alarming state before going off.

In the ultra-bright living room, she looks unreal. Not because she's magic, but because she's fashion perfection while a constant stream of displeasure—intermittently broken up with sucking on a cigarette—spews from her. Her form-fitting, knee-length dress is tailored to fit her willowy frame perfectly. The stilettos are Christian Louboutin with scalloped edges along the ankle, solid white, except the underside is blood red.

He can appreciate how magnificent she is because she's not directing her ire at him.

"I've never even met Topher. She didn't want to involve the boy in magic if he didn't have any, and look how well that's turned out. It's conceit, really," she continues, nearly chewing on the cigarette in her aggravation. "But if you ask her, she's a martyr. The martyr no one asked her to be." *Martyr* sounds harsher than *silly bitch* with the way she draws it out.

"Hello. My name's Ophelia," Ophelia finally says when it's clear Ulla's just going to keep chain smoking and talking at them.

Ulla exhales the first plume of smoke since arriving, and levels a long, disinterested—but obviously interested—look at Ophelia, and Mateo's uncomfortably aware that there is a dynamic brewing between the two women that will either be amazing or a nightmare. "Ulla Kindell. But you know that. What is all this? Why's he dressed like that?"

"He's shy," Ophelia says.

"Mateo Borrero," he puts in, not wanting this to sour but unsure how to question someone whose whole vibe implies you shouldn't ask them things. "You know Linnéa how?"

"Sisters," Ophelia and Ulla both say, then narrow their eyes at one another. Holy shit.

Ulla extracts another half an inch of chemicals through her cigarette, gaze moving from Ophelia to him. Her eyes aren't unsimilar to Topher's now that he's looking. A darker, more normal hazel. She must dye her hair. Topher's and the missing mom's are pale blond verging on white. Ulla's is black, pulled back into a second skin of a ponytail. Or Hamingjas can look like anything. No clue. All the things he'd ask if he wasn't trying to get Topher out of jail right now.

"What's wrong with you?" She gestures with a vague circle at Mateo's face. "Your mother's a horrible person, but she's still a person. You're not."

Harsh. And true. Mateo reaches up and takes the shades off. Her eyes widen fractionally, and she sucks on the cigarette with more fervor. "My mom, the horrible person, did something to me a long time ago. I accidentally . . . set it off. As utterly unbelievable as it sounds, it's not related to this Topher-in-jail-for-murder thing. Just an unfortunate complication. Why were you looking for my mother? And no, I still don't know where she is. I meant that."

The lip curl that revelation causes could sear skin, melt paint, and make babies weep. "There's blood magic at play. At my sister's house and around that dipshit Christopher. When Linnéa disappeared, I started keeping tabs on Topher, including his little jaunt to Seattle, where the most horrendous blood witch I know happens to live. I went to ask if she had anything to do with it, but all I found was you."

So many dots connected.

He's jarred from potential musings by Ulla stalking forward and leaning down to stare into his face, suddenly very close. "Take it all off," she demands.

A sideways glance to Ophelia, who shrugs, so he peels off mask and gloves and rolls his sleeves up. Ulla doesn't lean back even an inch. She has a deeply uncomfortable stare.

She straightens. "You've lived the last—what are you? Fifteen?"

Wildly incorrect. "Twenty-three."

"The last twenty-three years without this horrible face popping out. Just bring the other one back to the fore." She says it with real disdain, like even an infant can hide their demon face.

"I'm not disagreeing with the concept," Mateo says, though he might be. "But if I could do that, I would."

"Try harder," she says unhelpfully.

Closing his eyes, he tries to try harder without actually knowing how to do that. Ophelia and the—he is just now realizing unnervingly not-human—luck spirit are silent while he doesn't say what the problem is. He's only been like this for a few hours, but he's having a marked inability to recall his normal eyes, mouth, or teeth.

If casually asked if his hands have always been demon claws, he might say yes. Which is disorienting because he also keeps missing things he's reaching for, the claws ending way beyond where his fingers used to.

"Open," Ulla says, and his eyes snap open to a phone screen held an inch from his face. An inch is too close, so he leans back and sees it's Ophelia's phone displaying a picture of someone flipping double middle fingers.

It's like he's doused in cold water while also taking a bucket of cold water straight to the face, up the nose, down the throat, and into his lungs. The shock forces out a gasp. Ulla's saying something—presumably about the picture but that's a guess from context clues because the picture makes no sense. **The picture is terrible. So terrible he can't understand anything she's saying around staring at it. He wants to grab the phone, smash it on the ground, smash it down her throat that isn't actually her throat but a throat she's chosen to wear, frustration building because she's forgotten what it's like not to be limited like this, stuck in a tiny meat sack, forced to use lungs to pull in air through feeble flesh balloons and use gelatin eyes to see this hateful world.**

The phone is gone, replaced with Ophelia's face, her hands on his cheeks. **She's warm, calming, perfect. Lips to his forehead, then his face in her hand, and he wants nothing else.**

"Look," she says softly, **and he makes a desperate keening to behold another awful picture from the phone. He wants to pull away, but her arm is around him, her mouth against his ear, and she's whispering. The meaning is lost in a riot of confusion, brain rebelling against the new picture, but the soft tone keeps him rooted. She wants him to look, so he looks.**

Ophelia's in this photo, flipping double middle fingers with someone he doesn't want to look at. He tries to focus only on her, but Ophelia doesn't take pictures with other people. She doesn't like other people. Only him.

Her family moved in next door when he was eleven. Ophelia's older sister, Juliet, caught him creeping and called him over and trapped him in a perfectly normal pre-teen conversation he couldn't follow because he never hung out with anyone and was barely allowed outside. He'd been unsociable, even in pastels, hadn't known what to say, and so had given her a lot of one-word responses. The whole time Juliet had talked, Ophelia had been crouched in the yard a few feet away in shorts, a tank top with spaghetti straps, and bare feet, inexplicably ripping grass from the lawn in a methodical fashion. He'd finally asked what the hell Ophelia was doing. Juliet had rolled her eyes and said she was "being edgy."

But Ophelia, absolutely wretched human creature that she was, used one hand to keep plucking grass and the other to give him the middle finger, shitty smile in place and locking eyes while she did it. She would have held his gaze and the middle finger up all day if her mom hadn't come out and dragged Ophelia inside. Ophelia had flipped him off the whole time.

Enchanted isn't the right word because it implies something delicate, whimsical, and positive, not the feral nonsense feud that followed—but he's never come up with a better one.

They'd spent the next week engaged in a war of middle fingers, flipping each other off from afar, hanging out windows, and running by making weird noises so the other was tricked into looking. She'd found the perfect spot on her roof, just visible through his bathroom window, and waited, who knows how long, until he tried to use the bathroom and saw her. He took a photo of his middle finger and printed it out on his mother's crappy printer, folded it into a cute-looking note, and waited for her to emerge from her house to shove it through the fence between their yards. She'd cackled and ripped it up and started shoving it through the spaces between the fence and he'd started shoving it back, until they were in a frantic war over the scraps.

Real normal kid stuff.

At some point they were together every chance they could be. At some point, he'd beaten another boy with a length of lumber—cheap shots from behind—because the boy had stuck his hand up her shirt. At some point she'd stabbed a boy in the thigh with a dull steak knife because the boy had shoved Mateo off the top of the slide on the derelict playground the too-old kids hung out in.

They were completely savage and senseless about one another. **So he hates whoever is audacious enough to pose with her. The meat is tall and skinny, with dark eyes, well-shaped brows, black hair in a messy shag swept to one side, black eye makeup and lips, and a really slick jacket with a fluffy collar.**

Oh.

It's the other him.

No.

The human him.
The only him.
Him.

The picture is replaced with Ophelia's face, her fingers in his hair. "There you are. It's okay," she whispers, her words suddenly coherent.

"What the hell?" he manages around an inability not to breathe like he's just been forced to run a mile. But he can already tell what the hell because the arms he wraps around Ophelia aren't claw-tipped. No blade-teeth meet his tongue. He reaches to his eyes, which are still wet, fingers coming away with black, but Ophelia assures him softly that they look normal again.

"Interesting," Ulla says in the tone of someone who doesn't find it interesting at all but has other things to do because it's not her drama. "What's the plan now?"

"Give him a minute," Ophelia snaps.

Where she touches feels like what he imagines being irradiated feels like, electric and hot in every cell as if too much pressure might make it all slough off. He can't stop wiping his cheeks, amazed that he's only smearing around what was already there. The leaking had felt natural, like of course shit just comes out of his face all the time, and now it's weird not to have it. His life is so messed up. "How did you know that would work?"

"Lucky guess," Ulla says with a raised eyebrow. It's such a bad joke.

"Okay. Human-faced again. Thanks for that," he says, trying not to stare at his hands. They feel wrong even though they're the hands he's had his whole life. "Quincy took Christopher to bail out Topher. When they're back, we get everyone in the same room and talk."

"Pedestrian," Ulla says, which isn't a rebuff because she doesn't follow it up with a counter or complaint. She might be incapable of enthusiastic agreement. Her gaze shifts to Ophelia. "You. What do you do?"

"Astral projection," Ophelia says readily, uncharacteristically willing for interrogation.

"Possession?" Ulla asks. A flicker on Ophelia's face. Surprise? Then thoughtful.

"No," but Ophelia doesn't say it firmly. It's almost a question.

"I cannot believe this is the help I've found. Infants who don't know how to do anything," Ulla complains, but it's nowhere near the heat of the complaints about her sister. She starts pacing, another cigarette between her lips two steps in. "Fine, fine. Topher will be safest here. My sister is annoying, but she loves her son. The house is warded a particular way that isn't obvious unless you're well versed in my sister's flavor of protection craft. It won't allow entrance for anyone with ill intentions against Topher."

She gives Mateo a pointed look. And suddenly he knows why she'd agreed to meet them so easily. Just being in the house meant he was on Topher's side. The first good thing to happen in fully 72 hours. Magic had actually helped them prove their intentions.

"Every day I expected this house to expel Christopher," Ulla gripes, blowing a perfect smoke ring. "But he cares about Topher in his own horrible way. He's just also an asshole."

An earlier disquiet returns, one he should have thought of before he sent Christopher off to get Topher, but there'd been a detached certainty to a lot of his actions of the past few hours. "Are we sure Christopher isn't involved in whatever's after Linnéa? I heard tales of abuse."

Critical, storm-cloud gray eyes turn to him. "Bullshit. He used to worship the ground she walked on, and when that faded, he recognized the free ride she was. She fell out of love with him as soon as he made it clear he was a poor father, but they had an understanding."

Huh. Mateo had only been in Christopher's presence a few minutes total, but the narrative seemed sound. It was easier to think that Linnéa hadn't been honest with her sister. In his mother's book, Christopher's entry had said *useless*, but his mom was also an asshole. Useless could mean dangerous to other people. "Linnéa wanted out of their contract. Could you see him getting abusive then? That could have been Christopher in the evil wizard outfit. We couldn't see who was in the outfit and they were tall."

"Who's Quincy?" Ulla asks, ignoring his concern entirely.

"Topher's driver," Mateo says, knowing what she's getting at. "He doesn't have anything to do with any of this but volunteered to help."

She doesn't need to say anything for the expression on her face to make him feel like a fool. If you don't know Quincy, sure, that weak-ass defense sounds suspicious. But Quincy had been so consistently solid and helpful. He'd been cool with everything. Including magic existing and Mateo's demon state.

And.

It's weird that he was so cool about it, isn't it?

Ophelia's phone bings. "Quincy," she says. "Says Topher's being processed for release."

Mateo gives Ulla a look. Like *see, I'm right about Quincy*, who he's suddenly feeling defensive about. He really had helped a lot. Or it's that it would be amazingly ironic if, after all of this, they'd sent the evil wizard right to Topher. But he wouldn't text if that was the case.

Ulla makes a displeased noise but there's nothing to do but wait, so she wanders away to do whatever angry luck spirits do in their sister's ex's homes when no one's around.

Mateo and Ophelia lie down on the gray living room couch. It's L-shaped and Ophelia's short, so she takes the arm of the L and Mateo takes the stem, the tops of their heads nearly touching. It's not a comfortable couch but he's exhausted, and Ophelia can always sleep.

Curled on his side with eyes closed, the weight of the past few days somewhat slides off of Mateo. Topher's nearly free. Sure, there's a whole murder charge to deal with, but maybe Topher's rich enough that it'll just go away. Mateo's demon thing is seemingly in check too. Nothing's fixed, but at least it's no longer actively broken.

These are good things. Great, even. They should mean sleep.

But his brain is trying to relive the past few days in a way he has zero emotional capacity to deal with. Maybe it's just that the demon can't relax until Topher's in this hideous house. Mateo has no idea how long processing takes, but he imagines Topher's arrival should be any moment now. Quincy hadn't texted that everyone in jail was dead or anything—he'd have led with that—so hopefully Topher's brush with incarceration was uneventful and not extremely traumatizing.

"You're fussing," Ophelia says, and Mateo tips his head to see her also tipping her head and staring at him.

"*You're* fussing," he counters like a child.

"You're worried about him," she says, which is a response out of absolutely nowhere. That she means Topher but hadn't said his name and that he was actually just thinking about Topher makes it embarrassing.

"*You're* worried about him," he counters again like a child.

"I am. I like him. He's weird," she admits easily, as if they're people who admit feelings. She studies his face from her nearly upside-down-to-him vantage point. "Are you heartbroken?"

"Should I be?" He doesn't mean to ask it, but she's forcing him off balance with her upsetting eyes. Or maybe being a demon all day did something to his wiring. He doesn't want her answer. Doesn't want words put to whatever it is they are to one another. If they never say it, it's not something else for them to lose.

Her horrible azure gaze studies him critically, mouth tilting into one of her more scathing smiles. "You're so stupid."

Something in his chest loosens. "Yeah," he agrees, looking away from her, admiring the ugly décor. Loving how gray and square and featureless it is.

She takes pity on him just long enough for him to think she's dropped it. "You like him, too," she says. Proving she is trying to catch him off guard.

"Totally. His most attractive feature is his bank account, and who doesn't love a murder rap. If anyone likes him, it's the demon. It's being *so* weird about him," Mateo says with too much forced glibness in his voice. "Why the hell do you think I like him? He's alright. I'm not saying I hate him or anything. If I were into nervous mice that are ninety percent eyes, he'd be my first pick."

"You've described him as at least seven different animals to me." She says it like it explains anything, but when he turns and stares at her like she's the dim one, she adds: "You don't describe anyone to me. You don't notice anyone but me. Outfits don't count."

Huh.

Floundering for a denial, all he can think of is that he'd even searched *animals with large eyes* on his phone to add to the mental list.

He's saved from inner reflection—thank fuck—by Ulla walking loudly into the room.

"This is taking too long," she declares.

Mateo and Ophelia both sit up, dig out phones, check against the clock, but they honestly don't know what's too long here.

So they start texting.

And they wait.

And wait.

Mateo even forgoes text for horrible actual call. Six rings and a *leave a message*. Quincy should have answered. Even if he were driving, he'd have answered. He had that phone-through-speakers thing Ophelia's car is three decades too old to have. He tries Topher's cell too, in case it's back in his possession, but no dice.

He even tries Christopher, but it goes right to voicemail.

No one's picking up or texting back.

CHAPTER THIRTY-THREE

"There *is* a lot of traffic," Mateo says, eyes on the red line on his screen representing the cars crawling on every side of Ulla's white BMW they all ride in. "And an accident."

Ophelia makes an *uh-huh* of humoring agreement, and Mateo clicks his phone screen off just to click it on again a few seconds later. They're traveling the same path Quincy would probably take from the jail to Christopher's house, though in reverse.

Why?

A vague hope that they'll spot the other car.

And because sitting in the house doing nothing while no one calls them back hadn't been a viable option for any of them. If they get all the way to the jail without anyone calling them back, at least Ulla can storm in and ask questions. She hasn't said a word since they got into the car but is driving with an aggressiveness that should be impossible at five miles an hour.

Dark smoke appears as they crest a hill, still a dozen car lengths ahead and on the other side of the freeway. Checking his phone again, it's clearly the accident that's making everything slow, and though it should cause relief—Quincy is dealing with this same traffic—it doesn't explain no one calling back.

People think about emergencies as hectic, sped up things happening too fast to react. Sometimes that's true, but mostly emergencies are slow-motion avalanches of poor decisions and unnecessary actions reaching a critical mass and then tumbling down at the regrettable pace of San Francisco evening traffic. It's ridiculous that he's only now realizing they've been in an emergency this whole time, everything falling too slowly to notice, and there's not a damned thing he can do about it because he was always going to be too late to this.

They're still not close enough to see it, but Mateo knows it's them.

A sharp breath beside him as they creep closer, and Ophelia makes the same conclusion he has. "Oh no . . ." she whispers.

Ulla swerves and cuts across three lanes of freeway like an absolute asshole, not giving anyone any choice but to let her across, and takes the nearest off-ramp. They barrel down a few surface streets and then they're back on the freeway in the other direction.

They edge forward for what feels like years, and finally get within eyesight of the wreck.

"Just the car," Mateo says quickly.

Not immediately seeing a body is the only possible upside here, so he grasps for it, insides shaking. The Mercedes is between a cop and a tow truck, resting drunkenly on its side like a giant kid got sick of playing and tossed it there. The drag of traffic inches them closer and he sees the hood crumpled in toward the nonexistent windshield. A white powder coats the ground and Mateo's dimly aware it's something to suck up the gasoline. The scent is making him nauseous. Mixed in with the white, twinkling on the glass, neon on the edges of the broken windshield, is blood. He can't keep his gaze off it, and it's upping the nausea, making his head floaty, detached. Is that his demon thing? Or is seeing the wreck of three people he's been spending a lot of time with—two who he cares about—getting to him?

The car's crushed all to hell but it's unmistakably Quincy's.

"I'm pulling over," Ulla says in a not entirely level voice, sliding her car unrepentantly in front of the wreck and jarring them to a stop. Mateo cranes around and catches the cop looking less than thrilled about it, walking briskly toward her bad park job. That pace slows when Ulla steps out. Her all-white situation and the severity with which she exists is universally arresting.

"You can't!" Mateo hisses.

Except she can. Ignoring him and slamming the door, she approaches the cop.

They wait in the car, Mateo's gaze slipping from the serious-faced cop again and again, to a strip mall off the freeway. A vacuum repair shop keeps drawing his attention. It's weird that one should exist. Like, with everything happening—Topher and Quincy might be dead, Topher's mom and dad might be too, and Mateo might actually be a demon now—it's unfathomable that someone in San Francisco might need something sucked.

The thought is mildly delirious, like his mind's trying to find a light comment to make to Ophelia but he can't bring himself to verbalize it.

She has her cell gripped in one hand, eyes closed. Is she *Watching* Ulla? Did her soul float out there to have a listen? She's probably able to do that from here. He doesn't ask, scared of her doing it but also scared to know what's happening.

Ulla stalks back to her car and gets in. "All that fool knew was that someone was sent to San Francisco General Hospital, in critical condition," she snaps.

Someone isn't three people.

He goggles at Ophelia, like she can make sense of that extremely wrong math, but she just stares at him. Missing's almost as bad as dead when you have no clue where to look.

"It's not one of his accidents," Ophelia says, a combination of fury and fear warring in her eyes, but her mouth's all pissed off. "I can see blood magic all over the car."

Does that mean it was Christopher or Quincy? Maybe even Christopher *and* Quincy.

"Do we go to the hospital?" he asks, brain spinning and empty of next steps. Whoever's at the hospital might be able to tell them what happened. Assuming whoever it is doesn't die before they can get there.

"Are you shitting me?" Ulla says in her most irate voice yet, but she's not talking about Mateo's question. She's got eyes on her phone and, with no explanation, dials someone. "Where in the hell have you been?" Not really enough time for an answer. "No. I don't care. Where are you now?" Pause. "Don't move. Not a step." She hangs up and puts the car in drive, civilly rejoins the flow of traffic for three seconds before cutting across four lanes, again, like an absolute asshole to take the nearest off-ramp. "My twit of a sister is at the airport. I'm going to get her before she gets herself snatched up like the pigeon-brained imbecile she is."

Mateo rips his gaze from behind them where it had instinctively gone when Ulla peeled out next to a cop—who takes no notice. "She's alive?" An hour ago, that would have been the biggest news yet, but he barely cares right now. "Wait! Let us out! Someone has to go to the hospital. We don't know who's there, and they might know what happened."

Another ill-indicated turn and Ulla pulls over at the edge of a strip mall.

"Can't she take a car to the hospital?" Ophelia reasonably asks.

"I don't trust her to cross a street right now," Ulla says with heat. "She knows something's happening and she's just senseless enough to make everything worse. In the name of *helping*." She pops the lock on the doors. "Get out. Text me what you find and don't do anything reckless. I'll bring her to the hospital."

Which is how they end up in front of a Country House of Waffles while one of their friends might be dying in a hospital or spirited off by an evil wizard.

Mateo gets as far as *San Francisco Gen* in the rideshare app before realizing that Ophelia's rooting around in her purse with purpose. "What?" he asks.

She squats in the parking lot to upend her bag directly onto the concrete. After a brief chaos of riffling through every lipstick she's ever owned, she finds what she's after, stands, and thrusts a small gray piece of fabric at him.

He unfurls it. "Underwear?" he asks in slow confusion. Not just any underwear. Topher's underwear. The pair he'd soaked and left with them to launder and return. The pair Mateo had yet to return because he hadn't worked out a good time to give a guy a single pair of underwear back. Ophelia had seemingly just been carrying it around in case the moment presented itself. Recognizing this doesn't help. "What?" Mateo adds.

"I can use them to track his energy. Find out if he's the one at the hospital or somewhere else." Ophelia tries to snatch the underwear back, but he doesn't let go.

"No way." He has no intention of arguing this point. The fact that they have no idea where Topher is makes it untenable.

"You could follow his energy into oblivion for all we know." Now they're glaring at each other, about to have a tug-o-war over Topher's underwear.

Except when he pulls, she gasps, and he remembers her hand—burnt from dragging him away from his mother's evil spell book when it lit him on fire. He wavers and she snatches the underwear away with a sneer.

"You're not the only one allowed to risk themselves, you jackass," she yells. Like, a proper yell, extremely loud in front of a breakfast place. "If he dies because you stopped me from doing something I was made to do, I'll never forgive you."

Mateo wilts. In the twelve years he's known her, she's never yelled at him.

Everything inside of him wants to yell back *no*. She wasn't made to astral project; she was forced to. By a manipulative bunch of assholes in a cult. Her family ran away because Ophelia was gifted, which meant the cult leaders had big, dangerous, cult-y plans for her. But gifted or not, her connection is damaged. The greater the distance she travels, the higher the likelihood of losing her way back to her body.

When astral projection goes wrong, it goes really wrong. See: Her entire very dead family. He spends a lot of his life thinking about walking in on her dead.

They stare at each other for a long time, her eyes wild because she's mad and his eyes wild because he's scared. Fear's the only emotion properly piercing through the curtain of numbness since he untransformed.

But she's not wrong. He could have died a half a dozen times in the past week. She'd hated it. But she hadn't stopped him. She'd helped, even.

Which is how they end up *inside* a Country House of Waffles while one of their friends might be dying in a hospital or spirited off by an evil wizard.

Mateo orders coffee and says they need time to decide on food to keep the waiter away.

Ophelia slumps down in the booth, bare feet appearing on the bench beside him as she gets as close to lying down as she reasonably can in a chain restaurant while clutching underwear to her chest.

"Don't die," Mateo says uselessly, and she gives him a grim smile and closes her eyes.

Setting a timer for thirty minutes—arbitrarily chosen based on how much he doesn't like her doing this—he drinks his flavorless coffee and tries not to look like a creep who is definitely intently staring at a lady passed out in front of him. At the seventeen-minute mark the waiter's circled enough times to be suspicious in an undefinable yet soon to be actionable way.

But Ophelia's eyes pop open. In the terrible yellow light of the restaurant, they're the neon blue of a highlighter.

She's got something.

CHAPTER THIRTY-FOUR

Ophelia has to be familiar with a person's energy to find them in the astral plane. A personal item helps strengthen that connection—and it doesn't get much more personal than underwear—but her Traveling isn't GPS. Catching the edges of Topher's energies still means Ophelia has to wander around playing *hot or cold* to follow it to the source.

An extremely awkward rideshare later, Mateo types in a generous tip to a baffled driver and gets out of the car. He has to jog to catch up with Ophelia, who's already half a block away.

"It's pastel," Ophelia says as he comes up beside her, gaze directed at a particular picture-perfect, cute-ass San Francisco row home.

With what the Evil Wizard had been wearing, Mateo expected spires, dark brick work, and some stained glass. "Hiding in plain sight?" he suggests.

Ophelia frowns at the pale blue home. "Same energy as Christopher's office and Linnéa's door. Same bad cleanup. And I can see a line of Topher's weird haze if I concentrate."

Seeing Topher's haze here is good, right? Because seeing it means Topher's still alive. Probably. He doesn't ask in case the answer is *not necessarily,* and they keep standing there because their plan hadn't gone any further than *find the place and text Ulla.*

Mateo flexes and unflexes his hands, trying to will the claws out. Unfortunately, his new weird shit isn't interested in being helpful, his hands offering only normal human nails that could use some polish. Amazingly typical that it won't come out when he wants it.

They really should wait for Ulla and Linnéa. They're not human. Way magic. Scary. Ulla has a dagger. She'll know what to do.

Except, standing yards from where Topher might be dying, it's obviously impossible to wait for the luck sisters who are an unknown amount of San Francisco traffic away.

He doesn't discuss this bad idea so much as just starts doing it. "Should we knock?"

Ophelia joins right in. "I guess."

He cranes around to see the neighborhood. Pristine little flower boxes. Unassuming. He turns back to the house. An L-shaped staircase with two pillars carved with floral flourishes leads to the front door. The cost and view must be insane because it sits on one of those vertical streets San Francisco's famous for, right on the edge of the neighborhood and overlooking the bay. The other homes are in neat, connected rows, but this one's got its own lot.

Topher is being held in one of the most charming houses Mateo's ever seen and it's extra scary suddenly. The lack of a plan, their cluelessness, and the fact that Topher might already be dead. There's no sign of Mateo's constant companion despite the adrenaline—not even sharp teeth. He's just a guy, back slick with sweat because Ophelia's just a girl, and basically made of spun sugar.

"Maybe you should wait out here," Mateo tries.

"No," Ophelia says, shoving her hand into her knit bag, rummaging, and presenting a switchblade. "If things go weird, we run away screaming. The nearest house is right there." Intentions established, she drops the blade into the volume of her flowy dress where a pocket must exist, and starts for the house.

Mateo catches Ophelia's skirt and shares an exchange of meaningful looks based on years of exasperation. He can't stop her from coming, but he should be in front.

The whole way up the steps, Mateo expects a single shot to ring out. A magical lightning zap. Something. But now he's in front of the door and nothing's happened, so he pushes the doorbell. A merry little tune, the kind that seems like it would get annoying real quick, is audible through the door. Evil Wizard is a masochist, then. Terrible addition to the lore.

The song plays for a good twenty seconds, and Mateo strains to hear anything around it. Belatedly, he realizes there's one of those peephole cameras that hook into an app and that the Evil Wizard might have been staring at his face this whole time. But then the door opens.

A very California woman in yoga-lady prime form stands there. She's blond, tall, and fit as all hell—six-pack abs on display in a matching yoga pant and crop tank set. The whole thing is that horrid purple-pink color all girls' things come in to show that femininity isn't bad but pink is going too far so here's this one oppressively florid purple. Her hair is in a high ponytail, her feet are bare, and there's not a single drop of sweat anywhere.

"Hello," she says brightly, like she loves having strangers drop by. It's disorienting, especially because she's rocking an expertly applied natural makeup look, the barest gloss of pink lips with evenly applied primer and concealer, and perfectly clump-less mascara. There's no reason he's focused on this except his brain is having trouble with the idea that the Evil Wizard is a fitness nut who works out in a full face of boring makeup.

"Hi," he says, thrown and unsure how to recover. This is the place. Ophelia saw magic and auras. This is the Evil Wizard. Or the Evil Wizard is in the house. The Evil Wizard is somewhere, so they have to get inside. "Is your spouse home?" he tries. Her outfit is cute, which is a far cry from the all-black industrial getup worn while throwing him out a window.

Her smile somehow brightens. "Oh, sure. You're clients?" She steps back, holding the door wide for them to follow.

"Yep," he says, and looks at Ophelia. Her shoulders pop up in a shrug, so they follow Yoga Wife in.

As soon as boots cross threshold, he expects a wall of force or a two-by-four upside the skull. There's just a low shoe rack—they remove their shoes—and then they're led into a home office. It's old-timey, tufted velvet couch in teal, low coffee table with smart person books atop, and built-ins on one wall filled with more pretentious-looking books.

"I'll let him know and bring some tea," Yoga Wife says serenely, leaving them there without so much as a sideways glance. If she thinks it's weird her possibly Evil Wizard husband has a goth and a boho chick over unannounced, she isn't showing it.

"There's no way it's a different house?" Mateo asks under his breath, moving to the bookshelf to look for evil clues.

"No way," Ophelia says just as softly, her interest in the desk at the window side of the room. It's neat like the rest of the room, but there's a few notebooks she starts leafing through.

Unless you love the magic of reading, there's nothing magical on the shelves. Classics, leatherbound with gold foil titles of tiresome two-word names from the eighteen hundreds. His fingers hover over a small section of newer paperbacks, but they're about the economy, like a boring English professor who has an eye on retirement.

He's about to ask if Ophelia's found anything, but a haunting aroma fills his head, flash baking his throat and sinuses. It's exactly like getting a pound of masticated saltines shoved down his gullet plus the scent of rotting cheese. It's been over a decade since he's experienced this cloying, paralytic scent. It's the same half-remembered noxious yellow smoke his mother used on him as a child.

He doesn't realize he's stumbled until his hand catches the edge of the bookshelf. It only holds for a second before he drops, smacking into the ground without even the barest attempt to brace or soften the impact.

Dimly, he's aware that it should have hurt, but the world, his body included, is underwater a million miles away. Even duller beneath that is panic, forcing his gaze to track across the room, trying to see Ophelia. That might be her hand, sticking out behind the desk, but the haze is increasing, suffocating, and his vision swims violently.

For a hysterical moment, he thinks it's his mother. The half-buried memory of yellow smoke, helplessness, and pain awakening a primal terror he hasn't had to deal with in years.

Bare feet come into view. Pink painted toenails.

Not his mother.

There's no relief in this realization.

He wants to look up but he's a boneless and gasping fish on land, unable to summon the coordination of limb or strength to turn his head. One of those feet lifts, presses to his chest, and rolls him onto his back. From this new angle he can see up into the face of the Yoga Wife. She's holding something loosely in one hand, a black metal base all he can see from the floor. Wisps of yellowed smoke vomit gently out of it. He's transfixed for a moment, but then drags his gaze up.

Her bright, unrelenting smile is the last thing he sees before everything cuts to black.

CHAPTER THIRTY-FIVE

It's, like, the fourth time he's passed out in forty-eight hours, and it's starting to feel like a real problem. When he wakes up this time, the pain's not as bad as that one time he broke his neck, but it's quite a bit worse than that other time he lit himself on fire. His week's been shit.

A groan slips out because something brutally reeks, like if strong cheese made of ass kicked him in the face. At least he's not on the floor anymore—he's now seated—but his brain is a badly balanced load of laundry slopping around in his spinning skull and it takes real effort to lift his head. Dry tongue against sandpaper lips as he takes in the dark room. Cold. Exposed wood walls and bare concrete floors. No windows. There's the dank, vague feeling of being underground. It takes his brain a long time to spit up *unfinished basement*.

Someone's put minimal effort into nice-ing the place up with floor pillows. Gauzy curtains hang from the ceiling a few yards away, obscuring the depths of the room.

His vision is doing that drunk thing where the world is a movie playing at a strange frame rate, a little too slow so that his brain struggles to string the disparate images together coherently. With this sluggish thought comes the understanding that Ophelia's nowhere in sight.

He looks around more pointedly, a firm tug of arms proves that the only give is that of his body. The chains—chains?—have his arms secured tightly behind the chair he's seated on, and are wrapped around his lap, torso, thighs, and ankles.

Conclusion: He's really fucking chained to a chair.

He's having a hard time holding on to panic. The very pertinent thoughts: *Where is Ophelia?* and *Oh my God I'm chained to a chair!* feel like they're dripping out of his ears.

He takes a deep breath to clear his swampy thoughts, but the smell assaults him again and he retches, eyes tearing up, and gets to spend a few moments trying not to vomit on himself. The smell is definitely magic, but like every other moment of his life, being able to clock the obvious-magical-bad-thing doesn't help.

Ophelia, Ophelia, Ophelia. It's the thought of her that keeps dragging his attention away from abject misery and back to the room. He can't sit tied to a chair nearly vomiting and reminiscing because he doesn't know where she is. Topher too. He's here to find Topher.

With momentary focus, he spots a brazier on the ground to his right, a lazy stream of yellow smoke twirling from little holes around the rim of its intricate metal lid. This is the thing hurting him and it's only about four feet away, but it might as well be on the sun.

He strains against his bindings but it's exactly as ineffective as it was the first time. Whatever. Keep your head up and look around, asshole. Don't get hung up on the thing you can't reach. This is when he realizes the brazier is sitting just outside the edges of an intricate magical circle scrawled into the concrete in what looks like blood, salt, and ash.

Following the circumference of the ring like a lifeline, he tracks it to the left, to black shoes, up black-clad legs, to hips, then an arm, and to a masked face.

Mateo jolts—or tries to—the ability to control his body is a dicey thing, so he's got no idea if he did it. Evil Wizard is right in front of him, and it's hysterically disconcerting that they might have been standing there the whole time.

"Ophelia?" Mateo says because it's situationally better than hello, but he's surprised by the slurring of the name, like he'd barely gotten his mouth open to say it.

Evil Wizard cocks their head the smallest amount, like a dog catching the edge of a sound and trying to work it out, but not cute. And they must work it out, because they step around the circle, careful not to touch it, and walk to one of the gauzy curtains a few yards away. Having never been in a scary wizard's murder basement before, Mateo's concerned about what might be behind there. The wizard draws it to the side, giving Mateo a clear line of sight.

Seeing Ophelia should calm the panic clawing for purchase in his sluggish brain, but it only heightens it. She's so small when not in motion, crumpled on her side on two of the floor pillows, hands bound in silver tape and hair a massive, obscuring mess around her face and upper body. Normal for her hair but upsetting in this context.

"Topher?" Mateo slurs next.

The wizard releases the curtain, hiding Ophelia from view. Not seeing her tied up is worse than seeing her tied up, but the wizard is indicating the ground to the left of Mateo.

"Oh shit." It's out before Mateo's syruped brain fully recognizes the form on the ground. You'd think a second large magic circle with a whole guy in it would be hard to miss . . . and yet. "Topher!" He's not sure why he yells it. Topher's clearly not awake. More raw panic slices through the haze as he struggles like he's developed bending-metal strength in the past minute.

Topher looks rough.

No. Correction. He looks like he's been in a car accident.

There's grime smeared down half of his face and his normally flawless gray outfit is still gray, but now it's with road filth. Breathing, Mateo's pretty sure. And bleeding.

While he strains against chains with zero success, the Evil Wizard must have walked back to their original position in front of Mateo. Or they'd moved magically. Who knows? Could have been teleporting all around the room because such feats as *look beside oneself* are difficult for Mateo right now.

He and the Evil Wizard stare at one another. Probably. The end-of-days warlock could be looking anywhere with that full-face obscuring ski mask on, but it seems to be at Mateo. Why did this perfect Cali-bodied suburbs rando do all of this? Why's she after Topher and his mom?

Except Yoga Wife walks into the room from a door he hadn't noticed and can't keep track of once he looks away. Meaning, Yoga Wife isn't the Evil Wizard. She's an evil extra in workout spandex.

Smiling a plastic, dead-eyed smile, she moves to the smoking brazier and picks it up. Mateo cringes, expecting her to shove it at him and knock him unconscious again, but she backs up a few paces instead.

It's like removing a rope from around his neck and a fist from around his brain, the sudden release of pressure so desired that an honest-to-God sob escapes Mateo's lips. The disorientation melts away, not totally, but enough for him to pull in the first full breath in years and have a coughing fit about it. He looks at the Evil Wizard again, eyes hot and wet from strain and discomfort. "What's happening?"

"That was going to be my question," the wizard says.

Ethan says.

Even with the mask on, the voice is unmistakable. He's waiting for Mateo to react, except Mateo doesn't know how to react because he doesn't know why a broker from the office of the dad of the guy that hired him is the Evil Wizard. "What the fuck is happening?" Mateo repeats with much more fervor.

Ethan rocks a little on the balls of his feet, like he's considering this magic-kidnapping-murder-basement situation he's completely to blame for, and pulls off his goth ski mask. Despite knowing it's Ethan, it's still shocking to see his face sticking out of the dystopian garb.

"Your outfit's ugly," Mateo spits.

"Be mature," Ethan says, but fusses with his layers a bit, deciding to take off his gloves.

"You threw me out a window!" Mateo yells and sends himself into another coughing fit.

Ethan waits till it's under control. "I was trying to throw *him* out a window, not you."

"That's not better, Ethan," Mateo rasps.

Squinting and holding a thumb and index finger one inch apart, he says, "It's a little better. And a perfect example of *my* surprise." Ethan stuffs the gloves in his pocket and squats outside the circle so they're more at eye level. "I think Linnéa's finally back and I walk in on you three. And whoever the hell that witch who threw me down the stairs is. Who was that?"

"What's wrong with Ophelia?" Mateo asks instead and Ethan has the gall to look offended.

"Nothing. Just sleeping. Perfectly fine. I'm not going to hurt your little friend."

"And Topher?"

"Less fine, but don't worry about that. I can make sure you still get paid," Ethan says, absolutely missing the point of his concern around Topher, taking on a distracted tone as he examines the circle Mateo's at the center of. Assured by whatever he sees, Ethan looks at Mateo again. "Consider it from my angle. The hot guy who I thought was a bullshit con artist milking an asshole manager's rich son out of some money, keeps getting in my way. He shows up at my work and evades the ward my intern managed to get under the conference room table—something with nine wormlings from bones into flesh. She was so proud of her work and so disappointed you spotted it. She's dead now, so whatever. Then, I've got the sweetest signal ward primed on Linnéa's door for her return, and it goes off, but when I show up to grab her, it's him again. And yes, I threw him out a window, but he should have died, and he didn't, and I was even really bummed about that, okay? But then he texts me the next day about my jacket. I thought I was being punked. While I'm trying to figure that one out, he decides to show me—" he gestures at his own face. "Whatever that was. You've been running around messing up my whole week. What the hell are you?"

"Why should I explain anything to you?" Mateo snaps. Despite what should be a terrifying general dynamic, he's deeply agitated by the tone Ethan's taking. With the daze of the shitty smoke lessened, his temper is clawing to get free, wanting out but unable to grab a footing.

Standing from his squat, Ethan gives his wife—who's still standing with the brazier raised—an exasperated expression. Now that Mateo's really looking, it's becoming clear that something's super off about Yoga Wife. Like not-blinking off.

Mateo's agitation tilts back toward fear.

"You've got this all wrong," Ethan says, still looking at his bizarrely motionless wife. "You think this is a good guy versus bad guy situation."

"I'd gesture at Topher's battered body beside me, but I'm tied to a fucking chair. It seems pretty bad," Mateo says.

Ethan looks at Mateo, hand moving to the base of his skull, running up the bald back of his scalp like he's honestly feeling badly or struggling with something here. Which is insane. "Okay. Fine. Yes. It's not great. But that doesn't mean it can't be."

"Is this the part where you tell me your evil plan and try to seduce me to the dark side?"

He's not serious, but Ethan drops his hand and looks him soberly in the eyes. "Yes. It is."

Mateo's read on the situation dissolves. Tied to a chair while Ophelia and Topher lay unconscious, all of them held against their will, seems pretty clear-cut, but Ethan's acting like there's a very valid reason for it all. That would be great.

Sensing Mateo's softening, Ethan's quick to fill the silence. "I had a whole situation going on here. I've taken a pledge to Marbas. In exchange for my devotion, he gives me secrets lost to time. I've got—" he actually pauses for dramatic effect. *"Amazing* powers." Really draws out the middle *a* in *amazing*. "Knocking you out that window was nothing. I have to be one of the most powerful witches alive."

Ethan looks at him like he wants a cookie or a head pat from Mateo for this brag about his own attempted murder. Is he supposed to know a Marbas? Not wanting to show off that he has no idea what Ethan's talking about but annoyed again, he says, "And you've kidnapped Topher because . . . ?"

Some of the expectation pinches off of Ethan's face but he presses on. "It's his mother I wanted. I always knew Christopher was doing something uncanny. The man's an idiot and has this stupid laugh that carries. I could be seven rooms away with the doors locked, on a call with headphones on and still hear his donkey caw." Completely unrelated detail but Ethan needs to get it out, it seems. "But his picks always pay. Always. And then I saw her and knew. She wasn't mortal. I thought fae, that Christopher had guessed her name or stole her coat or whatever fairytale bullshit, but she wasn't some minor spirit. Everyone I sent after her missed. She was completely untouchable."

Ethan is losing himself to his own drama, forgetting that he's talking to a captive audience who's still nauseous.

"I had no idea Topher even existed. Christopher never talked about his family. Too busy talking about himself." Ethan is incapable of delivering the story without interpersonal office politics slipping in. "When his wife vanished, Topher showed up at the office and got so spectacularly dismissed by Christopher I actually felt bad for him. Having that for a father. Gawd, I'd have cut his brake line. I thought Topher was standard issue because that asshole wasn't treating him like a money maker. Which made him perfect for snatching to lure the mom out. So, imagine my surprise when everyone I sent after Topher died."

"Holy shit," Mateo says and doesn't expect to get Ethan's enthusiastic agreement.

"Right? Nearly my whole coven. Do you know how hard it is to train up a practitioner from zero?" Ethan says it like they're reacting to the same thing here. "Just finding people who won't be weird about it at work is a nightmare. A lot of time and effort lost. The little shit might be more powerful than his mother. Or at least more destructive. I thought arranging for his arrest would flush Linnéa out, but then you fucked that up, so I just went for it. Had to toss six spells at that car to get it to crash."

He starts complaining about Quincy's driving, but Mateo's stalled out on the part where Topher wasn't accidentally killing random people. He'd been unconsciously protecting himself.

"But why were you after either of them?" Mateo interrupts.

"Marbas requires a tithing from his devotees. The more powerful the tithing, the more awesome the secrets revealed," Ethan says like it's obvious.

And Mateo's too slow on the uptake. Too magical-smoke-messed-up not to have startled at the words. Because *tithing* when combined with *unconscious on a magical circle* can only mean *sacrifice*.

Ethan notices Mateo's surprise, and something in his expression changes, any excitement to share his story replaced by naked curiosity as he studies Mateo. "Are you not pledged to someone?"

It feels a lot like Ethan's asking if he has a significant other really dramatically, but Mateo knows that's not it. Who the hell is Marbas? It's vaguely familiar but not in a useful way. If he just says a name with a lot of consonants, will that work? But he's not quick enough.

K. Valentin

That horrible cat piss, fish, and hate incense reek flares and Mateo barely has time to register that Yoga Wife had come closer, has the brazier only an inch away from his face.

Mateo gags, slumping in his seat, the little bit of strength and focus he'd managed strips away. And for the fifth time in forty-eight hours, he passes out.

CHAPTER THIRTY-SIX

"There he is," Ethan says merrily, fuzzing into view along with consciousnesses as Mateo wakes. There's blood smeared deliberately all over Ethan's face. A horrible addition to the situation. The brain fog from the stink-smoke is gone, as is the chair, which one might think is an improvement but is not.

Mateo's on his back, strapped to something metal, and he can't move even harder. Arms above his head, legs spread some, bound at the wrists, ankles, hips, and thighs. He strains but there's no give.

Conclusion: He's really fucking chained to a table now and misses the chair.

"Don't get worked up," Ethan says at his feeble struggles, moving out of his line of sight briefly, the sound of something sliding against concrete, and then Ethan's there again, stepping up onto the table Mateo's strapped to. The outfit's been downgraded. Bare feet, just the pants, and no shirt. Ethan's chest is a series of freshly carved symbols on top of long healed ones. Mateo can't recognize any of them, except in that way anyone can recognize bad shit and know it's bad.

Ethan considers him from above, and Mateo realizes there's a knife casually gripped in one of Ethan's hands. No. A dagger. Magic-ass-looking dagger that everyone but Mateo seems to possess.

Mateo tries to thrash. It's very underwhelming when he can only move his head. Metal chains dig tightly everywhere, including around his pelvis and high around each thigh, like horrible chain undies.

At his renewed attempt, Ethan kneels over him, knees on either side of his hips, and leans close to his face. The blood smeared all over him is still wet. Fresh. The idea that some of it's Ophelia's or Topher's courses through him but is quickly dismissed. It doesn't smell like them. Disconcerting realization as he'd had no idea he knew what their blood smelled like, but he'll take the bizarre reassurance.

"I get it," Ethan says in an inexplicably gentle tone, pressing Mateo's hair out of his face with one hand. "I thought you had a pact, but that's not it. You even told me earlier. You don't know what's wrong with you. But I do. It's obvious. You're possessed."

Accurate assessment and in no way calming. "Ethan, what are you doing?" It comes out shakier than he means it.

"I'm going to exorcise you," Ethan says, like it's nothing. Like he does it every day. "I'll get it out, and then you can make a pact with it, if you want. Which you should want. It's been feeding off you all this time. You should get something from it. Then you'll understand all of this. Why it's worth it. Even if it's a minor spirit, the power will be amazing. I'll teach you how to use it, make it bend to your will. You can join my coven. Be my student. I've got a few openings as of late." He smiles, like he's not leaning over Mateo with a dagger while he's tied down.

Mateo doesn't want to humor Ethan for obvious, everyone-is-kidnapped reasons, but Ethan's offering something he needs. Something he's been desperate for his entire life. If Ethan can get the demon out, everything will be different. He wouldn't have the slow degradation of mind and soul hanging over him, strangling all possibilities of a future. He could focus on Ophelia. Figure out what happened with her and her family, use Topher's payment to find experts in projection, make sure she won't just drift away again.

And if he can figure that out, they could just live.

Also, and more critical to this moment, it's not clear Mateo's getting a choice about this exorcism so much as it's just happening. "Whose blood is that?" Of all the potential questions, that's the one that forces its way to the top.

Ethan's smile falters. "I'd think you'd be a little more excited." Ethan looks to one side and Mateo follows his gaze as best he can. He's startled to see Yoga Wife is still right there, standing dutifully beyond the edges of the magical circle Mateo's still at the center of. Both arms are dripping freely onto the floor, blood running down from deep cuts at the inner elbow. "Don't worry, she's not real. It's a flesh body but she's a construct. Another gift from Marbas."

"You're extremely bad at being reassuring," Mateo says, and Ethan smiles again.

"Everything will make sense after," Ethan says serenely, catching the dagger on the collar of Mateo's shirt and slicing all the way down to navel. He pushes the ruined shirt aside and lines up the dagger with the center of Mateo's chest. It's nothing like any exorcism Mateo's ever seen on television, which doesn't mean a lot, except that it's extremely distressing and isn't helped by Ethan's next words: "This is going to hurt."

Like butter. Mateo's always thought that description was a gross way to describe cutting into anything but butter. Then the blade slides into his skin and scrapes against bone exactly like a knife pressing through butter, clinking against the porcelain plate beneath. His chest offers no resistance even as Ethan drags the blade around, carving a wide circle. Black blood wells and Mateo chokes down a shout, his useless thrashing proving useless yet again, and now he understands why the chains are so tight.

Ethan pauses his downward cut, but it's not because he's doing a wellness check. He uses his other hand to wipe up some of the black oozing out around his blade. Completely ignores the sharp gasp and that he's still got the blade tip buried in Mateo.

"How long have you had this demon in you?" Ethan asks, studying the tackiness of the black blood between fingers. It's always been more viscous than actual blood, more goo than liquid. Slightly warmed putty.

"My whole life," Mateo says raggedly, trying not to think about the blade so indelicately located in his chest.

Ethan makes a thoughtful noise, but keeps testing the blood between his fingers. "I've never seen this before. It's . . . different."

"Ethan, the fucking knife," Mateo pants, and Ethan finally drags his gaze back to him.

"Sorry, that's just—" but whatever it *just*, he'll never know because Ethan pulls the knife out, repositions it to cut more, but pauses again. Fingers run indelicately up the length of the cut he'd already made, and another expression Mateo would rather

Ethan not make while trying to wield unknown dark magic settles on his face. "It's healing."

"So do it faster," Mateo says with a clear edge of hysteria. It is of critical importance that Ethan not become more interested in the strange qualities of his body than exorcising him.

For a heart-screaming moment he thinks Ethan's going to alter course, ask a dozen more questions, maybe start slicing and dicing to test him out—but then that dagger slips in.

And it's absolutely wretched.

Mateo has no idea what he's carving, circles and lines that are probably meaningful, but not to Mateo. Ethan works quickly, and soon the whole of his chest drips and burns with a dozen deep-carved symbols and Mateo's not trying to be quiet about how much it hurts, gasping and panting the whole time.

When it finally stops, his vision narrows and Mateo's afraid he's going to pass out. Luckily, the next step of Ethan's secret-knowledge exorcism involves pouring what feels like a cocktail of lemon, salt, and acid onto Mateo's cut up chest. It keeps him really conscious, throat raw from screaming and chest a misery.

"Almost done," Ethan soothes, his face a mask of blood and sweat and Mateo realizes Ethan's been muttering something the whole time.

He tries to focus on Ethan's mouth, but the words are nonsense, a language he doesn't know. Latin, if he had to guess, because Latin feels like the right flavor for Ethan's magic.

Muttering turns to chanting, and it's like they've both spent the last hour in socks sliding around a carpet, hairs standing on end and the air charged. If this gets the demon out, he'll owe Ethan his whole life. Which will be awkward since Ethan is definitely an asshole and a murderer.

These concerns are washed away as Ethan's chanting gets louder, the dagger glowing, the intricate pattern carved into the blade giving off a red light. In concert with the blade, the symbols on both Ethan and Mateo's chests also glow. On Mateo, the half-healed cuts heat with renewed intensity and reopen.

Ethan raises the knife in a very *about to stab* way, eyes sheened with the same glow as his blade and all Mateo can do is scream.

CHAPTER THIRTY-SEVEN

The blade hovers, Ethan's eyes searching . . . and then they just sort of keep searching. And they're staring at each other. And Mateo's scream flags and then stops because he can't scream that long.

No stabbing.

No more magic words.

Ethan looks mystified.

"Not that I want you to stab me, but what's happening?" Mateo asks shakily, voice raw.

Ethan lowers the dagger, squinting at Mateo's eyes and then at the symbol he'd carved into his chest. The magic heating Mateo's chest is dull now, so whatever had reignited the pain is already wearing off, leaving only an inflamed ache and blood mess in its wake.

"I don't know," Ethan says, staring at his own cool chest cuts, and Mateo realizes he's double checking his work. He even slips a phone out of his back pocket, turns the camera around, and checks his magic blood face paint. "It . . . didn't work?"

"Are you asking me? If so, that's extremely bad!" Mateo might be shrieking. He honestly can't tell. Some emotion lodges in Mateo's chest—underneath what is still a lot of pain. Anger? Disappointment? Relief? That last one rings the loudest in his brain and is the most alien to his actual wants and needs, so he maybe starts freaking out a little bit.

Ethan looks around, checking the magic circle on the floor of his murder basement. "I don't get it," he says slowly, in no hurry to deal with Mateo's upset, but his gaze does eventually return to the person he's sitting on that he just cut up a bunch. "That should expel it. That's always worked before." He puts his phone back into his pocket and sets his dagger down beside their legs on the table before running both hands down Mateo's chest indelicately.

The slashes are no longer slashes, only red welts, but it's all still raw, and Mateo grits his still very human teeth in pain.

"Do you know anything about what's possessed you?" Ethan finally asks.

"Not really." There's no reason to be coy when the situation hasn't changed. Strapped to a table. Maybe this guy can help. Or maybe this guy's going to murder him in a minute here. "My mom did it when I was a baby. It's not something I remember."

"Your mom?" Ethan repeats, bemused as he settles on Mateo's thighs, seemingly not prepared to get off him yet. "She's a witch? What order?"

"Uh, I don't think she plays well with others." Mateo's not actually sure that's true. She went missing a lot before the final time. She might have been running off to witch meetups. She might have been using Witch-Tinder. He'd never had any idea what she'd been doing.

"Borrero," Ethan says slowly, and badly, and it's clear he's made a connection, summoned the name from some recess of his mind. "The Blood Witch?"

Ethan's saying it like a proper title. Mateo's never heard her called that before, but it would make sense. "I don't know what other people call her. But I'd sure like you to let me up now."

Ethan doesn't let him up, eyes dithering as he falls into a contemplative silence that Mateo's not loving. "I don't think I will . . ." he finally says.

"You're not going to get anything out of her," Mateo says quickly, trying to counter whatever extortion plot Ethan's just concocted. "She bounced five years ago, and before that, she barely cared if I lived or died."

"I had shit parents too," Ethan says, like whatever his deal was is comparable. Maybe it is. Mateo has no idea how someone becomes a stockbroker, let alone an evil wizard. "Don't worry. I'd still rather have you than her." This is the least good thing he could have said, but he says it with a hand on Mateo's cheek, like he's soothing him. "But knowing she did this changes things. I've never met her, but I've heard stories. I'll show you to Marbas. He'll know what she did. What it is. And how I can control it."

Ethan starts to dismount, and Mateo struggles anew, the word *tithing* blaring through his mind. "Ethan, wait! What are you going to do to get information?"

"It's very noble that you're giving this little job your all," Ethan says, feet on the floor now so he leans over Mateo's face. "But this is deep knowledge. You don't get it for free. You know that's how the world works. If it's about the money, don't worry. You don't need Topher. I'm rich. I'll mentor you once we get whatever's inside of you under check. That transformation earlier. The healing. The blood. That's power. That's useful."

"Here I thought you liked me for my personality," Mateo says, still struggling uselessly but with a much more frantic edge. Fuckity fuck! He's going to sacrifice Topher. Ethan can't fathom Mateo wanting Topher alive for any reason other than getting paid—which might have been true a week ago but definitely isn't now. "Isn't Topher useful too? He makes luck."

"I make my own luck," Ethan says easily, leaning closer to speak softly. "I understand this is difficult for you. We're all paying a price, okay? I'm going to waste my extremely hard-won tithings on you, so show a little gratitude and just let this happen." He straightens. "Now, stay put."

"Ethan! Wait!" Mateo yells, panicking, because that was a joke, and Ethan is one thousand percent stone-cold enough to ritually murder Topher.

The room isn't huge. Just a normal basement. A good size but not massive.

Which means fitting two large, person-holding magical circles side by side, really means side by side. There's less than a foot between the two magic captivity rings. When Ethan turns, Topher's right there.

But he's no longer on the ground.

He's on his feet in only the most technical sense of the word, swaying, shirt bloodstained and eyes like a hunting owl.

CHAPTER THIRTY-EIGHT

Topher throws himself at Ethan.

None of them expect it.

Not Ethan, not Mateo, and somehow least of all Topher, who's the one doing the bodily throwing.

Ethan makes a bird squawk of surprise and stumbles, catching Topher's weight awkwardly and both of them spin out of Mateo's limited sight.

At the same time, creepy Yoga Wife steps right up to Mateo's side, strong yoga fingers pulling at chains.

"What the f—" he starts to ask, but she interrupts.

"Shut up, Teo. This is crazy hard."

It's Yoga Wife saying it, Yoga Wife squatting her yoga thighs to tug at chains beneath the table, trying to work out how to loosen them. But the words are Ophelia filtered through the suburbs. Her body's still behind the ugly curtains, he's pretty sure, but she's somehow possessing Yoga Wife. A thing she absolutely couldn't do yesterday, but there's no time to celebrate. The pressure on the chain around his neck increases alarmingly for a moment, and then slackens completely, the sound of metal dropping onto concrete jarring in the space.

A glance to Topher and Ethan, and they're having the stupidest fight he's ever seen. Topher very obviously doesn't know how to fight so he's just slapping, and Ethan maybe does know how to fight, except he can't land a solid punch through a series of stumbles, frantic weaving from Topher, and a badly placed floor pillow that takes them both down again.

"Phee," Mateo pleads softly, but he doesn't say anything else. Her hands are shaking, that prim blush pink lipstick that Ophelia would never wear set in a grimace of concentration.

On the floor, Ethan and Topher roll around—still looking ridiculous—and Ethan manages to get himself on top of Topher. But Ethan hears the second chain hit the concrete, the one that was strapped across Mateo's pelvis, and he finally looks.

"Hey!" Ethan yells upon seeing his horrible wife trying to release Mateo, and he struggles to get off of Topher.

Except Topher's having none of it, wrapping arms and legs around Ethan like an uncomfortable Cirque du Soleil contortionist experience. And he's committed, looking like hell but holding on for all he's worth.

Ethan's struggling to get an arm between himself and Topher to push him off while also looking at his horrible wife in dismay. "What the hell, Becky?"

"You named your evil wife Becky?" Mateo shouts.

"Oh, shut up!" Ethan yells back, slipping an elbow between Topher's upper body and his own. "Becky, stop." She doesn't. "Becky, I command you to stop." Still nothing. He manages to get his lower arm against Topher's throat, grimacing as he pushes down and yells: "Unmake!"

It's a power word. A spell. Yoga Wife's body, leaning over him as Ophelia tries to get the chain from around his thigh, shudders violently and then crumples. The tight-ponytailed head hits the metal edge of the table with a thick crunch before sliding to the floor.

"Ophelia!" Mateo doesn't mean to yell, knows it's not her body, but she's never possessed anyone before so he has no idea what getting damaged in someone else might do.

It's exactly the wrong thing to say.

Ethan turns in the direction of Ophelia's body, but he's still got Topher squirming and clawing at him, turning blue beneath Ethan's forearm and the weight of his upper body against his windpipe. He lets up enough for Topher to get a single ragged breath but it's not out of charity. Whatever protection Topher's luck offered outside of an evil wizard's home, his body's still that of a hundred-and-thirty-pound computer guy. Ethan punches down viciously and it's exactly as devastating as a boxer hitting a baby. Fist to face and back of head to concrete, Topher stills with the solid sound of his skull being hit from both sides.

It's the second most terrifying thing Mateo's ever seen. He has to believe Topher's just unconscious; that Ethan needs him for his sacrifice—but he doesn't actually know that.

"Fuck, fuck, fuck," Mateo pants, struggling against his chains again. He can almost sit up, abs burning as he has to use his nonexistent core muscles to pull at his arms.

Ethan drags himself to his feet, approaching the curtain. "She's a Traveler?" he asks the room at large, haphazardly ripping the curtain down. Ophelia's still lying there, bound and curled on her side, but her eyes are open and completely white.

"Don't you fucking touch her!" Mateo yells, trying to split his attention between freeing his arms, Topher unmoving on the floor, and whatever Ethan's doing in front of Ophelia. The chains won't budge, the metal cuffs around his wrists digging in painfully as he pulls. Ethan's ignoring him, has the back of his hand on Ophelia's forehead, and Mateo can't allow it.

Between the cuffs and his body, he only needs one of them to give and this body is more malleable than the metal. He strains and the edges of the cuff cuts, rips, and then peels skin. A series of cracks and another vicious blood-slicked tug and one hand is free, scraps of meat left behind. The yell that escapes him draws Ethan's attention, though Mateo's unaware he's shrieked in a way that's not possible for something human. And unaware that Ethan's looking stressed for the first time.

Hands up in surrender, Ethan says, "Hey, hey, I stopped! I stopped!"

But words don't matter now, because Mateo can rip himself free and that's the only way he can make sure Ethan doesn't hurt Ophelia or Topher anymore. One of his hands is a ruin but the other is still cuffed. An animal impulse to be free at all costs overtakes him. He smears blood all over the trapped one, ignoring the naked muscles on display as he wrenches again. Blood oozes and something in his thumb cracks.

And then Ethan's on top of him, mounting his middle, trying to force him back down onto the table.

Mateo bucks frantically, and it's more effective this time because he's partially unchained, but Ethan has a wealth of experience doing horrible magic shit to people—and possesses actual muscles—so he maintains his position on top.

"You just got too high maintenance," Ethan says, and the dagger is out again.

Mateo catches the descent, but his hand is still shredded, slick with gore, missing critical muscles, and his grip isn't good.

Using body weight, Ethan forces the point down, aiming for Mateo's chest. Aiming for his heart. Mateo strains against gravity, trying to stop the descent but there's so much blood. His hand isn't doing what he needs it to. Another shout as the blade's tip pierces skin.

"Shh, shh, shh," Ethan says softly, though he's shaking, straining, face red as he forces the blade deeper. It slides against bone horribly, skidding against a rib.

He can't. He can't die here. Not with Ophelia all dead-eyed over there, five foot nothing and only barely still alive in the first place. Not with Topher coldcocked on the floor, the least helpless most helpless person on the planet. What was the fucking point of any of this if he gets them killed? He was trying to help Topher. He was trying to get his own shit together enough to help Ophelia. And he knows life isn't fair. He's not deranged. But isn't he supposed to have some horrible, evil thing inside? Something that needed to be locked away? But he's losing an arm wrestle to a jagoff!

Hand hellish with pain, he struggles to keep Ethan's arm up, losing his hold millimeter by bloody millimeter. Ethan will feed them both to his patron Marbas; will trade them for magic to increase his stock portfolio or however the hell Wall Street works and it's just wildly unfair.

Ethan grits his teeth, trying to angle the blade better, to get at the black and beating heart beneath. And he's going to do it. No amount of gumption or impotent fury can do anything about the fact that Mateo's never worked out a day in his life.

Mateo's only begged one other time in his life. Not when his mother wouldn't tell him why she did this to him. Not when she cut him, hurt him, used parts of him for her spells and craft. Not even when she disappeared, leaving him without a single hope of figuring out what was wrong inside.

It was only when Ophelia died.

Curled up next to her corpse, there was nothing he hadn't begged to. He's not so broad with his plea this time. If he's going to die anyway, he'd rather die for them.

"Please," is all that makes it past his lips before Ethan has the angle right, Mateo's bloody hold slips, and the dagger sinks in to the hilt.

CHAPTER THIRTY-NINE

Ophelia screams but the body around her refuses. Not a whimper. Not a tear. She can't even part its lips.

She can only watch from the floor, caged within the Yoga Wife, who is now devoid of whatever magic let it move. No matter how she rages, it won't obey, and it won't let her go. She can't even move the eyes, only able to see what was in their line of sight the moment Ethan dismissed the spell that powered this spandex and pumpkin spice freak.

This is hell.

This is worse than hell because she's been in hell: three days trapped outside herself, watching Mateo try to die for her.

But he's not *trying* this time. He's done it.

And it's her fault. Again. If she hadn't agreed to come in with him. If she'd made him wait for Ulla. If she hadn't agreed to take the job in the first place, a thing he was only doing in his roundabout and nonsensical way for her. She could stop him. She could always stop him. There was nothing he wouldn't do for her. That was their whole *thing*.

But in those critical moments, she never stops anyone. Not her sister Juliet, not her mother, not her father, not herself, and now not Mateo.

And she knows why she hadn't. Because she likes Topher. But also because of Mateo. Because he likes Topher and that's so rare. Precious. A seedling to be nurtured, set on a windowsill, moved from room to room to follow the light without direct exposure to the elements. She'd wanted a friend for him so much. Someone more positive than her.

Somewhere in her happy and softly fucked up life with Mateo she'd forgotten the fundamental truth of herself.

Everyone else dies.

Ethan dismounts Mateo's still form and vomits onto the ground on the opposite side of the table from Ophelia in the Yoga Wife's body. Whatever's wrong with Ethan, he needs a few minutes heaving. She hopes he heaves out his entire fucking guts.

Eventually, Ethan wipes at his mouth with obvious distress, gets to his feet, wobbly, and starts circling the table. What's left of Mateo is dripping onto the floor all around her, the steady *splitch* and Ethan's ragged breaths the only sounds.

A moment of savage hope pierces Ophelia's soul at the slow and considering way Ethan circles. Something had been happening to Mateo as he'd struggled with Ethan, that black stuff bubbling out of his eyes, mouth, nose, and ears, like his insides had liquefied and they all wanted out of his head at once. Her angle for it was bad and hasn't improved.

She can't see what Ethan's seeing now. Can't see why he leans close to the head of the table, over where Mateo's face is. Ophelia's world constricts to Ethan's expressions. Is Ethan seeing movement, signs of life, something to indicate Mateo's still alive?

Ethan grimaces. "Fucking yuck," he mutters, then turns his attention to her.

All those years ago, she hadn't been confused about why Mateo's reaction to seeing her dead was to crawl into death beside her. She was the only thing that had ever loved him, and he didn't have it in him to return to existing without her. But that kind of sad surrender isn't her. Even without a body, she continues to voicelessly rage. She's nothing but misery, no tactile senses or flesh attached. As always, her anger can exist even when no other part of her does.

Mateo thinks Ophelia never cries, but she just never lets him see it. It upsets him. But he isn't here to see her cry. And she isn't here to actually cry. So, she screams, sobs, and curses and it doesn't matter, the same way it's never mattered to anyone but Mateo.

Ethan squats beside her, but it's not her he's looking at. He rolls the Yoga Wife onto its back, gazing right into her face, a hand beneath the nose to check for breath. His face, still streaked with red and black blood, twists into annoyance. He doesn't know Ophelia's in there. Wouldn't care if he knew. The aftermath of their lives is a series of annoyances for this wizard cosplay Wall Street prick.

Ethan stands. Leaves her. Approaches Topher.

There is no heart in the chest she occupies but a phantom sensation of thumping starts as she's racked with impotent terror and anger anew. Yoga Wife's head lolled to the side, so she can see Topher crumpled on the floor, only a few feet away, seemingly still alive, with a trickle of blood trailing from his nose and pooling under his face.

This can't happen. Not again. She can't be the only one to survive again. Though *survive* is a laughable way to describe this prison she's stuck herself in.

A bare foot to Topher's hip and Ethan shoves him onto his back. Topher groans but doesn't otherwise stir. Ethan walks away again, but it's only for a moment. When he returns, he ungracefully dumps Ophelia's actual body onto the floor beside Topher. There's no disorientation at seeing herself over there. No novelty. She's used to that view.

Ethan squats and starts repairing the circle around Topher and her empty body. Ophelia—while piloting Yoga Wife—had broken the edges of both magic circles to let Topher and Mateo out. Which at least means Ethan wants Topher alive for now. What will it mean if Ethan traps her body in there? Will she get sucked back into it? Trapped out of it forever?

Whatever the answer is, she'll figure something out. She'll ruin him.

Using the blood dribbling from his fresh chest slashes, Ethan works on the first ring. He's nearly done when his attention shifts back toward the table beside her.

Ophelia can't see what he's reacting to, can only hear the liquid squelch of Mateo's dripping blood. Though, the sound is different now. Thicker.

Ethan stands, approaches the table, and squats beside Ophelia as he examines something on the floor. Disgust flickers on his stupid face, and then he delicately picks something up. It's a wet, palm-sized mass, black and dripping. With obvious revulsion, Ethan tries to make sense of the thing, locating the edges and picking at them until he's holding up a sodden piece of paper with the tips of his fingers.

The background noise of drips and dribbles is interrupted by a solid thwack, like raw meat impacting concrete, but Ophelia can't see the source.

Ethan jerks, drops the paper, head turning sharply toward the table Mateo's corpse is on. Then he's up, a frantic lunge at the smeared, broken parameter of the circle around them. Whatever he meant to do, he doesn't. He's shuffling around panicked, a confusing scramble of limbs trying to distance himself from something she still can't see. Ethan ends up crab-walking backward, nearly beside her again, breathing heavily.

She follows his gaze as best she can. Something is crouched in the circle with Topher and her body, just at the edges of her vision. It's hard to look at, a flickering, undulating darkness. Some basic humanity within her shies away from it, a flickering of nightmare images without detail or form. She can't see them, but she knows there are teeth. There are claws. And even in her disembodied state, its hunger is suffocating, the sensation of a mouth opening and opening.

It's Mateo, she realizes with a victorious shriek of her soul.

Except it's not.

Because the thing hunched over her physical body is only comparable to a human in that it seems capable of standing up. It's like if dark could hurt like light, the shadow blinding, and the eyes of the Yoga Wife are watering as Ophelia uses them to look at it.

The dark thing is pressed close to Ophelia's physical body, but she can't tell what it's doing. *Is* it Mateo? She doesn't know. But if it's not, if it's the demon, she hopes it kills her. Let them be together, even if together is dead inside of it.

A slap of feet, and Ethan, thus far ignored by the creature, makes for the stairs.

The creature doesn't move, and Ophelia's going to die furious if Ethan's the only one who escapes. But something is happening, and she's slow to understand. The thing that used to be Mateo isn't just a mass of shadows, it's leeching the light from the basement, smothering Ethan's ocean breeze–scented candles. Rapidly, she's not just trapped and immobile, but in the pitch dark.

There's no noise but Ethan, the loud groan of stairs as he takes them two at a time. He must be nearly to the top when there's a scuffle, shriek, and crash. She still can't see anything but has to assume that was him eating shit off the stairs.

"I'll pledge myself to you!" Ethan screams, voice shrill in hysteria.

More silence. Ophelia waits because it's all she can do. Is it killing him? Is it considering?

"I can be helpful. Useful. Get you people. Whatever you want," Ethan assures it, his voice loud and quivering in the darkness.

When it speaks, it's a whispering voice she can hear inside even this stolen body, scraping against the very bones. **"I'm just not that into you,"** it says.

Ethan draws in a sharp breath that would be Ophelia's if only she had working lungs.

"Mateo?" Ethan tries, voice desperate. "You don't have to do this. I've made some mistakes, yes. But we can figure this out. Get you help. Help your friends."

The laugh is a lance, hurting teeth that aren't hers. It's not Mateo's laugh. Not a human laugh at all. But she loves it desperately.

"What are you?" is the last thing Ethan says before the darkness is shattered by his screams.

They go on for a very long time, and she loves that too.

CHAPTER FORTY

Something is exceptionally wrong. A nagging thought he can't make sense of as he licks sweet blood off the palm of one hand.

Hand?

Since when does he have hands like these? Not a normal hand made from the formless throng of body, of which he has many, but one of two that are different. Corporal. Constrained by rules of biology that can be bent, as he's done, but not entirely broken.

That is one of the problems, isn't it? These two hands contain rigid substance other than that which is nothing.

Solidity.

Meat and bone.

How can he be meat and bone?

And there is more of it. All over. Encasing him.

Him? Is that right?

He looks around the room, which is also wrong, because *look* and *room* aren't things he does. He should not *look*, because his perception has nothing to do with sockets and wads of jelly-filled flesh. He should not be *inside a room*, because he exists in the place where nothing else is.

This is somewhere, and the somewhere sucks.

Along with the knowledge that something is majorly boned about the situation, exists an unease. A fear. A concept foreign to the substance that is both brain and nothing like the soft, salty gray matter he's just eaten—the matter that he is starting to suspect lives inside the skull anchoring him to this ugly room.

The fear isn't of the place, which is good because it doesn't make sense to fear walls and stone. It is an intangible concern, like he's misplaced something precious, even though he's never considered anything of particular import.

There. On the ground.

They lie in a pile, which is a very meat thing to do but the sight of them causes a savage fury that hasn't been felt in units of time he can no longer understand. Careful, because their shells are meat and meat is so easily destroyed, he lifts them off the stone. The tacky floor pillows are as good as it's going to get so he sits them there, dragging more pillows to frame their limp forms so they don't slump.

The soft, pale one moans, the thin layer of skin over eyeballs flickering. Opening. Opening more and more. That feels normal, the unease in his gut he shouldn't have softening, shifting to pleasure at being goggled at.

He focuses on the other one, knowing an empty vessel by scent. Searching around the room, he smells the air, easily catching an essence he knows as well as . . .

Weird.

The thought can't be completed.

An absence of memory. Is that what's wrong? His memory is gone? But gone isn't right. He knows some things. He knows he isn't supposed to contain this density of material. Knows these carved off pieces aren't supposed to be sodden and floating around inside of him. Knows he isn't supposed to have this silent mass of soft tissue at his center. Knows it isn't supposed to be stabbed through with a shard of metal.

And he knows her.

Even in another shell, he will always know her.

Reaching a hand—not the clumsy flesh ones but the correct kind—into the Lululemon-wearing meat crumpled on the ground, he ever so gently pulls her out.

Unlike last time, she doesn't need much to go back to her shell, soul and flesh connected.

Soul and flesh connected? That thought frustrates him. Alarms him. Something is so fantastically wrong and his mind—that he shouldn't have—feels slippery, a greased egg on a tilted countertop.

A cage.

He's been caged.

Certainty swells for a moment, the puddle at his core expanding, deepening and widening into a bottomless pit of fury. As he moves a hundred real hands to sink claws into the prison, rip it from off of him, he hesitates. That doesn't feel right either. He is made of the wrong things, in disconnected pieces, not properly whole, yes, but . . .

"Teo?" A voice he would sooner cease to exist than not listen to, whispers. Then hands, sliding to cheeks that he shouldn't have, direct a face that he also shouldn't have to focus down on her.

Ophelia.

His Ophelia.

But in a reciprocal way, not that he's a creep about it.

Basement grime and blood coating her dress, she gazes up at him with a brow creased in worry. He doesn't like that expression on her face, a sliver of panic thrumming through the destroyed heart motionless in his center.

"Are you okay? I mean, you're not okay, but . . . are you okay?" This voice is vibrating with nervous energy, but even so it is accompanied by thin fingers, unerringly finding one of the two meat-arms in his mass of dripping shadow and, frankly, a lot of arms and things like arms, and even teeth.

Topher.

He wants to attach a neat yet meaningful summation to that name, like he'd done with Ophelia, but his meat brain skitters around a few different possessive descriptors that make him uncomfortable and don't necessarily feel mutually agreed upon.

Luckily, there is blood to focus on.

It oozes from Topher's hairline, down cheek, chin, and throat, and he can smell it on those fragile hands lost in the pulsing blackness of his body. This blood is Topher's, and the earlier rage sweeps through him again. The sight of Topher prone, hurt, bleeding, then awake, trying so hard only to go down again, the brutality of the hit, the way his delicate skull impacted unyielding stone—it is intolerable and unforgivable, yet he's already consumed the cause.

His strange matter pulses in agitation, but he gently moves his face from Ophelia's grasp, drawing Topher closer to bring bloodied hands to some of his mouths. So carefully he drags tongues around each finger, across each palm, mindful of teeth. Each hand is licked clean before pressing tongue to the sweet mess streaming down Topher's brow and then cheek. Another laps up shoulder blades and neck, to the back of Topher's scalp, mindful of where skin has been mashed against bone.

A soft noise from Topher and he pulls back slightly, concerned he's hurt his frail flesh in some way. Gray orbs quiver, but not in pain or even fear—which is wild because some part of him is aware that too many mouths are in play. The maelstrom of emotion in those storm-cloud eyes drags his attention down to that defenseless mouth, remembering blunt teeth, a questing tongue, and the honeyed press of pale lips.

A kiss he hadn't reciprocated for reasons more difficult to grasp than the unreality of his form and the fracturing of his memory. Whatever the reason, he wants to correct it now.

Careful to use only the mouth connected to the prison, teeth receding to wherever teeth go when not eating, he presses lips to impossibly soft lips.

Topher's response is tentative, only lips and breath, soft and hesitant but underneath that, eager. One of his now bloodless hands slides up to grasp at the place between neck and jaw, unerringly finding it in the dripping ichor and shadow. Once Topher gets the hang of it—or the assurance that teeth aren't going to eviscerate him—he leans in, lips parting, and eyes closed. Like he isn't kissing a monster at all.

"Hey, I'm totally for this but we've got stuff to do right now," Ophelia says, letting them keep kissing for a moment more before catching his cheek and directing his face back to her. Those eyes are cerulean and beautiful but marred in the unhappiness of her delicate housing. She strains on tiptoes, trying to press her forehead to his but she is only, like, three inches tall, so he sends a wave of shadow beneath her bare feet, lifting her up so they can meet. "Mateo Borrero, come back," she whispers to him, lips close enough to brush at least one of his mouths.

This nonsense jumble shocks him, forcing a clarity he hadn't known he'd lacked.

He knows suddenly that he can do what she asked, but if he does, there is something he'll miss. A swell of unknown enticement sits just out of reach, and he stands on the precipice. One step and he can understand, but if he steps, he can't un-step. He will fall.

"Mateo Borrero, come back to me, or I'm going to be mad at you forever. So will Topher," Ophelia says less softly.

He doesn't just back away from the edge, he turns around and sprints—metaphorically speaking.

What his body does is shed shadow like he's one of those inky cap mushrooms on overdrive, a violent expulsion of ichor that leaves him naked and unstable, holding Ophelia around the middle with Topher latched on to one of his arms. He can't support Ophelia's weight, so he drops to his ass on the ground, dragging both of them down with him.

CHAPTER FORTY-ONE

"I did what?" Mateo asks, wearily seated in the chair he was earlier strapped to. A horrible combination of the first two things Ophelia alighted on in Ethan's closet cover his person, which means he's ruining a nice pair of Saint Laurent pants and a gaudy Prada cardigan—he feels less bad about the cardigan because it's ugly, but still.

"You ate him," Ophelia says, fluttering around the depths of Ethan's magical murder basement like a fairy, shoving ugly curtains aside and studying shelves. He wants to remind her to be careful but he's not sure he has the right anymore . . . on account of the eating of a live person.

"But. Like . . ." he starts, but he's not sure what he meant to say. His attention keeps diverting to the mess slowly making its way back to him across the floor. Alarming chunks of demon gunk casually worming their way to his bare feet where they just sort of disappear into him. He remembers feeling like he was fragmented, confusion, a lot of anger, and then he so very vividly remembers the eating. But it's distinctly unreal because that part was exactly like his dreams, but this time it for sure happened because other people around him totally saw him do it.

"He deserved it," Topher assures him, reaching a hand up to awkwardly pat Mateo's knee. He's seated on the concrete at Mateo's feet, cross-legged and loose-limbed. That hand lingers, and Mateo realizes he'd absolutely had those fingers in his mouth, the memory a sudden fire hose turned full blast directly into his brain. He'd demon-mode made out with Topher *so* much. And Topher's just patting his knee and not looking deeply traumatized about it. Aside from the fact that too many mouths were involved, Mateo doesn't feel weird about it either. Which is, itself, extraordinarily weird.

Maybe it's just exhaustion on Topher's part. He's actually in worse shape than Mateo by virtue of an inability to heal—which is saying a lot because Mateo's got a dagger in his chest.

And, actually, both Topher and Ophelia are taking this whole cannibalism thing really well.

More distressingly, so is Mateo.

He's not even grossed out, though he can taste Ethan's blood in his mouth—Topher's too, and he's trying not to think about that. This lack of distress is so deeply distressing that he folds it up tightly, stuffs it in a waterproof bag, vacuum seals it, and shoves it into the furthest depths of his *things Mateo refuses to emotionally deal with* lockbox where it will hopefully die.

It's really hard to ignore the reality of the situation, though, not just because of the dagger that is, again, still in his chest, but because he also can't stop looking at the large stain at the bottom of the stairs.

They'd told him the particulars of what had happened—mostly Ophelia while Topher anxiously chimed in. How Ophelia had maneuvered Yoga Wife around the room while Ethan and Mateo had exorcism fun. She'd messed up the magic circle around Topher to free him, had been trying to find something for Topher or her to hit Ethan with, but then things had gone to shit.

Then he'd been stabbed in the heart and transformed into something else. The demon. The thing inside him. He'd called out to it right before the knife went in and it had acted.

Except.

It hadn't felt like *something else*. He hadn't been sitting on the sidelines watching the demon pilot his body around. Confused, half out of his mind, and furious about everything, it had felt like him.

If not for Ophelia thinking to mess up the circle around Mateo before going for his binds, he'd have stayed trapped, and they'd all be dead. The *they* that didn't include Mateo. Because he had been dead in a way he's absolutely not going to deal with right now. Which means Topher's not wrong. Ethan deserved it.

Ophelia returns, squatting first in front of Topher, hands on his cheeks, making sure he's not about to pass out, and then she straightens and looks at the dagger in Mateo's chest. "We should get that out."

"I was thinking of keeping it. Like a hardcore piercing," Mateo says, unwillingly dragging his attention from the spot where he ate a man to the spot where said man stabbed him. He can feel it in him. Like. A lot. It's absolute shit. And if he concentrates, he's very aware that his heart isn't beating around it.

"What are we talking about in this wretched basement?"

From the top of the stairs, the unmistakably displeased tone of Ulla calls down, followed by the sound of stilettos picking their way unerringly down the steps. She halts before the last step, gazing at the stain there, then takes them all in.

"Oh good. None of you died." She actually hops over the stain, a dainty little leap that looks insane because she's still in her flawless white power skirt blazer combo and four-inch heels. When she gets closer, she amends her comment. "Oh. One of you did die. Well. Two out of three isn't terrible."

She, exactly as Ophelia had done moments before but with negative ten thousand degrees Celsius warmth, squats, takes cheeks in hand, and regards Topher. Having never met her before, with no obvious indication of who she is, Topher allows this because he's too awkward to stop a stranger from grabbing his face.

"Topher," she says, voice taking on a tone that feels impossible for her. Which is to say, soft and sympathizing. "I'm your Auntie Ulla. Your brainless mother's warding the house upstairs. She's perfectly alright and will join us in this grubby little room in a moment. Your father is dead."

The entire delivery is the same soothing tone, so it takes them all a beat to process the last line.

"Oh," Topher says and then reasonably starts weeping. It's devastating-looking because Topher's all mussed, with a huge red welt forming under his half-closed right eye, the sclera filled with red and now leaking silent tears.

Ulla leaves him to that, surveying Mateo and his whole dagger situation. "Isn't that where hearts are?"

"That's such a disconcerting way to ask that," Mateo counters, but then she wraps her fingers around the handle. He tries to yell *wait* or *don't*, so what comes out is a shrill, "want!"

Which she ignores and jerks the blade out.

Sagging forward, blood dumps out of his chest, onto lap and floor, splattering everything with black. Ulla makes another affronted noise. He hopes she got splashed as he gasps and uselessly tries to stuff blood back in with his hands. Something thick and sodden splats into his fingers. It looks like soggy paper, but as soon as he has the thought, it slurps back into the gaping wound in his chest. Which is just one more thing in a day with a lot of shit. The torrent slows, then stops, and he sits back gasping.

"Not. Cool," he says between ragged breaths.

"If it didn't keep you dead just sitting there, it wasn't going to coming out." She has the nerve to sound annoyed, but she's also looking at her shoes in disgust. Small victories.

The scent of fresh-cut grass fills the room, and Linnéa Nystrom walks through the doorway.

She's a lot, but in a totally different way than Topher. *Amazon* is the word that comes to mind, like an uncanny but upsized fairy queen. Makes absolute sense that Ethan saw her and thought Christopher was pulling far above his pay grade. She's also the whitest lady Mateo's ever seen ever. The same platinum blonde hair as Topher but turned up to a twelve, nearly glowing it's so light, falling in pristine sheets on either side of her face. He can see her white lashes from across the room. To make her all the more surreal-looking, she's in pale jeans and a simple button-up long-sleeve slate top. Perfectly pleasant mom-wear, and he has the thought that Ulla dresses to up the uncanny, but Linnéa's trying—and failing—to downplay it.

Mateo starts to sweat, which is strangely encouraging because it means he's still capable of getting nervous. He hopes Topher's gigantic mom isn't, like, mad at him or something. Maybe hamingja hate demons. Everyone hates demons. There's a whole genre of movies about how much no one wants them around. And here he is, dumping blood on her sister's shoes, eating people near her delicate son. It would be exceptionally poetic to make it twenty-three years and deal with an evil wizard just to be snapped in half by the lady he was trying to find.

But she doesn't care about him. Stepping through the horrible bloodstain with no mind, she moves to Topher and sweeps him into her large mom arms and bosom where he cries more miserably—possibly partially in relief now.

Ophelia, unmoved by intense mom action, says to the room, "We need to get out of here." And then to Ulla. "Get your car into the garage. These two can't walk far. Then come back down here and help me steal anything that looks valuable."

He expects Ulla to protest, but she only mutters something under her breath and gingerly makes her way back to the stairs.

A cursory look at Topher clinging upsetly to his mom and Ophelia then comes over to Mateo. She waves a hand in front of his face and he starts—so he must be trying to pass out. "Teo? We're going to get you two out of here, but we have to do something about the wife."

Mateo stares at her, then connects meaning to those words and turns to stare at Yoga Wife. She's sprawled beside the exorcism table. A whole spandex-clad body just right there.

"Can't we just burn down the house?" Mateo asks weakly, because he should, his brain already broiling with a thought he can't quite bring himself to say.

"We can't start a fire," Topher says in a small cry-voice from his mother's arms. "It's too dry here. We might take out the whole neighborhood, the hills behind it, the whole forest."

"Also, a fire will make investigators come here," Ophelia points out.

"Is she really dead?" Mateo asks. Because he should ask that—should care about that.

"I'm not sure she was alive in the first place." Ophelia walks to the body, using a bare foot to shove her arm. Yoga Wife is mad dead. "*Something* was in there when I first possessed her, but it definitely wasn't after Ethan dispelled it."

"Sentient magic. An old god's will made flesh," Linnéa says in a startlingly thick Swedish accent. Topher sounds like he's from California and Ulla has the accent-less and over-annunciated tone of someone aggrieved at having to talk to buffoons.

There's not a good way to say it—such a bad first impression—so Mateo doesn't say it in a good way. "I could eat her."

Ophelia turns back to him, lips parted, a rare moment of visible surprise on her face. Nothing comes out of her for a moment, and then a soft, "Teo." It's all she can counter with.

He can't relish the one time he manages to shut her up because this is too big of a deal, and he needs her not to get upset. "If there's no bodies, there's no crime." Like it's logical. Factual. No other choice.

They stare at one another.

"Let's just put her in the trunk. Figure it out not here," Ophelia tries. But an hour-from-now-them isn't going to be any better than now-them at body disposal. She knows it. He knows it. Topher's face knows it too. He's doing a fantastic job looking solidly pathetic and exactly like a guy punched square in the face by someone way stronger than him and then told his dad is dead, clinging to his mommy. He's watching Mateo with the same face he'd walked into the print shop with. Desperate, with no ability to help. That first time, Mateo had been excited to see such naked need. Now he hates it. Wants to do anything he can to make it go away. And maybe that's the demon making him feel that way, but maybe he doesn't care if it is.

"What if you get stuck again?" Ophelia tries, keen eyes watching for any sign of doubt.

So, he doesn't show any. "I won't."

"If he does, we'll bring him back," Topher surprises them both by saying. There's a confidence in his voice despite his ragged look or his watery eyes. Like it's nothing. Easy. They'd just done it. They can do it again.

"Teo," she says again. Almost has her. She's scared. Doesn't want to leave him to do something so awful.

"Phee," Mateo pleads, soft enough so only she can hear. "Get Topher upstairs. I can do this. I'll be fine. Please."

She puts her hands on Mateo's cheeks, leans down, and kisses him. It's soft and warm, and in direct contrast to the violence he's just promised to do. He closes his eyes briefly, relishing it and missing it even though it's still happening.

When she pulls away, they stare at each other and he knows without hesitation or fear, that he'll be anything he has to be if it'll keep her safe. He absolutely doesn't give a single shit. Her unnerving blue eyes are wet. Because she knows it too. And because she knows, she leaves Mateo there and urges Topher and Linnéa up the stairs.

Alone in the basement, Mateo's gaze tracks slowly back to the Yoga Wife, teeth already sharp.

CHAPTER FORTY-TWO

It's surprisingly easy to get away with murder when there's no body or reasonable expectation that you had anything to do with the missing people. Helps if there's no public record of you existing. Double helps if there's been a streak of broker- and finance-related weirdness in San Francisco as of late. Thanks for that, Ethan's shitty coven.

Not that Mateo has anything to do with their clean getaway—aside from body disposal.

He spends an unclear number of days sleeping, roused from time to time and made to move here or there, but mostly everyone lets him be. Which is great because he feels like shit—psychologically but also extremely physically—and being awake means thinking about things.

His dreams are blessedly absent, so when he closes his eyes, it's to darkness.

Bits and pieces get to him via Ophelia, who keeps trying to feed him. He hasn't been hungry in days.

Fun fact he learns on something like the second day: the little lady statue he'd found under Topher's bed was of Linnéa.

A good luck charm she'd left near her son. Really sweet except for the part where Mateo removed it, ensuring that all of this was a little worse than necessary.

Quincy's the one who was at the hospital. He'd been in rough shape at first but ended up with only his arm in a sling and some whiplash. A miracle, considering Christopher Nystrom died at the scene of the crash.

Mateo sees Topher briefly three days later—after Topher gets some much-needed medical attention. His eye looks even worse. A deep, baseball-sized black bruise has settled around the cavity and the eyeball's still red. Mildly concussed but alright. Or as alright as you can be when your dad just died from an evil wizard–induced car accident because that same wizard wanted to sacrifice you and your mom to a demon and said mom—who is a magical luck spirit—finally came back from her unannounced Cancun hideaway to learn you have magical powers.

Speaking of Linnéa, Topher explains that the blood on the couch of her house had been to throw off her pursuer. She'd wanted to make them think someone else had gotten to her first. She'd had a whole plan to wait them out in another country. Not knowing that Topher had powers made her think he'd be safest if she was as far away from him as possible.

Literally anyone knowing that would have been fantastic and saved a lot of people a lot of trouble, but Mateo can't fault her when he's made ten thousand bad decisions in the past week.

Mateo lies awake in one of the previously unused guest rooms of the late Christopher Nystrom's house. The furnishings are aggressively gold, but there's a bed, so that's fine. He's on his back staring at the ceiling and playing a new game called *Is this normal disassociation because of all the cannibalism or is this a demon thing and I'm never going to feel things properly again?* The scent of freshly mowed grass fills the room, and Mateo sits up in alarm.

Linnéa Nystrom fills the doorway. They haven't said a word to one another in all of this, her busy with Topher and a dead husband; him busy trying not to think while prone on a bed. Striking gray eyes survey him before settling into a softly inquiring expression. "I hoped we could speak?"

"Sure," he says, unreasonably concerned that she's asking politely to yell at him. It just feels like he's done a lot of stuff a nice mother should be upset about.

She sweeps into the room and perches on the end of his bed. It's big weird to see that she and Topher have the same fluttery movements. On her it seems enchanting and on Topher like he's ten seconds from a breakdown of some sort. Mateo's gaze flicks to the door, and though he can't see him, he suddenly knows Topher's right out there, hovering just beyond the doorway. Topher smells like lavender, iron, and a little bit of something sweet. Honey, maybe. Mateo is now deeply aware of how everyone smells.

At least Topher's presence probably means she isn't going to snap him in half.

It takes Mateo a distracted moment to realize Linnéa's hands are being offered to him, palms up. He stares at them in confusion and then slowly puts his hands in hers—which is the right answer from the way she squeezes his warmly in return and doesn't break them off.

"First, I would like to offer my thanks for your deep friendship to my son," she says. Mateo can hear a small sound of dismay from the hall. "He's told me of the ways you have helped him in my absence and my heart is moved." Extremely dramatic rundown, but okay. "My dear Topher, sister, and Ophelia have told me of your troubles," she continues, still holding his hands.

Just double-hand-holding with someone-you-know's mom. He's sweating to find out what *troubles* those are when she says, "I know of your mother."

"You know my mom?" He nearly yanks his hands away for no reason except that he's shocked, and it feels difficult to comport himself while touched. "Do you know where she is?"

Long pale fingers squeeze his. "I'm afraid she is the keeper of her comings and goings. We have always been two different winds, she and I, traveling in opposite directions. But we have passed one another in the night. We have spoken. But more to the point, after hearing of your situation, I think that we have spoken of you."

All the spit in his mouth is suddenly absent, making swallowing difficult. What could his horrible mother possibly have to say to this magical nice lady holding his hands and looking directly at his face in naked concern? "What did she say?"

"She had questions about my existence in this realm. How I came upon a human form." She keeps a constant pressure on his fingers, like she can keep him calm by holding him still.

This isn't even anything yet, nothing actually helpful or actionable, but his heart is hammering—it started beating again about a day after dagger removal. "What did you say?"

"For me, it was love." Like her son, it looks exceptionally devastating to see her strange features wrinkle in misery. It's only a flash, the love in question only recently dead, and even if Christopher had been a dick, once upon a time he must not have been to her. She takes one of his hands and presses it alarmingly to her bosom. She doesn't say anything, only waits.

Mateo gets extremely uncomfortable, not least because Topher's a few yards away. But then he pulls in a hard breath. "You don't have a heartbeat."

"This form was Christopher's ideal in the dreams we shared." An unwanted look into Christopher's psyche, for sure. "When he asked me to marry him, I took it. Made it my own. My kind has always existed alongside this world. Because of our love for one another, it was no great thing to come here. These answers weren't what your mother sought. When I said all of this, she laughed and asked if the same could be done with hate instead of love. With flesh instead of dreams."

"What did you say?" Mateo asks, and she releases his hand, cups his cheek.

"Yes," she says. "Emotions and intentions are power. All of them."

He knows he doesn't want the answer but asks it anyway. "When was this?"

"Not so long ago. Before my dear Topher, so I suspect before you," she says it gently, thumbing away a tear he hadn't known he was shedding.

He's not upset, exactly, but there's something breathtakingly demoralizing in hearing that his mother did whatever she did on purpose. It wasn't an emergency decision—dire straits where she had no other choice. It was a premeditated and conscious action. He shouldn't be capable of surprise, it's par for the course with her, but now he knows this thing, and it sure does feel worse.

A theory is forming in his brain—one he doesn't want to form, but too many things are clicking together. Because a human body shouldn't be able to maintain a demon possession for so long; an exorcism oughta exorcise the thing that's not supposed to be in the body; a demon possession doesn't make a person into a cannibal; and his horrible mother once asked a woman who was actually a creature from another plane of reality, how she got here.

Ignacia Luisa Reyes Borrero trapped a demon inside her son's body. Except that didn't mean what he'd always thought it meant.

It didn't mean she put a demon in the body along with her son's soul.

It meant she turned a demon into her son.

The one thing she'd tell him about his situation was that he was possessed, and that using magic would make everything worse. But that was a lie. Every single thing his mother told him was a lie. What in the fuck is he supposed to do with any of this?

Something of his internal devastation must show—or it's the black tears—because she murmurs, "You poor child," and then engulfs him in her large arms, pulling him into her chest. Mateo's no hug expert. Aside from Ophelia, he's not really the hugging type, but if he were to rate the hug on a scale from one to ten, it would be a solid twelve million. It's a good hug. If he wasn't fantastically embarrassed to be twenty-three and getting an extremely long hug from someone else's mom, he'd stay in it a while. But he is, so he pulls away, palming at his cheeks, only barely stopping himself from wiping them on his borrowed shirt. He's rocking what is basically a belly shirt on him in the form of one of Topher's nondescript gray tees and he doesn't want to stain it with demon yuck.

As if sensing his dilemma, Topher steps in, a box of tissues held in front of himself like a shield. He's out of breath, which means he'd run to get the box. This fucking guy and his nice-ass mom. Mateo doesn't know what to do with them both in the same room as him while he's trying to be despondent, but he wants a tissue, so he gives Topher a weak smile.

It's all Topher needs to approach.

An Amateur Witch's Guide to Murder

Mother and son share a silent back and forth while Mateo cleans up. It's a lot of Topher making his eyes too wide and his mom smiling like she has no idea what he's getting at, but then she turns to Mateo and says, "I didn't disturb your rest just to distress you. I had hoped to help in some small way. Ophelia mentioned a missing book?"

CHAPTER FORTY-THREE

Mateo sits at the center of the same uncomfortable gray couch where he'd eaten Christopher's finger a lifetime ago. Topher, of the recently concussed, isn't allowed to help, so he's beside Mateo, buzzing.

"She's fairly confident," Topher says, watching Linnéa and Ophelia move about the room, setting up a large magical circle around Mateo.

Probably hoping for a response but the last time someone prepared a ritual around him, Mateo had eaten them. Ophelia's dutifully sprinkling a mix of rue, basil, and rosemary around so there's obviously a level of trust here between Ophelia and Linnéa. Mateo hadn't been witness to it—busy lying on his face in a bedroom realizing he's maybe not actually a human being—but it's intensely uncharacteristic of Ophelia to info-dump his backstory. She must really think Linnéa can help him.

Not a single one of the symbols she's drawn are familiar to him, but that just means whatever her magic is, it's not extremely evil, like everything he gleaned off his mother. A lot of pleasant-looking leaves and even some peaches are in play around the ring. Not a single drop of blood involved. He's rating it loads higher than Ethan's work.

"I'm not entirely human either," Topher whispers, dragging Mateo's attention back to his suddenly way too close face, which is leaning in and up to deliver this earnest message. With way too much clarity Mateo remembers that he fully licked his face.

Linnéa straightens and draws both of their attention—thank fuck—her features alight with excitement, edges of pale lips tipped up in the more confident version of Topher's baby deer smile. It's like she's just been told she's going to hang out with a bunch of puppies for an hour, not that she's about to start a ritual to find Mateo's mom's evil-ass spell book. "We will begin now, Mateo."

She beckons Topher from the circle, and he joins Ophelia a few yards away, clear of the herbs and chalks. The pair stands with arms linked as Linnéa moves in front of Mateo and kneels.

Mateo catches Ophelia's gaze briefly. Her lips quirk and she mouths "relax."

So, he does, attention flicking back to Linnéa.

"Ophelia has explained your attempt to contact me with the charm I left Topher. That you had the Blood Witch's spell book, and that something went wrong with your casting. But that isn't what happened. It did not go wrong. You did contact me, Mateo. A shout in the dark, but because I was pursued, I resisted this call, assuming you were an enemy. It was a powerful call. A powerful magic that you performed. I am an ancient being. That it could pierce what I protect myself with is no small thing."

Mateo blinks hard, remembering the charred little figure that had been Linnéa and how angry and scared she'd felt. She'd left that statue with Topher so it had probably looked extra bad when he'd used it to call her.

"Intentions and emotions. These are the most powerful things," she says, watching him steadily. "Where is the book?"

"I don't—" he tries, but she puts a finger on his lips, silencing him.

"You do," she interrupts, and despite the physical shushing happening, she's still smiling, still pleasant about it, like she's trying to coax a toddler into counting properly.

Mateo chances a look at Ophelia and Topher, but they're just watching, Topher's lips parted in wonder, Ophelia's gaze hard and attentive.

When it's clear Mateo doesn't know what to say, Linnéa tries a different question. "Why don't you have the book?"

Is this a trick question? Ophelia had to have told her it disappeared, meaning he doesn't know where it is or why he doesn't have it. Maybe Linnéa wants a more hippie-dippy answer? When he tries to speak, the pressure of her fingers lessens some, so he manages, "It's not mine?"

"Is that a question?" Linnéa asks sweetly, and he gets the sense that he's done something right but has no idea what.

"It's not mine," he repeats more concretely.

"Why isn't it yours?"

"It's my mother's."

"The Blood Witch?"

"The Blood Witch."

"And whose blood is in your veins?" Linnéa asks.

He hesitates because, again, it feels like a trick question. His blood is literally black. His mom did something really fucked here and it's not what he'd always thought. But she's looking at him with her placid eyes, waiting for him to answer her *what color is the sky* baby question, so he must know the answer she wants.

"The Blood Witch?" he tries.

"Statement," she corrects softly.

"The Blood Witch's blood is in my veins," he says and is greeted with that radiant smile.

"Then the book is yours, by blood," she says, and the world turns to ice.

For a moment Mateo's terrified he's on fire again. Then he leans forward like he's going to spew but from his heart. With a shudder, the book drops out of his chest with a lot of black stuff and a solid *splish*. It feels like he's finally coughed out something that's been lodged in his throat for a month and he's left panting.

Linnéa, somehow sensing this absolute nonsense thing was going to happen, had taken a few steps back and miraculously avoided all splatter. "Very good," she says with the pure delight of someone watching their toddler do a little dance just for them.

"I ruined your couch," Mateo says weakly, lightheaded and disoriented from the magical vomit.

"It's okay," Topher offers from across the room. "We don't like it. Or need it. We're selling the house."

Mateo is still staring at his mom's spell book. No. *His* spell book. He reaches a hand down and tentatively taps the cover. It doesn't do anything—like light him on fire or disappear—so he picks it up. He tries to shake it clean, but then realizes the black stuff is sliding back up the simple cover and into him.

Spreading the spell book open on his lap, he runs fingers over the bright white pages and the small black script. When he'd found the book in his mom's office, there'd been a steady pull, a thread of connection trying to get him to use the book.

And when he had used the book to try to talk to who he later found out was Linnéa—for at least a few moments—everything had felt right.

Then he'd gotten freaked out, the spell had gone to shit, the book had gone inside him, and he'd partially transformed. But why did the spell book go inside him, and why did he transform?

Studying the cover of the book, he focuses on how touching it makes him feel. Content. And angry. While transformed, he'd been furious and confused about everything, but one of the clearest thoughts had been about not fitting together correctly anymore.

He'd assumed his mother had always had this spell book, but what if she hadn't? What if she'd made it after he was born—or summoned or whatever the fuck. Because the cover looks like him, the pages are written in his blood, holding it feels correct, she definitely did something to him when he was young with that ass-smelling yellow smoke Ethan had also used, and nothing she told him about himself was true.

It really isn't his mother's spell book at all. It's his. It's the pieces of him she carved away.

But just having the book isn't why he transformed. Between the first partial transformation and the second *cannibal time* transformation, the book had been inside him.

Linnéa keeps telling him intentions matter. Topher was in jail and then Ophelia and Topher were both in danger. He'd been desperate. He'd wanted to use the demon's—*his*—powers. Before the first transformation he'd gotten scared and it had half messed up, but before the second one, he hadn't given a single fuck.

Having the book and wanting to use his powers is why he transformed.

Ophelia drops down beside him as he carefully closes the book on his lap.

"Looks like the magic was inside you all along," she says with a completely serious face.

She is the absolute worst person on the entire planet.

* * *

Two days later and he hasn't eaten anyone else—or anything at all—so it's determined that Ophelia and he should go home. Topher and Linnéa have a funeral to prepare for and an entire life to re-figure out. They decide to rent a car to drive back to Seattle. It just doesn't seem prudent to trap Mateo in a tube in the air with a bunch of people right now.

Mateo spends way too long folding and refolding the mismatched assortment of clothing he's borrowed over the past week. He runs fingers appreciatively over a gray V-neck t-shirt that's unreasonably soft yet bears no tag to tell him the material. There's a metaphor for Topher in there somewhere, a smile curving his lips because he'd made such a stupid yet apt comparison. Still doesn't finish folding, moving to fuss with a pair of sweatpants he belatedly realizes must have been the late Christopher's because they're way too big to be Topher's.

It's not that the folding is hard or anything, it's just that, once he finishes, he has to hand the pile to Topher and say goodbye. Topher's been an exceptional host, possibly playing the same *avoidance except when absolutely necessary* game Mateo is.

Or he's just, like, grieving.

Or remembering that time Mateo ate a guy a foot from him and feels rightfully spooked.

Or it's the reality of finding out he's not entirely human and his powers killed a lot of people.

Or maybe he's uncomfortable about how much demon tongue Mateo put all over him.

That last one makes Mateo stare unmoving into the middle distance for a really long time. It's cosmically unfair that he's the singular being able to unlock a whole new level of mortification based on things he did while dead and transformed into another state of being or whatever.

Although . . . Topher hadn't seemed particularly uncomfortable at the magic book vomit ritual, which could be politeness or the concussion. And really, didn't Topher always look uncomfortable? How was he supposed to parse what was Topher's default *nice guy who is normal uncomfortable* versus *nice guy who is exceptionally uncomfortable*? Not that Topher had looked uncomfortable while he'd been actively putting tongues all over—

No. Absolutely not. He can't finish that thought. He folds the sweatpants with urgency.

This is stupid. He's being stupid. Get it together, you absolute jackass.

Rising from his bedside crouch, he gathers up the very folded clothing and makes his way through the ridiculously long halls of the house, aiming for Topher's room tucked into the back. The hope that someone will waylay him finally dies as he reaches the open door to Topher's room.

The space is in scandalously slight disarray—startling only because the room had been so sparse and neat before. Now the bed is unmade, the night's pajama pants hanging limply off the end of it. More books have appeared on the desk, another laptop, and a pile of things that look like they have something to do with computers. Square flat boxes with wires and a power strip that weren't there before. There's even a bowl of what was once cereal but is now a single fattened O floating in an inch of milk, sitting atop one of the stacks. It's almost like a totally normal room that someone actually lives in—albeit someone rich enough to have multiple computers and a wall of windows.

Back toward the door, Topher sits curled forward at his desk, cross-legged in a rollie chair definitely not meant for that, attention on a laptop. Weird-looking black headphones curve around his earlobes, and with the way he's lightly bobbing his head and scrolling around with abandon, he hasn't heard Mateo come in.

All at once, Mateo's seeing Topher in his natural habitat, without the stress of an accidental murder, a dickhead dad, or a missing mom threatening from every angle. His hair's puffy but corralled backward, the worry lines that have been knitting his brow since moment one are gone, and he's mouthing something—maybe the words to whatever he's listening to. None of that vibrating tension of anxiety rolls off of him. Taking advantage of this voyeuristic moment, Mateo also checks out his outfit: dark gray joggers with a trendy seam down the front of each leg and an oversized linen tee in pale gray with raw hems. He's like a soft custom rain cloud, scrolling and vibing out to what sounds suspiciously like screamo music.

It takes Mateo a moment to realize what he's scrolling through. Job listings on a pay-to-play site—the kind of site Mateo's never seen the inside of. Salaries listed boldly because they're amazing six figures, and the people who apply for them are at a premium.

Topher is at a premium.

Right. What the hell was he being nervous about? This is a goodbye—of biblical proportions.

He'd done what he'd been paid to do—albeit in a really roundabout way—and he's going home. Topher's going to be in San Francisco, hacking things and getting paid piles of money on top of his piles of money. This had been . . . fun. Confusing. Ultra weird. No small amount of traumatizing.

Mostly, it had been temporary.

"Hey," Mateo says.

Topher draws in a sharp breath as he turns to the right, but his startled woodland creature expression shifts into a smile when he realizes it's Mateo. He returns a whispered, "Hey."

Which sands some of the forced indifference off of Mateo's next words. "Got your stuff. All clean and only sort of stretched out. No demon gunk, at least."

Bare feet drop to the floor and Topher stands, taking the pile of clothing without so much as glancing at them, dropping them onto the seat he'd been occupying.

They are suddenly way too close. Like Mateo had creeped right up to him without realizing it. So now he's basically all up on Topher and those massive gray eyes are vibrating, directed up at him, the bruising still stark against pale skin in a way that makes Mateo's chest hurt.

"Are you leaving now?" Topher asks.

"Just about," Mateo says, meaning to ask if Topher wants an itemized receipt, or maybe joke about leaving a good Yelp review if he ever gets a website up, but the idea that this is it, the last chance, muddles with the memory of Topher's head hitting the concrete in Ethan's basement.

Instead of saying something stupid, he presses the stray hair away from Topher's bruised eye, coaxing it back behind an ear with a careful touch that he lets linger till he's sliding fingers to the back of Topher's neck.

It's not a decision so much as a necessity, like they were both waiting for this except Mateo hadn't realized until now. Topher's gaze steadies, lips parting slightly, and Mateo leans down to meet them. It's not a frenzied kiss, though his heart is pounding. He keeps it gentle, like he's still afraid he might hurt Topher even without the maw of sharp teeth. Really, he just wants to take his time, savor this moment that's never going to happen again, commit it to memory, and maybe overwrite some of the other stuff. The less good stuff. Anything that isn't the knee-weakening-ly sweet way Topher's kissing back, a hand gripping Mateo's shirt hem, the little sigh he makes, and the way he tastes like sugar and smells like cinnamon and grass.

It takes a delayed moment of more warm kisses before Mateo's brain drags up the fact that the grass smell isn't a Topher thing.

"Oh my," Linnéa says from the door.

Mateo backs up so quickly he rams ass first into Topher's desk with a swear, scrabbling not to knock the laptop or the bowl of milk off before throwing hands up in surrender. Last thing in the world he wants is for Topher's mom to think he's eating her son face-first or something.

But Linnéa's doing that same patronizingly delighted smile from the book vomit ritual. "I'm so sorry to interrupt you boys," she says in amusement. Which is the most embarrassing thing she could have said. "Ophelia asked me to find you, Mateo. She's ready to leave."

Absolutely one thousand percent did Ophelia somehow do this on purpose.

"Well, I gotta go," Mateo says as the most inadequate good-bye ever, hands still raised but managing to look at Topher and not his mom. "See ya."

Topher's dropped into his rollie chair, haphazardly on top of the clothes, face bright red. "Absolutely. For sure. Yes," Topher stage whispers, eyes back to vibrating.

Mateo's desperate to get out of the room before he completely ruins his cool-guy-leaving moment, but Linnéa catches him in a long, awkward—but at least a different flavor of awkward—hug. He manages to extract himself and finds Ophelia, who knows exactly what she did by the smirk on her face as she directs him to help her finish loading up the rental with the stuff they stole from Ethan's house.

Once that's done, they're off.

Ophelia drives, Mateo lying down in the backseat because he's still pretty run-down—and chest-vomiting a magic book that's actually part of him hadn't helped.

The music's low enough for conversation but they don't talk for a while.

Not in a bad way.

She's letting him try to deal with everything, and talking never helps.

Staring at the tops of trees and sides of buildings whizzing past the window across from him, Mateo torturously replays the goodbye. The kiss had been really good. And he'd almost been *so* slick, up until that part where he got scared of Topher's mom and knocked a bunch of shit over and ran away.

This is pointless to worry about. He's never going to see Topher again.

Which.

Like.

So why the fuck had his brain supplied *see ya* as his departing line?

Forcing his thoughts to something actually relevant, he clutches the spell book to his chest. It's going to take some effort, but he's going to learn every spell in it. He's going to learn what his mother knew. What she took from him. Maybe that'll make him worse, but he's already eaten two people. How much worse can it get? And maybe *worse* has always meant more of what he actually is, and maybe it's not bad if he becomes that. Because demons aren't evil, they just don't interact well with the material world. It's whatever the human involved does to get the power, or with the power, that's capable of good or evil. And maybe he's not actually human. But he's also not just a demon. So maybe he can be whatever the fuck he wants to be.

He'd been on the verge of something after Ethan's knife sunk in. And he can't shake the feeling that the thing he'd transformed into had been a hell of a lot more informed than his current self. But being like that, knowing whatever he'd almost known, had felt like a one-way street sort of deal. If he'd walked down it, he's not sure he'd be able to come back, and there are things here—people here—he needs.

"Talk," Ophelia says from the front.

Talking never helps, except he'd nearly lost the ability to ever talk to her again.

So he talks. Tells her everything.

The dreams, the shadows, and the almost-knowledge he'd punted aside in that basement.

That kiss. The two before it. That they don't matter. That they do matter. That they can't matter. That he'd thought it was the demon who was being weird about Topher, but it wasn't. And it's kind of a relief because the idea of something else controlling him was horrifying. But if not something else, that means the one actually being weird about Topher is him and he has no idea what to do with that.

The Ethan stuff. So much Ethan stuff. There's no emotional guide about what to do when you thought someone was cool and you sort of hoped they'd be your friend but instead you eat them. He explains how he keeps waffling between knowing it was a perfectly valid response—sort of—and regretting it. And it's double terrible because he's crying about this while in the coolest jacket Ophelia could spot in Ethan's closet. Balmain, double-breasted with a chunky zipper detail and an oversized cut. It's magnificent and Mateo's glad she grabbed it, even though wearing it makes him want to lie down on the road a little bit.

And somehow this guilt is coupled with an utter lack of guilt that is extremely wide and bone deep because he's furious at Ethan for touching her. For touching Topher. For seeming cool and being shitty. For trying to help and then trying to kill him. For actually succeeding in killing him.

Most nonsensical of all, he's mad at Ethan for dying.

And beneath that Mateo has a blindingly bright fear. That he'll do it again. Eat someone again. Because a week ago he thought he was human and today he knows he's not. He's something else and that something is hungry. But it's also not a fear, it's a certainty. He definitely will eat someone. He knows he will. He's excited that he will.

He spews out all the things he's kept from her for years and years for no reason other than that saying them makes them real but it's all real anyway so he might as well say it.

And when he finishes, she says, "We'll deal with it."

And he says, "I love you."

And she says, "I know."

CHAPTER FORTY-FOUR

"Nice lipstick."

Mateo Borrero pulls an earbud out, muting the furious screeching and synth to see if the comment was sincere or sarcastic.

Difficult read.

Three guys in Seattle-chic—flannel, jeans, and beards—stand in a loose pack in front of a coffee shop that boasts butter coffee and acai berry bowls. The one who'd probably spoken holds a smoothie in one hand and has a half-smile on his lips.

Mateo almost shoves the earbud back in, not wanting to deal with this. Harassing or flirting. Doesn't matter which. He doesn't want it. But the guy's manner is ambiguous enough, so he chances an answer. "Nyx Cosmetics. Got it at Walgreens."

"Cool," the guy says, and Mateo slowly turns around, deciding to count to ten before putting his earbud back in. He gets to eight.

"Hey." Closer now. Smoothie guy. The one in blue plaid and blue jeans stands just to his right. A guy in some guy clothes. About to use his guy mouth to say some guy things. "You busy this weekend?"

Comparatively, it's probably the better option, but it's the one that makes Mateo inwardly cringe the hardest. If he'd been being an asshole, Mateo could have just eaten him.

It's his own joke, but he hates that he made it.

"Seeing someone," Mateo says instead.

"No worries," the guy says, which is also probably the better option, but same joke about eating him.

The ping of the crosswalk sounds and Mateo crosses without incident. Which is fantastic because he doesn't have time for anyone's bullshit today.

He checks his phone. Nothing new from Ophelia. The last text reported that Topher had landed but SeaTac is an annoying distance away, even with a paid car. Why exactly Topher's coming in person, Mateo's not sure. Ophelia had seemed excited, so Mateo hadn't questioned it, and it's not like he doesn't want to see Topher—except in an existentially confusing and horrified way where he doesn't know what seeing Topher will feel like so deeply dreads it. Still, he'd closed up early to try to beat Topher to the house.

Despite his best efforts at getting fired with seven days of no-call no-show, Mateo is still gainlessly employed. Angelica was his unlikely hero. She'd covered for him, worked his shifts, and said he was super ill—which is also how he explained it to her. It's not like he can tell her that he'd been a demon and it took a while to feel something resembling human again. Now he owes her a life-work debt—the most sacred kind.

Though Mateo's had no direct contact with Topher since fleeing his state, he's been kept abreast of him by Ophelia, who's better at texting than him.

Which is a cop-out.

Mateo's not bad at texting so much as he never knows what to say to Topher, and adding a funeral and weird powers to the mix doesn't help. It's not like he can say, "Sorry your dad I kind of hated whose finger I super ate—did I even tell you that?—died. That sucks for you. Also, how are those wacky powers going? Kill anyone else trying to kill you? I think about the way your blood tastes a lot."

Total dick move on Mateo's part, he knows, but trying to study baby's first extremely evil magic book while also trying to re-form himself into something like a human being is taking a lot, and he hadn't trusted himself not to make it weird. Topher had enough to deal with.

Which is why his teeth are sharp and he'd had to put on his shades—his eyes leak black when he gets worked up now—by the time he unlocks the front door. He's unreasonably nervous as he kicks his boots off and yells into the house. "He here?"

"Almost," Ophelia calls back, emerging from the kitchen with a tray of atrocities. Not just because food is gross to him now but because she is gross. It's an array of fruits left out in the sun to die, cardboard that's meant to be crackers, a cheese that smells like absolute ass.

"What the hell?" he says, shucking off his backpack and hoodie.

"It's charcuterie, you swine," she says with no bite, setting it on the table along with a bottle of wine.

"Why are we having charcuterie?" he asks, but honestly, he's delighted. She, without anyone asking, made a horrible food thing. Like civilized people do. It's Ulla's influence, which is an insane concept because Ulla's the only person more unpleasant than Ophelia—thought affectionately. Ophelia hadn't just been keeping in touch with Topher, but specifically Ulla, who knew a thing or two about astral projection. She's been helping Ophelia practice possessions, and just like Mateo, having some actual forward progress has done wonders for her general mood.

"Because Topher's fancy and I've missed him," she says and gives Mateo a cutting look that says things like *and you do too, you jackass, but you won't say it because you've been avoiding him, but you can't do that today because he's coming over.* She says all that with one shitty smirk and he hates it, so he retreats to the bathroom to wash up.

He doesn't hear the knock—of course—but he hears the front door open, and hurriedly dries off, checking himself in the mirror. If he doesn't linger, he can see his face enough to make sure his lipstick is still crisp before his face becomes a voided-out silhouette. Good enough.

Stepping into the living room, Topher's just, like, there. Scrawny, anemic, and recently through a wind storm. The black eye lingers, a yellowed splotch on his pale skin and only a touch of red at the outside edge of his eye.

Topher just stands there, so Mateo just stands there, and they might have done that all night, but Ophelia directs Topher to the couch. Topher has the demeanor of a small bird that's recently flown into a window, only barely managing to avoid breaking its neck, and is now afraid of all large surfaces. Impossible to tell if that's the normal look or some extra special more-bad kind and is secretly the reason Ophelia wanted him to fly up.

Having never worked out what he'd say to Topher if he was ever in the same room with him again, the myriad of conceptually correct greetings flee his vicinity. But this is Mateo's chance to say something reassuring. Apologize for the radio silence.

Assuming Topher hadn't wanted that.

Which he probably had.

An Amateur Witch's Guide to Murder

Topher hadn't texted either.

"How's your mom?" is somehow what Mateo goes with. Cool. Spot on. Absolutely what you say to a guy who just came from a funeral.

"Good. Really good," Topher says, seeing the charcuterie tray on the table and picking up a shriveled apple slice.

Mateo takes a seat on the couch—not too close—and Ophelia hovers just behind the couch, between him and the kitchen as if to block a means of escape. She puts a hand on Topher's shoulder and squeezes.

The frantic expression smooths off Topher's face and his lips form an alarming and unhappy line. "No. That's not right. She's only *okay*. Making it work. I think. With dad, um, dead, there's been a lot to do. Aunt Ulla's helping. Mom was still in the will. So, that's good. We have an offer on the house. Mom's house too. She's thinking about going to Sweden to scatter dad's ashes. Maybe stay a while. I can get work from anywhere, but I don't know if I wanna go with. That was their place." A sad little smile sits on his lips at that.

"Makes sense," Mateo says weakly, reaching desperately for something to say to shift them away from the dead-dad talk. Unless he should be talking about the dead dad. Is that cathartic for Topher? Is that insensitive of him? "How's the magic going?" He can feel Ophelia's gaze on him, and he wishes she had the power to kill him with her mind.

"Really good," Topher says more easily, nodding too much. "Mom's been teaching me how to deal with my powers. To be intentional with them. How to tell when they're happening. How to make them happen on purpose. I'm still not very good at it, but she says that just takes practice. It feels weird to call them powers... mostly I just don't want to accidentally kill people. That feels bad. I mean. Of course, you know. We all know. Everyone knows that. Not that there's anything wrong if we do accidentally—" He has the sense to stop himself midsentence, the sticky moral issue of *is murder okay sometimes if you super didn't mean it* still too raw for all of them.

"Right. Cool." It's all good stuff. Or as good as things can be given the circumstances. Sounds like Topher's figuring it out with a nice mom-based support structure. Thriving. About to set out on a new life adventure. And now Mateo knows. So he can close that chapter. Go back to his own shit and Topher can go do his own thing. Which is fine. Best, really. For everyone.

Except the weight of Ophelia's eyes are still on Mateo, and when he glances back at her, she's looking at him in that special way that means he's being extra dim.

She wants him to say something civil, probably. Like a supportive friend, right? Like, this must be "friends"? If you help a guy not be sacrificed and he watches you eat another guy and still comes to your house? That's gotta be friendship at least.

He can do this.

He can say normal friend words to this guy who's looking at him with forlorn loris eyes. And yes, he'd looked that one up.

Mateo opens his mouth. Condolences would make the most sense. Sorry his dad died. Sorry it's been rough. Sorry for not texting. He could ask about Quincy, double-check he's doing alright—though Ophelia had confirmed that a week ago. There's the small-talk thing. Ask how the flight was? How long is he in town? Is he staying nearby? Hell, he could just admit that he'd wanted to see him, talk to him, might have even missed him. That Topher sitting here right now, staring in his way too intense but also sort of charming way, makes the thing that's inside of Mateo—that's just Mateo—sort of happy.

An Amateur Witch's Guide to Murder

There's half a million things Mateo should say, stacked neatly on top of whatever it is he actually wants here. Which he's absolutely not going to verbalize, so instead he says, "There's an empty room here. Rent's $700 a month plus a third of utilities. Want it?"

Topher's eyes widen, but he doesn't stumble over the reply. "Yes."

End

ACKNOWLEDGMENTS

This book wouldn't exist if not for a lot of people, so let's go! First and foremost, thanks to Jake, who had to read this story seven thousand times in seven thousand forms. You're my first reader and my cheerleader. You're simply the best. Better than all the rest (except Bug). I couldn't ask for a better partner in life. Thanks to Adriana, who had to read this story six thousand times in six thousand forms. You're always enthusiastic about my ridiculous ideas, and you're there in a pinch when I'm having a five-alarm writing fire. Thanks to my sister and mother for their excitement and support and dealing with how all I can do is reference publishing-related stuff now.

Huge thanks to my agent, Cameron, who is endlessly patient for when I write a book where I don't explain anything that's happening in it but then excitedly put all the details in an email and you have to be like "How about you put that in the book?" Thanks for supporting me, getting all my stupid jokes, and having such a big brain that forces me to write better stories. Thanks to everyone on the Alcove Press/Crooked Lane Books

Acknowledgments

team! Most special thanks to Rebecca, my amazing editor, who somehow lined up fate to offer on Halloween (impeccable vibes), and helped hammer this book into a cuter, funnier, funner story. Your enthusiasm and support has been amazing. Thanks to Thai for helping usher this book into creation. Thanks to Mikaela and Dulce on the Alcove Press side and Crystal, Grace, and Leilani on the BookSparks side for all your hard work making this book seem really cool. Thanks to Debbie for fixing ten thousand incorrect comma uses and for supporting my abuse of: —

Thanks to everyone in MSMF, my fantastic writing group full of extraordinarily talented writers. Thanks to Katiee and MK for dealing with this story when it was a 10-page short story that obviously should have been a novel. Thanks to Arwyn, Sara, Anja, and Gina for quick turnaround edit sprees. Y'all are the best CP's for reals. Extra special thanks to Cristina, Stacie, and Emily. Cristina is responsible for the big climax actually being good. Stacie is responsible for peer-pressuring me into querying this book. I'm ready to blurb you! And Emily unlocked my pacing problem with the simple words "what if this was the aunt?" Hero. Thanks to Waverly for day-job commiseration. Let us one day not stress. Magical sparkle sunshine thanks to Jenni for being my caps-on-purpose freakout friend. You are so smart, amazing, and kind, and none of us would have met without you.

Special thanks to my two longest running bffs. Karlee, every chaos woman I write is secretly you. Devin, I legit could not have done this if you didn't always have my back.

Acknowledgments

Thank you to the extremely goth FedEx manager who sparked the initial idea of this story. I never spoke a nontransactional word to you, but your style was amazing. Last, but definitely not least, thanks to anyone who picked up this book and gave it a chance. I hope you liked it!